I0737807

DREAMS OF WINTER

THE FRACTURED UNIVERSE #1

CHRISTIAN WARREN FREED

Copyright © 2020 by Christian Warren Freed

Excerpt from *The Madman on the Rocks* 2021 Christian Warren Freed
Cover design by BroseDesignz
Cover copyright 2021 by Warfighter Books
Author Photograph by Anicie Freed

Warfighter Books
Holly Springs, North Carolina 27540
https://www.christianfreed

Second Edition: January 2021

Library of Congress Cataloging-in-Publication Data
Name: Freed, Christian Warren, 1973- author.
Title: Dreams of Winter/ Christian Warren Freed
Description: Second Edition | Holly Springs, NC: Warfighter Books, 2021.
Identifiers: LCCN 2021930781 | ISBN 9780578645858 (trade paperback) ISBN: 9781735700038 (ebook) Subjects: Science Fiction | Fantasy | Space Opera

Printed in the United States of America

10 9 8 7 6 5 4 3 2 1

of the band - to worry about them and want them to do the 'right thing'. He adds depth to the characters through their actions and his dialogue is very realistic."

ARMIES OF THE SILVER MAGE

"Armies of the Silver Mage was a great read...any fan of Lord of the Rings or Game of Thrones will love this book. I'm looking forward to next book."

"The book is almost an homage to the great classics like Sword of Shannara and the Lord of the Rings. The author has cleverly used his past military and combat experience to make the battle scenes more realistic."

The Northern Crusade

#1 Hammers in the Wind
#2 Tides of Blood and Steel
#3 A Whisper After Midnight
#4 Empire of Bones
#5 The Madness of Gods and Kings
#6 Evens Gods Must Fall

The Histories of Malweir (all stand alones)
#1 Armies of the Silver Mage
#2 The Dragon Hunters
#3 Beyond the Edge of Dawn
Immortality Shattered
#1 Law of the Heretic
#2 The Bitter War of Always
#3 The Land of Wicked Shadows
#4 Storm Upon the Dawn

The Fractured Universe
Dreams of Winter
The Madman on the Rocks
Anguish Once Possessed
Through Darkness Besieged
Under Tattered Banners
A Time For Tyrants
A Good Day For Crows

D.E.S.A. Files
Where Have All the Elves Gone?
One of Our Elves is Missing
From Whence It Came
Of Elves and Men
Save the Queen!

<u>The Lazarus Men Agenda</u>
>The Lazarus Men
>Repercussions
>Daedalus Unbound
>Exile's Fury
>Prodigal's Return
>The Icarus Dilemma

<u>Crimson Spiders</u>
Zero Hour
Against All Odds
One More Again*
Last Shot at Glory*
Behind Enemy Lines*
No Quarter*
Kill Box*
Spiders in the Night*

Tomorrow's Demise: The Extinction Campaign
Tomorrow's Demise: Salvation

The Children of Never
Coward's Truth

A Long Way From Home: My Time in Iraq and Afghanistan +
So, You Want to Write a Book? +
So, You Wrote a Book. Now What? +

+ Nonfiction   * Forthcoming

For my wife Annie.

ONE

3187 A.G. (After Gods)

A single drop of rain fell. Lost quickly amongst the dust and grime of the village street, the raindrop went unnoticed. Who could have guessed that a single drop would alter the course of events set in motion thousands of years ago and change the face of the universe forever?

Autumn's bite was crisp this year. Sharp winds blew in from the northern sea, forcing people inside. Whole fields of crops were lost to the pre-winter freeze that gripped the land. It should have been a time for celebration, a time to pay tribute to the gods for their generosity bestowed. As winter drew closer the people prepared for the worst. Not everyone chose to hide in the safety and warmth. Two friends sat on a porch, staring off into the surrounding fields. Light mist clung to ground, curling up the porch and around their ankles. Frost kissed the few leaves that had not yet fallen.

"I cannot stay here much longer," Mollock Bolle whispered.

An angry wind blew his stringy gray hair across his face, forcing him to push it aside with a frown. Deep lines creased his face; the bags beneath his eyes were dark and haunting. He'd lost much weight over the past year. Sleep did not come easily anymore. Perhaps it was a sign of things to come, though Mollock did not believe in premonition or any such devilry.

Fenrin shook his head. "What are you talking about? You just arrived a few days ago."

"Doesn't matter," Mollock distractedly replied. His dark brown eyes focused on the night. A glint of fear danced around the corners of his eyes.

The wind howled; the cry of a thousand wolves. Fenrin shivered. His small plot of land on one of the surrounding hilltops overlooking the small farming village of Parnus was one of the larger vineyards in the region. Fields of grape vines filled the gentle slope off his back porch. Frost covered those vines now, frost and the first hints of winter. A half-moon hung high in the early night sky, shying behind the stratus clouds. He knew, lost among the stars, a million ships sailed between worlds.

"Something is going on, tell me," Fenrin persisted. "This doesn't sound like you."

Mollock eyed his friend. They'd known each other for almost four decades; childhood friends in a way that no amount of time could threaten. This made Mollock more uneasy. He didn't know how to tell Fenrin something he himself couldn't explain.

"It is a feeling. Perhaps just a dream," he shook his head. "I don't know."

Fenrin narrowed his eyes. His curiosity peaked. "What do you dream of?"

"Do you have nightmares, Fenrin?"

He wasn't sure he liked the direction of conversation; the menace behind Mollock's tone. "No, not really."

Mollock rose and went to the porch rail. His eyes scanned the nearby tree line, watching for things that his mind screamed couldn't exist. Every shadow haunted him, threatened his life in a special way known only to the lords of darkness.

"I do."

Fenrin rocked uneasily in his chair. The strained squeak echoed in the empty night. Dried leaves scrapped across the porch.

"If I didn't know you better I would say that you are starting to frighten me, old friend."

Mollock grimaced. Not even his long years of military service prepared him for this. "You should be frightened. I am."

His heart skipped. Fenrin felt his mouth water. Hands shaking, he reached into a pouch and drew out a long stem pipe. He packed in the tobacco and lit it, drawing deep on the soothing smoke. Fenrin wasn't scared. If anything he was confused.

"Mollock, I never heard you speak like this. We've been through wars together. How many times have we stood against the enemy and come out alive?" He exhaled a thick plume of bluish smoke. "None of what you are saying is making any sense. Come back over here and have a seat. I have some wine inside. It will ease your mind some."

Mollock Bolle smiled softly. "You have been a good friend to me, Fenrin and I have wronged you. I shouldn't have come here. I cannot say why, but I feel that every moment I stay here threatens you with danger. I must leave soon."

"You still haven't told me why."

Mollock stared at his friend, his face drawn and severe. "They are coming for me."

Fenrin's face paled. He leaned forward. "Who?"

"I don't know."

The darkness erupted. A flock of birds fled from the nearby stand of pine trees. Fenrin opened his mouth in shock, the pipe spilling embers on the old wooden porch. Mollock spun and drew his sword. His breath came quickly. They watched as a monstrous shadow crashed through the trees, coming closer to the house. There was no subtlety, no stealth. The creature was unafraid.

Mollock fought the urge to piss on himself. He closed his eyes tight. *Not again*. The beast roared; a dreadful wail that withered every tree and plant around it. Its massive bulk easily batted aside trees that had grown for over a hundred years. Their thickness meant nothing to the raw power exhibited. His mighty head rose higher than the tallest tree. The air grew rank, fetid. The beast was death, and nothing on the face of the world could withstand its awesome power.

"What in the name of the gods is that?" Fenrin stammered. His words were pregnant with slowly realized fear.

Mollock shook his head in denial. He couldn't believe he had been found so easily. He quickly regained composure. There would be time enough for chastisement in the future, hopefully. Mollock sheathed his sword. The weapon would be of no use against a creature of shadow.

"Get back inside and lock your door. Douse the lanterns. It won't bother with you once I am gone. It is me it's after." His voice was hurried, urgent.

Fenrin rose, hand scrambling for his aged rifle as the beast drew closer.

"Damn it man, if you ever listened to me do it now. You cannot fight this. I must run," Mollock insisted. The harsh tone of his words broke the beast's grip on Fenrin. "Gods willing, I will be able to come back and explain what is happening."

"And if you don't?" Fenrin asked.

Mollock grimaced. "Then I am dead."

Gathering up his back and walking stick, Mollock Bolle moved to the edge of the stairs. He turned and looked back at his friend. There was much to be said, but he had not the words for it. Instead he gave a haphazard smile and said, "Winter."

Fenrin was confused. "What does that mean?

"You asked me what I dream of. I have dreams of winter."

And with that he was gone, just another shadow in the growing darkness. Fenrin thought to call after him, to demand an explanation. The beast in the forest cautioned otherwise. Instead Fenrin ran inside and bolted the door. Every footstep of the beast shook dust from the rafters and threatened to bring the house down around his head. He hurried to extinguish all the lanterns and candles, silently thankful he hadn't built a fire yet. The beast stalked closer. The ground trembled. The air became fetid and rank with the odors of death. Fenrin vomited in his chamber pot. His heart raced. His hands became sweaty.

And then it too was gone. The nightmare creature of shadow was gone. Fenrin struggled to his feet and, on shaky legs, ran outside hoping to catch a glimpse of the terror. Rather than finding the beast he saw a wide swath of destruction from the forest through his vineyards. The world had turned to death and decay. Fenrin murmured a quick prayer to Aris, goddess of protection and wisdom, for his friend. He knew Mollock Bolle was a dead man without the help of the gods.

The Bloody Man arrived at night. Twice the size of a mortal man, he didn't move, didn't even blink. The villagers of Kovlchen were both frightened and amazed. No one had ever seen anything like this before. Prayers were whispered, blades sharpened. The man was heavily muscled, sculpted almost, and completely covered in dark crimson blood. Arms at his sides, he stared out at the world with empty eyes. Villagers flocked to see the Bloody Man, if such a being might be called a man. Those daring enough moved closer, eager to get a better look. Mothers hurried their children home, lest they become contaminated or infected.

A week passed and with it the novelty. People talked less of the Bloody Man. The mayor and constable decided that, while the man had not so much as blinked during in the time since his arrival, something had to be done. They sensed a latent threat and gave voice to that paranoia. A town meeting was called in the local tavern.

"The question is not what as much as when," Mayor Zenningberg told the assembled audience. "This bloody man represents a danger we have never experienced."

"But he has done nothing," farmer Aenni reasoned. The old man was well known for his wisdom. "How can we act against a being that doesn't even seem to breathe?"

"That is not the point! Sure, the bloody man may not have acted against us yet, but that is not to say he won't soon," Zenningberg insisted.

A chorus of cheers and murmurs filled the room. The people were frightened. That much was certain. An undertone of fear laced the smoke thickened air. Old and young alike could feel it. Danger lingered just beyond the borders of common sense. The bloody man was a danger. He must be dealt with.

Zenningberg held up his hands for silence. It took a moment, but the crowd finally stopped their chatter long enough for him to continue.

"My friends, I love this village. I have spent my entire life here and devoted the last fifteen years to making it the best village in the middle kingdoms. The Baron of Berchenfel has used this as his model community. That being said, we cannot allow this *thing* to remain here. The longer he stays the more danger we are in."

"Danger from what? He hasn't moved at all."

Zenningberg caught the familiar face of Prentiss. He snorted. The lad was the local troublemaker, a youth who did not see the value in the wisdom of his elders. The boy needed to keep his mouth closed and go about his business.

"Prentiss, imagine what would happen when he does move. That creature has got to be nearly ten feet tall. And look at the muscles on him. He's a beast of man and I for one do not wish to find out what he means to do." Zenningberg smiled to himself. He could feel the mood of the crowd shifting back in his favor. "Let us not forget that he came here by supernatural means!"

"Prove it!" Prentiss shouted.

"How can you deny otherwise?" came a frail voice from the back of the room.

All eyes turned to see Father Dorchea, the spiritual heart of the village, striding towards Zenningberg and the podium. The Father was the most respected man in the village. When he spoke, people listened.

His stern eyes leveled on the crowd. He was a thin man, old and covered with liver spots. His hair, what was left, was thin, close cropped and streaked gray.

"This Bloody Man is a message, sent to us by the Gods to confront our sins against the Fathers," he told them.

"Father, the gods do not always interfere with the whims of man. What have we done to draw the wrath of the gods?" asked the mayor.

Father Dorchea slid through the crowd to stand beside his friend. "My friends, who are we to question the creators of all life? Are we not the children of gods? The very spark sent unto this world to bring joy where once only darkness reigned. This is not an easy thing of which I speak. My heart aches from the signs before my eyes. The Bloody Man is a bane to our continued existence."

Arguments spread through the crowd. Some for, some against the continued presence of the Bloody Man. Perhaps the worst part of the situation was that gnawing uncertainty buried within each of them. Uncertainty can be a powerful emotion; strong enough to spark unabashed fear or peak the highest curiosity. Fear slowly won out. The tide of emotions turned towards the bitter prospects of the potential horror the Bloody Man represented and how best to deal with the situation.

It was all talk until Jarris Thoom came in carrying the limp form of his youngest daughter. Tears streaked his cheeks and his voice trembled as much as his waning strength. "The Bloody Man! It was him! He killed my Elisa!"

Zenningberg bellowed for quiet. "How Jarris? How did he do this thing?"

Jarris sank to his knees. He cried uncontrollably, gently placing Elisa's body on the dust covered wooden floor. "Those kids," he whispered. "I told them not to go near him. I told them, I told them, I told them." He looked up into the panic stricken eyes of both the Father and the Mayor. "They just wouldn't listen. They had to go play near this monster. And he killed her!"

Zenningberg passed Father Dorchea a sidelong glance. In a voice just loud enough for the two to hear, he said, "that settles it. We have to get rid of him somehow."

Dorchea nodded and dropped down to comfort poor Jarris.

"Everyone, listen to me!" the Mayor roared to be heard. "Go to your homes and find what weapons you can. Tonight we will end the threat of this Bloody Man. Go now!"

"And what of the gods? Will they not punish us for what we seek to do?" Prentiss asked accusingly. "I don't believe much in gods and signs, but if what the Father and poor Jarris Thoom said are true then something must be done, but violence is not the answer."

"There is no other way!"

"He has already killed once, are you so willing to let him do it again?" Zenningberg asked.

Prentiss shook his head. "A moment ago we all preached peace and now look at you! Nothing more than a blood thirsty mob! We were not raised this way. This village has avoided going to war for three generations and now we throw it all away on the whim of a single incident? I cannot stand for this."

"Our paths have already been chosen!" Father Dorchea replied. "The gods demand action."

"And if we die?"

"Then the gods decreed."

The simple answer was chilling. An eerie silence settled over those gathered for a tender moment. The atmosphere stifled. A choking feeling hung at the back of everyone's throats. Jarris Thoom solved it all in a single act of violence. Hatred and rage collided in his mind, creating a super emotion that no sense of morality or reason could overpower. He looked up at the young Prentiss.

"That thing killed my little girl!" he roared. Jarris moved quicker than anyone anticipated. On his feet and dagger drawn before they could react, he plunged the old, nicked blade deep into Prentiss' chest. The youth fell with a cry, dark blood flowing down his tunic.

In that moment every bird launched into the sky. A thunderclap so loud it shook the foundations of the world began a whirlwind. The Bloody Man blinked once. The emotions he felt were indescribable, but he'd felt them before. More than once he had been forced to act in response, lest they become too much even for his soul to bear. Strength filled his muscles and his skin danced with electricity that glowed blue in the dark of night.

The first to die were those closest. At nearly twelve feet tall and thicker than three men put together, the Bloody Man swung his fists like clubs, smashing and crushing bone and muscle. Men and women ran screaming. Some tried to make a stand, but it was not enough. Nothing was enough to stem the tide of violence pouring from the Bloody Man. It was a scene from Hell. Broken bodies began to pile up. Hatred so deep it set fire to every building in sight consumed the village. The Bloody Man did what the gods had created him to do. He killed. And killed. And killed until there were none left to oppose him.

Mayor Zenningberg died from fright. His old heart couldn't comprehend the sights opened to him. Father Dorchea knelt before the Bloody Man and prayed for those few moments before his head was crushed like a piece of rotten fruit in the Bloody Man's mighty fist. And then the Bloody Man stopped suddenly. His eyes opened and he saw the devastation he had caused for the first time. Not a soul lived in the village of Kovlchen. Even the smallest dog and youngest child had been killed, their bodies a travesty of human form. Homes and shops were leveled. The entire area looked as if a massive earthquake had ravaged it. He tilted his head back, horrified at what he had done.

"NOOOO!" he cried and dropped to his knees in misery.

Not again, he shook his head. Not again. Tears spilled from his eyes. The destruction burned what was left of his heart, ate at the depths of his soul. Pain and suffering seemed his eternal companions and he didn't know why. These people had done nothing to deserve the horror he'd unleashed. Murder. That's what it was. Sheer, brutal murder. No one would ever learn what had happened to the quiet village of Kovlchen on that dark autumn night. An entire people were destroyed before the sun had the chance to rise.

The Bloody Man cried for them all. Every last soul he sent back to his father caused a tear so large it created a sea of raw agony. He sank to his knees. The old doubt had returned to his soul. He remembered why he had fled humanity so many centuries ago. He wasn't made for this life, but there was no alternative. The Bloody Man yanked himself to his feet. His movements were timid, like a scolded child.

Ever had he been this way. The gods had cursed him. The Bloody Man walked through the carnage, praying for a sign of life. Death mocked his efforts. Agony filled faces stared back at him. He heard their twisted laughter echoing back from the depths of Hell. This seemed his lot in life. Suffering. His soul cried through the dark hours of the night.

And then he found it. Found that single spark of life that suggested hope had not died. He knelt down beside the body of a small child and gently cradled her in his massive arms. A tear fell, splashing on her cheek. The girl groaned and breathed deep. She opened her eyes; radiant green and speckled with fear.

"Shhh," he whispered. "Do not be afraid. I will not harm you."

She screamed and struggled in his grasp.

"Please," he pleaded. "I will not hurt you."

He finally set her down, expecting her to flee. But she didn't. She stood fast and stared back in wonder.

"What happened to my momma?" she asked. Her voice was strained and broken.

He bowed his head. "I am sorry."

The Bloody Man stood and turned to leave.

"Wait," the girl asked. "Who are you?"

He stopped long enough to look back over his shoulder with pained eyes. "Sorrow. My name is Sorrow."

TWO

No one knows the origins of the universe. Gone was the knowledge of creation; lost to faded memories and the advance of time. History became legend, legend became myth. It is said the gods, flawless emperors of all, opened their hearts and gave life to hundreds of worlds. That love nurtured and evolved into utopian grandeur. Humanity prospered, every day reaching new heights. But all was not well. The gods were unhappy. War loomed ever on the near horizon. Realizing their plight, the king of the gods gave birth to three sons; would be kings to rule.

All was well for a time. The godlings matured into fine young men always eager to please and learn. The universe was their playground but even that was not enough to stay the drums of war. Doom threatened to end the reign of the gods and they were powerless to stop it. Most historians agree it began with the Three. Meant to bridge the hostilities, the Three served to widen them. Lesser gods became jealous. Plots formed. The Three slowly became corrupted. One fell into shadow. One fled and went into hiding, the pressures simply too much for him. But the third remained and struggled throughout his entire life in the pursuit of goodness and purity. His efforts did not go in vain. War was temporarily averted. Humanity prospered. Mighty empires rose and fell. Civilization became more than a handful of caves. Men learned to fly to the stars. Life was grand, advanced and cultured.

Unfortunately, the third brother did not get to see the rewards of his efforts. His was a life of constant emptiness. As much as he longed to be with what he considered his children, he needed his brothers more. One day he went to the golden halls of his father to ask why theirs was a tortured existence. Their father, king of the gods, grew angered and cast his son out. No one in the history of life had ever dared question the rule of the king. Blood or no, his son had broken the cardinal law. The son was cast down from the heavens, forever destined to roam the universe in search of unobtainable answers and join his brothers in exile.

That decision provided the spark, the catalyst for war. The gods formed sides and did battle with one another. The war was long and terrible. Much of the glory of the age was lost. Those few worlds that willingly gave their assistance were swept under a tide of devastation so terrible their worlds crumbled from the core. Wrath and vengeance dominated all life until there was nothing left to give. What gods remained met on a quiet planet far from the center of the universe, Occanum, and made their final battle.

What happened is speculation, but it is said the gods destroyed themselves in a great explosion. The golden age of the gods was over but the gods themselves were not destroyed. Deicide is easy. All one needs to do is stop believing. The king of the gods knew this and set his plans in motion. Their physical forms evaporated, but the universe was not done with them. Galactic winds pushed their essences out across the universe. Each one drifted to a planet and settled; into the water, the ground, the very air men breathed. Time watched as civilizations evolved in the worship of specific gods, partaking of the essence in the earth. No god awoke, however, for the king knew that should the gods awaken they would return to their warring ways and finish what had been started.

But the gods were not the only victims of their appetites. The brothers never regained their unity. The madness was infuriating. It was too much for even their godlings minds to comprehend. Lost to the strain, the brothers turned on each other. Good and evil did battle in an eternal war. Their struggles destroyed entire worlds, leaving millions ruined in their wake. The first brother wanted no part in the war and remained in hiding. The fate of the universe would fall upon the shoulders of three brothers determined to hate one another.

3210 A.G. (After Gods), Prophet Isle, planet Crimeat.

Clink-clank. Clink-clank. The jingle of cold iron keys slapping against Evdar's thigh echoed menacingly down the dungeon hall. It stank of mold and decaying flesh. The only light came from a single torch at the end of the hallway. This didn't bother Evdar. He'd been a warden here for nearly nine years. He heard the familiar scurry of rats and spiders moving in the shadows. They were the closest thing he had to friends. The caress of cobwebs breaking across his face was almost welcome.

Evdar came to the end of the hall and unlocked the last door. Massive and ancient, this door hid the world's worst criminals. The damned dwelled within. Only certain death awaited those unfortunate enough to find themselves locked inside. Evdar strained his muscles to turn the key and pushed the old oak door open. A single beam of moonlight filled the center of the cell, pale and anticipatory. Shadows danced like faceless assassins from the corners un-kissed by the sun. An occasional wisp of cloud interrupted their dance, but only for a moment.

The walls were stark, stained white and covered with latent disease. The floor smelled of old flesh and human waste. A slop bucket sat in the corner next to a half-emptied plate of food. None of that mattered. The main attraction sat hunkered down in the center of the cell. He was huge, a monster of a man. The iron ring around his neck collared him to the ground. Not even a beast from the depths of the Great Barrier Jungle could have broken the chains.

His breathing was shallow. The echo of his heartbeat reverberated from the padded walls. *Thump-thump. Thump-thump.* His wrists were chained behind him, carefully placed so that he could not break free. Long strands of thick, black hair hung in front of his face, concealing it from Evdar. The warden snorted in an attempt at bolstering his weakened confidence. The prisoner, enormous compared to normal men, held latent horror for any unprepared to look upon him.

"Time again, Evdar?" asked the Shackled Man.

Nervousness spread like a foul miasma through the cell. The voice was deep, subliminally threatening. Evdar halted, his feelings of danger whispering quiet warnings. The warden waited until his mind cleared. He'd been through the same mind games with the Shackled Man for his entire tenure, but they were not a thing to get used to. Something wicked lay in the prisoner's true identity. There was enough confusion to make him wonder who the real prisoner was. Evdar placed the new plate of food on the ground and stepped back.

"I don't think I want to eat this tonight," the Shackled Man said. He still hadn't looked up, making Evdar even more nervous.

"I don't care what you want, Amongeratix," he replied. "It is the same food you have eaten since you've been here."

He snorted. "Food. I have dined with gods and kings, and you dare call this food? How low humanity has fallen."

Evdar refused to rise to the bait. "Eat it or not, I don't give a damn."

Amongeratix looked up. His movements were in slow motion, deliberate and haunting. Eyes the color of coal stared up at Evdar. The unrestrained hatred gave him pause. "Are we having problems, Evdar?"

The warden struggled not to reply. He knew this game, for it had been played far too often. Amongeratix delighted in the cruel tortures of conversation. He purposefully baited Evdar time and again for nothing more than sheer pleasure.

"Can you feel the call of the moon, Evdar?" He closed his eyes, fondly remembering days wild and dangerous. "It burns through my blood; gives me strength. It makes me feel like a beast again."

Evdar shook his head. He knew full well why this monster was shackled before him. Amongeratix was accused of killing more than a hundred people in a violent prison escape on another planet. The Inquisition had locked him in the foulest prison before managing to convince the Conclave to set the death sentence.

"Your days as a beast are over."

Amongeratix's smile was lost in shadows. "And that is where you're wrong. The beast cannot be contained. Not with chains or mortal bonds. Every month for the past thirty years I have waited for this night. The warmth of the moon lights the fire in my soul."

Evdar bit back a laugh. "What soul could you possibly have?"

"So much more than you might possibly imagine. Sometimes you should just sit and watch the moon."

"The moon offers me nothing," he replied. Evdar blinked rapidly. It was always part of Amongeratix's manipulations that subliminally prompted the guard to stay, waging a war of words he couldn't win.

"Nothing but the nightmares lurking on the edge of darkness," Amongeratix lowered his head. "I remember times when these pathetic cities of yours didn't exist. A time when mother moon saw armies of bloodthirsty axes rise and fall through long nights as they clove the armies of the day. You have never had the privilege of seeing fields of fire that drain your blood. The night can be such a dangerous mistress. If only you could have seen it, my dear Evdar, if only."

Evdar took a step back. The warning bells screamed caution. The baiting had taken a new direction. Amongeratix was calmer, more calculating. A foul twinkle fired the depths of his black eyes. Evdar realized that, for the first time, he was scared.

"Sometimes when the moonlight strikes my face and cool breeze blows my hair back, I can feel a tiny pain in my mind. The pain turns into seething fire, a rage so fierce it is all I can do to control it. Insanity grips me and takes me to the edge. I just want to kill." Amongeratix shuddered. Dormant muscles rippled and flexed. Evdar moved further back until he touched the fetid wooden door.

"Do you know why I killed all of those people?"

Mountains of fear stole his voice. Evdar could only shake his head. He couldn't deny that there had always been that quiet sliver of curiosity, though he was afraid to know the truth.

Amongeratix drew out his words. "I killed because I enjoyed it. If I could do it all over again I would. There is such power in taking a soft neck and squeezing. You squeeze tighter. The face turns different shades. The breathing turns to choking. At first the victim struggles, mistakenly thinking there is still hope. And then…**SNAP**. Oh Evdar, there is such joy to be had in seeing those final moments of life drain. Hearing that last gasp as the gift of your gods leaves forever."

"You're insane!"

Amongeratix barked out a dark laugh. "I won't be in here forever."

Evdar's fear reached its zenith, and he fumbled with the lock. He couldn't escape fast enough. His heart raced. Sweat dripped from his face and palms. His stomach threatened to revolt. Evdar slammed the door shut behind and ran, forgetting to lock it.

"The blood will flow again, Evdar!" Amongeratix howled from his cell. "I hear it call, and once more the universe will see the glory of my nightmare unleashed. There is no escape. You are all doomed!"

Amongeratix threw back his head and let loose a roar so tremendous it shattered every window in the prison. The time had come. Signs spread across the world. The old heard and felt their hearts stop. Death rode across the small village like a tidal wave. No one was safe. A distant clock tower chimed midnight. Lightning crashed down from the heavens, sparking wildfires across the surrounding hills. Somewhere, rain began to fall, hot and acidic.

Amongeratix surged and strained so hard his eyes rolled back into his head. Rage and the overwhelming desire for freedom tormented his mind. He felt the bonds of his chains weakening. He heard men charging down the hall towards him. The familiar clang of steel echoed to him. Swords. The guards had come to kill him. Fools, he thought.

Too late would they realize they were no match for his malevolence. Amongeratix felt the old hatred rise from the back of his throat.

The cell door burst open, and six guards rushed in. Cruel weapons that sparked bright blue beckoned in the empty darkness. Amongeratix surged upwards, but his bonds were too strong. The guards swarmed him, beating and pummeling him with clubs and violence. He took the pain. It was a welcome song, a boon companion. Each touch of the electroprods sent fifty thousand volts of electricity into him. Blood frothed at the corners of his mouth. His eyes burned. Evdar wormed his way around so that Amongeratix could see him. The guard smiled, cold and wicked, before cracking his club across Amongeratix's temple.

Darkness. A sharp thud.

"Is he secure this time?"

Evdar jerked the heavy chains and nodded. "He won't get out of these."

The captain of the guard blew out sharply. "He shouldn't have gotten out of the old ones. I still think this was all in your imagination, Evdar. You know he prides himself on his ability to manipulate." The man lashed out with a sharp kick to Amongeratix's ribs. "We should just cut his tongue out and be done with it. This son of a bitch is more trouble than he's worth."

"The Conclave voted against it," Evdar reminded. "They want him alive and unspoiled for when they hang him."

"Hang him? They need to draw and quarter the bastard and then burn the pieces. Lethendweil would be a better place without his filth."

They quietly exited the room. Once in the hallway, the captain turned to Evdar. "I want a double guard from here on out. Cut his food and water ration in half. I don't have the patience for his damned games."

He stormed off, angered at being disturbed so late and confused as to why one of his best guards would act so irrationally. The captain shrugged and kept walking. There was nothing else to do for now. Evdar waited for him to disappear in the gloom before leaning back against the slime and moss-covered wall. He exhaled a long, nervous breath.

"Shit," he whispered.

Shapeless patches of color danced behind his heavy eyelids. Sweat and blood dried on his face. His body was sore. The beating Amongeratix had taken would have killed a mortal man. Fortunately, he was far from mortal. His broken bones were already beginning to mend, his internal bleeding slowing to a halt. His heartbeat crept back to normal. Consciousness worked its way back into his system.

He struggled to rise but found the chains had been replaced with heavier, stronger, and ensorcelled ones. Amongeratix snarled quietly. Moonlight gleamed menacingly from his fanged teeth, and he decided that he had had enough. The foolish games of mortal men had run their course, and it was his time again. Gathering his full strength, the shackled man surged upwards and broke his bonds. The music of shattered metal striking the cold rock floor careened off the walls. Amongeratix stretched for the first time in years, his muscles sore and underused. The room was barely high enough to contain his massive twelve-foot frame.

Amongeratix ignored the cramps and jets of pain shooting through him, and wicked grin creased his aged face. He was one step closer to freedom. The moon seemed to shine a little brighter, harkening old memories of violence. He turned to face the tiny window.

"Finally," he whispered.

As if on cue, a hellish bolt of lightning struck the window. Glass and stone exploded as if hit by a cannon round. Amongeratix was knocked to his knees as dust and debris choked the night, and a purple-tinged light formed in the center of the room, dancing from one broken shadow to the next. Hectic instability pushed the light into a hazy orb. Amongeratix sat in muted remembrance; he had since this once before. Fierce winds slashed into the cell, forcing him to shield his eyes lest they be put out by flying shards of his prison.

The orb came to hover directly in front of him, but for a moment only. Raw energy surged into the ruined chamber an instant before the orb smashed down into the floor. Amongeratix was thrown against the wall. The entire prison trembled and threatened to break. His eyes darted back and forth, eager to catch his first glimpse of an old acquaintance. Purple gave way to an unimpressive blue, and the floor dropped away in massive chunks until all that remained was the tiny square upon which he stood. Amongeratix summoned his strength and peered into the fog of the abyss.

Dark faces leered up at him. Wreathed in flames, they taunted him. Beckoned him to join them. He snorted. They were the souls of those he'd so enjoyed killing. Tongues of blue flame shot from the depths. A sound came to him, one reminding him of a witch's cackle on the day of the dead. Amongeratix bowed his mighty head, letting long strands of pitch black hair hang in front of his wide face.

"I have long awaited this day," he said.

"The time is at hand at long last," rasped a thin voice from the depths. "The universe has become diseased, a wretched memory of past greatness. The quality of humanity has failed."

Amongeratix smiled fiercely. "I have carried out your bidding as best as I could."

"The time for battles is over. Now is the time for war. The gods are scattered. Their ancient power is broken. Many refuse to wake for fear of what humanity has become. Your father sleeps."

"My father!" he snorted. "That title means nothing to me. He abandoned us long ago."

"Yes, all because of your brother's impudence. He is the cause of it all. He must atone for his crimes. Find him, Amongeratix. Find your brother and cast his soul to me. Only then will you be able to shake loose the chains and take your proper place in the pantheon of the gods."

Amongeratix closed his eyes. The promise of revenge traced his lips, but he dared not give in to the temptation of those dreams. Not until his brother lay dead and broken at his feet could he finally become what his master desired. The floor trembled for a moment only, long enough for the illusion of despair to fade. Amongeratix stood free in the ruins of his cell. Raw power coursed through his muscles. A strength that had long lain dormant surged back to life, and he became hatred.

His attention was drawn to a commotion in the hall. The guards had recovered enough to return. He turned to meet his enemy. This was a day he had dreamed of. Amongeratix stepped back away from the door.

"Stand back!" a voice cried from the other side.

The shape charge exploded. Wood and metal slivers shredded the air, tearing into the prisoner's flesh. Guards poured in with the cloud of fumes. Amongeratix waited long enough for them all to enter. None caught the glint of teeth flashing in the scattered torch light.

Amongeratix attacked. Faster than human reflexes, he ripped and tore through the guards. Ropes of blood splashed against the walls, burned hotly on his cheek. He reveled in the violence. He killed and killed until only one remained.

Evdar knelt in the center of the room, bleeding from a torn abdomen. Amongeratix slowly walked closer to his tormentor. Gone was the haughty arrogance and air of superiority Evdar had once directed towards him. The guard was bleeding to death. His flesh had already lost color. His eyes began to glaze. Amongeratix knelt and cupped Evdar's chin, lifting the head so he could stare him in the eye.

"Evdar, my dear Evdar," he mocked. "Welcome to my misery."

Evdar tried to shake his head but lacked the strength as his blood flowed. "You're…insane."

Specks of blood dripped from his mouth. It hurt to speak, to breathe.

"I am tired of your help. You and all your pathetic kind. The universe belongs to greater beings, yet instead we are cursed with lesser sons that don't deserve the breath they draw. My time has come, Evdar. Look around you. All of your friends lay dead, their dreams and aspirations no more than dust torn in the wind."

He kicked the nearest corpse. "This is the promise the gods left you. Death and decay are all that remain for you, Evdar."

"There are no gods," Evdar coughed. "The world is what man has made it."

Amongeratix tilted his back in fierce laughter. "Is it? There are secrets, forgotten dreams that humanity has lost forever, that remain elusive. Your kind does not deserve to live. The Conclave will fall." He knelt. "Before I am done with you, my old friend, you will beg for the gods to end your life."

Darkness engulfed the room but could not drown out the screams.

THREE

3210 A.G. (After Gods), Prophet Isle, planet Crimeat.

Moffo Kain was a shallow man. He preferred the calming virtue of shadows to the bright lights where trouble had a habit of finding him. Here, he was all but invisible, which was the exact reason he'd been contacted. No names had been given, and, to be fair, he had been at the beginning of a drunken stupor when they had contacted him. *Go to Prophet Isle and await further instructions*. That was it. Cryptic, but the purse full of gold coins had enticed him to the point where he couldn't back out. Moffo was also an opportunist. He had awoken the next day to a pile of scattered coins and a naked woman in the bed.

His nose was fat, swollen from too many breaks. High cheek bones had lost their prominence with the roundness of poor health, making his light brown eyes seem smaller than they were. Moffo constantly felt tired, wishing he weighed less. His black hair was long and stringy; the grease all but dripped from the tips. The cut of his cloth was poor and showed little quality. He was poor, downtrodden, and hopeless. He was the exact kind of person *they* needed.

Moffo hired a small boat to take him across the sea to Prophet Isle. He was told his contact would meet him in the shanty town of Breld. Five days and nights he wandered the town and became a regular at the bars. He scowled at the sky, angered at having to come here in the rainy season. Not even his new cloak, thick and forest green, managed to keep the rain completely off. Miserable, he settled down and waited until the raw beginnings of impatience set in. Breld was nothing special. Most of the buildings were of flimsy construction. The roads were rutted too deeply for a wagon to roll through. Stray dogs barked and fought over scraps in the alleys, occasionally scoring a meal with a random corpse left to rot.

Finally, when Moffo was ready to abandon his task, a stranger approached him, his face hidden behind a mask. Moffo's suspicions instantly rose, though not enough to dissuade him from accepting the rolled piece of leather. Moffo started to ask a question, but the stranger turned and left.

He paused only to look back over his shoulder, saying, "Tell no one."

Moffo enjoyed the secrecy of it all though he still had no clue as to what he'd been hired for. He accepted the challenge and soon found himself climbing over aged boulders and fields of spiraling trees. Prophet Isle was plush, making the desolation of Breld curious. Flowing fields of verdant grass turned into forests of trees hundreds of feet tall. Deer and smaller animals were abundant. Streams of silver water divided the land, the soft bubbling echoing far away.

It was the boulders that first whispered caution. Dark grey, they stared back at him in silent warning with weatherworn faces. Moffo found it odd but did not stop. He was too close now. Foreboding grew the further he went. He felt something, evil perhaps, in the air. The notion was ridiculous. What could possibly be evil in such a paradise?

The answer was most unexpected. Moffo crested the final rise and looked down upon a sight both serene and frightening. The building was tiny, no more than a minor castle back on the mainland. Walls of pure onyx glittered, sucking in all light. Barred windows, circular and so small that he doubted his head would be able to fit through, sporadically dotted the sides. A strange humming warped the air. His head pounded. *What is this place?* Dread spiraled clinging fingers into his heart, clutching and tearing at him.

Whisper-thin clouds danced across the night skies, occasionally crossing the bright full moon. Sparse winds tickled down his spine, reminding him of a childhood spent hiding from his father. Moffo eased just a little closer to the odd building. His every instinct screamed for him to turn and flee, warring with his natural curiosity. Moffo chose to stay. This was it, he decided. Moffo slid down behind a particularly foul-shaped boulder and withdrew the piece of rolled leather from his inner pocket.

Fat fingers, deadened from the cold, struggled with the ties that had swollen with the dampness of the island. He cursed and finally gave up. Moffo drew his slender dagger, the metal cheap and overworked, and cut the straps. The leather unrolled of its own accord. Its cryptic message played out before his eyes—and made absolutely no sense. He frowned and reread it, hoping to find some semblance of meaning or worth. Again, nothing.

The one you seek will find you. Escort him safely back to Breld. We will be waiting.

Moffo Kain cursed again. He hated games. He decided that the stranger in the mask had played him for a fool. Only a fool would come to such a place as this, he reasoned. But the gold! If not for the gold, he might have abandoned this foolishness altogether. The gold was real. That meant that whoever hired him was real.

The ground shook. Moffo slipped and fell to the ground. A sharp rock dug into the fat roll on his right hip. A snake squirmed away, disturbed from the impact of his body on the ground. Glowing eyes blinked and stared at him from the darker shadows. A hairy spider crawled over his left hand and made him jump back with a gasp.

Lightning ripped through the heavens, striking the onyx building with nightmarish fury. Stone and glass exploded in a shower of sparks and dust. The concussion knocked Moffo back down. Random crashing sounds came from the forest behind him. Large animals raced by, clearly spooked. Moffo glanced skyward and wondered where the lightning had come from. The sky had barely a cloud in it. This was not right. Again, his mind begged him to leave, and again his greed dominated. Moffo Kain was willing to forgo his own safety for the promise of a trickle of gold running across his fingertips.

The dust began to clear, giving him a partially clear view of the building. A gaping hole spit bland light, mocking the dark of night along the upper levels closest to him. How was this possible? A howl danced up from the forest and was echoed by a dozen more. The mournful sounds reminded him of old women wailing at a funeral. He felt fear for the first time this night. Moffo suddenly doubted if he would leave this place alive. The world seemed in revolt, but from what he did not know.

A strangled scream rang out, and the world stopped. Moffo felt his blood chill at the sound and hurriedly rolled over into a crouch. A myriad of violent colors clashed inside the hole. The scream multiplied, and Moffo swore as he saw a body fly from the gap. The violence escalated before abruptly ending. Moffo rose and dashed to cover behind another boulder. A light rain began to fall. The drops were just cold enough to spark a shiver each time one struck exposed flesh.

Silence settled over the building. It reminded Moffo of a graveyard just past dusk. He was not a superstitious man; too much in life was explainable with a little thought. Looking up into the hole in the wall, however, Moffo realized that there were monsters in the world. A hulking figure twice the size of a human lumbered into the rift and leapt to the ground. Lightning wreathed the skies, giving Moffo a glimpse of this new nightmare. His heart beat a little faster. Fear made him salivate. His fingers twitched. His mind screamed that what he saw could not be possible.

The giant landed with a crack, and a cloud of dust billowed around him. Rising to his full height, the giant looked around as if relishing his newfound freedom. He spread his arms and roared to the skies. Defiance. Moffo caught a thick tone of the emotion pulsing from the giant. The winds picked up sharply, blowing the giant's long black hair wildly as he approached the crouching man. Lightning continued to stab the sky, marking each step the giant took. Moffo took morbid interest in the man, for it clearly was some kind of man, if twice Moffo's size. His clothes were torn in a hundred places. His flesh was burned, and he bled from a handful of minor wounds. The hands caught Moffo's attention. They were massive and capable of crushing skulls. Moffo wanted to turn and run, but his legs froze him in place. The giant came to a stop a few meters away and stared down at him with utter contempt. Moffo awaited the killing blow.

"You are the one I am supposed to find?" the giant snorted.

Hot urine flowed down Moffo's leg. The giant noticed the growing stain and barked a terrible laugh.

"Answer me before I rip your head off," he snapped.

Moffo Kain jerked his head up and down. "Y…Yes."

Amongeratix looked down on the insignificant man and clenched his fists in subconscious rage. Ancient power coursed through him, and he reveled in it for the first time in centuries. Much had been stolen from him since his imprisonment by the Inquisition and their damned Blood Witches. His life and dreams were nothing but hollow shells of what might have been. Still, he managed to repress the sudden outbreak of violence and refrain from killing the man.

"Who are you? Speak your name," Amongeratix demanded.

"I am called Moffo Kain."

Amongeratix sneered. "Why have you come to me, Moffo Kain? What game is being played?"

Moffo struggled to come up with a viable answer though he did not truly know why he was here to begin with. Too much had happened too soon. Faceless strangers and greed tempted him here, in front of his deepest nightmare.

Finally, he remembered. "I am supposed to take you to Breld."

Amongeratix stepped closer. "What is important about this place?"

Moffo never got the chance to answer. The giant tilted his nose to the wind. His eyes narrowed with newfound intent. Moffo watched as his muscles tightened, threatening to rip from the constricting flesh. Amongeratix snarled, surprised by what he smelled and then sensed. A sneer twisted his face. The presence was one he had not felt in hundreds of years. All thoughts of freedom evaporated and were replaced with the desire for revenge.

Lightning crashed between them. Moffo rolled over and clapped his hands to his ears. The smell of burnt hair gagged him. White spots continued to flash across his vision, and he feared he was blinded. Moffo struggled to rise but had no strength. The spots faded enough for him to make out bits of the second giant, the one called Tannus. He was much the same as the first monster. Easily twelve feet tall, Tannus was the vision of chiseled perfection. Moffo was reminded of one of the grand statues in front of the palaces in Vaade. Blond hair close cropped and neat topped his muscular face. The hint of a scar poked from the collar of his shirt. Moffo doubted that either giant had the ability to best the other, so closely were they matched in size and stature.

Amongeratix turned, eagerly hunting his prey in the enlightened night landscape. The Shackled Man couldn't see him, but he knew without a doubt that he was here, hiding and waiting for the right moment to show himself.

"Brother," Amongeratix whispered. "At last we can begin our final game."

His hair danced across his face and massive chest. The faint howl of a restless wind echoed across the fields of rocks. Emptiness mocked him. Amongeratix grew impatient as years of pent up frustrations and detailed plotting surged against each other. Moffo stared up at the giant with newfound horror. Such things simply were *not*. Amongeratix ignored him. Frustration wore at him. He'd waited so long for the revenge freedom promised only to find it remained just out of grasp. Whether his prey hid out of cowardice or mild dramatics, he couldn't tell, but Amongeratix fought the rage gnawing his nerves. All the pain and little agonies, the sheer indignity of being shackled for so long, constantly tormented him. Amongeratix wanted revenge.

"Tannus, I know you are here!" he bellowed. Sweat stung his hate filled eyes. "Show yourself, already! Show yourself to me!"

A twig snapped. Heavy footsteps crushed fallen leaves. Heads turned. The Shackled Man smiled. Moffo slinked backwards, suddenly eager to be away from this scene. He blinked rapidly as a second monstrous figure emerged from the shadows. Never in his darkest dreams had he imagined beholding such terror. Unlike Amongeratix, the newcomer was content with waiting. After all, a few more minutes were nothing compared to the eternity of time. Amongeratix flexed his hands. His breath came out in hot plumes. He was being toyed with, an old tactic of his brother's. He forced himself not to abandon caution and charge into the night. They'd been adversaries for so long that each knew the other's ways and would be prepared. No, it was better to wait for Tannus to step into the light and begin the confrontation.

Silence crept across the area. Even the sound of the wind died to nothing. From across the field Tannus watched Amongeratix passively, as if uncertain how to react. The convenience of it all was puzzling. Tannus had been halfway across the universe when an anonymous message had come to him. It warned of his brother's impending escape from the Inquisition prison. Tannus had gone into reaction mode and chartered a flight to Crimeat without so much as an extra thought spared to how anyone could possibly know in advance the events to come. Not even the fabled Blood Witches had the power to predict the future.

As soon as he'd arrived on Crimeat, he'd gotten the feeling that a thing was about to happen that went far beyond the war with his brother. Tannus almost felt helpless, an unusual feeling, to be sure. The planet was boiling with contempt; he just couldn't figure out against what.

Regardless, he couldn't worry about that now. Amongeratix was free, and it didn't matter how. Tannus knew the story of his imprisonment, and it was by sheer luck that the Inquisitor managed to take Amongeratix so easily. Tonight was not going to be so easy.

"Tannus! I can smell you. I can hear your breath, ragged as it is. Let us embrace as brothers should." Amongeratix had grown tired of waiting. Instinct and impulse urged him to attack. Visions of ripping his brother to shreds were only dissolved by the fact that he had failed to do so over the span of centuries.

Tannus moved so fast it became a blur. Moffo Kain tripped and fell back before the second giant closed the distance. Anger and spite radiated from the brothers. Theirs was an ancient hatred, one so deep it threatened the core of civilization. The ground trembled. Fires erupted in violent gouts from rents in the earth. Thick clouds poured in much too fast to be natural and blanketed the sky. Intense heat threatened to choke the life from Moffo.

"Ever have you lacked patience, brother," Tannus scolded.

Amongeratix sneered. "Patience? I have spent more time in secret prisons rotting from boredom than you give me credit for. Perhaps you would like to be shackled to the ground like a wild beast? Keep your patience; I have my hate to push me."

"You made your choices, and now look at the monster you have become. How many did you kill inside of there?"

Amongeratix smiled. "One more would be nice."

"You have never managed it before. What makes you believe you can be successful tonight?"

"A new power is rising, brother. The universe will be right again, and it is I who will stand at the front. Our war has extended far too long, Tannus. Our little feud is rapidly approaching the blood-filled end promised all those years ago. No one can stand on the side and watch. This is the end of it all."

Tannus looked for any sign of humanity in his brother, any trace showing that madness had not claimed him. He came away disappointed. Delusional fancy streamed off Amongeratix. His rationale was so eroded that all his focus narrowed to a singular point, and that point was the ultimate destruction of the universe.

Tannus had never understood his brother's lust for power. There were underlying truths to it, but in the end Tannus believed it was more about acceptance than power. Amongeratix had always felt as if their father had not truly loved him. That misinterpretation drove his innate rage and filled his soul with undying hatred.

Tannus held out his hands, a final gesture for peace. "We do not need to do this. Our father has been gone for too long for us to continue this pointless feud. Set aside your hatred and let us be brothers again."

His settled then, moody and threatening. "We have not been brothers in a very long time."

Tannus let out a deep sigh. Reason was forgotten. "This can only end badly for you, Amongeratix. The universe does not need your murdering ways. You will beg for the cold comforts of your prison cell before this night is done."

"You continue to mock me, Tannus," Amongeratix ground out. "A time of reckoning is coming, brother. You are no longer father's favorite. Your light will burn out."

Tannus stood unaffected. He was used to the taunts and impotent threats. Of all his brothers, Amongeratix was the most easily provoked. Tannus counted on that fact now. He doubted he had the strength to match his brother's aggression and needed every advantage he could find. For unexplainable reasons, Amongeratix seemed to be getting stronger.

"There is no power in this universe capable of such a thing. Go back to your cell and forget this mad quest of yours. You are beginning to bore me, *brother*."

Madness sparkled in his eyes. "Am I truly?"

Amongeratix twitched, his fingers flexing at his sides. The slightest hint of luminescent green power radiated off his flesh. Years of captivity fueled his rage. He had been waiting for this moment for a very long time. Generations were born and had died, and still he had rotted in prison, robbed of all the glory he deserved. Amongeratix was filled with hatred, and Tannus was the perfect target.

"Come to me, brother," he bade. "Let us dance once more."

Lightning struck the prison, sending great gouts of dust and rock out in waves. Amongeratix attacked. Moffo Kain was both impressed and horrified at how easily the giant moved. His muscles were tight, rippling against his skin. Each step Amongeratix took was like water passing down a stream. Effortless. Flawless. Moffo Kain had no doubt that he gazed upon physical perfection and knew that man should not have to witness such. Fierce winds ravaged the landscape around them, adding nightmarish elements that toyed with Moffo's mind.

Tannus stared coldly at his brother. Conflicts as old as the sun remained between them. Amongeratix was evil, corrupted and diseased by the quest for more power. Still, they were brothers, and that was a bond that could not be easily shattered. He hesitated. Tannus only wanted to stop his brother, not kill him. Amongeratix grinned wickedly, savagely, and broke into violent laughter. It forced Tannus into action. The giant reached behind his back, under his dark cloak, and produced one of the largest guns Moffo had ever seen. It would have been a cannon in the hands of a mortal man.

Thunder roared, forcing Moffo to cover his ears as Tannus squeezed the trigger. Bluish flames shot from the barrel. Chemically infused, each round was designed for the jacket to disintegrate upon contact, allowing the chemicals to penetrate the skin and render their targets immobile. A steady stream of fire belched from the mighty gun, sleek and black against the moonlight.

Amongeratix dodged with uncanny reflexes, twisting and leaping high into an arc over the sudden battlefield. He came barreling down behind his brother. "You'll have to aim better than that, Tannus. Imprisonment has not hampered my abilities."

His eyes lit up a sulfurous yellow, seething with hatred. Tannus spun, firing in anticipation of Amongeratix's next move. "We need not do this," he repeated. "Come back with me. It is not our universe anymore. Times have changed. Come back and let us end this feud."

"You always were shortsighted. Do you forget that this is all your fault? That we would not be in this position if not for your impatience? No, Tannus. I will not return."

Amongeratix launched into attack. He charged into his brother, ducking and twisting out of the way of a hail of bullets. His eyes rolled into the back of his head, his hands flexed with immeasurable strength. Froth spilled from his lips as he allowed the ancient battle rage to consume him. Clouds raced to cover the moon, showering the land in ethereal darkness. Amongeratix began to glow, building power as he ran. He roared, a sound that reached down into the bones of the earth. Bolts of energy pierced the clouds toward Tannus. Using unimaginable reflexes, Tannus targeted each bolt and fired his weapon. Unerringly, he intercepted all of them, small explosions of raw power shaking the world.

Acrid smoke filled the area with haze. The smell of burnt flesh and hair choked Moffo as he watched the titans battle. The thunder of the assault weapon was lost to him. His eyes could not widen further. He knew that the shock of what he witnessed would haunt him to his dying day—which he forced himself to admit might be tonight. Stone and tree burst apart, fragments and splinters shredding everything within sight. Moffo whimpered and ducked deeper.

Brother crashed into brother. Lightning struck again. Tannus' weapon flew away in a shower of sparks. Fists struck. The wet crunch of pounded flesh echoed again and again. The giants slammed into the ground. Amongeratix pressed his advantage, hammering into his brother with centuries of aggression. A tooth flew off in a rope of blood and spit. The snap of a nose breaking. A rib. Tannus fought back with equal ferocity. Each blow was sharp and precise. He rolled right, forcing Amongeratix to miss. The force of the blow drove a hole in the softened ground. The distraction allowed Tannus to bring a knee up into his brother's kidney. Amongeratix howled in pain and jerked back just enough for Tannus to kick him off. He flew back and broke the nearest tree upon impact.

Tannus struggled to his feet. At least two ribs were broken, and blood splattered his once perfect face. Anger broiled in his eyes. It had been a long time since he had been forced to bleed. He stalked over and picked up the pieces of his rifle. Broken. It wouldn't serve as a club in its current condition. Tannus scowled. He had not wanted it to come to this, but he knew deep in his heart that there would be no choice. Always his brother failed to listen to reason. The disappointment would have been heartbreaking had it not been so familiar that Tannus found his heart callused to his brother's depredations.

Amongeratix was in equally bad shape. The violent yellow in his eyes had faded. Much of his rage was gone, lost amongst the beatings he had taken and given. Wisps of breath formed streams in the chill night air. Tiny beads of sweat trickled down his forehead. Muscles tightened and then loosened. Much of the adrenalin had left him, abandoning him to a feeling of shaded uselessness. Amongeratix spit blood and forced a smile through cracked lips.

"You are growing weaker, brother," he chided. "There was a time when I would not have gotten so far. Your power wanes."

Tannus shook his head. "I told you we did not need to do this."

Amongeratix dismissed him with a wave. "This was mere foreplay. Our actions today will give birth to the grand design for tomorrow. Once again, we shape the future of the universe. It is better to wait out these next few months in the anticipation of events to come."

"I have never known you to run from a fight, *brother*," Tannus replied. He wiped the blood from his cheek.

He failed to notice the wicked gleam in the corner of Amongeratix's eye. Unmitigated power surged through him. He gasped at the rawness. Tannus took a menacing step forward and was met with all Amongeratix's pent-up rage. Waves of brilliant blue power funneled off the Shackled Man and struck his brother with full force. Tannus flew backwards, driven all the way back to the main prison building. His massive body shattered trees and boulders, rendering him unconscious well before he was crushed through the thick wall. Smoke and dust poured into the night sky. Miniature explosions rocked the ground. Amongeratix collapsed, exhausted.

Moffo Kain struggled to close his mouth. Never in his wildest dreams had he expected to witness such things. Signs of apocalypse were everywhere. He felt as if he'd been part of a war between titans. So much destruction would have once pained his heart, but now it held an empty sensation. Yet, as afraid as he was of these giants, curiosity demanded more. He wanted to know what they were. Who. The bitter testimony of their potential paled his flesh.

"Moffo Kain."

Startled, Moffo snapped out of his daze to find Amongeratix addressing him. A queer look lingered in the Shackled Man's eyes, as if he'd just lost some small part of himself.

"We should be going now. He will not remain so for long," Amongeratix told him. The Shackled Man had recovered, barely, and was back on his feet.

"He's not dead?" Moffo could hardly accept that. Nothing could or should survive such punishment.

Amongeratix shook his head ruefully.

"Aren't you going to kill him?" Moffo asked.

Amongeratix sneered down at him. "Come. We have much work to do."

FOUR

3210 A.G. (After Gods), Krenz, planet Vau Prime.

Tolde Breed could not sleep. Ill had been his dreams of late, frozen nightmares of a time long past. He did not know what they meant, only that they returned night after night. Tolde began to despise the night. He took no comfort during those precious few hours a day when his body demanded rest. Wiping the sweat from his face, Tolde sat up and looked out the window. Dawn was still some hours away. Darkness reminded him of his self-inflicted miseries. The longer it went on, the more he was convinced that he had unfinished business left somewhere in the universe.

Already an old man, Tolde was well into his late eighties. A lifetime of service to the Inquisition had left him scarred. Conspiracies haunted the corners. Shadows played at the edge of his sight. Faceless whispers taunted him from the recesses of forgotten memories. He had seen too much, done too much. The years of his life had been spent for good cause, however. He had served the Order of the Inquisition faithfully, defending humanity across the stars from the threat of the gods awakening. Tolde was not close to death, leastwise not from age. Regeneration technology and extended healthcare provided most citizens with almost unnaturally long lives. Tolde expected to live for at least another fifty years. Age. He snorted. Some things did not get better under the cold progressions of time.

Much was forgotten of the Old Times. Men did not recall what had happened to their gods or why. All they knew was that the gods slept and had not been seen or felt in over three thousand years. Every child was taught the story of history turned myth. Long ago, the gods went to war. A great explosion occurred, destroying their physical forms and sending shards of their essences to every planet in the universe. Those planets evolved in the worship of the god that touched them. It was a convoluted system, but the elected head cardinals of all of the religions gathered on the central planet of Vau Prime.

Tolde slid from the stark white sheets and went into the refresher. He carefully dabbed a washcloth in the cold water and

31

cleaned his face further. Simply wiping the sweat away did not make him feel clean. He gazed into the mirror and felt…he wasn't sure what he felt. The aged face staring back at him was somehow alien, lost. He closed his eyes and went back to bed. Perhaps sleep would find him and cradle him away in its tender embrace.

He crawled back into bed, the soft sheets clinging to his lean body. Most of the fat had been eaten away by a high metabolism and a rigorous training regimen that all Inquisitors went through. His bald head touched the pillow. Its coolness was comforting. His once sharp grey eyes closed and opened a moment later when a high-pitched chime announced he had a visitor. Almost grateful for the distraction, Tolde got up and threw on a navy-blue robe.

The face he saw upon opening his door was young, much younger than he had been when he was first recruited into the Inquisition. That youth did not translate into confidence. The boy trembled at the very thought of disturbing one of the senior ranking Inquisitors at such an untimely hour. Tolde sighed. He felt that the Order had lost much over the last few decades. It was a strength they could not get back.

"Well?" he growled when the boy made no effort to speak.

Swallowing hard, he replied, "Senior Inquisitor, I am sorry to wake you this late, but the Inquisitor General has ordered a council with you."

Ordered? Normally it would be requested. Tolde suppressed a frown. This was highly unusual, especially for a man old enough to be almost irrelevant. Almost.

"Inform the Inquisitor General that I shall be there shortly."

The youth nodded and left just fast enough to appear urgent without seeming to run away. Tolde imagined the look of relief that boy must have. He certainly would not have wanted to wake up a senior official in the middle of the night. Tolde let the door hiss close behind and went to the large bank of reflexive windows. He pushed the controls that opened the heavy curtains and stared down into the heart of Krenz. The principle city of both the Inquisition and Conclave was alive with activity. There was nothing abnormal about the fact; Tolde quickly came to learn that this city, perhaps even the planet, never truly shut down. There was always something else to do.

Mighty columns speared into the sky in tribute to the majesty of human imagination. Sculptures and intricate carvings crawled around most of them. Krenz was the history of the universe. It was here that the light of the gods first helped humanity rise from obscurity. The great columns were erected in the gods' honor. As large as a city block, the massive structures pierced the sky. Lights, the strongest in the universe, were mounted inside the columns and never dimmed. Whoever had initially planned it all had been smart enough to realize that the columns needed to be taller than most buildings to let the light shine. Tolde remained impressed with the architecture. The lights were visible from space, offering a feeling of homecoming whenever he returned from a task. One for each god, the tribute lights of Krenz provided continual light for those in distress as well as those keeping the faith.

Tolde had always held an affinity for the columns. He liked to think that mankind was bigger than itself, that there was some measure of care inherent in them all that could rise above the petty ugliness and find sanctuary in the hearts of all. Decades of service to the Inquisition had provided ample evidence that this was not always so. He'd lost track of the number of people he had been forced to hunt down. Some had died; some were imprisoned for crimes against the Conclave. All were convicted and labeled heretics. The columns of light offered Tolde hope.

Sighing, he left the skyline and dressed. The Inquisitor General was not a patient man, and if it was urgent enough to rouse Tolde in the middle of the night, he was probably not a happy man either. Tolde opened his closet, pulling out a freshly cleaned and pressed uniform. It was not every day one was called into audience with the highest-ranking Inquisitor in the universe. The boots. The tunic. The dark grey pants. The off-white jacket with his rank epaulettes and insignia. Tolde was as comfortable wearing the uniform as he was breathing air.

He traced a fingertip over the blue tinged red rose on the left breast of his jacket. The rose was the symbol of the Inquisition and a memory of where they had come from. Inquisitors were taught that the red was for the blood spilled to preserve peace, and the blue was for the promise the future held. Tolde wasn't convinced in the simplicity of the message, but he did believe in the Order. Humanity believed in the Order. It and the Conclave were the two most pivotal organizations in history. Between them, order was maintained, and the gods continued to sleep. Tolde knew, as did the others, that if just one of the gods managed to awaken, there would be an imbalance, and all they had worked for would fall apart. Anarchy and chaos would consume the universe as a singular god went on a campaign to undo his brothers and sisters. That was the true meaning of the Inquisition—to smash the various cults and heretical movements trying to revive their gods. Tolde Breed often prayed that those dark times would not happen on his watch. Recent events made him think otherwise.

Dressed, the Senior Inquisitor slipped on a pair of white gloves and left his apartments. A driver awaited him in the building lobby.

"Another long night, eh, Inquisitor?" The driver smiled.

Tolde gave a sharp nod. "You know that the Order never sleeps, Aron."

Aron grinned, less brightly this time, and opened the door for Tolde. The night air was crisp. Late autumn had come to Krenz. Soon, the winter snows would fall, and the city would shift modes. Vau Prime wasn't an overly large planet, despite being the center of the universe. What it lacked in spring and autumn it made up for with the harsh summers and equally harsh winters. Tolde was never one to appreciate either extreme, but he had grown used to them over the decades. Thankfully, for much of his work he was in the field and not stationed here.

His current assignment kept him close to home. The office of the Inquisitor General had assigned him to the training cadre at the Order's basic training facility. Easily as large as a small city, the Order's main base occupied an entire island off the main continent. Normally, Tolde would have stayed in his quarters there, but he had been forced to take leave after five months of hard training.

Aron waited quietly, shutting the door gently behind the Inquisitor once he was comfortably seated. A light rain sprinkled the windshield, blurring the orange glow of the streetlights. Aron pushed the ignition button and pulled back on the controls. The air-car hummed and shook slightly as it lifted from the ground. Tolde looked out the side window with mild interest. The cryptic message from the Inquisitor General soured his mood for reasons he did not fathom. Memories from a time long ago flooded back. He had been summoned to the Inquisitor General's office once before, early in his career. The events that had followed had not only shaped not career but defined his life. He prayed such was not the case this time.

The city blurred by. Most of the people were still asleep, souring Tolde's mood considerably. Still, he had chosen this life. The

Inquisition was not bound by a typical duty day. Their offices never closed, their members remaining vigilant against cults and heresies spanning the universe. It was a hard life. Each Inquisitor came with an individual brand of social awkwardness. Relationships were difficult to maintain. Tolde was proof. He had never married, never truly considered it. He had no sons, no daughters. When he died, so would his bloodline. Such facts were trivial; Tolde was thoroughly dedicated to the security of the Conclave worlds.

"It looks like it is going to turn out to be a pretty good-sized storm," Aron commented from the front seat.

Tolde tore his gaze away from the city below. "I like it when it rains. It feels like the world is being cleansed."

Aron, used to Tolde's off comments, nodded once. "It smells nice, too. Sometimes I think we get too wound up in our daily affairs to notice the simple pleasures in life."

"Those are the trappings of such an advanced lifestyle. We often lose sight of what matters for trivial pleasures," Tolde replied. "Do you have a family, Aron?"

He beamed, silently thankful that a senior ranking official took the time to inquire into his personal life. A failing of leadership was that they often forgot the men and women who did the trivial things in life. Tolde prided himself on knowing the people who worked for him, recognizing their contributions to the total effort.

"I do, sir. I have a wife and three daughters," he replied, banking the air car onto the main avenue.

Redemption Boulevard was one of Krenz's main spectacles. Statues of previous Inquisitors and members of the Conclave lined the road. Willow trees ran the length down the middle from the Cathedral of Conclave all the way to the offices of the Inquisition. Their yellow leaves adding pleasant contrast to the stark grey buildings as branches blew in the breeze. Tolde looked down and smiled. Redemption Boulevard always reminded him of summer.

"I envy you, my friend," Tolde said. "You have a luxury that I never will."

Aron did not know how to respond. Much of what he took for granted was alien to the men and women he worked for. That saddened him for reasons he couldn't explain. The domed towers of the Inquisition Headquarters slowly came into view. The massive structure stalled any additional conversation. It was easy to take the majesty for granted. Tolde had come and gone from here for more than fifty years. The heart of the Inquisition, the faded gold walls represented all that was good in humanity while at the same time sending stark warning to those who would usurp the status.

Every curve was familiar to him. A massive dome in the center spawned dozens more on three surrounding sides. They reminded him of mushroom caps in the wild. Banks of windows met his gaze like empty eyes searching into his soul. Daunting, to be sure, but gratifying. The main dome reached up to nearly two thousand feet and dwarfed the rest of Krenz for miles around. Aron followed the well-used path and brought the air car down.

"Here you are, Inquisitor," he said after hitting the door button.

Tolde Breed climbed out of the small vehicle and nodded his appreciation. "Thank you, Aron."

"Do you need me to stick around to take you home?"

Tolde had a mischievous twinkle in his eyes. "Between you and me, I have no idea how long I am going to be. Go home to your wife and children. They deserve you just as much as the Order does."

"Thank you, Inquisitor."

The door shut, and Tolde was alone again. Squaring his shoulders, the Senior Inquisitor began the short march up the Penitent Path to the massive iron doors. Along the way, he reflected, as was the tradition, on what the Inquisition meant and how his actions impacted the lives of others. However, Tolde was in no mood for such superstitious habits. Instead, his thoughts swirled around the mystery of his summoning. Dawn was still some hours off, and this entire affair smelled foul. He stopped to present identification to the black-uniformed Prekhauten Guard on duty and continued. The Inquisition might be the Conclave's gun, but the Prekhauten Guard was the bullets.

Tolde had always appreciated their military might. Most were exceptional people, not just sharp instruments of war. The Guard and the Inquisition worked hand in hand to enforce the Conclave's will. Tolde marched past several more as he wound his way through the white marble corridors. He had tunnel vision, as he usually did. The only reason to be here was for business. Tolde saw no point in exchanging unnecessary pleasantries with men and women he barely knew. He made the occasional nod or slight wave but did not slow—at least not until he noticed a stern looking man in a dark Guard uniform.

"Senior Inquisitor" the Guardsman said, "it has been a long time."

Tolde stared back at the man's hazel eyes. "Sergeant Matthias. I haven't seen you since Keltoo."

Matthias smiled. "It's Sergeant Major now. Someone thought I was responsible enough to run my own division."

"Responsible, but not mature?" Tolde grinned.

"Something like that. I heard a rumor that you have been summoned to the Inquisitor General's office."

Tolde's eyes narrowed reflexively. Inquisition business was not common knowledge.

Matthias held up his hands submissively. "Don't worry; I am here for the same reason. Guard headquarters decided to assign me to you since we had such a memorable showing the last time."

Dark memories haunted the pair. Bodies frozen in space. Eldritch powers threatening to unravel the fabric of the universe. Matthias had lost half of his men that day, and their faces continued to mock him from the mirror. Atonement seemed impossible. Tolde was no better off. Everything that made him who he was had almost come undone on the bridge of that ship. Deep space choked them almost as much as the power of the Blood Witch they had brought along. Try as he might, Tolde Breed would never be free from those nightmares.

He grimaced. "Hopefully this time will be less intense."

Matthias shrugged and fell in step. "Senior Inquisitor, it is in my experience that we seldom get to make that choice."

They arrived at the outer offices of the Inquisitor General without further conversation. Enough had been said. Tolde was never the sort to waste time wondering *what if?* He would have his orders soon enough, and that was all he needed to know. The crisp uniforms of the Guards on duty contrasted with the dazzling white marble. Tolde often wondered if the color scheme had been set on purpose. The Guardsmen nodded respectfully to Matthias and ushered the men into the antechamber.

Old memories flooded in as if they were from yesterday. Tolde passed a cursory glance around the chamber, impressed that virtually nothing had changed over the last fifty years. Tradition was an integral part of the Inquisition. He glanced down at the ancient wooden table in the center of the chamber and felt content. The table was a relic from the very first Inquisition. It represented a time when humanity rose above petty differences and united in common purpose. The crystal vase in the center changed with age. The dark red rose tinged in blue was replaced daily, but the table had been then since the beginning. Tolde found comfort in the rose. Beautiful and dangerous, the rose had long been the symbol of the Order.

The Inquisitor General emerged from his private study. Inquisitor and Guardsman bowed reverently. Alain Nye had only been Inquisitor General for a decade but had aged several more during his time in office. His once chestnut hair had faded to grey. Stern lines creased his face, and spots had formed on his hands, and he had lost weight under the pressures of office. Still, the honor of leading such a prestigious organization was something he would not have passed up. Fifty years ago, he had been a mere adjutant for Farius Graeme, the previous Inquisitor General. That association had opened doors and offered him the world he now occupied.

"Gentlemen, please. There is no need for ceremony, not now," Alain told them. "I apologize for calling you here at such a late hour."

"We came as soon as we could," Tolde replied for both.

"I thank you for that. Times are troubling, now more so than ever," Alain admitted.

Tolde stiffened at the remark. The last time he had heard such had nearly left him dead. He passed a curious glance to Matthias. The Guardsman remained impassive, his face as stern and unreadable as a faded statue.

Alain noticed their rising apprehension. "Do not worry yourselves over this now. The others are awaiting us in my study."

The Inquisitor General led them into the expansive room. It smelled of old cedar and polish. Bookshelves lined the walls of the semi-circular room. Tolde had only graced this room once and was equally amazed. The sheer volume of knowledge contained here was rivaled only by the Conclave archives. Inquisitor Generals were required to be well read, highly educated people. What Tolde did not expect to see was the Cardinal Seniorus and the commanding general of the Prekhauten Guard lounging in faded leather chairs sipping a particularly rare vintage of brandy. Both he and Matthias snapped to attention.

"Stand at ease, gentlemen," Lorenu Phos said. Her voice was crisp, melodious. Her time with the Guardsmen had inured her to their form of speech. General Strannan offered her a bemused smile. "As it is already late—or early, if you choose to see it as such—I will not waste any of your time. Senior Inquisitor Breed, you once served the Conclave on a mission of most serious consequence. Sergeant Major Matthias and you were responsible for the capture and imprisonment of one of the Three. I am afraid that the Conclave has need of your special talents again."

"Cardinal Seniorus Phos, I humbly submit that I have no special talents. I was asked to perform a task, and I did it. There is not much more to tell. That was a dark day for the Inquisition and the Conclave. Many paid with their lives."

She smiled at him before turning her gaze to Alain. "I am most impressed with your Inquisitors, Alain. They are very formal and proper."

Alain tipped his head in acknowledgment.

She returned her gaze to Tolde and Matthias. "Unfortunately, this is not the time to stand on decorum. Amongeratix has escaped from his prison on Crimeat."

Tolde felt his blood run cold. Panic flared within and threatened to overwhelm his senses. "Escaped or been freed?"

"We do not know. The Blood Witch spells that contained his evil were shattered by an unknown power. A handful of guards were murdered, and Amongeratix has disappeared. I wish I had more answers to give."

Awkward silence settled. Matthias and Tolde each thought back to the hardships of bringing the monster in the first time. Too many had died. It had taken them over a month and a chase across the stars to finally succeed and only then when Amongeratix wanted to be caught. Tolde suddenly felt an unexplainable sinister purpose forcing his actions. He already knew why he had been summoned. There was little room for doubt.

"Cardinal Seniorus, I am not an ignorant man. Amongeratix was my problem once. I understand why you have summoned us. When do you want me to leave?"

General Strannan cleared his throat. "It is not as simple as the first time."

Strannan was a bear of a man. Matching scars crisscrossed his face, lingering results of a strange encounter with religious fanatics on one of the moons of Ko early in his career. He had opted to forego reconstructive surgery for personal reasons. The scars, combined with his near perfect white hair, lent him a menacing appeal that furthered his reputation.

"How do you mean?" Tolde asked. He knew Strannan more by rumor mill, having met the man only a handful of times.

The general absently traced a finger up and down one of the pencil-thin scars. "We know that he had help in escaping. There are reports coming in that confirm Amongeratix in the presence of another man shortly after we believe he broke out of prison."

Tolde's mind wandered back to theories and conspiracies he had spent decades idling over after he had taken Amongeratix to Crimeat. "That is nothing new. There are cults and heretics across the universe dedicated to worshipping the Three."

"Tolde, the Three have the ability to undo the very fabric of being. It is no accident the Inquisition and Conclave have worked so closely together over the millennia. I fear what might happen if just one of the Three awakens to his full potential," the Inquisitor General added.

He hesitated. "I fail to understand where you are taking this conversation, sir."

"Tell him," Lorenu Phos motioned towards Strannan.

"We think that Amongeratix battled one of the others immediately following his escape," Strannan admitted.

Tolde and Matthias both stiffened measurably. Impossible. Neither of the other two had been seen in centuries. Amongeratix was the only one to continually resurface in some brutal capacity. History spoke of the last time all the Three had met. An entire world had been devastated, left as a lifeless rock drifting through space. Over five billion human lives had been lost. By the time their war had ended, not a single blade of grass grew. It didn't take much for Tolde's imagination to summon images of a universe in flames.

"Are you sure?" Matthias asked.

He, too, was haunted by the faces of men he had lost hunting down Amongeratix. There was no desire for revenge; rather, he fervently wished to never cross paths with any of the Three again. The very thought was enough to inspire unheralded panic.

Strannan nodded slowly.

Lorenu Phos looked at them intently. She was an older woman, having earned her title after her predecessor, Utharian Dal, was found dead in his chambers twenty-three years ago. Rumors that he had been poisoned circulated through the Conclave, though none could prove it. Lorenu had been voted in after a tightly contested debate. Lithe, she bore a grace and elegance that many lacked. Her shoulders sat squarely, her head tilted just right to command attention. Vibrant blue eyes showed compassion and intent. She was the sort of person who immediately took control of a room just by being there.

"I am afraid so, Sergeant Major," she replied softly. "The Conclave is working to keep this from becoming common knowledge. Fortunately most of the universe has forgotten what the Three are. What I need from you is to keep it that way. The Three managed to destroy an entire world the last time they met. I will not be the Cardinal Seniorus who allowed that to be repeated. Tolde Breed and Matthias, I do not ask this of you lightly. The potential for death is all too real. You have already confronted one of these monsters and paid for it in lives. I am afraid it will be worse this time."

"Cardinal Seniorus, I believe I can speak for Sergeant Major Matthias when I say that we would be honored to undertake this task," Tolde replied formally.

The acceptance in his words ended there. Instincts screamed for him to say no. Self-preservation struggled to win through the waves of duty and patriotism he felt. Tolde knew he was living on borrowed time. Memories of his last encounter with Amongeratix confirmed it. Death was stalking right around the corner. Tolde idly wondered if death had finally come to collect its dues.

Matthias offered a nod of agreement.

Strannan added, "You will not be acting alone. There are a thousand Guardsmen stationed on Crimeat with another five thousand in the neighboring systems should you require aid. I have already given orders that they are to give you full support."

"We also have two Inquisitors assigned there," Alain told them. "Tolde, it is no secret that I was the one to recommend you to Farius Graeme the first time. You showed promise and the potential to make a positive difference to the universe. You have my full trust and confidence now as well. Succeed or fail, the Order of the Inquisition is proud of you."

Too many emotions conflicted within. After so long, Tolde Breed was about to confront his demons.

Lorenu Phos waited for the door to slide shut before addressing Alain. "Do you think they will be enough?"

The Inquisitor General rubbed his chin. "I do not see why not. They managed the first time with little trouble."

"Matters are different now," she reminded.

"Cardinal, my men are the best in the universe. If Sergeant Major Matthias cannot bring Amongeratix down, it cannot be done," Strannan added.

She thought carefully before replying. Her eyes narrowed, her cheeks flushed. "It does not feel right. I have read Inquisitor Breed's reports. Even then he believed that Amongeratix was not acting alone."

"Breed spent decades looking in dark places for hidden conspiracies and cults that might have been involved," Alain replied. His face was passive, eyes lazy. "All he found were whispers and empty holes. I do not doubt your suspicions, Lorenu, but I must caution that our sole focus, for the moment, needs to be on stopping the Three. We cannot allow them to destroy another world."

Dawn broke across the eastern horizon, pale shafts of light ripping into the veil of darkness. Soon, the sky would fill with a violence of color. Red and orange would drive the purple and blue away, if only for another day. Lorenu found portent in the dawn, for it reminded her too much of the coming struggle against the Three. She prayed it would not come to all-out war, for the implications were heart-stopping. That simple fear inspired incomparable dread. The entire universe would change as violently as from night to day but without the raw beauty. Ugliness would devour what light was left and leave a burned-out hull of society.

"Is it enough, though?" she asked. "Davith, I think we should put the army on alert."

Davith Strannan cocked his head, his face taut with thought. "That might be too much. We have nothing to go on, only that Amongeratix has escaped and is supposed to have been seen with one of his brothers. The Prekhauten Guard is certainly up to the challenge, but right now we would be wasting our time. You can't expect fighting men and women to stand on alert for an extended period of time."

Nye tilted his head. "I agree with the General. We should wait. Prudence and caution are our allies now. Let Breed and Matthias do their jobs. They have not failed us before, and I can see no reason to expect such now. This might just blow over."

"Inquisitor General, I cannot risk the future of the universe on might," Lorenu said.

She turned back to the bay windows to watch the battle of colors, all the while wondering what the future held for them.

FIVE

3210 A.G. (After Gods), Prophet Isle, planet Crimeat.

Boots crunched over the broken wood and stone, small dust clouds puffing up with each step. Black and highly polished, the boots whispered authority. Senior Inquisitor Tolde Breed surveyed the room with a mix of disdain and horror. Decades flashed by, sending him back to the first time he had stood in this very cell. Amongeratix had been chained and drugged, left here to rot for his crimes. Senior Inquisitor Breed had harbored deep reservations about the facility on Prophet Isle successfully containing the prisoner. After all, the Shackled Man had already escaped from the nearly impregnable prison on Keltoo, and there seemed even less security here on this populated planet.

Tolde spent the next three decades rooting out conspiracies and following rumors of dark cults working to undo the Conclave and free Amongeratix. And now, back where it had begun, his greatest fears were being realized. Tolde had known deep inside that the Blood Witch's spells would never be enough to keep one of the Three imprisoned for long. As powerful as the witches were reputed to be, the power of the Three was much greater. He shivered at the thought of both entities colliding before refocusing on the task at hand.

The air had an iron taint. Blood. The dark substance coated large spots on the floor and walls. Ruined corpses lay at broken angles. All that remained of the guards were the empty cries in the afterlife. Amongeratix had proven why he deserved to be executed, but this did not explain how he had escaped. Tolde Breed scanned the cell, hoping for some clue, some fragment of information that might lead him back to the trail, to the hunt. Stepping over a body in the doorway, Tolde frowned. He never understood the need for senseless violence.

The wall to his left was smeared with blood as if it had been ripped open and made to bleed. Tolde gingerly ran a gloved hand over the jagged stains. Specks of dried blood flicked away on his fingertips, raining down to the floor. The body at his feet was on its back. The head twisted in an awkward angle. Tolde had no illusions that any of what had happened was his fault, but a small measure of guilt still ate at him.

"This is worse than Keltoo," Matthias whispered from over his shoulder.

Tolde nodded. The level of violence was certainly more severe than their first encounter with the Shackled Man. There had been no mercy, no side effects from the radioactive nebula nearby. This was plain murder.

Matthias gently tapped his boot against the nearest body. A rattle escaped the corpse's lungs followed by a thin cloud of greenish haze. "The Conclave should have let us put him down when we had the chance."

Tolde frowned at the idea. How does one kill a force so infinitely powerful as Amongeratix proved to be? "The Conclave has their reasons for doing what they did. It is much too late to reflect on it now."

"Do you think he is still on the planet?"

Tolde shrugged. The senior leaders of the Conclave seemed to think he was, but that didn't make any sense. His last escape had ended with him booking transport and fleeing to another world. There was no reason to think this time would be different. Still…. "I do not know. His brother being here might keep him here longer. Amongeratix is cunning; we know that from personal experience."

Matthias moved to the massive hole in the wall. The sheer amount of destructive force went beyond his ability to process. "Do you notice that the blast came from outside? The debris pattern goes from the wall out to the hallway."

"I did."

"If he was the one to break the Blood Witch spell, the force involved would have blown outward."

Tolde squinted. "He had help in escaping, powerful help."

More bodies, or at least what remained of them, decorated the chamber with gruesome splendor. This was not Tolde's first time stalking through such horrors. His life as an Inquisitor took him from world to world in seemingly vain attempts at halting heresies and secret cults. More often than not, murder and death trailed in his wake. This time was different, though. Tolde felt his heart darken. Something sinister and hidden was at work here.

"What force could have done this?" Matthias asked.

The Guardsman moved to the edge of destruction and looked down. Blast marks scored the outer wall in a wide circle around what used to be the window area. His initial assessment was that it would take a large bore howitzer to blow a hole so large. Unfortunately, there was nothing so large on Crimeat.

Tolde looked sharply at the mutilated body at his feet. "I don't think I want to know. This feels wrong."

"It couldn't have been conventional. The blast pattern is all wrong."

Of course it is. "We can rule his brother out, whichever one was here. They have no love for one another, if what the archives say is true."

Matthias nodded absently. "I believe them. You need to see this."

Moving next to the Guardsman, Tolde looked down and cringed inwardly. The landscape for as far as he could see was ruined. Trees were broken, ripped from the ground. Massive boulders were shattered into gravel, others jutting upwards like broken teeth. Patches of grass and weeds were now blackened spots that nothing could grow in. A light miasma of suffering hovered just above ground level. The brownish mist was like a pall.

Tolde and Matthias looked down on a scene of pure chaos. Matthias rubbed the left corner of his jaw. "That must have been a nasty fight. Everything in the area is dead, right down to the grass."

"There are no weapons in the universe capable of doing this. I think we need to find the local Inquisitor quickly."

"It might already be too late," Matthias countered. "Amongeratix might already have jumped planet. I would."

Tolde narrowed his eyes. "No. We cannot afford to take that chance. He might easily be hiding under our very noses praying we make the mistake. One thing is for certain. This will not be as easy as the last time."

Matthias offered a sympathetic look, recalling the way his men were systematically killed in the attempt to capture Amongeratix. "Easy is not the word I would choose to remember it by."

More than half of his squad had died on the derelict spacecraft Amongeratix had used to escape from Keltoo. Memories of those frantic weeks haunted him still. The chase spanned the stars before finally ending in deep space. Not even the psychic powers of a Blood Witch had been enough to keep his men alive. Amongeratix had sliced through them with terrifying ease. Matthias himself had nearly died.

"No one ever said ours was an easy life," Matthias quipped to ease some of the tension.

Tolde gently shook his head, dazed by the level of destruction below. "No, they certainly didn't."

"Which brings us to our next issue."

"That being?"

Matthias slung his rifle over his right shoulder. "How are we going to explain to the local Inquisitor that a Senior Inquisitor is on the planet without his knowledge?"

"That I have an answer for. We are under the edict of the Cardinal Seniorus. The local Inquisitor did not need to know of our arrival."

Even as Tolde spoke the words, he forced back a wince. Most of the Inquisitors he knew, himself included, took pride in knowing everything that happened on their worlds. Having a senior ranking member of the Order arrive under suspicious circumstances was more than an insult. Inquisitors might be the sworn defenders of the universe, but they were still human in the end. Jealousies and unbidden conspiracies would undoubtedly come to mind.

Matthias held back from replying and looked back down. They had clearly come to an end here. It was time to move on. He gestured towards the clustered Guards. "Sergeant Fies? Form ranks. We are heading back to the transport." He glanced back at Tolde. "Do you have any further instructions?"

Tolde thought for a moment. "No. I think it is time to visit the local Inquisitor. We also need to exercise discretion. There may be cultists or spies anywhere just waiting for us to announce ourselves. I have a feeling that this is going to turn into a very dangerous situation for us."

Matthias gave a halfhearted grin. "It wouldn't be a job otherwise."

Tolde stared at him for a moment, his eyes lacking clarity. Violent memories mocked him. The last time they had tangled with Amongeratix had almost gotten them all killed. Now there were two of the Three involved. The potential for disaster grew with each passing moment. His focus shifted back to the ruined bodies strewn across the cell. Glazed eyes stared back accusingly. His blood chilled. Tolde desperately needed to know what they had seen before that final strike had claimed their souls. Reluctant as he was to admit it, he was out of his depth here.

"We need a Blood Witch," he said suddenly.

Matthias jerked at the name. The witches were an enigma to the universe. Many theorized that they weren't human anymore, if they ever had been. He had a latent fear of the ethereal creatures. Everyone did. Their arcane arts took them too close to the darkness. Rumor whispered of a rogue witch who had destroyed Regal IV some years back. Her powers had become so uncontrollable the planet virtually disintegrated. Matthias heard the rumors the same as everyone else. Those doubts manifested in his conscious. Still, it was only through the powers of a Blood Witch that any of his men had managed to survive Amongeratix the first time. The debt was more than he was willing to consider.

"That is…dangerous. There is no way to control one of *them*."

The Inquisition often employed the witches. Their help was invaluable to preserving order and justice. Tolde would just as soon tackle this situation head on without the need for backup, but he recognized his shortcomings. "They did well for us the last time, Matthias."

"How can we be sure they will do the same now? The Cardinal Seniorus wanted this to be a discreet operation. We won't be able to maintain that with a Blood Witch present."

Tolde felt cornered. Matthias was right. Blood Witches were scarce, though widely recognized by their grey robes and wispy appearances. They came from only one place in the entire universe, the Acumensiis Comet.

He gestured to the damages around them. "I do not believe we will remain a secret for long. Someone discovered that we imprisoned one of the Three on Crimeat. It won't be long before Amongeratix attacks again. We need to seize any advantage we can if there is any hope in containing his hatred."

"He was making for Occanum the last time," Matthias offered. "Perhaps he aims to do so again."

Occanum. The battlefield of the gods. Tolde had traveled there on his own after their first encounter with Amongeratix. The world was all but dead, rendered lifeless by an impossible battle millennia ago. Tolde rubbed the ache building in his right temple. There were too many variables to consider without getting extremely depressed and lost. He gestured down at the ruined landscape.

"No. He is still here. The arrival of one of his brothers will keep him here for a while at least."

"I don't like this game. Too much can go wrong."

"None of our choices are good. Our actions are all that stands between the return of the Three and a universal conflict," Tolde insisted. The look on his face soured. Dark times, indeed.

Sergeant Major Matthias sighed heavily. Concern tweaked his flint colored eyes. "We are wasting time. If this is indeed what you propose we do, the trail is only getting colder."

Tolde Breed gave the desolation a final glance and contemplated the future and sputtered endings.

The local office of the Inquisition was unworthy of the title. Crimeat was not considered one of the more sophisticated worlds. The only true relevance it had was from its location along the main space lane for shipping and travel. Tolde and Matthias took the short two-hour shuttle flight from Prophet Isle to the capitol city of Vaade researching the local and political situations. Tolde was surprised to find Crimeat was still ruled by a feudal system filled with dukes and barons and such. Most worlds elected to be governed by the Conclave. The antiquation of Crimeat might prove a severe obstacle.

Their shuttle landed at the local spaceport, and they were quickly ferried through the awakening city to the Inquisitor's office. The driver and attendants were polite enough, their manners etched with the proper amount of fear and respect for the Inquisitor and his Prekhauten Guardsmen. Matthias struggled to contain his grin, recalling a time when he had been just as impressed to see a squad of Guardsmen march by in combat fatigues.

Dawn broke over the eastern ocean. It reminded Tolde of a wound, the red sun bleeding through the dark clouds on the horizon. He wondered if it was merely a testament to the benevolence of the gods or a portent of tomorrow. Such dark times clouded the ability to find beauty in the simple.

"This is a far cry from Krenz," Matthias commented.

The streets, paved with white stone, were mostly empty. Various shops and merchants were established along the main avenue. A fountain with four large horses carved from swirled marble rearing up in the center, water spewing from their mouths, filled a small square not far from them. Matthias suddenly felt out of place. His dark uniform and combat gear drew accusations and suspicious stares. A stray dog yipped and darted down a side street.

Matthias turned to Fies. "Sergeant, have your squad secure lodgings at an inn. The Senior Inquisitor and I will be along shortly."

A flash of relief eased over Fies' face. "Yes, Sergeant Major."

Tolde watched them march off. Much of the tension had left them. They walked like men relieved from the possibility of certain death. He almost envied them, but the grim reality offered little escape. They were all going to die before this mission ended. Inquisitor and Guardsmen marched down the center of the avenue. An air of dominance surrounded them. Those few out and about shuffled off to the side, giving them a wide berth. Senior members of the Inquisition were rare on Crimeat, though not enough for men to be careless.

The office of the Inquisition was a small concrete building, unassuming and almost invisible among the city streets. A single sign was all that marked it as an official building. The dull grey background only made the blue-tinged rose stand out that much more. It seemed almost out of place among the streets of Vaade.

"Do you know anything about this Inquisitor?" Matthias asked.

"No. I know only his name," Tolde replied. His words were simple, but the tone hinted at an undercurrent of mistrust. Matthias let it go, reminding himself to ask at a better time.

The duty clerk snapped his head up as the door opened. A thin cloud of dust blew off of the top of the door. Tolde and Matthias marched in without waiting to be called. Stern looks passed down to the clerk who suddenly found himself fumbling and shuffling through papers.

"May I help you?" he asked.

"My name is Senior Inquisitor Breed, and this is Sergeant Major Matthias of the Prekhauten Guard. We are here to see the local Inquisitor," Tolde announced with an authoritative voice.

The clerk snapped to at the mention of rank. A lowly person in the hierarchy, he valued the potential for promotion. "I am sorry, Senior Inquisitor, but Inquisitor Prowl is not in at the moment."

"I did not come all the way from Vau Prime on a sightseeing tour," Tolde snapped. His patience was already at an end. "Where is he?"

The clerk paled. His right hand started to twitch, almost imperceptibly. "He…he is at the Council building. The Council is in session today. All twelve of the Lords of Lethendweil are in attendance."

"When is he expected to return?"

The clerk shook his head with the slightest movement. "I do not know. There are rumors of an uprising in the western half of the continent. Inquisitor Prowl often sits in on the council meetings. He could be there for the rest of the day. I am sorry, Senior Inquisitor, but we were not expecting you. There was no word from Krenz."

"No. There won't be, either. We are here at the discretion of the Conclave. Inform the Inquisitor that we shall be staying at the inn at the end of the street. I expect him to contact me at his earliest convenience."

"Of course, Senior Inquisitor. I shall relay the message."

Tolde and Matthias left the clerk to his worries. The morning sun had climbed higher, struggling to burn off the nightly mists. The clash of cool and building warmth soothed Tolde. He had never cared for the night. Too many unanswered questions and faceless horrors lurked behind the darkness. The phobia stretched back to his childhood, but for reasons he would not explain to anyone. Tolde Breed served the light, darkness be damned.

"That was uncharacteristically kind of you," Matthias commented.

Tolde passed him a sidelong glance. "I can't fault him for not being here. This is a close-hold assignment."

"You're still debating bringing him into it, aren't you?"

A nod. "The fewer people who know of the Three, the easier our task will be. Amongeratix is a worthy foe, Matthias. You of all know best. We need to handle this as much on our own as we can."

"This trouble the clerk mentioned might prevent that from happening," Matthias countered with a serious tone.

"Let's not jump ahead of ourselves. I want you to draw up the local arms and armory. We need to know what we are getting into before the hunt begins again. I will look into the political situation, especially which god Crimeat worships."

"And the Blood Witch?" Matthias asked.

Tolde paused. A crisp autumn breeze caressed his face. "I will need a secure communication uplink for the request. The Three are more dangerous than we know. Amongeratix most certainly had assistance, and we can't chance being discovered this early in the quest."

"I don't like this at all," Matthias admitted suddenly.

Tolde forced a smile. "What is there to like? We are about to go to war with one of the three most dangerous beings in the universe and have strict orders to keep this all to ourselves. Fate is stacked against us."

"Inquisitor, it has been in my experience that Fate doesn't give a damn about us. The only thing we can count on is each other. I am going to start cleaning my weapons. Something tells me we are in for a rough time."

Tolde kept his tongue, though his heart bore the same warnings. He couldn't help but feel as a small pebble preceding the coming war. Odd, he thought. There weren't any indications of war, yet his soul ached from the idea. Change was coming and the universe was never going to be the same after.

The hooded man watched until Inquisitor and Guardsman returned to the inn. A frown creased his hidden face. This was unexpected and troubling. No one had mentioned the possibility of more Conclave resources being dedicated to Crimeat. He stroked his thin beard, eyes narrowed in thought. Plans were already in motion, yet they teetered on the edge of failure with the unexpected arrivals from Vau Prime. He snarled. They could only be here for one reason. They *knew*.

He tilted his head back slightly as the sun finally broke free of the clouds, shattering the night with a chill morning. For a moment, the light struck his face, and he blinked. His eyes were gold flecked through with orange. Satisfied, he hid his face and ducked into the nearest alley. Winding a path through the back streets, the man silently made his way through Vaade. Small groups of people were coming out now, merchants and shopkeepers ready to begin yet another day. None passed the cloaked man a second glance.

He came upon a rundown-looking antique shop. Two ancient sets of armor stood on guard on both sides of the wooden door. A multi-colored banner blew overhead in a waving rainbow of homeliness. Jerking the door open, he stormed in and slammed the door shut.

"You!" the shopkeeper said with surprise. "You shouldn't be here."

The hooded man remained emotionless, lest his building rage break loose and he slay an old friend. "Be calm, Toms. I have information the movement needs."

Toms nervously scanned the rest of his shop. He rushed forward and locked the door before turning on his caller. "You know better than to speak this way in public, Darka Jorm."

He flinched at being named. No one spoke his name and avoided the consequences. "I must get word to the Baron."

Toms snorted derisively. "Then go to the palace and request an audience. I imagine the council will be in session for some time yet."

"I am not here to play children's games with you. What I have to say needs to be said now, not at the convenience of some administrative clerk who does not know the truth of what we do."

Toms brushed off his concern. "Speak plainly. I am no good with riddles."

Darka Jorm scowled, his gloved fist clenched. "Give me ink and paper."

He waited impatiently, occasionally peering over his shoulder. Caution and suspicion blended into an unrecognizable mess. His mind raced over what he knew and what was yet to come. The Senior Inquisitor spooked him good and proper. There were too many variables to find any comfort. The dawn of revolution was breaking, and he was destined to stand on the horizon. Darka snatched the paper from Toms and started to write.

"Say, I've never seen you this way before," Toms said. A worried look crossed his aged face.

"You never will again. I do not plan on returning here again."

Toms was an old man. His hair was mostly gone now, leaving a scalp filled with wispy patches of stringy, grey hair and liver spots. Much of his former strength had faded, leaving him gaunt and wiry. His clothes were of poor cloth, and he was a shrewd businessman. Association with men like Jorm was not good for his health. Darka Jorm's words would come back to haunt him, though he knew it not. Still, Darka's tone was enough to fill him with his own personal dread.

Finished, Darka rolled the paper and handed it over. "Get this to the Baron immediately. Crimeat is not safe. The Conclave knows."

Toms stared back blankly, the color draining from his face. Even out here, dozens of planetary systems removed from the middle of the universe, the Conclave held a certain terror. Be they truth or lies, men feared what they did not know. Toms finally tried to speak, but Darka Jorm was unlocking the door and leaving, taking time only to check each direction for signs of detection. The door swung shut with a groan. Toms unfolded the tiny paper Darka had handed him and read the poorly scratched writing.

The Conclave knows what we are about. We must begin at once.

Toms dropped the paper and slumped down onto his chair. Cold dread filled his heart.

SIX

3210 A.G. (After Gods), Durn, planet Crimeat.

Dawn served no purpose for her. The glory of the day was lost, broken amidst the crashing waves upon jagged rocks. Her soul was rent, torn away by foul memories that consumed her a little more each day. She was a wreck, helpless and alone. No warmth from the golden rays, no joy from the sound of songbirds. Each dawn was bleak and threatening. Elisa sighed, wiping away the now permanent tears that stained the corners of her autumn eyes.

A deep snort broke her misery. She glanced up at the roan mare stabled beside her and smiled. Unexplainable understanding shown in the horse's eyes.

"Another day," Elisa told it warmly. "Perhaps today I will find what I have been looking for."

The horse gently tossed its head. Elisa looked around. None of the other animals stabled in the barn seemed to notice her. She shook her head, still disbelieving how her life had spiraled so low that she was forced to scrape for a place in a barn to sleep. Not that it mattered. The only thing important in her life was finding the Bloody Man and killing him for what he had done.

Elisa was in her mid-fifties now. Five decades had passed since that fateful day when the gods had turned their backs on her. Her once lustrous red hair was streaked grey. Her blue eyes had lost some of their shine. She was tall, her face gaunt. When her hair, normally past her shoulders, was pulled back, it gave her a severe look. She was thin but dangerous.

The cruelties in life had forced her to grow hard. She'd grown up with a foster family in a neighboring village. Her foster parents had done their best to raise her, to make her forget. But the constant sorrow was ever-present. She had taught herself the arts of battle and weapons.

Elisa had left her foster home as soon as she was old enough, and then her quest had begun. Odd jobs had come and gone along the way. She had worked as a bounty hunter for a few years, a mercenary for more. The jobs helped pass the time as she worked her way across the continents of Crimeat.

The hunt had finally taken her to Lethendweil, a rich land with many climates and troubles of its own brewing ever on the near horizon. She felt odd being home again. For it had all started in the kingdom of Berchenfel. The rolling grass plains no longer held any comfort or special feeling for her. It was as alien as one of the great star liners making port in Vaade. Her quest had taken her across Berchenfel, over the Gaic Mountains and to the town of Durn—Durn, which dwelt ever in the shadows of the Great Barrier Jungle and the rumored horrors therein.

She shivered as she looked across the empty field. The jungle simply began, a wall of thick trees and undergrowth that devoured the sun, stretching from one side of the continent to the other. Men did not go there unless there was great need. Elisa feared that such need was now upon her. Scattered talk led her to believe that the Bloody Man was on the other side, hiding in the land of the Ugri. Pain and horror awaited her in the jungle. It was a pain she was almost unwilling to find. Almost.

Elisa stretched, forgetting her quest for the moment. Her muscles were tight, sore. Endless nights in one barn after the next had done her no kindness. She was hard where she should have been soft, aged where she should have been young. The lines on her face betrayed any youth she desperately clung too. Gathering up her personal hygiene items, Elisa made her way out back behind the barn to a small running stream. The water was crisp and felt good. She washed her face and hands, feet and privates, and then packed up.

A dark-skinned man in a military uniform stood awaiting her in the doorway. She repressed her instinct to reach back and draw her dagger. If there was one soldier, there had to be more. He saw her apprehensions and held out both hands, palms forward though his expression remained the same.

"You have no need of a weapon," he told her in a deep voice, "yet."

"Who are you?"

"My name is unimportant for the time being. I was sent to find you."

Her eyes narrowed sharply. "By whom?"

He gave her a surprised look. "By General Shiramon. These are his lands, and he is lord."

"What would a lord have to do with me? I am just passing through," she lied.

The soldier frowned. "His business is his own, but I know that he has heard of you. He knows the bounty hunter Elisa and requires her services."

A shiver ran down her spine. "Suppose I am not her?"

"You still come with me. I am not here to bandy words with a broken woman begging for scraps in a farmer's barn, if indeed you managed to pay for your board. You have five minutes to get dressed, gather your belongings and meet me outside." He turned and left the barn. "Oh, and do not think about sneaking away. I have men watching all four sides. Hurry up."

Elisa closed her eyes with a tight frown. She had almost made it through the kingdom without being caught. Nothing for it, she threw down her gear and started getting dressed. Her pants were worn, thick for all seasons. Her boots threatened to give out on her. She wished she had taken the time to get them resoled in the last village, but she was too close to her quarry to stop now. Her faded brown leather jerkin bore the scars of multiple knives and an arrow or two. Elisa threw her grey travel cloak on and collected her items. She tied her red hair back in a tail and slung her pack over her shoulder.

"Let's go," she told the soldier once she was outside.

He turned to give her an appraising glance and nodded once. A sharp whistle brought his men out of hiding. All were on horseback and armed for war. Their dull silver armor gleamed in the morning light. Strong shields of iron hung from their saddles. Swords were strapped to their hips, and single-barrel ion rifles were slung over their shoulders. Elisa could just make out the blackened tips of the energy weapons poking up by their necks. She smirked. They weren't taking any chances, but with whom?

She didn't get the feeling they had come to arrest her. That could only mean one other thing. This General Shiramon had a job for her. *Lovely*, she thought, *just as I am this close to ending my quest.* Resigned to whatever cruel distraction fate had designed for her, Elisa strapped her pack to her horse and swung into the saddle.

They rode in silence. Every so often, she would catch one of the soldiers staring at her. Elisa shivered. She found it odd how out of place their ion rifles were. Much of Lethendweil, indeed all Crimeat, rejected advanced technology. The Conclave didn't mind. Universal policy was to let planets evolve as they saw fit. She could have afforded an air car with all of the jobs she had done, but it didn't feel right. There was nothing as comforting as an old rifle in her hands and a horse beneath her. The rest seemed impersonal, offensive. That is not to say that there weren't advancements comparable to those of other planets, but the people and, more importantly, the ruling bodies, were content with what they had. If anything, it made the population easier to control.

The castle of Durn dominated the hillside it was built upon. Battlements overlooked the rolling valley that ran to the near edge of the jungle. Small villages and towns surrounded the castle. Elisa was unimpressed. She had seen the great fortresses of the world, and Durn paled in comparison. Built of iron and stone, its massive grey walls reached up into the sky, daunting and imposing should the Ugri ever decide to attack. General Shiramon was shrewd and took great pride in his military and defenses. Elisa knew none of this. The affairs of single rulers were small and beneath her interests. Unless the Bloody Man dwelled therein, she cared not.

The thick, black portcullis was raised at their approach up the single lane causeway. Arrow holes and catapults scarred the walls. Men stood ever ready to rain down an impossible defense upon any attacker. Rumors of war were everywhere, though war against whom she wasn't so sure. More guards stared down at her as if in judgment. They passed through the gates and came across a wide, empty courtyard. Barracks lined the side walls. Each was capable of housing a hundred men at arms. Random pairs of soldiers moved here or there.

Elisa glanced up, noticing for the first time the banners of the general. Black with a red dragon breathing fire. She took that as a bad sign. Men like Shiramon spent their lives in pursuit of empty glory on some distant battlefield. The universe was much crueler. Elisa was convinced that pain and despair were the future. Whatever power the gods held, it must surely be vile to have created such beasts as the Bloody Man.

A well-dressed man with a pencil-thin moustache and shifting eyes emerged from what she assumed was the command building. He was tall and thin, just muscular enough to fill out his uniform. His hands were clasped behind his back, and his gaze was intent. Still, there was the slightest hint of pleasantry.

He faked a smile as they were brought to a halt. "Welcome to castle Durn, Lady Elisa. I trust my men were not severe with you?"

She stayed in the saddle, using the time to size up her questioner. "They came unbidden while I was busy."

"That is unfortunate, but I am afraid I sent them on a very important task. What good are men at arms if they cannot perform the tasks assigned, eh?"

She folded her hands over the pommel and waited.

Seeming to recognize his error, the soldier bowed curtly and said, "Forgive my rudeness. My name is Commander Piett. I am the second in command when the General is away."

"Why have you brought me here, Commander?" she asked.

Faint redness crept around his collar. "As I said before, the General has need of a person with your qualities. This is quite the important task for us here in Durn."

Elisa swung to the ground and faced Piett. "Who do you want me to kill?" she asked in a flat voice.

Piett grinned. "A woman to the point. I appreciate that. Come inside. Business such as this is best discussed where prying ears cannot pierce."

Dismissed, the escort squad rode off to the stables and a warm breakfast, leaving Elisa with Piett. He pulled out a red leather-bound chair for her to sit and waited until she did before taking his place behind his mahogany desk. Crossed sabers hung on the wall behind him. The rest of the walls were decorated with various flags and trinkets collected over a lifetime of military service. And always there were General Shiramon's colors. She felt ill at ease.

"These are dangerous times," Piett began. "Long have our people protected the rest of Lethendweil from the Ugri and their fowl craft."

She interrupted, "Commander, I am not interested in the politics of Durn or of any other nation. Please, tell me who I am hunting so I may be about my business."

"Mind your tongue before I forget who summoned you and why," he snapped. "There is no call for discourtesy here, miss."

Her jaw clenched. Her teeth ground. "You contacted me, or perhaps abducted is more appropriate. I am not in the habit of carrying on casual conversations, Commander. For that I apologize, but my time is very valuable to me. There is much I must be about."

"We are well aware of your quest, the General and I. In fact, you might say that it has much to do with you sitting in my office right now."

He rose and placed his hands behind his back. She guessed it was his comfortable position. Piett stalked over to a wall map. "Are you aware of what happened recently on Prophet Isle?"

"No, should I be?"

"Perhaps not. The Conclave and its Inquisition pets kept a very dangerous prisoner there for decades. Reports are still fragmented, but people say that prisoner escaped a few nights ago."

She was intrigued, but not enough to tangle with both the Conclave and the Inquisition. "I don't understand how this affects me."

He smiled. "Conclave prisons are warded through use of the Blood Witches' foul arts. It is all but impossible for one to escape without outside help. The Council and General Shiramon are convinced that this prisoner had the support of a powerful network."

"And you wish for me to find this prisoner?" she asked.

He struggled to keep from openly mocking her. "No. Let the Conclave deal with its own problems. These are matters that I believe none of us wishes to become involved with. The General is interested in the one responsible for freeing the prisoner. There are rumors, whispers really, that he is making his way through the Barrier Jungle and into the Ugri lands. He must be stopped and brought to justice."

"Justice? By whom?"

He paused. "We could, of course, turn him over to the local office of the Inquisition, but there is a certain level of distrust between us."

Political manipulations aside, Piett had no desire to explain how doing this small deed would build Shiramon's standing in the Council. Durn was not a rich land. Any bounty or reward would amplify their coffers and set Durn ahead of its peers.

"You propose a dangerous business," she warned.

"Yes, I know. One does not go against the will of the Inquisition without facing consequences," Piett replied. "There is much unsaid at this point. What if I were to tell you that war is coming and this person of interest might have a key role in it all?"

"Rumors of war are constant. I don't see what this one man can do or how he can be solely instrumental in orchestrating a war," Elisa told him.

Piett snorted. "Rumors are endless. Many are nothing more than a bored man's fancy. Secrets, now that is a subject worth exploring."

"I don't understand, Commander."

"Rumors serve no purpose," he explained, "but secrets are nearly as good as the coin in your purse."

She frowned. "What secrets could this man have that are so important?"

"Secrets born in shadow."

He held up a staying hand before she could ask the obvious. "I will say nothing more of this. We wish to hire you to hunt down this man and bring him back to Durn. You will be handsomely paid for your efforts."

Elisa feigned thinking. Her mind was made. Catching the Bloody Man was the only thing of importance in her life but the rewards from finding a man wanted by the Conclave could easily fund her quest for years to come.

"What is his name, and what does he look like?"

Piett kept his smile hidden. Reaching down on his desk, he produced a black and white image and slid it across the desk to her. "Reports say his name is Mollock Bolle, though he may be using an alias."

She studied the picture. He was old, certainly too old to be of much trouble. A long salt-and-pepper beard hung below his chin, and his eyes were almost hollow. His cheeks were sunken, making his pointed nose seem that much longer. Elisa had seen dead men look better.

She glanced up at Piett. "When do you want me to leave?"

"Tomorrow at the latest. I would like to extend the full hospitality of Durn to you. How good would it feel to sleep in a real bed again, if only for a night? Food, drink and access to my armories. Rest assured he is a dangerous man."

"Why not use your own men?" she asked.

"We cannot become involved in this. There are many in Vaade who would wish to see us fall from grace. It is best this way. Naturally, I expect your silence in this matter."

She noticed the predatory glare in his eyes and nodded crisply, not from fear or respect, but from necessity. Men like Piett offered golden smiles with knives behind their backs.

"I have a man waiting in the courtyard. He will see you to your quarters for the rest of the day. And please, take advantage of our hospitality. Whatever you require will be covered by the General."

He waved her out the door, taking the time to light a poorly rolled local cigar. Piett's eyes narrowed, boring into her back as she walked off. Bounty hunters, he scoffed. And a woman at that! A woman should know her place. Clasping his hands behind his back, he began a stroll up to the ramparts to enjoy his smoke and the evolution of a beautiful day.

Secrets born in shadow. Elisa tried to fathom what Piett had meant when he had said those words. The world was plagued with secrets, littered like a forgotten battlefield on distant shores. She scratched the corner of her mouth with a half-chewed nailed. Secrets. Shadow. The ominous tone in those two words might have chilled her marrow if she had not been tempered by hideous events as a child.

Bounty hunting was an episode from her past. She liked to think she had evolved beyond the need for part-time jobs and passing fancies to keep her occupied. Crimeat had grown more dangerous over the years, or perhaps it was just her maturing and seeing more of the world than the sleepy village she came from. The violence and the horror seemed perpetual, eager to reciprocate onto the next victim lest it be thrown to the back of broken memories. The priesthood benefited from the loss of morals and growing sin. Conclave enrollment rocketed as the days grew darker.

There had been a time, long ago, when she might have gone to the nearest temple to pray. Surely the gods would answer her. But no, each time she bent her knee and let the wounds in her heart bleed out to them, the gods were silent. Their mighty statues stared down almost mockingly as if she were beneath their concern. What point was there in gods if they did not answer the faithful? It was not until later in life that she had recognized the core problem. Her faith was gone, evaporated like the deep winter's snow on a pale spring morning.

"Damn them all," she cursed softly.

The room Piett had furnished was Spartan at best. There was a small cot with an equally small writing desk and a two-drawer bureau for what few possessions she had. Elisa remained packed. There were small things that didn't sit well with her here in Durn. It didn't make sense to send a large military escort to bring her in if she was expected with a smile and open arms. Piett was hiding something. Secrets born in shadow. Elisa wondered whose shadow had given birth.

The midday bell chimed from the town's tower, reminding her that she had not eaten today. Stomach snarling, Elisa strapped her weapons on, wrapped her cloak about her, and set out to find something to eat. Surprisingly there were no guards positioned to confine her to quarters. She made her way through the gates uncontested and down into the village. People shied away, often looking the other direction rather than risk gaining her attention. She frowned. Most villagers she knew were quiet, decent folk, but the ones in Durn were almost beaten.

Finally, she found the Gilded Barrel, one of the cleaner establishments in the village. The door squeaked open. Elisa passed her gaze across the common room, finding it unimpressive. A light coat of dust blanketed the floor and half of the tables. The benches and chairs were worn to the point of disrepair. Cracks and splits ran the length of the bar in the rear of the room. She sighed. At least the fire was warm and almost comforting. A serving maid presently made her way over.

"What can I get for you, miss?" she asked pleasantly enough.

Elisa blew the dust away from the area in front of her and said, "Whatever you have to eat."

"We have a boiled potato soup and fresh dark bread with green apples."

She smiled. "That is fine."

"What would you like to drink?"

Elisa thought for a moment. "Water."

The serving maid almost looked disappointed but said nothing as she whirled and went back to the kitchen. Elisa would have loved the taste of cold ale, but her suspicions of Piett continued to rise. She scanned each of the five other patrons and, once satisfied that none appeared threatening, settled back in her chair to await her meal.

Mollock Bolle glanced up at the irritating sound of the door opening. He couldn't say why, but the sudden arrival of the tall red-headed woman set him on edge. She bore the look of a hardened killer. His mind instantly turned towards bounty hunters and assassins. No stranger to the like, Mollock was surprised to find them looking for him this close to civilization. He had been hunted for the last fifty years, always staying barely a step ahead of his pursuers. That old paranoia settled in, so familiar he hardly noticed when his right hand began to jump.

He knew too many secrets and had paid for them with his life. He damned his inquisitiveness but was afraid he was already too late. His soul had to be doomed; if not, what was it all for? He thought of his friend, Fenrin, and that terrifying night in Berchenfel so long ago. Fifty years later, he still had no idea whether Fenrin had survived the night or not. The shadow beast seldom discriminated when hunting prey. Countless innocents had been slaughtered in the pursuit of Mollock Bolle. He often tried to imagine what hatred drove such a being, what intent moved a being with such singular intent.

The redhead took a seat at an empty table with her back to the bar, giving her a clear view of every entrance to the common room. Almost every entrance. Mollock concealed a childish grin and finished his mug of ale. It was going to take more than blind luck to snare him. He motioned the same serving girl over and flashed her a semi-toothless grin. His upper gum was mottled black, and the teeth, what few remained, were stained faded yellow. She frowned as she noticed the stray hairs protruding from his ears.

"What can I get you?" she asked as politely as possible.

Mollock wiped his upper lip on his sleeve. "Jennelle, that girl there, who is she?"

"Dunno. She just got into town," Jenelle replied nonchalantly. "There's been plenty of strangers coming and going lately. I think the General is up to something against the Ugri."

"The Ugri?" Mollock asked, eyebrow arched nervously. "What have they got to do with anything?"

She scowled. "Are you going to order anything, or do you just plan on wasting my time, old man?"

He refrained from commenting on the old man remark and let her go about her business. Mollock was already thinking into the future. There was still much to be done before he would be able to rest. Tossing a handful of copper coins on the chipped wooden table, Mollock slunk his way towards the kitchen entrance. His eyes never left the strange woman sitting on the far side of the room. He barely managed a sigh as he slipped through the door without being noticed. The hairs on his neck stood on end for reasons he still wasn't sure of.

Mollock jumped at the sound of the heavy butcher's blade chopping through a duck neck and into the hard counter. The cook offered a wry grin as he wiped the blood away and pushed the head on the floor for an old hound to gnaw on. Mollock's stomach turned. A chuckle escorted him out the back door and into a gravel alley. Wasting no time, Mollock Bolle dashed off into the growing shadows. Dusk was fast approaching, and the town of Durn was closing. Whispers and rumors drove the citizens into their homes faster than in most of the other kingdoms. Mollock enjoyed it; it made the conduct of his business much easier.

An armed patrol marched by without as much as a glance in his direction. The appearance of another vagabond worked in Mollock's favor. The old man worked his way to the front gate with a drunken wobble, lest the guards take interest in him. Mollock was soon through the gates and casually marching towards the Great Barrier Jungle. He didn't normally bother getting involved with the causes of others, but the Ugri would pay well for the information he had. And he needed a place to hide.

SEVEN

3210 A.G. (After Gods), Vaade, planet Crimeat.

"Order!"

Lord Emleth, elected head of the Council of Nobles on Crimeat, roared at his fellow councilmen. His baritone voice vibrated through the large round chamber with silencing effect. He narrowed his faded blue eyes. His fists balled in building rage. The hour was late, and his patience had waned.

Satisfied that civility had returned, he continued, "This is a diplomatic authority, not a barracks for raw recruits. I trust you to remember your standing as nobles. As head of the council, I will not condone a course of action that threatens our entire civilization with unmitigated war. It has been a generation since the last Unified Army was forced to act. I refuse to believe that such strength is needed now, in our time."

An elderly man, bald and overweight, leaned closer to his younger counterpart seated on his right and whispered, "It would appear your arguments weren't persuasive enough, Scura."

Baron Scura sneered, his face a twisted mess of ill will. Black hair shimmered in the artificial light of the chamber. "We shall see."

Scura rose. He was a man of average height and build yet deceptively aggressive beneath his mild demeanor. Deep, almost hypnotic hazel eyes bored unflinchingly into a man's soul. Scura was one of the younger nobles but a powerful voice with a growing following. "Lord Emleth, if I may. I believe I can speak for the entirety of the western kingdoms when I say that none would go against the voice of the council. However..."

Emleth's eyes narrowed. He drummed the fingers of his right hand impatiently on the carved ivory tabletop.

"How do you propose we solve the question of the Ugri? My own people will no longer tolerate the loss of life and lands beyond what has already been suffered. What promises will I be able to take back to them to assuage their fears? Not only have the Ugri been a threat to the west, but now we are confronted with the disaster at the Inquisition prison on Prophet Isle. I fear that our efforts are in vain."

Scura faced his peers with arms outward in appeal. "Fellow nobles, only through the combination of force will we be strong enough to end the threat of the Ugri for good and set peace to our lands. The strength of the Unified Army can and will drive them back to their mountain caves and reclaim the lands stolen through endless generations. No longer will we have to live with a threat looming over our shoulders. Children will not have to be afraid of the night. My forces can be mobilized within one calendar month. The time for talk is ended. It is time we acted. I implore you all to join me and help save us all. Let us be strong, decisive and unified for the good of all our peoples."

Inquisitor Ursal Prowl sat with one leg crossed over the other, mildly amused with the pomp and grandeur on display. Born a common man, Ursal had no interest in politics and the petty games that decided the fates of millions. The universe might be a better place if the Inquisition and the Conclave were finally able to control all the worlds and bring them under one system of leadership. He glanced over at Danja Stall, the Conclave's representative to the council. The older

Stall fidgeted under his dark blue robes. The white trim only served to make him look older rather than regal as was its design.

Scura continued despite the menacing glare from Emleth. "How can any of us rest when our children, the continuation of our species, lie at risk? How many graves have been dug across Lethendweil because of those monsters from the west? This body must act now! We must send a clear message to both peoples that the Ugri shall no longer torment us as they have for so long. My people deserve freedom. Your people deserve freedom! It is time we gave it to them. Now is our hour!"

The twelve nobles erupted in arguments. Any semblance of order that Emleth sought was lost beneath the passionate fervor Scura created. Jealousy flared to life. Thirty years older, and he had never been able to inspire his council with such passion. His was a legacy of cunning and deviousness. Born and bred for battle, Emleth was a tribute to the ancient warrior kings that had ruled before the Conclave had arrived and illuminated the world to the gods. Killing, he understood. Politics and games of intrigue, he often left for others to twist their minds with.

The council chamber, symbol of the most powerful people in Lethendweil, amplified the acoustics through a high-domed ceiling and alabaster pillars that stretched nearly fifty feet. The round chamber was large enough to hold hundreds of people and was dominated by a large mahogany table at the center. Hundreds of years old, the table was as much a symbol of the unified leadership of Crimeat as it was of strength and power. Black marble, streaked with rich veins of gold, made the floor serious, almost menacing. Banks of solar-powered lights lined the ceiling in circular patterns, constricting until they reached the oculus in the center of the roof. Golden sunlight streamed down on the bickering lords.

Ursal Prowl sat in the back of the chamber lamenting their behavior. He frowned at their failure to recognize the true power here. Lords and nobles were nothing compared to the strength of the Inquisition. None of their doubts would amount to much if they had the nerve to simply ask for his assistance.

The Inquisition had a mixed reputation depending on which planet you were on. Crimeat was not as deeply committed to their god as other worlds; Ursal constantly found himself investigating reports of heresy. His idle gaze caught Emleth's. The briefest flicker of recognition flared and then died in the old man's eyes.

Emleth sighed, a gesture so small only Scura and Ursal noticed. He reached up to stroke his thin grey beard as his peers raged to new depredations. "Battlefields contain more civility than these proceedings. When did it become more acceptable to assault each other rather than facing the issue at hand?"

"Getting us to agree to the point of action is the point, Emleth. Or perhaps you are too old to remember," Scura said slyly.

Finding an almost predatory feel to Scura's words, a haunting of days long past when the world had evolved at the tip of a sword, Emleth almost wished these problems could be solved by brute force. Violent memories comforted him when he closed his eyes, memories of blood and despair from his time on the battlefield. Armies of frightened men, steeled against the charging enemy a moment before the lines collided. He breathed deep, desperately hoping to regain those lost feelings. The sounds of cannon fire, brutal and horrific. The smell of cooling blood and unmitigated destruction. An odd serenity came with the chaos of war. His wife had never understood him, never understood the need to stand on the line, leading men. Endless nights alone in their bed had offered her ample reason to slip away before giving him an heir. *The bitch*, he cursed inwardly. His line was ending, and with it the three hundred year rule of Vaade. Broken.

The hollowness of his legacy mocked him from the nearing shadows of demise. Anger suddenly welled to life, and he entertained the thought of drawing a sword and rifle and charging into the fools surrounding him. What better way for the descendant of great warriors to meet his end? Surely the ghosts of his fathers would approve. He watched Scura with a predatory gaze.

"I believe you have our esteemed noble's instincts prickled, my boy," the bald and fat Count Blathk whispered as Scura settled back into his chair.

Scura disregarded the older man, disdain briefly flashing across his boyish face. Instead, he took to his feet again and, with a voice loud enough to drown out the rest, said, "Lord Emleth! You are a man of gun and sword. Surely you of all can recognize the need of our peoples?" Reluctant silence settled over the nobles.

"They call to you, to all of us. It is by our word, our very bond to the lands we serve, that the people are kept free from slavery and worse. I would not be the man I am if I returned to my people with news of failure. The pride in my soul would force desperate actions. I pray none of us are forced to spend the remainder of our days mired in self-indulgent misery. But I speak of affairs too close to remain objective. Perhaps it is time to hear from our esteemed Priest of the Conclave and his Inquisitor?"

All eyes shifted towards Danja Stall. The nobles provided a mixture of feigned interest and avid anticipation. Danja cleared his throat, his fingers twitching nervously. It was an old habit he had never been able to shake, not since his first presentation before the Board of Cardinals on Vau Prime.

"These are…potentially dangerous times. Much uncertainty shrouds our decisions, making them ill-advised or brash. The unexplained events on Prophet Isle only serve to strength the rising fear amongst the population. We must question if the Ugri truly are the great enemy we believe them to be. I spent much time in the temple today. I prayed for wisdom and guidance."

"What answers were you given, priest?" Emleth asked, almost reluctantly. His devotion to the gods was not perhaps what it should have been.

"Communion with any god is not easily achieved," Danja snapped in reply. "How those intimate moments are translated takes time."

"Spare us the plague of riddles, Danja," Scura demanded. "We have heard this all before. The Conclave is the sworn protector of the universe. How are we, mere nobles on a singular planet, expected to overcome heresy and doubt when our very own priest will not deal straight with us?"

Danja Stall fired malevolence at the young man but had the grace to swallow the hatred threatening to spew forth. His fingers, aged and spotted, stopped twitching. "Very well, I will tell you what you wish to hear. No riddles, no hidden truths. The world is spinning out of your control. There is a new apprehension in the universe. Your actions are but the catalyst for the coming storm. Be wary of your desire to spill blood so recklessly. The horrors you sow will be repaid before the end."

"Who are you to question the voice of the Conclave?" Ursal Prowl shot up and barked at them all. "You owe your allegiance to the gods and to the Conclave, or would you have me report to the Inquisition that you whisper heresy?"

Though anger flared amongst them, none of the nobles were bold enough to challenge both the Conclave *and* the Inquisition. Men had died for less—or worse. Emleth moved quickly to quell the rising tensions lest blood be spilled in the council chambers for the first time in centuries.

"No one is debunking what our esteemed Conclave representative says. You must understand our position, Inquisitor," he spoke up. "Our peoples have been threatened for a very long time. That threat has grown over time until now it brings us to the brink of inescapable confrontation. We do not enter into this matter lightly, else we sunder our souls from the glory of the gods. Would that we had an army of the Prekhauten Guard to augment our forces; then, tensions might not be so high. The cold fact is that we do not. You have only a token force, and those must be given permission from Guard headquarters half the universe away. No, Inquisitor, we are alone and are now feeling the strain of that singular truth."

Placated, Ursal Prowl sat down, receiving a comforting pat on the shoulder from Danja Stall. Uneasy silence dominated the chamber, giving the nobles a chance to reflect upon what had been said and how they might interpret it. True to Emleth's admission, going to war was not an easy decision to make. Empty beds and grieving widows awaited any return, victorious or defeated. What sane man willingly sacrificed the lives of those beneath him for a vain attempt at glory on some distant field that might not be remembered?

Face flushed with mild discontent, Emleth said, "I will not deny that my heart desires to take to the field and lead men in combat, but these are different times. The current situation is vastly changed from the time of my youthful fury. Any army we try to build now will take weeks before we can wield them in the field. The Unified Army is a powerful tool that should only be used in the direst of situations. Leadership and logistics will hamper our efforts as much as our lack of viable intelligence of the Ugri.

"That said, I implore each of you to return to your lands and discuss this matter with your own councils," Emleth instructed. His face, once old and losing intensity, now hardened with resolve. "War is a difficult decision. Unless all twelve lands are unanimous in support, I will not allow it. This meeting is adjourned until the next moon. The gods willing, there won't be a need for such movement on our part."

General Shiramon slammed his fist onto the table with unabated fury. The hard lines of his face were like granite. "This is absurd! The army must be mobilized without delay. You won't be there. None of you will, and once again it will fall upon my shoulders to bear the brunt of the Ugri assaults. My people shed their blood so yours can sleep safely. Even now my border guards are embattled against these damned creatures. They are all that stand between life and certain death. When the dawn comes and the bodies are counted, I will have to inform the relatives of those who are not coming back. Strike now before the Ugri can break through my defenses. My vote is yes."

"Your zeal threatens us all with ruin, Shiramon," snapped Duke Parkhol.

By far the youngest of the council, Parkhol was duke only due to the untimely deaths of his father and older brother in an air car accident. Whispers suggested that it was his hand behind their demise, though proof was decidedly absent. Brash as his youth suggested, he wore crimson robes trimmed in light purple. His face was youthful, missing the cruel creases of long years of leadership and heartache. His auburn hair fell to his shoulders, framing his slender body.

Shiramon spun on the youth. "Bah! What does a boy know of the ways of men? I killed my first man before your father got the idea to find a consort and plant his seed, and you dare offer advice? Go back to your mother, boy. This is no game."

"All you have done is prove your great age," Parkhol laughed, "certainly not the wisdom one would associate with long years of ruling a kingdom. True, I may not have the experience of most of you, but I recognize folly when I hear it. Have any of you even seen an Ugri? Has anyone? You propose we march an army into unknown lands against an army of unknown strength and accuse me of immaturity? Your desires will damn us all if left unchecked by reason."

"Boy or no, we are all nobles of Lethendweil. All of Crimeat would bear down upon us were it not so," spoke the aging Lord Whitel. At one hundred and ten, he was the eldest and most respected of the council.

All bickering ceased. The lords of Lethendweil paused their arguments in order to consider his words.

Suffocated tranquility returned once more, only a spark away from bursting back into open flame. Much of the fever had bled from the air. Nobles closely watched each other, eager for others to show some sign of the same emotion that they were struggling to keep buried themselves. Still, any semblance of calm was gone, shattered like so many mirrors under the pounding of hammers. Scura patiently waited. A thin smile so crisp it was almost a sneer decorated his thin face. He had done his part. Events were now in motion that could not be undone.

Scura had spent his childhood watching and learning from his father. The mastery he possessed would see him to the throne of Lethendweil, or so he dreamed. The time of fossils like Emleth was over. For the land to progress, the old must be purged.

Whitel continued, "As Lord Emleth said, war is no easy thing to commit to. How do we readily throw our soldiers into harm's way without giving any thought to the consequences of our actions? Go back to your families, my friends. Back to your people. Let them decide which course to choose. For if the voice of the people strengthens our needs, then there is no way the gods will let us lose."

One by one, the nobles filed from the council chambers. Only Ursal Prowl and Danja Stall remained seated, locked in quiet discussion. What concerned the lords of Lethendweil did not necessarily concern the greater Conclave or Inquisition. Scura took note of this as he collected his obsidian cloak and departed.

"A word before you return to Reven, Master Scura," came Emleth's now calm voice. The fury and passion with he had addressed his peers with was gone, replaced by an oddly disturbing collectedness.

Scura quickly put on a false smile. "Of course, my lord. I am at your disposal."

The two marched in silence to Emleth's private studies. A pair of guards, dressed in light plate armor a combination of blues and greens on their chest and legs, snapped to attention and opened the door. Emleth thanked them and bade the door closed until he was finished. The study stood in opposition to the rigid formality of the council chambers. Rich teak panels lined the walls, reflecting the gentle licking flames of the fireplace. A thick rug of crimson and white patterns added homeliness to the leather furniture. Rows of books, mostly on Crimeat and galactic laws, decorated the wall behind the massive desk of the head councilor. A stuffed and mounted frazael bear stood on hind legs in the far corner, always eyeing the occupants with its three eyes. Scura found the creature disgusting and was glad they were now extinct.

Emleth gestured for Scura to take a seat while he produced a bottle of spiced wine and two crystal glasses carved to resembled birds. "These are troubled times."

Scura slowly nodded. Natural apprehensions arose. It was not unheard of for treachery and assassinations to occur amongst the noble class. Coming to the inner sanctum of the opposition was a dangerous act. Logic demanded otherwise. Emleth needed him. He'd seen it in the man's eyes. The only way Emleth could hope to remain in control of the council was through the support Scura held.

"That is a fair estimate. Forgive my impassioned outbursts, but our peoples have suffered much, and I find it hard to control my emotions. It pains me to know that more is in store for them if we fail to act."

Emleth handed him a glass. "Indeed, and I tend to agree with you. Scura, you and I have never been friends. I know little of your personal nature, but your demeanor gives credence to your character. Lethendweil could stand for more of your quality. There has been a lack of good leaders more interested in their people than themselves of late. If only you and I could set aside our differences and put the needs of the land first. I trust you understand my position?"

Scura concealed his bitterness. "Of course. It would appear unseemly if the head of the council eagerly advocated war. It is my belief that cooler heads will, in fact, prevail once matters become clearer. General Shiramon is not the most elegant of speakers, but his heart is in the right place."

"Shiramon is a pain in my ass, and that is no exaggeration. Military officers should not be in charge of kingdoms; otherwise, we would all be marching from one battle to the next on a tide of blood and bodies. Bah! Perhaps I am just getting old." He sighed and took a seat opposite to Scura. "Scura, I carry no illusions towards peace. I simply urge caution. War is a terrible beast that can easily grow out of control and consume us all. We cannot allow ourselves to give in to animalistic emotions without proper preparation. The use of force remains a viable option, but I am of a mind to try another route first. I want you to consider heading an envoy to the Ugri. Peace must be our priority! Should the Ugri reject us, I pray for future generations of both races."

A murmur on his heart, Scura paused, taken off guard by the sudden proposal. His most vocal opponent on the council had just asked—no, begged—for his help. He nervously scratched at the corner of his mouth. This new twist might be his salvation or damnation, depending on how it all worked out. Both choices present unique dangers, and that little nagging feeling warned him from the back of his mind.

"I…do not know what to say, Lord Emleth," Scura replied in carefully measured words.

"Say that you accept and will remain objective throughout the process."

Easier said than done. "I think I might like that assignment. Perhaps I will be able to determine what is truly happening in the west."

"Move quickly, Scura. Time is our enemy here. We must have answers."

Baron Scura finished his wine and excused himself. He had much to plot.

Vaade was the orignal city, founded when men first came to Crimeat. The Conclave had showered the city with lavish gifts and equipment to build an empire with. A delegation of priests had petitioned for acceptance into the Conclave, and, for a time, Crimeat had been the golden jewel of the universe. Time and decaying interests had reduced the planet to an afterthought, a pleasant reminiscence of better times. The once grand and modern architecture of Vaade was old now. Thousands of single-story buildings comprised the main city. White cobblestone streets provided an inviting atmosphere.

Shadows swirled around him like ripples across a river. Vague reflections of starlight twinkled off the green and blue forests surrounding Vaade. Nestled between the Korsl River Basin and the southern end of the Bothwel Mountains, Vaade offered breathtaking views from every angle. The ocean was not far off, ever enticing with the supple splash of water on sand. Crimeat's twin moons hung high in the night sky. One glowed a dark red, the other tranquil blue. The peacefulness of the scene made it hard to believe the land was a deep breath away from open war.

Militiamen patrolled the streets, offering a false sense of security. Still, the Ugri were hundreds of leagues away and certainly not the imminent threat the western kingdoms faced. The blue and black uniforms of the militia were accented with dark brown sashes. Each guard carried a shoulder-fired long rifle with a hand blaster and stun bar belted to his hip. They were not so much a military force as one of defense. Peace was not an issue here. Vaade had no prisons, no jails. Law breakers were mostly dealt with on the spot and brutally. Those deemed bad enough were deported to a prison barge sailing the coast. Order ruled the streets of Vaade—order and a healthy dose of fear for potential law breakers.

Wrapped tightly in a dark cloak, Baron Scura felt a part of the shadows. He enjoyed the anonymity darkness offered. The intricate decisions of his life were made infinitely easier under the protective cover of night. A noise to his right jerked his head. He snarled as an old street dog snatched up a rat and dashed down the alley to eat before others came to rob him.

"You should relax," whispered a voice behind Scura. "The night poses no danger for one such as you."

Scura didn't bother to turn. He knew he would find no one. "We play a dangerous game. Now is not the time for complacency."

No reply. Scura sensed a pair of figures behind him and tensed. The possibility that they had been hired to kill him was not inconceivable. Stale winds shifted through the alley, bringing the rot of old food and human waste. A man of his stature could have, should have picked a more appropriate place for this meeting, but he was not eager to risk being seen. What he intended was best left unseen.

"Did I not say to relax?" the voice said with soft laughter. "We would not be here if there was a hint of danger. People often see what they choose to rather than what is truly there. It is the great failing of your race. We are perfectly safe, Baron."

So you are not human after all. Interesting. "Those same failings can also be our greatest strengths. The instinct to survive is too strong to ignore."

"Perhaps you worry there is a blade aimed at your back?"

"I am a politician. It comes with my job."

Rustling in the dark. The voice took a different tone, ominous, potentially threatening. "Why have you summoned us?"

"It is time."

Hissing. Scura imagined the pair was communicating in their own language. Fingernails scratched down his spine. He was no stranger to intrigue and dangerous situations, but these two carried the aroma of predators.

"You understand what you ask? Once we take contract, there can be no turning back, no return to what you view as normal. Your life will no longer be the same."

"I understand." He found the words harder to speak than anticipated. Years of plotting were about to come to fruition. The sheer gravity of it threatened to steal his knees from under him. "How will I know when you are finished?"

"You will know."

Not the most calming of answers. Scura spun. The shadows swirled, and the figures dissipated before his eyes, but not before he caught the glimpse of black robes and golden masks devoid of everything but eyes. Vaumagian assassins. Scura toyed with the thought of what he had gotten himself into, though in truth it was much too late. Once the order of assassins accepted payment, the contract would be fulfilled. Scura stood alone in the dark alley and struggled against the oppressive weight bearing down on him.

Ursal Prowl finished his conversations with the Conclave Priest and began the long trek back to his offices. A nervous twitter made his legs dance. He dreaded what awaited him. His mind raced through what might have gone wrong; what could he possibly have done that the Inquisition was unhappy with? His next scheduled inspection was not for another three months, which left him with an unfamiliar gnawing feeling twisting through his stomach. People passed by offering casual greetings, but he failed to notice a single one. His office came must too fast for his liking.

Ursal reluctantly pushed the door open. His eyes immediately scanned the outer room for signs of his guest, and he was not disappointed. An Inquisitor sat, one leg over the other, casually read a data pad. He was sitting at Ursal's desk. A mild look of anger warmed his naturally hardened face. Ursal swallowed. Here was a man unused to waiting. This might prove worse than he had originally dreaded.

"Senior Inquisitor, my apologies for not being able to attend you earlier, but my presence is occasionally demanded by the council," he began, studying the rank epaulettes.

Tolde Breed gently set the pad down and looked up, his face now a blank mask. "I was not aware that Inquisitors were subject to local laws."

Ursal shook his head. His cheeks flushed bright crimson. "Not quite like that. The planet Conclave representative and I are considered adjunct members of the council. We are often called to participate in local affairs, at least in what they deem the important ones."

Tolde didn't move. "I see. Well, it is not my place to criticize your actions. Besides, I am here for more important matters."

"I was not informed of your coming, Senior Inquisitor; otherwise, I would have been here," Ursal replied cautiously. He hoped to worm out that vital piece of information that would explain everything, thus alleviating growing fears and apprehensions.

"I am Senior Inquisitor Tolde Breed."

Ursal Prowl paled. *The legendary Tolde Breed.* Inquisitors for the last fifty years had studied Breed's mission to capture one of the fabled Three. It was a keystone in their professional development and a lesson for all who would heed it. Men like Breed came along once in a generation, and from looking upon the hardness and distance Tolde projected, Ursal was glad. Any more than one and the universe might shatter.

Ursal unconsciously rubbed the sweat from his palm before offering it. "It is an honor, Senior Inquisitor Breed. I am Ursal Prowl."

Tolde should have been used to it by now. His celebrity amongst the Inquisition was practically unmatched—and, in his eyes, unwarranted. He had not asked to be assigned to that nightmare mission to capture Amongeratix. Dark dreams still visited in the lonely hours of the night. And now that beast was loose again, free to ravage hapless souls with his personalized hatred and darkness. Woe to any caught in his path.

"There is no need for formality, Ursal. I assure you I am not the statue that your generation makes me out to be. I am just a man. One small piece of the greater good."

His words rang hollow to Ursal, his mind already spinning through multiple scenarios.

Seeing that he had to continue the conversation if anything was too get done, Tolde added, "The Inquisitor General and Cardinal Seniorus deemed this secret enough not to inform the planetary officials ahead of time. And as you know, we are but humble servants. I do not expect to impose too much on you, Ursal."

Hints of casual betrayal flashed briefly in Ursal's dark eyes before he managed to regain what little composure he had remaining.

Politics among the Inquisition members was often complicated and dangerous, especially for amateurs. Whispers circled around the empty chambers and dark shadows of Inquisitors suddenly disappearing. Corruption ran deep, and Ursal Prowl suddenly found himself at the crisp end of a sharp rope.

Clearing his throat, Ursal replied, "Whatever I have here is at your service, Senior Inquisitor. My office is a small one, but we pride ourselves on ensuring the Conclave and Inquisition are properly served."

Tolde Breed nodded, silently approving of the only acceptable reply. He also knew that a man capable of passing the Inquisition trials was both cunning and dangerous, just like himself. Fragments of shattered loyalties clung to his boots like the detritus of so many wild beasts on the open plains. Uncommon, but by no means unusual, Inquisitors policed their own ranks, hunting down the disbelievers and heretics who veered away from the path. Tolde shied away from hunting down his own kind as much as he could. He found he had no stomach for it. Fidelity clutched his heart tighter than any love ever had.

"How big is your Prekhauten garrison?" he decided to ask, careful to avoid unwarranted accusations.

"Small. A five hundred man battalion is stationed across the planet. Most of them are here in Lethendweil, but we have compounds at all the major population centers. They can be deployed anywhere in the world in less than eighteen standard hours."

Another nod. "Pray that it does not come down to that, Ursal. I would like to link my Sergeant Major with their commanding officer at the earliest convenience. It is important that both units work together in the coming days and weeks."

Ursal gently cleared his throat, his sharp eyes never leaving Tolde. "Excuse, Senior Inquisitor, but you still haven't told me exactly why you are here. I must admit that I find your hints distressing."

If you only knew. "We all have our burdens to bear. I am not at liberty to discuss the details of my mission. The Inquisitor General will inform you when he feels you need to know. I can say no more."

Tolde left the obligatory I'm sorry off. He wasn't. Inquisitors worked through often nefarious channels that demanded intricate circles of secrecy. The Three were one of the most closely guarded secrets in the universe, and not every Inquisitor knew the truth about them. Tolde's orders were specific to the point that he would have Ursal arrested on charges of heresy and removed from his post if the junior Inquisitor discovered too much. Remnants of that same self-innocence mocked Tolde from the faded corners of his memory. He often longed for the simplistic lifestyle he'd had before his hunt for Amongeratix so many years ago. An entire life was never lived, potential futures crushed before that first precious breath fanned out.

"Inquisitor Prowl, I believe we have come to the end of this conversation. I do not mean to sound adversarial or even trite, but I have much to do. I will contact you with my needs when they arise."

Feeling mistrusted, Ursal did his best to maintain the tatters of his composure. "Of course, Senior Inquisitor. As I said before, my office is at your service. I will see you out."

"That will not be necessary. My detachment is staying right down the main boulevard at the Gilded Wyvern. I shall be in touch."

Ursal Prowl stood dumbfounded as the greatest living legend of the Inquisition marched out of his office. A lesser man might have been humbled by such a presence, but Ursal merely clenched his fists as the first inklings of humiliation burned his cheeks. Legends be damned, there would come a time of reckoning.

EIGHT

3210 A.G. (After Gods), Vaade, planet Crimeat.

The Night of Blood, as it would become known, was not unexpected. A miasma of discontent suffocated the world, choking down humor and good will with unrelenting oppression. Doors were locked, windows shuttered closed. No one could ignore the rising tension, threads of electricity vibrating under the city. Danger whispered on the kiss of the winds. Birds cowered in their nests. Stray dogs and cats bolted for hiding spots lest the vengeance about to be reaped turned on them. Only the foolish dared to venture out into the night.

Cool winds slashed through the streets, sweeping sand and dust across the cobblestones with enough fury to quail even the strongest nerve. Insects stopped chirping. The shadow hands of death stretched forth from the darkness, hungrily in search of the intended prey. All trembled and bowed before the vast wealth of intent burrowing into the very heart of the city. A whirlwind was coming, one so dire it threatened to tear the very fabric of existence from the womb of being.

Vaade slept uneasily. Shallow rot gnawed at the dreamers. Forest green and opal tiles echoed the haunting moonlight, turning the blackness of night into a kaleidoscope of reds, greens and black as it drooled over the rounded rooftops. Tendrils of smoke drifted up, but there was no warmth in any of the homes. Men and women of the city watch made their rounds with unnatural reluctance, as if they knew the dawn was going to abandon them. The most devout knelt at home altars or held hands around the bed with their children, mouthing prayers to the gods lest they be torn away in the middle of the night. An old woman rocked gently in her chair, smug with the knowledge that the Sickle was coming for her at last. A newborn cried uncontrollably for reasons the parents would never guess. Disaffected youth took to the rooftops with wine and spirits to watch the festivities, carelessly risking their own lives to the whim of angry gods. The city held its breath and prayed to awake with the dawn.

The drums of war pounded through the subconscious of everyone old enough to understand what horrors truly lurked. Political manipulations threatened to steal husbands away in the middle of the night, leaving families shattered wrecks. Greed and avarice drove the building storm. This night would be wreathed in blood. Silent and unstoppable, black robed assassins crept from their haunts and set about their grim tasks. All in the name of war, and the profit it brought only to those already wealthy. Death and nightmares were left for the poor to cling to once all else was crumbled to ash.

Gentle snoring echoed from the marble tiled floor. A candle burning low from a small bedside table broke the thickness of shadows just enough to highlight the rise and fall of the sleeping man's chest. On the floor, the bared fangs of a long slain and extinct garack wolf offered false protection. Teeth glimmered in the firelight. The absurdity of it was not lost on the men guarding the room. A common joke among the guards was that the wolf had seen more action from various escorts and mistresses over the years than it ever had when rutting with females of its own pack. Duke Parkhol certainly had extravagant tastes, not the least of which his proclivity for women, whether they chose to be with him or not. Far from the paragon of virtue, Parkhol found the need for more guards than any other councilman, save perhaps Emleth. Too many enemies lurked just a step away with a blade ready for his ribs.

Parkhol slept soundly, despite the electric atmosphere gripping the rest of the city. His master of assassins was one of the best in Lethendweil, and one of the most well paid. It never hurt to overpay the ones you relied on for private security. Plush accommodations surrounded the sleeping councilman. He had long held the position that Vaade was but an uneasy stop before returning to his ocean fortress of Carmak. Random women were generally the only visitors, women and the occasional merchant seeking to line his purse with misappropriated funds.

Outside the master bedchamber, a pair of guards clad in the rustic brown uniforms of the council stood like golems. It was a small courtesy extended to sitting council members, one of which Parkhol was not fond. Still, there was no practical reason to deny free security, especially during darkened times like these. Parkhol had smiled falsely as he accepted them into his temporary residence, all the while instructing his own men to watch the council guards for even the slightest form of treachery.

Night was now deep, and the storm had just begun. The guards were jumpy, their nerves frayed for unknown reasons. Each felt death reach out to tickle the nape of his neck but refused to admit it to the other. Men did not kneel before such fears. A soft wind rustled down the dark hallway. The guards exchanged a nervous glance, childhood nightmares crawling back into their weary minds. Shaky hands reached down for the comfort and illusory safety of their hip blasters. The obvious remained unspoken. There should not have been a wind, not inside with all windows and doors shut and locked.

"What was that?" Arkis whispered to his sergeant. His eyes darted back and forth, wide with unprecedented fear. Council guards were not supposed to engage in violence.

Sergeant Hoad frowned, grateful for the youth's impatience. "Quiet, boy. Nothing but the wind. A window must've come unlatched. Go on down and make sure it is closed again."

"What if it's not?"

Hoad snarled. "Go on now before you find my boot halfway up your ass. I ain't gonna take no lip from a boy like you. Now get!"

Arkis reluctantly obeyed his superior. Common sense said the window was unlatched, but common sense didn't feel right tonight. A thunderclap directly overhead shook the entire building, knocking dust from the recessed ceiling. Arkis cringed. Any pretense of bravado proved false, abandoning him now when he needed it the most. The young guard forced himself deeper into the shadows. Every footfall was like the pounding of some great beast over the plains of Berchenfel. Arkis felt his strength sap with each passing second.

Relief washed over him upon seeing the window rocking back and forth in the storm. Feeling foolish for succumbing to juvenile fears of the dark and the boogey men that haunt dreams, Arkis wiped the sweat from his brow and went to close the window. The latch clicked shut, and he forced a tired exhale.

It was the last thing he ever did. Arkis did not see the blade whip around his shoulders after he turned back towards Parkhol's chambers, did not see the chilling flash of a shining gold mask breaking the darkness for a fraction of a second. Hot blood flowed down his chest, his throat severed from ear to ear. All the warmth left him as his eyes rolled back into his head and his body was dragged away into the dark.

"What's going on down there?" called the sergeant as loud as he dared. The last thing he needed was Parkhol storming from his chambers with murder on his mind.

No answer.

"Arkis? Answer up, boy. This is no time for games. These storms have got me right spooked, and here you are playing around. I'm gonna tan your hide for this."

A strong gust of wind mocked him from the distance. Growling, Hoad set himself firmly to give Arkis a piece of his mind and the knuckles of a fist or two. The boy had to learn that being a guard was serious business. "Can't send him to do a simple task," he snarled under his breath.

Like Arkis, Hoad never saw the icy fingers crawl around his neck, moving more like smoke than flesh. Sharp pain pierced his chest. Hoad blinked once. Twice. The pain lanced hotter, and then he felt nothing. The pencil-thin blade that pierced his heart eased out with a tender sucking noise. A single drop of blood splashed on the carpet. Hoad's killer eased the body to the floor and continued. The real quarry was still ahead.

Embraced by shadow, the Vaumagian assassins slithered down the blood-stained hallway. The dark purple carpets would never quite get the stain out despite the cleaner's best efforts. Later generations would mark the spot as a shrine to men who stood up to darkness. Lost would be the reasons why. None of that mattered to the assassins. Lights went out as they passed. Shadows lengthened. An aroma of fear clung heavily to the furniture. The bedchamber door eased open without so much as a whisper.

Parkhol snored deeply, the sleep of the wicked without conscience. Two seasoned killers slid up to the sides of the bed, so quiet a wary predator wouldn't have heard. A casual gesture, no more than the flip of a finger, blew out the lone candle. Twin blades plunged repeatedly into Parkhol until his body shook with his last breath and the smell of urine and excrement fouled the room.

The Night of Blood had begun.

Providence was a fickle bitch. Legions of beggars held claim on land and titles, mockery of past lives driven destitute by changing times. The Night of Blood was not so discerning. Ruby flashes danced across the skies and through the massive thunderheads that seemed to settle directly over Vaade. Curious remains of some angry god's might often sparkled in the heavens, but this night was different. Man often made the assumption that the gods wanted to be involved in daily life. That misconception now threatened unprecedented vengeance upon Crimeat. Little did any in Vaade know that it all had next to nothing to do with them.

Lord Whitel sat on the old rocking chair on his second story veranda watching a flock of white sparrows launched from his private grove of orange baelbi trees. The red stripes running down the sparrows' breasts sang of home for reasons he never truly was able to comprehend. So much of life was wreathed in mystery. Whitel accurately guessed that much of it needed to be. Mankind simply was not ready to know the vast truths of the gods. As a result, those two most haunting words echoed in the emptiness of his soul: what if?

Fame and glory were already well behind him. Whitel often found himself sitting and watching the birds. The twilight of his life was closing in, probably should have already come and gone. He discovered that the more council meetings he attended, the lower his tolerance for greed and stupidity became. This morning was no exception. Too many nobles were too young to remember the pain and suffering of a continent-wide war. Capable in their own ways, Whitel saw the new generation of leaders as nothing more than inexperienced youth eager to prove themselves on the field of battle. Warfare was glory, at once hollow and filled with incalculable fame. Whitel wiped his hands of all of them.

Sadness nibbled away at his core. He tried to recall the harshness of his own lands. They stood in complete contrast with the plush luxuries Vaade offered. Orean bordered the edge of the great southern desert. It had few sparrows, few indulgences for an old man to occupy his time with. Such visions of beauty were often lost to the unending bitterness of the environment. The cast iron chair, faded dull green from years in the sun, suddenly felt harsher than he remembered.

There had been a time when Whitel would have jumped at the prospect of whetting his violent appetites against ageless foes. Those times were now lost. He was old and tired. A large part of him wanted to retire from public life. Retire and move his family here to Vaade or somewhere close by where a man might live the last of his days in peace. There was an infinite number of things to occupy his still-sharp mind. Orean's tanned buildings and brutal conditions did not compare to the near pristine streets of Lethendweil's capitol.

Whitel knew it was a raw fantasy. Unobtainable goals heightened by senseless emotions drove human compulsions. He was no exception. He feared what might become of his beloved kingdom should he resign now. Too many young wolves waited just outside the firelight, eager for fresh blood and the chance to prove themselves. Whitel could not quit, not now when his people needed the stability of reason the most.

Pressures of the council weighed heavily on his mind despite the simplicity offered by watching the sparrows. Sending young men and women off to a war they didn't quite understand was never easy. Most of the council saw things the way Whitel did, though a goodly number screamed for action. The divide between camps was obvious. Emleth commanded a peaceful settlement while hotheads like Shiramon and that damned Scura couldn't wait to shed blood. Complicating matters was the mysterious escape at the Conclave prison on Prophet Isle. More mysteries demanding answers.

Whitel shook off the harsh feelings building on his psyche and went back inside. The storm was near now, almost breaking over the white roofs of the city. Unnatural darkness seeped into every alley and cracked window. The elder noble smiled despite his rising misgivings and closed the double doors behind him. What little remained of the light echoed through the many panes. Safe again in his office, Whitel shuffled through a small mountain of paperwork, but his heart wasn't in it. Something about the jerky movements of the sparrows didn't sit well with him. Perhaps it was nothing more than an old man's superstition, though he strongly suspected it had much to do with those odd ruby flashes twisting the sky. He suddenly longed for the open air of the desert fringe. Whitel decided it was time for a walk to clear his mind.

As usual, his most trusted assistant, Danzer, awaited him in the antechamber with a patient look perpetually engraved on his face. The simple pleasantries a friendly face offered did much to improve the elder man's disposition. Pale skin made his green and white striped jacket stand out. Whitel wondered why a grown man would willingly dress like a child's doll but was too prudent to make any comment.

"My lord, you should be resting," Danzer politely told him. "Long hours of work aren't good for anyone, especially on a night like this."

"Ah, Danzer, you have a gifted tongue. It is a rare talent to rebuke your employer without offending him," Whitel said good-naturedly.

"I would never…."

"I am just teasing you, my boy. Events are transpiring faster than I anticipated. I have a feeling but do not know of what. These are dangerous times."

"I am sure those who came before us said much the same thing," Danzer replied as they started walking through the Orean noble's Vaade manor. Priceless paintings of wildlife and landscapes lines the walls, disrupted only by the occasional bust of some famous long-dead artist. Wall sconces under each painting made the manor seem like a museum. Whitel had the nagging sensation that it more like mausoleum. Crimeat was changing, and he was powerless to keep up.

They stopped under an ornate chandelier. A pair of poorly upholstered couches lined the walls. Whitel sighed and shook his head.

"Another trying session in council?" Danzer correctly guessed. His eunuch looks seemed fiercer in the wild light of the chandelier.

Aren't they all? "Worse than usual. The fools intend on plunging the entire continent into a war we do not need or understand. I wish I was young again."

Danzer felt his heart lurch. "How can we afford it?"

Whitel laughed gently. "In terms of money or lives? We have more than enough in our coffers to pay the bill. My fear is for the cost to our future. The Ugri are almost a myth to us. We know so little about them, but it does not stop us. Every spark of anger needs to be directed. And right now anger is consuming us all. I think a giant is about to awaken."

He saw the abstract horror glazing Danzer's eyes and gave him a halfhearted pat on the forearm. "Do not mind me. It is the ramblings of an old man who has seen too much and didn't die when he had the chance."

"Nonsense, my lord. It is a pleasure to serve at your side. I always find our conversations useful."

"You do not need to try and make me feel better, Danzer. I have lived a long and pointless life, and now the last thing I will see is a pointless war devour the land. Some might call that cursed. That damned Scura will be the death of civility. Would that his father still ruled."

Echoes of rumors surrounding the untimely demise of the elder Scura taunted Whitel. Lack of evidence kept pressure from the new Baron, enough for him to consolidate power and build his armies to nearly twice the level of previous rulers. The thought made Whitel cringe. Perhaps this war was more than just convenient. Perhaps the young Scura had been planning this for a long, long time.

"Trust in the gods, my lord," Danzer offered upon seeing the struggle behind Whitel's eyes. "They will see us through the coming storm."

Thunder rumbled, as if on cue, making Whitel grin. "Always a storm before it begins, eh? I wonder if the gods really care or if they are just figments of our imagination we use to justify our actions. At any rate, I hope you are right. Our faith might be the only thing that saves us from the long night."

An uneasy silence chilled the air between them. Danzer, optimistic for the most part, found it hard to maintain any positivity when doom and gloom burrowed into his fiber. Whitel noticed this and nodded.

"I think I will go for a walk in my gardens before the rain comes. I always like it right before the rain begins."

"Shall I summon your guard?"

"No, I think I will be quite safe within the walls of my own compound. Thank you, Danzer. Thank you for everything. You are one of the very best at what you do. Orean is proud of your work. Go and get some rest now. We are going to be extremely busy in the days to come."

Danzer bowed graciously and watched until Lord Whitel was outside. He almost followed despite Whitel's insistence. A foul presence tainted all of Vaade, twisting his stomach. He could feel…he wasn't sure what. Evil? Anger? Resentment? The possibilities were staggering, too much for a simple chamberlain to fathom. Danzer gave his lord a final glance and headed back to his bedchambers.

The coming storm drove out the heat, cooling the city enough to make it almost cold for a desert-dwelling man like Whitel. Winds kissed his face, driving a light mist across Vaade. Leaves curled up, giving off a strange sheen not quite metallic and not wholly organic.

Branches swayed. Whitel found peace here, surrounded by flowers and exotic plants that came from all over the universe. His expensive tastes were rooted deep in culture, if not precisely the legacy of his own. He often thought he would have made a better museum curator than a statesman. Too late now.

Whitel followed the red brick path until he stood beneath a centuries old willow tree in full bloom. The tendril branches lashed out to caress him like an old lover. Whitel was content. He wished that life was this simple. He closed his eyes and turned his face up to the blowing winds. He heard a soft click followed quickly by a thump in the soft grass at his feet. Whitel looked down at the small spherical object and knew he was dead.

The ultraviolet grenade exploded with a noiseless flash. Blinding purple-blue light flashed up and out, enveloping Whitel completely. The intensity of the light caused him to burst into flames. He died without a cry. Five seconds later, nothing was left but ash. The winds took the ashes of Lord Whitel and scattered them across the gardens he loved so much. It was a fitting epitaph.

The soft cackle of the fire did little to sooth Emleth's mind. Burdens continued to heap upon him, unwanted and thinly disguised to suit his needs. He couldn't remember the last time he genuinely smiled. Probably before his wife left him some twenty-odd years ago. Damn, that was too long to not be a man. Perhaps it was for the best. His position as council head left little time to pursue personal issues.

And now there was this business with the Ugri. He wanted to spit. The Ugri were an almost supernatural tribe that the eastern kingdoms knew very little of. No one had crossed through the Great Barrier Jungle and returned in more than a hundred years. Emleth toyed with the thought that it might be entirely possible the Ugri were extinct. There was no viable way to know. Satellites and flyovers showed nothing, confirming that they were a cave-dwelling species. And gods knew there were more than enough places for caves in the vast expanse of their lands.

Emleth looked down at Scura's empty cup and frowned. That man knew something he was unwilling to share with the rest of the council. Emleth felt like a puppet on a string. He idly wondered when he had started to lose control over the council. The Baron of Reven was undoubtedly charismatic but nowhere near the experienced leader

Lethendweil needed. Of course, that seldom stopped people. History was filled with rotten examples of greed spun out of control.

His own tenure was gently cascading down into those ranks. The implications of the future pressed heavily on his soul. Most nights were spent in restless slumber, if sleep bothered to grace him at all. Lately he had taken to drink. Spiced wine was his favorite vice. It helped steal away the pressures of the time. Emleth knew he was running, more like fleeing, from everything a leader should do, but it was too late to care. War was coming, and he did not have the power to avert it. *Nightmares for every night*, he mused.

Part of him knew that warfare was not a thing to be feared. He'd spent most of his adult life in the planetary mercenary corps, fighting from continent to continent for money, glory and fame. Killing came as naturally to him as taking a piss when he first woke up. A handful of worlds had felt the sting of his blades and the accuracy of his rifles. His name was remembered across the quadrant. No, not remembered. It was forgotten, like so much dust blown across the open savanna. The universe was deceitful in that way.

So now, instead of reaping lives, he was sending tens of thousands of others blindly into harm's way. Young men and women with no inkling of the politics behind the decision that was about to send them off to war would pay with blood and broken minds for the greed of others. Emleth scowled at the idea, never once stopping to think about what it had been like when he was one of the faceless soldiers. He poured the last of this latest bottle of wine and drained it from his cup just as fast. The winds began to howl, screams of warning against a lurking menace.

Damned wind. Emleth hated storms. They reminded him too much of the folly of his youth and the emptiness his adventures had brought him. Out of wine and lacking patience, Emleth decided to head into his bath. Perhaps a long soak might ease his rising tensions. Crossing the thick crimson carpet, Emleth shed his clothes and donned his favored granlet skin robe. The grey mountain cats were rare, thus making them a poacher's dream. It was one of the few personal luxuries Emleth allowed himself.

The marble in his private bath was rustic brown with thick veins of gold and black. Gold fixtures added to the overall feeling of wealth. Porcelain toilets and sinks presented pristine conditions that council heads had been enjoying for decades. The tub was enormous, easily capable of holding a dozen people. Crenellated columns circled the chamber, spearing up into a fifteen-foot domed ceiling. Emleth often felt like he was a bit figure in a grand stage play from countless years ago. The sheer size of the bath chamber made him feel small. It was good to be grounded from time to time, lest his ego grow too large for his position.

Emleth reached down to turn on the water. Jets of hot water flooded the tub in minutes. Steam rose in sheets. Emleth sighed. He could already feel the stress slip away. The only thing missing was wine. Satisfied the water was deep enough, he turned off the jets and shed his robe. The water burned as he gingerly sank first one foot and then the other in. He began to sweat long before he immersed his entire body.

"Music," he called once he was submerged up to his neck.

Wall speakers began softly playing his favorite classical piece, written by Lethendweil's most successful composer almost three hundred years ago. The music soothed his aggressions. Tension began leaving his body. Aches and pains bled into the heated waters, leaving him slowly calming down. Scented vapors drifted up from vents surrounding the bath. Emleth closed his eyes and tried to forget everything. *I'm not the man I need to be. Could it be I have lost the fire that once burned, once drove my spirit? Damnation. I need a drink.*

He didn't know how long he had been asleep. The tips of his fingers were pruned. His skin itched from prolonged exposure to the hot water. Thick clouds of steam shrouded the depths of the baths. He had half a mind to call for an attendant, but the urge to remain alone was too powerful. Only through solitude was he able to collect his composure and regain what little of his mind remained.

Click.

Emleth froze. The breath caught in his throat. There was no mistaking that sound. That distinctive metallic tone. Eyes slowly opening, Emleth tried to pierce through the gloom his carelessness had produced. Thunder crashed over the city, shaking buildings. The storm struck with all of the intensity of a meteor. The council head cringed despite himself at the shrieking winds tearing through the streets. None of it concerned him much. The storm, the sounds, the implications it held for his precious city. The only thing that mattered was that one sound that froze the blood in his veins.

His listened for another moment, praying that it was only his imagination. But no. Luck would never be so kind to him. He knew what he had heard and, more importantly, what it meant. Rising to his full, imposing height, Emleth balled his fists indignantly.

"Cowards. At least let me see your faces."

Four shadowy figures stalked out of the steam. Black, their robes concealed every feature but the golden masks hiding their faces. The fear betrayed in his voice now moved to his body. Gold masks. They could only be one thing. Someone had hired the Vaumagian assassins to eliminate him. Each assassin carried a snub barrel mark VII needle rifle. Capable of firing over one hundred two-inch razor-sharp needles a minute, the weapons were quiet and mercilessly effective.

The assassins moved in on three sides, halting a few meters away from the naked man in the tub. He was no more than that. Any pretense of being council head was gone, lost to the disrespect and embarrassment of being caught naked in his own private bath. A man in his position should have known better, especially during heightening dark times. Still, he defiantly placed his hands upon his hips.

"Don't lose your nerve now. This is the best chance you will get against me," he taunted. The real question he wanted answers to would go unasked. Who? Who sent you to kill me? The why was never that important. He might have been able to figure it out on his own if the Vaumagians left him alive. Not that there was any chance at all such absurdity happening. The Vaumagian order was the best in the universe. Emleth was already dead.

They opened fire. A bitter whizzing sound filled the bath. Pink mist sprayed from a hundred holes. His body was shredded. The message was clear. He was the example. Emleth was dead before his body slid back into the water. The only part left out of the water was a curled hand resting lazily on the rim. The waters turned dark crimson. Hope of averting the coming war drained as quickly as the spilled water down the drain in the floor.

One by one, the assassins concealed their rifles and disappeared back into the steam. The truth of what had happened would be discovered soon enough. The storm continued to rage unabated. Lethendweil would never be the same.

"Damned spooky night."

Jers glanced up from his cards with a frown. They were playing so they might forget the rage gusting across Vaade, and here was this damn fool bringing it right back to the front of his mind.

"Can't you just shut up for once, Haggle? We're in here all safe and sound. Let some other poor slob worry about the storm. It's your deal."

Haggle, nick-named for his ability to barter for everything from ammunition to a clean pair of socks despite the efficiency of the Prekhauten Guard supply system, tried and failed to conceal his grin. Jers was too good at cards to leave alone. He had to get inside the man's mind and shake him up a little.

"I'm just saying, it's a damned spooky storm. I mean, look at the way it just burst up on us. Ain't natural."

Sergeant Fies glanced up from his pipe. He sat with his legs stretched out, feet propped up on the window sill. The self-dimming glass reduced the need for curtains, and Fies almost wished for the old style. The storm was the blackest, angriest he could recall. And whatever mischief Haggle was up to, it wasn't natural either.

"I swear, you are going to swallow your teeth if you make one more gods damned comment like that," the now angered Jers snapped.

Annalilly chuckled, making Jers even angrier.

"I have no problem hitting a woman," he said through clenched teeth.

She spat out the wad of kerhak leaf she'd been chewing on and winked. She had just as much muscle as any of the rest of the squad. "Try it, pretty boy. I dare you."

Jers thought twice. Despite her attractive looks, Annalilly was quite possibly the most dangerous member of the squad. She wore her shoulder-length blonde hair up in a tail, even when off duty, and absolutely despised makeup and all of the typical things that society proscribed in the definition of a woman. She was a Prekhauten Guard and proud of it. Anyone who underestimated her deserved what justice she delivered.

"Mess with that one if you want to, but I value my balls too much," old Kastor told them. "I never heard a man with such a high-pitched scream as that fella over in Second Battalion, Third Company. Poor bastard had to join the Conclave choir after that. Shame, really. He had the potential for a great career."

Jers tossed his cards on the table and placed his head in his hands. Haggle burst out in contagious laughter.

"Oh, Kastor, you say the nicest things," Annalilly smiled.

The eldest soldier in the squad shrugged and went back to reading his book. Fies shook his head and exhaled a thick bluish plume of smoke. The rest of the squad was asleep. Most were restless, shifting and turning with each thunderclap. Only Beve, the heavy weapons specialist, managed to snore through it.

"Hey Sergeant, why are we here anyway?" Annalilly decided to ask once the laughter died down. The angles of her face seemed harder in the dim light.

The room was meant for conferences. It was the only one large enough to house all of Matthias's Guardsmen. Beds were brought in and lined up, reminding all of them of their basic training. Long, open bays with endless rows of bunks and absolutely no personal space. Sometimes life in the Guard was just grand. At least the food was good. No, that was a sharp understatement. The food was prepared by master chefs trained at the premier culinary academy in the universe. Only the best for the richest of Lethendweil.

Fies regarded his best corporal from behind the stoic mask he always presented when asked a stupid question. He scratched the corner of his lip, adding a dramatic pause that only served to irritate whoever he was addressing.

"Corporal, if the Sergeant Major wanted you to know, he would have told you."

Face still hidden in his hands, Jers added, "We are all going to die."

"Doesn't matter if we do, soldier. This is what we get paid for. Don't expect to stay comfortable in this hotel either. We have a Senior Inquisitor with us, and if that doesn't tell you anything you need to desert tonight. Whatever we are here for, it can't be good for anyone."

"That wasn't reassuring, Sergeant," she replied.

Fies pulled hard on his pipe. "It wasn't meant to be."

Scratching under his armpit, Kastor glanced up. His grey beard was sparse, more patchy than presentable. "Don't forget that Blood Witch they are sending for. You know nothing good can come from one of them being around."

Haggle squinted, deep in thought. "I heard that one of them saved the Sergeant Major's life a while back. In fact he was with this same Inquisitor. That has to count for something, right?"

"Only if you want things to get worse. I never liked them witches. Nothing natural about them at all."

"Kastor, I know you were around back when the Guard was created, but do you have to be so doom and gloom about us now? I'd like to see a little hope at least," Annalilly joked.

Kastor frowned. He hated being called old, especially by a young pup of a girl. "Look here, kid. I'm not about to take any lip from a youngster such as you. Mind your manners."

"You people remind me why I left home," Beve said out of nowhere. The hulking brute of a soldier hadn't even bothered to roll over.

Fies chuckled softly, recalling fond memories of his own brothers bickering back and forth until their father was forced to jump in the middle and end it. Usually it ended with one or more of their heads being thumped. Fies shook his head softly. When it came to family, the men and women in the bay here with him were as much family as he had ever known back home. He contended they were the best group of soldiers in the Guard and was willing to put that claim to the test any day of the year.

Haggle's eyes flew open in surprise, slightly angered that he hadn't seen the card he needed to win the game. Slapping it hard on the table he all but shouted, "I win. All because of this storm. I'm telling you, Jers."

"Shut the *fuck* up!"

Blood Witches and monster storms. How could this night possibly get any worse?

NINE

3210 A.G. (After Gods) Prophet Isle, planet Crimeat.

What do gods dream of? Is there a suffering of mortal excesses that propels them into the future on a collision course with destiny? The universe, vast and empty, is but a playground for the dreams of gods. None of these thoughts had ever manifested until now. Until he witnessed the awful events outside of the Conclave prison. The world, life, changed suddenly. Irrevocably shifting focus and meaning.

Moffo Kain sat glumly in the back of the cave he'd found outside of Breld. He had cringed as Amongeratix joyfully explained the full depredations of who he was, exulting in the vision of horror he had in store for the universe. Moffo Kain had once believed that Hell was but a figment of imagination used to frighten fools. He now knew better. Hell was a living, breathing thing, an entity that no living man or woman should ever have to witness. The very warmth of his veins was stolen at the thought.

Moffo glanced over at the sleeping giant in the back of the cave. Life. What cruel irony the Fates had twisted him into. This was not a life. Servitude demanded Moffo deliver Amongeratix to the others in Breld. Impulse and a lack of control had put him in the situation. He tried to imagine the nightmares that had led a being such as Amongeratix to this point, the depths of despair at being cast out from everything he ever knew. Most of all, Moffo Kain tried to imagine what life would be like as a god.

All his expectations and suppositions rang hollow. There was no grandeur in being a god. Life and death hung on the fickle emotions of simple human beings. Gods died when men stopped believing. How many worlds underwent massive change because of some zealot with firebrand religious politics? Humanity collected in violent mobs more easily than any were willing to accept. So, Moffo wondered, what spark was it going to take for all of Crimeat to turn into a blood-frenzied mob? He looked again at the sleeping giant, his own dreams of the future crashing down in cinders around them.

Amongeratix dreamed, fractured memories of an age now forgotten. Pain and suffering congealed in the hidden fabric of his mind. There was no love, no room for hindering emotions that chained the mortal soul. Worse, he dreamt of chains. And violence.

A clock chimed the eleventh hour. Voices howled. Tin cups rattled against iron bars. A rat scurried against the wall, eager to be free of the billowing madness. A man screamed. It was the sound of death visiting. Chime. Amongeratix sat hunched on the floor of his small cell and grinned. Madness was spreading through the prison. Heavy chains pinned him to the ground, cutting deep into his muscles in a vain attempt at breaking his spirits. The stench of the prison choked most men, a sickening mixture of feces and vomit. The occasional decomposition of a dead prisoner only made things worse as the hot summer nights came. Through it all Amongeratix thought of only one thing: the man who had put him in here.

Amongeratix closed his eyes and remembered days lost from the best memories, battles fought, blood spilled. All he once knew belonged to the eldritch powers of chaos and malice. The strength of his being centered on his ability to call forth powers no other living creation had the right to. According to his father, not even he should have been able to access that power. Every death, every shattered soul and broken dream built his strength, grew his legend. All that power sat latent in his veins. It seethed. It turned into rage and unabashed hatred.

The ancient clock tower chimed again, ever reminding him of his cage. His black eyes opened and stared passed the faded granite walls. His vision blurred. A dull ache pounded in the depths of his mind like war drums to a marching army. That army came into focus gradually, marching beneath the haunting glow of the pale halo surrounding the full moon high in the night sky. A storm growled on the near horizon, threatening to sweep in with full fury.

Amongeratix closed his eyes and tried to imagine how his brother had felt that day.

Endless plains spread as far as the mortal eye could see. Brown grass blew lazily in the wind. Dark shapes emerged from opposite directions. Massive beyond measure, the figures gradually turned into tight squares of soldiers. The exhausted armies continued at a slow pace toward each other. Neither was eager to engage the enemy after long days of marching across a barren land. Lightning showed glimpses of the armies. They were savage men armored in used boiled leather and rusted chainmail. Weapons were old and overused. None of it mattered, for this was meant to be the final battle, the last meeting between two ancient and hated foes. Every military-age male in both societies was recruited, forced into the ranks. Whoever won, the losers were promised annihilation.

Beneath magnificent standards stood a giant of man. Twice the height of his army, Tannus wore the finest golden armor and bore the best weapons a lifetime of searching produced. His normally soft eyes were hardened with a touch of exhaustion. He was tired of senseless combat and the waste of human lives it produced.

Tannus marched at the head of his army. The giant raised his mighty sword into the dim night, and the army ground to a halt. A mile away, the enemy did the same. It would take a few more minutes for each army to be ready to charge, so he decided to take advantage of the situation to address his men.

The very sweep of his gaze inspired hope deep in the hearts of men. It was both blessing and boon. His standard bearer planted the nine-foot pole in the dry dirt and waited. "Men. My friends! Across this sea of grass waits our ancient and venerated enemy. They are no strangers to any of us. We have met their kind before and come away bloodied. This war has been long, and we are all weary beyond measure. But take heart! I ask you to look deep into the warmth of your soul and find that strength not only you but the men to your right and left will rely on in the hours to come."

His voice naturally amplified so that the entire army, a hundred thousand strong, could hear as if he stood at the ear of each. Inspiration lighted in their eyes. Renewed faith, energy and vigor coursed through them in powerful undercurrents. They clanged their weapons against their chest armor, brandishing their blades in the sky.

"None of us wanted this war. It was thrust upon us with all the hatred and heartlessness a single being could manifest. None of us wanted this war, but it is ours to fight and win. We cannot surrender. We cannot retreat. All that we hold dear will be enslaved or worse should we fail here tonight." He passed his gaze across the entire army, making eye contact with as many of them as possible. Smiles reflected back at him.

Tannus continued, "The gods sit high in their heavens and pass judgment on us without bothering to come down and spend a day in our boots. I say let them sit. Let them watch from the clouds and do nothing. Tonight, this war will be won by men, not gods. It will be won by all of you. Embrace your faith. Make your prayers to the gods and give them praise, but look to each other to see us through to the dawn. Tonight, my friends, we fight the last battle in the last war. Tonight, we take our rightful place as victors in this pointless struggle that has claimed so many of our friends and loved ones. Tonight, we win!"

Men roared. The noise shook the ground and vibrated echoes into the cosmic heavens. It did not go unnoticed. Seated comfortably on their thrones, the gods watched events unfold below. Battle pleased them, and tonight promised to be most satisfying. Tonight, the Sickle would drink deeply in homage. Higher judges bowed their heads to the world below and silently watched their children play.

Tannus speared his sword indignantly at them. He alone was able to see them from the plain. Bitterness edged into the corners of his eyes, but there was something more. Something undeniably sad. A pack of wolves the size of elephants howled from just beyond sight. Horns bleated across the winds. Tannus looked across the battlefield and spied his brother. Amongeratix sat with a dour look upon a great horned monster with scaled skin and a whip-like tail. No doubt he was bored.

Slowly, Tannus brought his sword arm forward until it pointed at his brother's heart. "Bugler, sound the advance!"

One hundred thousand men surged forward. Enemy legions did the same. The separating mile steadily ground away. At a half a mile, the cavalry separated to the wings. At a quarter, the archers slipped into the front ranks. Tannus and Amongeratix led their armies closer to destiny. A horn blew. Archers halted and nocked. The creak of bowstrings was lost among heavy footsteps. The armies marched.

"Loose!"

A vibrating hum slashed over both forces. Shields were raised, some in time, some not. Screams drifted up, to the amusement of the gods. Men fell dead and wounded and were ground underfoot. BOOM BOOM, the drums pounded. A hundred meters were all that remained between the armies, savage men with killing in their hearts. Some of them wanted nothing more than to go home again. Others couldn't wait to reap lives in some sick fantasy.

Lightning crashed repeatedly as soon as the brothers clashed arms. The front lines met in all the glory the gods of war demanded. The sky filled with vultures and crows. A feast awaited. The noise was deafening ad sword met sword. Grass was trampled and the dry dirt slickened with blood.

Tannus grimaced as his swing was blocked by the bone sword his brother carried. His arm ached from wrist to shoulder. Amongeratix laughed at him. "Brother!" he bellowed over the roar of battle. "You cannot think to best me with this rabble. Look upon my might and know your demise."

Tannus gritted his teeth, forced to dodge a lunge by his brother's mount. Hot saliva dripped like acid. Tannus swung to force the creature back and jabbed upward. A white flash blossomed on impact. The beast roared the moment before Tannus's sword pierced its brain stem. Amongeratix toppled under the dying beast. Men fell by the score around them. Amongeratix pushed his dead mount off and rose to his full menacing height. He rolled his shoulders before leveling his gaze on his brother.

"That…was most impolite."

Tannus ignored the barb. He dropped into a high guard and waited. Amongeratix snarled at being snubbed. The raven skulls on his shoulders quivered with the wrath of his rage. He charged. Tannus quickly brought his sword up, blocking the overhand blow meant to cleave him to the groin. He used his brother's momentum to make a quick riposte before dancing back. The blade narrowly missed Amongeratix.

Hordes of hideously disfigured men raced past them. Claws and scythes were raised as they cut into Tannus's lines. Body parts spun away, trailed by thin ropes of blood. The carnage was spectacular. Not a single man from either front rank lived. Their last gasps were lost amidst the roars of their comrades. What more fitting tribute to a fallen warrior than for his friends to carry on in his name? Tannus struggled to hold back the tears that he figured should have dried up long since as proud warriors fell in the name of freedom.

Yet all was not dark. His army rallied. They stopped the crush of monsters. The line held. Shield bearers finally managed to pull on line and lock together in an impenetrable wall of iron. A surviving sergeant took charge, barking orders. The army behind him slowly returned to a ragged semblance of a phalanx. Pikes lowered, resting on the shoulders of the shield bearers. Tension doubled. Confusion danced in the eyes of the enemy. Everyone knew what was coming, but not a soul had the ability to halt it. Even Tannus and Amongeratix stood frozen as the battle ground around them. Then it happened.

"PUSH!"

Shield bearers surged forward. Pikes stabbed into enemy soldiers. The advance was slow. One step at a time. Tannus felt renewed strength flow through him, and he grinned savagely. This day was his. His army forced the enemy back with each breath. The monsters in the front ranks fell under steel and fury. Panic gripped them, and they broke. Survivors turned into the press, frantically trying to evade the cold steel ripping into their flesh. They died there, held up by rear ranks unaware of what was happening on the front line.

"Cowards!" roared Amongeratix. "They are but flesh and blood! Stand and fight, you dogs!"

Tannus laughed at the futility of the words. Brutality only went so far to inspire an army. Commanders across the universe and the span of time agreed that a healthy dose of fear was needed to maintain discipline among the soldiers, but Amongeratix's brand of violence served opposite purpose. The subtle transformation from man to beast changed only their bodies and spirits, not the humanity of their souls. Beneath the rotted flesh, his army was still mortal. They broke and ran under the punishing pikes of justice.

Righteousness flared to life. It drove the arms of the army as they continued to defeat the enemy in scores. Tannus straightened to his full height.

"Your army flees, brother. The day is mine."

Amongeratix snarled and spat. His knuckles turned white from the strength of his grip on his sword. His body trembled. The embarrassment suffered at the hands of his useless minions was witnessed by the gods, furthering his disgrace. Amongeratix let his rage swallow him, change him into a pure killing machine without conscience or mercy. Those were qualities of the weak. The weak deserved to fall.

"I do not need an army to defeat you," he growled through clenched teeth.

"Truly?" Tannus gestured up. "Our fathers watch. Even now they judge the cowardice of your actions. Do you not find misery in your deeds? Retire from the field. Take what is left of your forces and return to the shadows. Leave this world to what humanity remains. It is a small matter."

"Yield? To you? I will not."

"Ever have you dreamed of the glory I possess. You are a lesser son, Amongeratix. Your shame insults our heritage."

The battle had moved beyond them now. Sergeants and corporals continued to push their men. The shield wall was abandoned, thanks in part to the initial success of the pikes. Now it was sword work, fast and bloody. Corpses littered the plain. Winds picked up, driving the stench into the snouts of carrion eaters. Amongeratix and Tannus stood alone, just as they had for centuries.

The ground quaked. Rock and dirt blasted into the stained sky. The judgment of the watchers ruined the ground for miles. Lightning sparked wildfires, tender flames quickly spearing into an unstoppable inferno. Black smoke wafted in sheets. Acidic rain began to fall.

Discarded armor and weapons sizzled and melted through where the rain hit. Snakes slithered up from holes and beneath rocks, hungry to escape what was coming.

Amongeratix tipped his head back and barked a diseased laugh. His flesh sizzled. "Our fathers do not share your views, brother. It seems they wish for us to cross blades yet again."

Tannus hid his disappointment. He wanted to believe the gods were tired of war, tired of the senseless slaughter of uncounted millions in the name of a cause no one either believed in or understood. He was wrong. Their war was meant to continue for one more day.

"How many times must we play this tired game?" Tannus asked. "Neither of us wins, neither loses. Take what remains of your army and leave the field. I will not pursue."

"Touching, but you don't really expect me to bend a knee to your failed pleas, do you? No, Tannus, I mean to end our little war for good tonight."

Lightning laced across the sky, white-hot tendrils stretching like so many fingers into what remained of the night. The judges above were pleased.

Tannus spread his arms and said, "This will not end tonight, fool. We have a destiny that is not yet fulfilled. You fight for their amusement, nothing more. Break the cycle. Let us leave this all behind and find lives for ourselves. No more gods. No more empty pride. Have you never dreamed of true freedom?"

"No more words. You always talked too much."

Amongeratix attacked. Sparks exploded from their crossed blades.

"We don't need to do this."

Amongeratix smiled, a gruesome sight. "But we do. You of all people know better than to treat me with honeyed words. Sister Abyss awaits us, brother. Will you not embrace me long enough to feel her loving touch?"

"Father never gave you love. Your soul lacks charity's quality."

"Father! That bastard has no place in our quarrel. This is between you and me."

Soldiers began returning out of curiosity. Most were wounded. Bloody bandages dressed wounds until they reached the surgeons' tents. But the sudden sight of two armored giants about to engage in mortal combat made them forget their wounds and their mortality. In return, they were treated with one of the rare gifts of the cosmos: two immortals preparing to cross blades. Those with spears began rapping the butts on the ground, ragged at first, but slowly coming into unison. The sound amplified hostile feelings. The larger battle was over. Amongeratix's army was in full retreat. All that remained were the two demi-gods.

"Come," Amongeratix leered. "Feed me your hatred and anger. Give in to your fears. Attack me as you would a jilted lover, but know one thing, Tannus. Tonight, I will drink your blood."

Tannus leapt forward. Sword met sword. Sparks burned their arm hair. Thunder intensified. Blow after blow hammered into each other in slashes and blocks, parries and thrusts. Tannus and Amongeratix assaulted each other with unprecedented strength. The army howled approval, spurring the combatants on. Boots crunched as the brothers danced over the mass of corpses stretching across the battlefield. Broken bodies lay at obscene angles, run through with pike and sword. Ruined pennants stuck up amidst the slaughter. A halfhearted breeze blew them lazily in mock tribute. Sparks erupted each time blades crossed. The battle raged back and forth, neither gaining an advantage.

The brothers finally separated. Both drew ragged breaths. Slaying mortal men required little talent, and it had been long since they last battled each other. Tannus looked down and was repulsed by the accusing glares of dead men. Raw emotions pulled him in different directions. He was responsible for all of this. Thousands of shattered dreams lay heaped at his feet. His heart threatened to burst. Too much suffering threatened to overwhelm him.

Amongeratix tilted his head back and barked a laugh. "You were always the weakest of us, brother. Father should never have named you his successor."

"This is not what father wanted," Tannus gestured to the carnage. "We are meant for more than violence. Look at what our hatred has produced."

"Stop stalling. You are getting slow, Tannus."

His eyes narrowed menacingly. Sweat beaded across his brow, dripping down the bridge of his nose and into his eyes. The sting made him wince. "The flames are growing. Perhaps it is too hot for you?"

"You talk too much."

Tannus attacked, blade poised to skewer his brother through the throat. Amongeratix easily parried and sidestepped out of range. The force of the blow carried Tannus past while opening his back to a diagonal slash. White hot pain lanced across his shoulders. Blood ran down his back. He roared and spun, narrowly deflecting a punishing blow aimed at decapitating him. His brother, face contorted in uncontrollable hatred, continued to attack. Block and thrust, the brothers began scoring more hits. Blood ran from a dozen wounds on each.

"Neither of us will die here," Amongeratix mocked. He paused to glance at the nasty cut on his inner bicep. Part of the bone showed.

"We don't need to do this," Tannus pleaded. "Release your army, and I will do the same. This world has seen enough of our appetites."

As if in answer, a light drizzle began to fall. Steam rose in sheets. The flames gradually died away. Men and monsters alike turned their heads to the skies in wonder. The rain came harder, washing away the sins committed against each other. Blood and sweat were cleansed from their faces and hands. A pure white light broke through the clouds, striking the ground between Tannus and Amongeratix. The battle stopped. Flames faded. Amongeratix clutched the haft of his weapon tighter.

"It is over, Amongeratix," Tannus called.

"No, I will not let it end this way." He tilted his head up to the skies and roared. "You will not interfere again! This is my victory!"

Amongeratix dropped his sword, snatching up a double-headed battle axe. Both armies stood in muted shock. The giant lunged. Tannus barely reacted, jerking back an instant before the nicked axe blurred down. The axe bit the ground, and a great rumble deafened them all. A deep crack spread from the gouge. Rock and dirt collapsed in a wide circle. Soldiers recoiled and turned to run. Those closest to the rent toppled into the gaping blackness. Their screams echoed deep into the earth. Tannus and Amongeratix disappeared next, their blades meeting as they fell.

The gods looked down in amazement. Never had one of the Three ever shown such destructive capability. Whispers spread amongst them. One by one, they faded away until only one remained. Cloaked in shadow and gilded robes, the goddess extended her arms, and a golden shaft of light burst from her fingers. All still on the field were blinded. Many dropped to their knees in reverence as the light pulsed down into the hole.

Tannus was suddenly jerked back. Locked in the clutches of the light, Tannus felt himself being pulled back to the surface even as his brother continued to fall. Recognition flared in Amongeratix's eyes. The gods had spoken. Empty curses spit from his cracked lips as he disappeared in the eternal darkness.

Amongeratix opened his eyes and stared up at the dark ceiling. The fired had died down, letting in a light chill. The giant shifted uneasily, disturbed by his thoughts. Why was he meant to relive that single battle now? Meaning eluded him. The battle—in fact, the entire planet—was insignificant to him. Perhaps his recent battle with Tannus had awakened long forgotten memories. But to what purpose? Amongeratix closed his eyes and tried to go back to sleep.

Huddled within his cloak, Moffo Kain tried not to notice the giant when he awoke. Moffo was in no mood to be heckled or berated. He snuck peeks across the cave with the same thought swirling around in his mind. What did gods dream of? Potential answers proved unsettling, leaving Moffo rattled. He settled in for a long, cold night, failing to notice the sudden emptiness lurking in the hollows of his soul. It felt like the deepest aspects of winter. Was that what gods dreamed of?

The Breld chapel was quaint, deserving of the simplistic village it supported. Monks and priests were homegrown, spanning generations of the same familes. Caretakers tended the gardens year round, coaxing the flowers into full bloom and the trees to majesty. Round windows of stained glass fractured the light in a kaleidoscope of colors. A small tower held the village bell, bronzed and stained from centuries of service. Moss and ivy climbed the walls, giving the chapel a comforting appearance. Marble slabs lined the walkway from the main road.

The inside suited local purposes. Crimeat was a polytheistic world. Men and women were free to worship the god or goddess of their choice. Shrines and temples were littered across the four continents in dedication to most of the major deities known in the universe.

Villagers in Breld didn't care much about that. They kept to themselves and traditions that had sustained them for generations.

Bronze statues lined the outer walls of the chapel. Each faced the rows of stone pews in front of the pulpit. Fragrances of different incense gave the chapel a pleasant aura. Votive candles were lined in groups of twenty on both sides of the main walkway. A pair of monks scurried here and there, replacing candles or cleaning up some small mess.

Fresh-cut flowers decorated the balcony above the main stage. Blues, pinks and vibrant yellows added character and life. It was the one spot in the chapel where pure sunlight could filter in. Priests of decades past had decided that the flowers presented enough grandeur that stained glass was unnecessary. So it remained. Villagers came and prayed to their gods in private worship. No one questioned or influenced another in vain attempts to superimpose their god above the rest.

Moonlight filled the chapel now, adding an ethereal effect. The sanctuary was empty save for one man. He knelt before the statue of Aris, goddess of wisdom and protection. The shield in her right hand complimented her open left hand, as if beckoning those stranded souls to come into her reach. He knelt, head bowed. What he had in courage he lacked in guidance. Too much was happening too quickly for him. He truly felt as if events were spiraling out of control and was powerless to halt them. Still, he took a small measure of comfort in being only a minor player in the wide arc.

A door groaned open, forcing Darka Jorm to raise his head. His golden eyes flared with bright orange as a hand slid down to the small blaster he kept holstered beneath his jacket. Light footsteps told him it was a woman. Worse. His fingers curled around the familiar worn plastic grip.

"It is late to be seeking guidance from the gods," a light voice spoke.

"Time does not matter to the gods; why should it with us?" he replied.

"Come with me. There are some who greatly desire to speak with you, Darka Jorm."

He winced. She said it; she just had to say it. Darka let go of his weapon despite his sudden misgivings about being named openly. *Damned civilians. They never understand what they are getting into.* Rising, he turned on the woman. Darka wasn't surprised to find her swathed in dark robes from head to toe. These sorts of conspirators shied from anyone learning the slightest detail about them but had no scruples about giving away the identities of their confederates.

She was slight, hardly more than a hundred pounds. He frowned. She barely came up to his shoulder, but there was something about the way she stood that gave him pause. Quiet dangers lurked with this woman. He quickly decided that this was no mere messenger. She was a dangerous player.

"Do not be so casual as to use my name in public. You never know who might be listening," he scolded with less intensity than he'd originally planned.

She laughed; the sound was golden and musical. He couldn't figure if she was mocking him or dismissing him. "Relax, you are among friends here. There is nothing to be concerned of."

He doubted that. Men like Darka Jorm didn't live long making friends from place to place. Giving her his most charming smile, Darka buttoned the bottom of his tanned leather jacket and gestured towards the entrance. "After you, if that is the case."

"You are a nervous sort, aren't you?" she teased. "The spies you search for simply do not exist here."

"It's been my experience that spies are always where you least expect them," he fired back. He didn't like being spoken down to like a child.

She did not reply, choosing instead to lead him through a winding path through the rear gardens. More statues poked out from meticulously manicured shrubs and bushes. Darka shied from their accusatory glares. Worship was something he rarely remembered to do and only then when he was truly in need. Being surrounded by so many deities left him ill at ease. He ached to be free and back on his own.

The strange woman led him to a small enclosed gazebo, hundreds of years old. Vines draped over the sides, concealing most of the partially rusted interior from prying eyes. His muscles tightened reflexively. Impulses and fragmented instincts warned of a trap despite there being no point in one. Not here at any rate. He hadn't found any noticeable threat in Breld since arriving two days ago.

Pulling the vines aside, his guide gestured for him to enter. "Please, they would speak with you now."

A strange fragrance tickled his senses. Strange; he knew that smell but couldn't recall from where. Darka cleared his mind and entered. There would be plenty of time think on it later. First, he must deal with men too craven to show their faces. It took a minute for his eyes to adjust to the gloom. The orange flared, giving him an almost demonic appeal. Murmurs shuffled between the four awaiting him. He frowned, cursing himself for being right again. They were cowards, one and all. Darka Jorm placed his hands on his hips and waited.

"You have finally come," said the tallest.

Darka snorted. "It's not like I had much choice. The Conclave and Inquisition are putting more resources on world. I had to get out of Vaade."

"Yes," replied another, a woman. "Disturbing patterns are emerging. We have received word that some of the council have been murdered by Vaumagians."

His throat constricted. He hadn't been told the assassins were on the loose. Scura was playing a dangerous game. *But what is his intent?* Darka feared the answers.

"They have nothing to do with me," he said with unfelt confidence. "Why have you summoned me?"

A soft hand touched his shoulder. The woman from the chapel. "It is time."

The soothing tones of her voice eroded some of the rising tension pinching his neck, but not enough for Darka to lower his guard.

"Speak plainly. I am not into games."

"Very well," the same woman said lightly. "Amongeratix has finally been freed. Right now, he is awaiting us in a cave along the shore. Our agent has confiscated a small boat to get him up to Breld, but the harbor patrol has been doubled."

"And reinforced by Prekhauten Guard," the first man cut in angrily.

First assassins, now Guard. Darka frowned. His life had just become infinitely more complicated. "Why use the harbor? Most of the coast is unwatched. There must be an easier way to get him here."

"It is not getting him into Breld that is the problem."

Darka was beginning to lose his patience. His fingers ached to circle around the pistol grip again and punch a hole in the arrogant bastard's face. "You are beginning to waste my time, *friend*."

"Perhaps you should learn some manners," the first woman scolded the man. "After all, Darka Jorm is here to help us. He is an ally."

He grumbled beneath his breath but otherwise remained silent.

She continued, "We need to get Amongeratix to the mainland. Only in Lethendweil will he be able to help our cause."

Help our cause? Were these people insane? Amongeratix, whoever he was, was a murderer. Only the worst got slammed into the prison here on Prophet Isle. Darka started feeling uneasy about the situation.

"Didn't you people listen? I just told you the Conclave and Inquisition are dedicating more resources to Lethendweil, and you want me to escort an escaped Conclave prisoner there? Madness! You are going to get me killed."

"I told you he lacked the nerve," growled another man, smaller than the others.

Darka gnashed his teeth. *Come outside, and I will show you my nerve.* "How much?" he asked instead.

"What?" asked the first man in disbelief.

"How much are you going to pay me to do this? You're asking me to risk my neck for a cause I don't believe in. How much?"

The first lady chuckled. "I did not know we had been sent a mercenary, but do not distress. You will be paid handsomely for your services." She leaned close enough to whisper into his ear. "Do this for us, and I shall personally reward you beyond your wildest imaginations."

His cheeks flushed at the supple touch of her breath. Darka looked down on the black maw of her hood, fighting back rising emotions. Who was this woman to command such passion? The offer was wickedly tempting, but he doubted it was worth his life. He shifted his gaze back to the others. They seemed content to let her continue the negotiations. Fine by him. They were little men. She was the real power here.

"The trick is avoiding Conclave satellites. I can get a ship out of the harbor without any trouble. Getting it down to Lethendweil is going to be the problem," he finally said after much thought.

"A simple request. We can generate enough interference that their satellites will be unable to detect you," she said with every confidence.

Powerful, indeed. "What about the prisoner? Is he marked in any way? Will they be able to track him despite your interference? I'm taking an awful risk here."

"Aren't we all?" she chimed. "Get him to Lethendweil and then to the Baron. Payment will be awaiting your success."

"What makes you think I can trust you?"

"What makes you think you cannot?"

"Lady, you don't know the half of it. Fine. I'll take the job. Once it's done, I am out. I didn't sign on to be part of some rebellion, and I damned sure don't want to get killed being an invisible hero."

"How dare you!" roared the tall man. He took a step closer to Darka but came up short when he noticed the gunmetal blue barrel of a blaster pointing at him.

Darka gave a wry grin. "I'll be in touch."

Not bothering to wait to see if any of them acted, he strode away confidently into the night. Men like that didn't deserve to see the barrel of the gun about to kill them. He smirked. Too many people wanted to play sneak and spy games. Darka wanted no part of it, but his instructions had been specific. So long as his true employer called the shots, he was bound to obey. Still, there was much to be said for the mystery woman. He found her intoxicating, alluring. One day, he hoped to come back and make sure she fulfilled her promise.

Too many temptations reached out to snare him. *Damn her!* He did not need the confusion, not now. Too much was at stake.

Darka Jorm walked away from the chapel feeling unsure of himself. Weakness forced his hand in a direction he'd not intended. Emotions betrayed common sense. Darka Jorm sighed heavily. The night air was more stifling than usual, or perhaps it was the fact that he had signed his life away for reasons still shrouded in mystery. Either way, there was no turning back. Hands stuffed in his pockets, Darka headed off into Breld to find a tavern and lose his concerns in a bottle of wine.

TEN

3210 A.G. (After Gods), Krenz, planet Vau Prime.

Lorenu Phos finished sipping her tea and set down the empty cup. Sunlight was fading, giving the soft willows lining Redemption Boulevard a holy glimmer. The reflection reminded her of happier times, times when she was just a simple girl from a simple village and her cares revolved around playing with friends and shying away from a boy's first kiss. A faint smile caressed her lips. She wrapped her cloak tighter around her thin shoulders. The first chill of autumn blanketed Krenz. It was her favorite time of year. The colors of change throughout nature offered proof that the gods still existed. It was a blessing she never tired of seeing.

"Cardinal Seniorus, you are going to catch a cold standing out there," a soft voice scolded from behind her.

Lorenu didn't know whether to frown or grin. "Aliz, I can hardly get ill from a few moments of fresh air. I think I will be fine."

"Still, I will not have the one person in the universe I am responsible for getting deathly ill," Aliz insisted with gentle reinforcement behind her words.

Lorenu finally relented and let the smile crease her aging face. Crow's feet collected around the corners of her eyes like so many waves in the sand. Her body was tired. Too many decades in politics had aged her tremendously, and she felt every bit of it. If it weren't for Aliz and those who came before, she would have retired from public life long ago and never made it to the rank she was at now. For them, she was eternally grateful.

"I don't believe I have ever thanked you enough," she admitted.

Aliz offered a skeptical look. "For being your nanny?"

"No, for being my friend. I have the most difficult job in the universe, and I often feel overwhelmed from the pressure. You somehow find a way to ease my troubles. It helps me sleep at night. So, thank you."

"Cardinal Seniorus, I am merely doing my job."

"Aliz, how many times have I told you that you do not need to use my title when we are alone?"

Aliz remained stern. Her cropped brown hair was streaked with grey. The shortness of it gave her small features a mousy quality. Aliz came from a small fishing city on the east coast. She'd been groomed for her position from a young age and beat out more than three hundred other women. Nine years later, she privately considered herself the second most powerful woman in the universe. That is not to say she had any aspirations of rising above her station. No, Aliz was content with serving the current Cardinal Seniorus and planned on retiring at the same time.

"You never know who may be listening. There could be bugs anywhere within your chambers. It would do for you to be a bit more careful. I have been telling you this for years, and you still do not think it important."

Lorenu laughed. "You sound like my mother. I know what I am doing. And if there were bugs, as you call them, in here, my opponents would already have come forward to remove me from office."

"We cannot afford to throw away caution. Not now with one of *them* resurfaced."

"What troubles you, Aliz? I rarely hear such concern in your tone."

Aliz crossed her arms over her chest and repressed a shudder. "I am afraid."

"Of what? We are in the most secure place in the universe, surrounded by tens of thousands of Inquisitors and Prekhauten Guard. The security here is the very best. If we cannot feel safe here, then where, I ask you?"

"The oracles do not share your confidence."

Lorenu frowned. "When did you go to the oracles?"

"This morning. I couldn't help it. My dreams have been feverish, and nothing I tried managed to console me. I am starting to feel lost."

That would explain all the tossing and turning in the middle of the night. "Aliz, look at me. You have nothing to worry about. The Three have been handled before, by lesser people. Between me, the Inquisitor General and General Strannan, we will find a way to prevail. The Guard and Inquisition have never been stronger. Our priests number more than three times what they did when last the Three threatened us."

Her words broke against the fear-hardened shell surrounding Aliz. Some fears were too rooted, too entrenched in the psyche to be dispelled with mere words. Not even the strongest were spared the indignity produced by that lonely, empty feeling slowly rising to swallow the soul. Lorenu looked deeply into Aliz's hazel eyes and forced herself not to balk at the growing horror. This was the moment she felt powerless. All of her speeches and words were nothing but empty promises lost on the dying horizon. No wonder or spectacle produced by humanity carried the strength to break that hold. Lorenu felt a small piece of her die.

But she was a fighter. Her life was hard, not in the way of a soldier or farmer, not even in the way of a mother raising her children. No, her life was hard because it was her decisions that effected trillions on hundreds of worlds. Hard edges developed in Conclave and through countless meetings with dignitaries and politicians softened upon seeing Aliz on the point of tears.

The obvious question was the one she did not want to ask, but she felt compelled to. "What did the oracles say?" Her voice came out barely a whisper.

"They warned of a great change coming."

"That hardly seems prophetic. Change is what drives society. Look through our history, and you will find scores of empires that collapsed in on themselves because they did not change when they should have."

"Lorenu, the oracles promise that the Three are the harbingers of a greater darkness. Schism is driving towards us, and we are blind."

Lorenu Phos eyed her assistant dubiously. She'd never been one for the drivel of the oracles, despite their closeness to the gods. Her faith was strong enough that she never felt the need to consult the mythical link between man and deity. Still, she was the last woman to insult others for their beliefs. The glory of the universe belonged in humanity's power of free will.

"The oracles are often misconstrued, Aliz. It takes a trained reader to fully comprehend their riddles. That is why they have no place in our politics. We must look to each other if we are to survive this mess. It will all sort itself out, hopefully without too much chaos or bloodshed. Our military and intelligence units are already working to contain the Three. I will not let them destroy the universe or bring about this catastrophe the oracles promise. Of course, I wouldn't go so far as to call it a catastrophe, not yet, at any rate. Let us consider it a mild inconvenience. I know, it is a poor attempt at humor, but I would be a horrible boss if I didn't at least try to cheer you up."

Aliz smiled thinly despite her misgivings. Twilight spread across the sky. Purples, blues and blacks swirled together, demonstrating the natural beauty of the cosmos. Lorenu and Aliz took the opportunity to enjoy the last moments of sunset. Promises of peace seemed to beckon.

"Thank you, Lorenu."

"Its what friends are for. Now come closer. I am starting to feel a chill."

Aliz leaned closer and gently kissed Lorenu's lips.

Inquisitor General Alain Nye set the data pad down and pinched the top of his nose. It was late. The sun had gone down hours ago, and night was well underway. Alain winced before opening his eyes. He hated computers, hated having to read the different reports and presentations on these small devices. He preferred the feel of paper; the familiarity of worn pages on his fingertips.

Alain picked the data pad up again and reread the communiqué. He suppressed a frown. Matters were already getting out of hand on Crimeat. Tolde Breed was on the verge of finding himself in the middle of a war. No doubt he would be hard pressed to find and capture Amongeratix amidst the chaos and confusion. Matters must be dire indeed for a Senior Inquisitor to so eagerly send for a Blood Witch.

Two of the Three present. Request the aid of the Blood Witches immediately.

S.I. Breed

Two of the Three. It had to be Tannus. Sorrow had not been seen for generations. This was most unexpected. Amongeratix was a living nightmare by himself. The two brothers together could devastate worlds in their blind hatred. It had happened before, and the Inquisition had intervened to remove the memory from the survivors. Mankind was not ready to learn that demi-gods traveled the stars. Alain reached down to hit the intercom button on his mahogany desk.

"Rothus, have my air car readied. Also, send messages to General Strannan's office and the Cardinal Seniorus. I request an emergency meeting."

"At once, Inquisitor General."

Alain glanced at the single red rose on the right corner of his desk. The blue tinge was most vibrant, almost overpowering despite the thinness of the petals. It offered little comfort. None of the virtue it stood for manifested in Alain now. He felt alone, abandoned to the whims of a violent future steaming towards the present. The Inquisition had been his entire life. Each thought and deed drove him deeper into the faith, deeper into the grandeur of the true path the universe intended for mankind.

Alain reached down to delete Breed's message. Hysteria would ensue should that message find a way to open channels. The universe was not ready, not ready by far to learn that there were real monsters in the dark places of the universe. He blinked as the message faded from his screen. Disappointment marred his face. He had hoped to keep the strange witch cult from getting involved. Their kind often proved more trouble than they were worth. Too many times in the past had they stretched their eldritch magics into mortal affairs. And now it seemed they would have the opportunity to do so once again.

He idly wondered if they served an individual purpose contrary to the Conclave and Inquisition. Pride demanded that the request from Crimeat go unanswered. The full might of the Inquisition and Prekhauten Guard were more than a match for any one of the Three, but at what cost? Thousands would surely die in the struggle. Far too many for Alain to sleep at night. No, the summons for the witch would go through. His hands were tied.

"Inquisitor General, your air car is ready," Rothus poked his head into the office.

Still looking at the blank data pad screen, Alain replied, "Thank you, Rothus. You may retire for the night. I fear I will be quite late with the Cardinal Seniorus."

Rothus nodded curtly and left. Long hours in the office of the most powerful man in the Inquisition left him ragged by the time he retired to his meager apartment. Alain waited for him to go before shutting down his equipment and collecting his cloak. The late autumn nights in Krenz were cooler than his homeworld, and, even after decades of service on Vau Prime, he still hadn't gotten used to the cold. The cloak was the darkest black, emblazoned with the lasting heraldry of the Inquisition sewn above the left breast. Alain took comfort in such things. They gave him purpose.

The glass-paneled doors to his inner office hissed closed, and he headed out. Guards snapped to attention when he strode past. He returned the gesture and continued to the loading pads. No time for small talk tonight. Much work was left to be done. Rothus had already given the driver instructions. In fact, everyone along the way was expecting him. Privilege of rank; he smirked and marched into the office of the Cardinal Seniorus.

The lines under Lorenu Phos's eyes stole some of their natural sharpness but did little else to diminish her stature. She sat impassively in the antechamber of her offices, legs crossed neatly, hands over the knees. Alain took notice of the sternness in her gaze. She was not pleased.

"I trust you have sufficient reason for this?" she demanded.

He bowed. "Of course. My agents on Crimeat require assistance, the kind that only the three of us can send."

The hidden meaning did not go unnoticed. Lorenu stiffened slightly at his tone. Certain tension filled the space between them. He smiled inwardly. *Not even the mighty Cardinal Seniorus is immune to the myths surrounding the Blood Witches, it seems.*

"You assured me your agent would be able to handle this without drawing attention," Lorenu said softly.

"Matters have changed, Cardinal Seniorus," Alain replied flatly.

Her back straightened at the sound of her official title. Normally, they were on a first-name basis when not in council, or in public. "General Strannan should be here momentarily. Would you care for a drink while we wait?"

"I think we will all need one when I get done speaking," Alain added.

Her eyes narrowed. "What games are you about?"

"No games, at least not this time."

Awkward silence settled in as two of the most powerful people in the universe settled back in waiting. Each wondered what secrets the other possessed and how it might affect them in the end. The escape on Crimeat was distressing enough, but Lorenu had no way of knowing how bad it really was. Devastation threatened them all and was barely a whispered breath away. All manner of strange and terrible things came crawling to the verge of humanity during the long hours of deep night.

"This had better be damned good," growled Strannan as he stormed toward them down the cold marble hall. His cheeks were flushed from exertion, and he bore a sour look. The flesh around his scars, normally pinkish, was now stark white, giving him a terrifying look.

"Good evening, Davith," Lorenu smiled tightly.

He glanced from her to Alain. "Evening? It's the middle of the god's damned night."

Alain felt his stomach twist. "Now that we are all here, I think we should go inside your office, Cardinal Seniorus."

They filed into the office, where Alain wasted no time. "I will be very blunt about this. Our worst fears are coming true. Senior Inquisitor Breed informs me that not only has Amongeratix broken free, but his brother Tannus is now there as well. Two of the Three, the most dangerous two in my opinion, are loose on the same world. It is logical to assume that they know of each other and have already made contact."

"Damnation," General Strannan hissed. "This could be the end of that world."

"The world, General?" Lorenu Phos asked. "The people of Crimeat stand at a precipice, but think what might happen should the Three take their conflict back to the stars?"

"Total armageddon," Alain finished.

"We cannot let that happen, gentlemen," Lorenu told them gravely.

Strannan traced one of the scars running down his face. "Nor do we have the forces to stop them. Not two of them."

"What do you suggest? Obliterate the planet from orbit?"

Alain cut in before the two could go any further. "Cardinal Seniorus, I think there is another solution, one we all know."

"Enough with my damned title, Alain. We are talking about the end of the universe as we know it. I think we can forgo formality."

"Fucking Blood Witches," Strannan snapped. "I would rather send in legions of Guard than deal with them."

"They would be slaughtered. All the archives tell us this. Why risk ruining another generation senselessly?" Alain fired back.

"For the chance to kill two of those bastards? I'd sacrifice thousands!" Strannan shouted. His fist clenched with building rage.

Alain let the snap go unanswered. Strannan was getting dangerously close to taking a swing at him. Insulting the martial prowess of the Prekhauten Guard had been unintentional, but a man like Strannan took insult easily. The Inquisitor General decided to change tactics.

"I am not debating the abilities you have instilled in your men, Davith. I am thinking in broader terms. We cannot afford to let Crimeat fall. The entire universe would learn the truth of the Three, and we would lose all legitimacy. Doubt would creep in until it festered. The Conclave and Inquisition would crumble, leaving your Guard stretched too thin to restore order on member worlds."

Strannan made to speak but clamped his mouth shut quickly. Thoughts and emotions collided in his eyes.

Lorenu Phos leaned back into the plush leather cushioning of her chair, hoping to dissolve away so she didn't have to deal with the situation. A lifetime dedicated to the preservation of life now reduced to a razor edge without any foreseeable escape.

"Like it or not, Alain is correct," Lorenu cut in. "We cannot risk a full assault. The witches may be our only viable option. It is not an easy decision to make, certainly not one that any of us are comfortable with, but it must be done. I will not throw away our resources and let open war rage across the universe. We must stop the Three now, and on Crimeat. Delay only furthers their agenda."

"Assuming they are working in concert," Strannan theorized.

"We shouldn't assume anything," Alain said. "The Three are volatile and carry just as much hatred for each other as they do us. I believe that Tannus has gone to challenge his brother."

"Why now? And how did he know to go to Crimeat at the precise moment his brother was freed?" Strannan asked.

"Do you really want to know the answers?"

"Gentlemen, this discussion is pointless," Lorenu interrupted. She had had enough of the male posturing. "The reality is that there are two of the Three loose on Crimeat. We must swallow our pride and act now. Summon the Blood Witches, and we deal with the consequences later. Agreed?"

Strannan exhaled deeply. "Agreed."

"Agreed," Alain said.

Lorenu Phos rose, collecting her robes around her. "Let us go to the summoning stone. The Grand Mistress is fickle at the best of times; perhaps we will get lucky tonight. I'd like to think they are already aware of the situation."

A gentle hiss announced the opening of a private panel in the far wall. The three leaders of the known universe collected themselves and followed Lorenu in. Very few knew of this chamber's existence. Even fewer knew the origins.

The large conical piece of jade was easily the size of a grown man. Hovering over the ground-out top of a round piece of granite, it spun clockwise with a low hum. Enchanting, alluring. Alain never ceased to be amazed by the natural beauty of it. No one living knew of its origin, at least no humans. The summoning stone was a gift, part of a pact made by the first Blood Witches and the original Conclave after man emerged from the shadows of the gods. As far as anyone knew, it was the only way to contact the near mythical beings. It also ranked among the most closely guarded secrets of the Conclave.

Lorenu, Strannan and Alain surrounded the summoning stone with grim expressions. Each held up both arms, flesh only millimeters from the smooth jade. Lorenu nodded sharply, and they began. Pricks of electricity stabbed them, and for a moment they were blind.

A pile of dead dragonflies clumped together decorated the center of the large table. Made of polished stone the color of a cold sunrise, the blue, purple and green of the large insects added a prism effect to the centuries-old table that pleased Grand Mistress Ruma Zzein. The dragonflies reminded her of distant nebulas. There was perfection in the collage of colors, one that was unmatched by any constructed object. Humanity's greatest flaw lay in hubris. Mankind thought themselves rulers of the known universe, denying the richness of knowledge kept by the elder races.

Ruma Zzein often felt saddened by that. So much violence, hatred and destruction had been wrought through the ignorant assumption of man that the universe was a lesser place. Continued generations of pale sons enhanced their ignorance until it was much too late. The elder races, those that remained, took to the stars and remained in hiding. Ruma Zzein knew the truth of this. The truth that one day soon those races would return and bring vengeance to man. The conclusion was inevitable.

The Grand Mistress of the Order of Blood Witches sat at her favorite stone desk, marveling at her collection of insects. Most of her time was spent in the inner sanctum; the tallest spire of the abbey. Protective shields fluctuated over the open windows that circled the chamber. Ruma Zzein was able to watch the entire splendor of space as the comet marched by on its course. The room was large and carved from dark granite, giving a gloomy feel. Golden runes marred the black floor, flaring to life whenever she touched one. Candles burned constantly from the four corners of her table. There was no chair or any other furniture. The Grand Mistress folded her legs beneath her and floated at the edge of the table. Her long gossamer robes lightly kissed the floor, billowing slightly in the unnatural breeze.

The endless vacuum of space offered solace from the measured lives ground out on so many worlds. Here, amongst the stars, there was no frenzy, no rush. Time was meaningless. Space stretched cold fingers into the ethereal eternity, disturbed only by the pinpricks of light from distant stars. There was calm here, a tranquility that could never be found aboard a ship or trapped on a planet. True freedom awaited those brave enough to sail the stars in search of what mysteries remained just out of reach.

The Acumensiis Comet was one of those mysteries, perhaps counted among the greatest. It was the home of the Order of Blood Witches. No one knew how they had managed to build their monastery on a comet the size of a small continent. No one much cared, at least not among the common citizens. Scholars and philosophers shared their opinions in universities and symposiums intended to show the vast wealth of their knowledge. Few could begin to guess the truth. Fewer wanted to. No good came from dealing with the women of the comet.

Ruma Zzein viewed them all with disdain. Her order had evolved beyond the simplicity of the human race. A gentle knock on the aged wooden door disturbed her private thoughts. She rotated, beckoning the door open with a glance. A cowled apprentice bowed, arms folded across her chest.

"Summon Sister Abigail," Ruma Zzein commanded. Her voice would have sounded no more than a whisper to mortal ears.

The apprentice bowed again and backed away, leaving the Grand Mistress contemplating events to come. Delay served no purpose. She had *seen* what came next. All the horror and mindless devastation. The minds of the Cardinal Seniorus and Inquisitor General were laid bare to her when they used the stone. Their deepest desires and most prominent fears belonged to her now. The difficult decision of whether to let the humans know their fate or not weighed heavily on her. War was unavoidable, but which war? The one envisioned by the leaders of the universe was of minimal concern, a mere precursor to a greater darkness. The Three were powerful, but only pawns in this game. Life stood on a delicate balance. One false step, and chaos would reign.

Ruma Zzein shifted her gaze out to the stars. She hadn't expected to find such difficulties. The Blood Witches were neutral, an independent entity. They got involved with the mundane only when it served their purpose. Ruma felt new obligations, and they disturbed her. She remembered what the humans called the war of the gods. Her kind had barely survived, much less the humans. Remnants of nightmares continued to haunt them through the following millennia. The same was now poised to happen again.

The stars looked like streaks of light, slowly drifting away as the comet went by. Lost out there was the truth. A truth that man was not ready to know. The Grand Mistress frowned. The decision to save the universe should not belong to one person. She decided that it was time to send her Sisters out into the cold night. Humanity was going to need them if there was any chance at avoiding annihilation. Ruma waved a transparent hand over the dragonflies, and they suddenly sprang to life. The gentle buzz of wings filled her sanctum. It was a soothing sound, one she often took great comfort in. Twisting her thoughts, she gave the dragonflies commands, and they funneled up and out of the room.

Sister Abigail marveled as the swarm flew past her head. Their colors sparked her interest, reminding her of the stars.

"Come in Abigail," called the Grand Mistress.

Abigail drifted across the floor until she stood reverently before Ruma. "Grand Mistress, I came as soon as I was summoned."

"Thank you. I am afraid I must ask you to take the Pilgrimage again."

"So soon?" she asked.

Ruma nodded, the movement almost imperceptible. "The humans have called for our aide."

"I am honored, Grand Mistress, but there are other more deserving Sisters who have not yet made the Pilgrimage."

"True, but I have need of you specifically."

Abigail tilted her head to the right. "Might I inquire why?"

"You have knowledge of this specific scenario. Five decades ago, I sent you to the aid of an Inquisitor on his quest to capture Amongeratix."

"Inquisitor Tolde Breed. It was a…delicate matter."

Ruma nodded again. "He is now Senior Inquisitor and has been reassigned to the same matter. Amongeratix has been freed. The Conclave has called for aide. I am sending you to work with this Breed again while our Sisters try to determine the mystery of his freeing. There is something else. Amongeratix is not alone. Tannus has been confirmed on Crimeat as well, and whispers of Sorrow come to us. This is a dangerous time, Abigail. I fear for your life but can see no other way."

"I live to serve, Grand Mistress," Abigail replied. Whether she felt anything was a private matter. The Order trained daily to prevent emotions from showing.

"Take no chances. The universe is at a crossroads. The future is still murky. We must take every precaution," Ruma continued.

"As you command, Grand Mistress."

Ruma drifted closer to Abigail. Genuine concern showed in her gem-like eyes. "I fear you may not return to us, and for that I am truly regretful."

"Sacrifice is part of our role. I will meet my fate gladly so long as it is in the service of the Order," Abigail said emotionlessly.

Pride swelled in her breast. Every Sister carried the same poise, the same selfless dedication to the morals and standards of the Order. When the Forever Night crawled across the universe, her Sisters might be all that stood between life and oblivion.

"Prepare to leave immediately. Time is now our enemy," Ruma Zzein commanded. "May the blessings of Men'sha'ie be with you."

"And also with you."

Abigail turned and left Ruma Zzein alone with the darkness of her thoughts. The abbey no longer felt as safe as it once had. Once again, the failings of humanity crept in to taint the purity. The Grand Mistress of the Blood Witches floated back to her stone table and turned her thoughts inward. Fingers steepled together before her face, she tried to find the true path of the future. The universe conspired against her, clouding all but the present. She frowned. Not even the past was clear. Ruma Zzein closed her eyes and contemplated the course of things.

Cold dread tickled the gray hairs on her nape. She feared she had sent Sister Abigail to her doom.

The Acumensiis Comet continued across the stars without heed for mortal concerns, leaving the Grand Mistress of the Blood Witches torn.

ELEVEN

3210 A.G. (After Gods), Great Barrier Jungle, Crimeat.

The humidity was oppressive. Every movement was sluggish, deliberated on. Nothing moved unless it absolutely had to. Insects swarmed around Elisa. She constantly had to wipe down her horse's neck to remove the myriad mosquitoes and flies. Her face and neck were covered with tiny bites, already red from inflammation. She snarled, cursing her decision to try and find this Mollock Bolle. Elisa checked her heat sensor for the hundredth time since entering the Great Barrier Jungle.

Damned useless machine, she snarled internally. Everything the jungle was alive, generating impossible amounts of heat to spoil the sensor. She tried to ignore the singular thought dominating her mind. Why had she come here? The mission was a death quest at best. No one willingly entered the jungle without expectations of not returning. Elisa had always thought herself a practical woman. Clearly, she'd been wrong. Her horse snorted and tossed its head back as if reading her thoughts. She snarled again and kept riding.

Durn was a week's ride behind her, as was the ridiculously chauvinistic Piett. His harsh tones and words came too easily for her to put much trust into him. Snakes whispered promises with forked tongues. Elisa sensed a snake. Piett was a military man, no doubt. A career of service to General Shiramon had steeled him into a keen weapon, making it confounding why they felt the need to hire a bounty hunter. Her eyes narrowed. The freckles on her cheeks darkened. She was a pawn in some foul game, only the reasoning was beyond her.

Elisa wanted to scream her rising frustrations but doing so would only make her a target. She had little illusion that she was here unnoticed. If the Ugri were half as uncanny as local legends suggested, they would have picked her up the moment she entered the jungle and had her under surveillance the entire time.

Her knowledge of the group was limited. She'd read a few descriptions before leaving Durn, vague as they were. The only thing of interest to her was their supposed war-like nature. Every record presented the Ugri as a premier warrior race capable of sweeping over the twelve kingdoms without pause. As intriguing as the notion was, Elisa highly doubted its authenticity.

No race on Crimeat was that powerful. She idly wondered if the Ugri were just another pawn in this game. The thought struck an undreamed of terror in the cold recesses of her soul. The Bloody Man reentered her mind. Why now? She'd willingly set aside her quest to find the monster responsible for murdering all she knew. Too many stray thoughts collided, confusing her to the point of making her cry.

Elisa exhaled softly and tried to focus on the task at hand. The important thing was finding Mollock Bolle and getting back to civilized lands. The rest would sort itself out later, or not. She couldn't focus on that. Impossible events happened all around her and weren't her concern.

A tree on her left rocked suddenly, drawing her focus as quickly as she drew her sidearm. A dark shape crashed through the branches overhead and growled once. A shower of leaves and broken sticks rained down around her. Elisa caught a pair of cruel red eyes glaring at her from behind a tree. Her pulse quickened. Survival instincts took control. Elisa raised her pistol and aimed. The beast, as if sensing an attack, ducked behind the trunk and pounded massive fists on the smooth bark. Echoing howls came from all directions.

Elisa felt her skin pale. It was a trap. She'd been decoyed by the ruckus in the trees, forgetting to watch her surroundings. Her horse jerked back suddenly, rearing up on its hind legs and nearly throwing her to the ground. Elisa gripped her knees to the horse with all her strength to keep from falling. The beast in the tree snorted down, signaling the attack. Six squat figures emerged in a ragged circle. Half primate, half reptilian, the howlers moved synchronously. Elisa realized that she was in serious trouble. She barely managed to bring her pistol down and fire off a single shot before the howlers attacked.

A pain-filled scream drowned the sound of the shot. Almost green blood spit from a socket when the howler's eye had been. Another howler leapt over the falling howler to attach itself to Elisa's horse before the first dropped dead. Fangs bit deep into the front left leg. Claws dug into Elisa's calf, shredding through her thick leather boot like paper. She roared and pumped a handful of sizzling ion rounds into the howler's skull. One of her ribs snapped suddenly as she was blindsided. Woman and beast tumbled from the saddle in a heap of flailing limbs and cries.

Sharp teeth latched onto her forearm, causing her to drop her pistol. Elisa struggled, at first trying to push the heavier beast away. At nearly three feet high, the howler had enough raw strength to match any six men at arms. Elisa quickly recognized she was outmatched and rammed her head into the howler's bottom jaw. The move gave her the opening she needed, and Elisa successfully drew the thin dagger she kept at her waist. Two crisscrossing swings later, the howler fell away clutching its gushing throat.

The attack slowed. The remaining howlers pulled back, suddenly wary of what they had assumed was going to be easy prey. Three of their number already lay dead and a fourth mangled by the falling horse. They spit and snarled but made no move to attack. Elisa's breath came in ragged gasps. Her wounds hurt, undoubtedly infected already. She managed to gain her knees and brought her dagger into a guard. That was enough for the howlers. They barked once in unison, as if saluting a fellow warrior, and disappeared back into the jungle.

Elisa lowered her head and tried to catch her breath. The corpses already smelled. It was only a matter of time before the jungle's larger predators came sniffing around. She struggled to her feet, wincing from the pain.

Elisa tied her flame-red hair back in a tail and assessed her situation. It was not good. Her horse was lame at best. She only prayed it didn't need to be put down. Otherwise, she was turning around and heading back to Durn. The odds of making it on foot were slim to none, but she refused to die in the jungle.

Elisa checked all the bodies just in case before retrieving her med kit from her saddlebags. Her heart had slowed finally, and she was able to think clearly. She was stuck in the middle of a hostile environment, at least a full day from safety, and had no clear direction to go in. Her prey was crafty enough to have avoided her thus far, and she knew next to nothing about him aside from what Piett had told her. She almost wished she had invested in an air car. This would not have happened. Worst case scenario would be getting shot down, but she highly doubted the Ugri had surface-to-air technology.

"What am I doing?" she asked herself, more for the comfort of hearing a friendly voice than with the hopes of getting an answer.

Her horse snickered before dropping its head back to the leaf-strewn jungle floor. Elisa felt honest pain at seeing her beloved horse so. They'd been through more adventures and hardships than she remembered; the horse was her closest friend. Elisa wasn't sure what that said about her life, but he was the one thing in all Lethendweil she felt she could trust. Losing him now would only solidify her decision to abandon this quest.

She sighed in frustration and began seeing to her own wounds. The horse was either going to live or die. Nothing she could do would affect that. The horse was one thing, but if she didn't tend her wounds she would die. She poured water over the wounds, washing away the already drying blood. The cuts stung, reminding her more of insect bites than anything else. The howlers, or whatever their real name was, no doubt secreted poison. She needed to act quickly to counter the effects.

Elisa took a deep breath and stabbed a syringe of anti-venom into her right arm. She bit back a cry as the burning fluid pumped into her veins. There was no guarantee that it would work, but it was better than nothing. Wounds clean, she set about stitching and bandaging. An hour later, she was done and wolfing down a pack of dehydrated rations.

She glanced about, relieved to see no sign of the howler's returning. Darkness was coming in too fast. Elisa passed a glance at her sleeping horse. She'd given it a few shots of antibiotics and treated the wounds but remained doubtful about a full recovery. The sun was already beginning to set. The temperature was dropping, much to her relief. A combination of heat and humidity had made her skin break out in bright red rashes all over. The cool night air would be most welcome.

"I guess we need a fire," she told her horse.

Elisa began collecting fuel and made her camp for the night.

Two faces, the color of fresh clay, exchanged cautious looks before nodding to each other. They had seen enough. Both wilted back into the thick jungle undergrowth.

Elisa rolled over, groaning. Night wasn't half done, and she had yet to sleep. The jungle, deadly in daylight, was even more so at night. Sounds from a hundred species of insects annoyed her relentlessly. Roars of predators and the cries of prey assailed her nerves. Her eyes were raw, bloodshot and jittery. Mosquitoes and other blood suckers darted in for a taste. She heard the slither of snakes, the gentle foot pads of massive spiders as they crept across the jungle floor. Elisa wanted to go home.

The only problem was that she had no home. No one to love. Nothing to take comfort in. The Bloody Man had seen to that. His arrival on that autumn night had been unheralded; no one in her village had dared to dream a being like that was even possible. A giant, easily twice the height of man, the Bloody Man had initially frightened her. Children had rub screaming to their mothers. Massive and muscled, the Bloody Man reminded her of pictures of old statues of the gods.

Eventually Elisa had worked up the courage to investigate. She'd stared up into those cold eyes and suddenly found the unexpected. There was pain hidden behind them. Whoever this being was, he was in terrible pain. She had tried to imagine what suffering drove him to cover himself in blood, what dark secrets haunted his waking moments. Try as she might, nothing had come to her. The imagination of a five-year-old girl had taken over, and she's seen him traveling through space, delivering a message too much for even him to bear. Such a thing could easily drive one mad.

Elisa blinked and watched as a spider with a body the size of a dinner plate crawled towards the edge of the fire. Black and red with hairy legs, the spider was carrying a dead bird in its mouth. Predator and prey. The scene reminded Elisa that life was constant struggle. Jubilation did not come without cost. Great pain must be endured before the soul found absolution. Elisa no longer prayed to the gods. They had abandoned her that day, fifty years ago, when the Bloody Man had destroyed her family, friends and way of life. Her absolution would come only at the end of a blade. She closed her eyes and tried again to fall asleep.

Mollock Bolle stared down at the outstretched skeleton nearby and sighed. Random thoughts entertained his solitude. He wondered who the man was. What dreams or torments might have inspired him to take the lonely path through the jungle? Eerie similarities sparked concern. The Great Barrier Jungle was no friendly place, certainly not one to invite travelers. The Ugri lands were even less hospitable. Vast empty plains and prairies offered little respite from the sun or the predators.

A crimson millipede snaked from an eye socket and into the nostril. Mollock cringed. The thought of ending like this poor fool haunted him with every step deeper into the west. But what choice did he have? That fool Strannan had put a price on his head so big he wasn't welcome in any city, village or hamlet east of the jungle. There were only so many places a man might hide in Lethendweil. And, frankly, he was tired of running.

A twig snapped in the gathering darkness. He stiffened. The Ugri had come. Mollock tensed despite what he knew. The Ugri were not so careless as to make any noise when they stalked their prey. Any noise they made was because they wanted him to know they were finally near. His breathing quickened despite knowledge of what was happening. Mollock held out his hands; palm up to show he had no weapons. The Ugri slowly emerged from the surrounding bushes.

There were seven. Each stood no taller than four and a half feet. They had flat faces with heavy brows and tiny eyes. Their noses were pinched, almost snubbed. The massive size of their heads made it appear as if they had no necks. Hairless, the Ugri had flesh the color of clay. Some were a bland grey while others were pale orange. Others were speckled in between. Mollock had been among them before but still wasn't used to the sickening sight. Clad only in loincloths, the Ugri were thickly muscled and bred for power. Their eyes were cold and black, offering no glimpse of what they were thinking. Each carried a short spear and a cruel-looking dagger strapped across the waist.

One stepped forward. His teeth were broken and crooked, like he'd been chewing on rocks. Mollock swallowed in revulsion. A foul aroma wafted from the Ugri, a mixture of excrement and dried blood. Strings of partially chewed flesh clung between his teeth. His thick fingers, all three on each hand, clutched his spear. For a moment, Mollock was unsure if he was a dead man or not.

"You should not have returned," the Ugri snarled at him.

Mollock looked the creature in the eyes. Anything less was taken as a sign of disrespect. "My apologies, but I had no choice."

Murmurs rippled through the others.

"You must leave now."

Mollock Bolle paused, knowing his life depended on his next words. "Great one, I bring news for Kulaam Lune. I must see him before it is too late."

The naming of their honored leader angered the Ugri much faster than Mollock had anticipated. Muscles tensed. Snarls echoed across the tiny clearing. He watched as their hands gripped their spears tighter and then move in closer. The Ugri leader leveled his spear at Mollock's chest.

"Outlanders do not speak that name," he growled menacingly.

Mollock bowed his head submissively but maintained eye contact. "I apologize again, but this matter is most urgent. War is coming to you."

"We do not fear battle."

"This one you should. But I will say no more. The rest is for your shamans to hear," Mollock said boldly.

The Ugri turned and looked at his warriors. They snapped at one another in their broken tongue. Mollock felt that he had not said enough and opened his mouth. The Ugri leader turned on him and lowered his spear, if only slightly.

"You will come with us."

Mollock finally exhaled. His death, once imminent, was now a secondary consideration. News of the other kingdoms' coming invasion would only carry him so far before Kulaam Lune either had him executed or sent back to the eastern kingdoms. He could always tell them the terrible secret that had haunted his life for the past five decades but doubted the Ugri held to conventional philosophies. Despite their warlike appearances, the Ugri were naturally peaceful and kept to themselves until provoked. The combination of war and his knowledge threatened to rip the fabric of their world apart.

Then there was the female bounty hunter. She'd been most persistent, forcing him to leave Durn in so much of a rush he'd had to leave most of his scanty belongings. Mollock had no doubt she was close. He recalled stories of a female bounty hunter with flame-red hair some years ago, and they now chilled him. If any of those stories were true, he was in trouble.

Mollock was no stranger to being hunted. His explorations left his life in ruins, forcing him to continually move. Capture meant death. It had taken him decades to come to terms with the startling truth he had learned in the Bothwel Mountains. Solitude became his boon companion, the only thing he could count on to carry him through the day. It was a lonely existence, but one he was forced to accept.

The Ugri blindfolded him despite his meager protests and led him through secret paths known only to them. Mollock stumbled and tripped more times than he could count. His lower legs became a mass of swelling and bruises. They paused long enough for him to relieve himself and drink water and then continued the march. The Ugri appeared tireless. Kilometers passed, and still they went. Mollock quickly lost track of time. Exhausted and starving, he practically collapsed when they halted for the night.

The Ugri leader finally removed his blindfold. Mollock winced in pain at the sudden light, rubbing his eyes and blinking rapidly to reduce the effects. He took careful measure of his surroundings. The foliage was slightly different, lighter and more brush-like. Mollock took that to mean they were closer to the western edge of the jungle. He collapsed against a smooth bark tree and tried to catch his breath.

His feet hurt enough to make him regret leaving his horse at the way station back at the far edge of the jungle.

Truthfully, the Great Barrier Jungle was less than fifty kilometers wide, but few easterners had dared to venture the entire way through. Inherent dangers kept them from entering the jungle, and the persistent threat of the Ugri kept them from thinking too hard on it. The Ugri took full advantage of that hesitancy. They developed trails and hiding spots, forward positions in the event of an assault. Mollock shook his head ruefully. The east had no idea what they were getting themselves into. An Ugri warrior came by and dropped a hunk of cured meat in his lap. He left before Mollock could thank him.

"Eat now. We leave again soon," the leader said from behind Mollock.

Mollock turned and looked up. "How far have we come?"

"Do not ask many questions, outlander. There are things you do not want to know."

Mollock frowned. He chewed on the tough meat and replied, "I came here to help, not be treated like a prisoner."

"You are not a prisoner. You may leave at any time." The Ugri leader gestured to the surrounding jungle and barked a laugh. "Be careful of the night. The jungle is not friendly when the sun fades."

Mollock tried to conceal his frown. They were still too deep in the jungle for him to think about getting away. Not that escaping was what he wanted. He was safe so long as he was in the company of the Ugri. Mollock Bolle resigned himself to the situation and sat back. The rest would not be long. The Ugri seemed intent on getting him to their war leader as quickly as possible. Perhaps they had taken his warning more seriously than he thought. If so, his chances for surviving the next few days improved dramatically.

"Eat fast," the Ugri reiterated and then left.

Two more days they marched at an impossible pace. Mollock, already an old man by most standards, was forced onto one of their shoulders several times. His legs gave out. His back spasmed, and the blisters on his feet swelled. He might have felt shame had he been amongst his peers, but the Ugri were not human. Their stamina was highly developed. He had no doubts he would have been left for dead if they did not find truth in his earlier statements.

At last, they emerged from the thick jungle canopy. Mollock breathed fresh air for the first time in over a week. The humidity dropped, and a cool breeze caressed his face. The blindfold was removed for the last time, allowing him to stare across vast, open plains. Brown and green grasses blew lazily in the constant wind, reminding him of a woman's hair caressing her shoulders. He could make out herds of deer-like animals grazing. Small mammals popped their heads up from underground burrows. Large boulders dotted the steppe, and the sky was a pale shade of blue streaked with dissipating clouds.

"This is beautiful," he said to himself.

A snort reminded him he was not alone.

"This is Ugri land."

"Keep moving!" the leader barked.

The race continued.

Mollock felt like he had been taken to the literal middle of nowhere. The steppes ranged as far as the eye could see in every direction. The only change as they approached was the tiny sprouting of thatch huts that appeared to be part of the earth. Dozens of Ugri emerged to witness his arrival. Curiosity and anger twisted their faces. Mollock swallowed hard despite himself. This was not the first time he'd had dealings with the Ugri, though never so deep into their territory. A motley assortment of weapons leaned against the huts or rested lazily on the backs of the Ugri themselves. Interestingly, there were no women or children. Mollock got the distinct impression that this was a war camp.

"Bring the outlander," the leader snapped to his warriors and then disappeared into the growing crowd.

Mollock was shoved through the Ugri until he stood before a massive stone throne. Granite gray, the throne was in the fashion of a typical human chair well over seven feet tall. He might have found that amusing if there hadn't been over a hundred Ugri warriors surrounding him. The noise dropped off once a wizened old Ugri emerged from behind the throne. Half as tall as the others, his skin was so leathered he look preserved. His bones showed through the taut flesh. A necklace of bones, most animal and some human, was his only garb. Despite seeming too old to be alive, the Ugri's eyes held acute awareness. Mollock swore he caught deviousness drifting in them.

The old Ugri smacked his bone staff onto the stone slab the throne sat on and held his arms to the skies. His cries were in the Ugri tongue and unknown to Mollock. All Ugri warriors bowed to one knee, heads lowered reverently. A gruff hand to his back forced Mollock to do the same. He cursed silently as small, sharp rocks burrowed into his knees. He dared to look up and was surprised to watch Kulaam Lune take his seat upon the granite throne.

"Why have you brought this outlander here?" Kulaam demanded once he eased back into his seat.

Solid and massively built, Kulaam had been the Ugri leader for nearly three decades. He had won the throne by challenging and defeating the previous ruler in unarmed combat. Kulaam was the strongest of the Ugri. His fists were as large as the balls children played with in Vaade. His eyes bore a strange mixture of compassion and vengeance. Wisps of hair sprouted down his back, marking his age. It would not be long before some young Ugri decided it was time to try him. Mollock feared for whoever was so foolish. The feather cloak draped around Kulaam's shoulders offered vivid beauty in an otherwise drab world. The rainbow of colors highlighted the Ugri leader's strength and presence.

"Great Kulaam, this *human* claims to bring word from the east," the war leader announced from his knee.

Kulaam Lune narrowed his eyes on Mollock, instantly judging the man. "Stand, *human*."

Mollock obeyed, his hands clasped at his waist so as not to pose a threat. The thought almost made him laugh. As if he could be any sort of a threat surrounded by so many warriors.

"Who are you?" Kulaam asked menacingly.

"I am Mollock Bolle. We have met before, Great Kulaam," Mollock replied with as much false confidence as he could muster.

Kulaam regarded him. His eyes were cold and sharp. "When?"

"Seventeen years ago. I came trading information and was granted an audience with you. I cannot be more specific as to the location because I do not know where I am."

"The shaman says *humans* should not be here," Kulaam pressed. "What news do you have for me?"

Here goes nothing. "An invasion is coming, Great Kulaam. The eastern kingdoms are uniting to move against you. Their armies will outnumber yours by thousands."

"For what? We have done nothing to them," Kulaam said.

"They do not care. Forces are already mobilizing close to the jungle edge. Their leaders believe that your warriors have snuck into their lands, killed their people and livestock and started this war," Mollock answered. The sorrow in his tone was genuine.

Quiet murmurs spread through the assembly. The Ugri had never ventured beyond the jungle border. They were nomadic and comfortable here on the steppes. Even though they were a war-like species, they fought only amongst themselves. Nothing in the east interested them. Mollock understood enough about the Ugri to know they would meet the coming violence with their own brand. It would end in slaughter.

"We will defeat the east," Kulaam roared to his people.

Mollock shook his head sadly. "You cannot hope to win, Great Kulaam. They have armored vehicles that protect their soldiers from arrows and bullets. They have craft that soar over the field and drop bombs. They have weapons that can fire large shells from miles away. They can kill your warriors without ever seeing them. It is a fight you cannot win."

Uproar broke out. The Ugri bellowed for his to be the first death. They called for war. They begged to be among the first to attack the easterners. Kulaam turned to his shaman, their words lost amidst the shouts. Finally, he returned his steel gaze to the Ugri, and silence crept back over them.

"My shaman tells me you are a spy," Kulaam accused.

Mollock felt his heart jump to his throat. "A spy?"

The shaman cast a wicked grin. Kulaam continued, "You bring another with you. A female *human*."

Female? Mollock struggled through the confusion until realization slapped him hard across the cheek. The bounty hunter! *That bitch is going to get me hung*. "Great Kulaam, I assure you I come alone and on my own accord. The other your shaman speaks of is hunting me. She wants to return me to the eastern lords for reasons I do not yet understand. You must believe me."

"Believe you?" Kulaam mused. "Spy or no, we shall capture this female and learn for sure. Take him away!"

Rough hands clutched his arms tightly. The Ugri leader who had brought him to Kulaam leered down at him as he was yanked to his feet and dragged off. Mollock Bolle realized his life was now forfeit.

The Ugri would catch the bounty hunter and execute them both as appeasement to their gods. War would come, and the Ugri would be wiped from the face of Crimeat. Tears crept from the corners of his eyes. He had tried. Tried and failed.

It was a recurring theme in his long life.

TWELVE

3210 A.G. (After Gods), Vaade, planet Crimeat.

Fear strangled Vaade. The streets remained empty. No one was allowed outside unless they had a valid reason that was necessary for the good of the city. Martial law had been declared the morning after the Night of Blood. Armed men and women patrolled the streets, arresting any dumb or brave enough to break the law. Paranoia opened the gate to hysteria. Men and women were found beaten in alleys and side streets. Accusations already ran rampant across the city. Priests bowed in prayer to every deity in vain efforts to find answers.

Whispers of the Ugri army drove conversation. Some spoke of treachery from within. Peace had reigned for too long, argued the old-timers. It was only natural that it wouldn't last. People begged for the Inquisition to get involved, but their offices remained closed. Not even the Conclave representative was ready to release a public statement. Not yet.

Hands gripped tightly behind his back, Count Brentor stared out his balcony window. The surviving members of the council had been hurried back to the council building and secured behind hundreds of armed guards. Brentor's eyes were hard, the poor dome of the Conclave Basilica the object of his attention. Grave injustice had been done. Three of his friends and colleagues were dead. His teeth ground with an angry sound. He couldn't think straight, couldn't eat despite several nervous attempts by his attendants. Rage threatened to consume him. Vengeance for lost friends begged for fulfillment. No amount of arguments or political disagreements justified murdering political officials.

The assassinations inspired despicable feelings inside. Brentor was a man easily angered but wise enough to stay his reaction until the proper target was identified. He strengthened his dedication to his friends, hardening his resolve to see vengeance done. But not yet, no, not just yet. Brentor was strong enough not to give in to his desires. Strong enough not to let ragged emotions assume control. Five decades helped clear his thoughts.

Age itself had not been overly kind. Time was beginning to show its effects. A few extra pounds collected around the waist. Thick streaks of grey ran through his thinning hair. Dark bags clung to his brown eyes. He'd lost a step or two through the years but still had enough to face a challenge. His life had been dedicated to the art of warfare. He'd often said that any fool could hack away with a sword or point a rifle and fire, but it took a master to understand what war was and to turn it into an art form.

His martial prowess helped secure the wealthiest kingdom in Lethendweil. The riches, beauty and strength of Houraf were well known across the world and the envy of many. Many said that not even mighty Vaade could contend. Brentor worked tirelessly to give his people the quality of life they deserved. His sacrifices had turned a poor seaside town into a wealthy city that, in his opinion, should have been the capitol. But now it might all prove for naught. The attacks of the prior night left him rattled. Whoever had done it make it look too easy; it couldn't be random killings. His mind turned slowly, mulling over every little detail that he knew. There was only one true order capable of committing such perfect crimes.

Still, he was a lord of Lethendweil. Brentor shifted his heavily muscled frame. Age may have slowed him slightly, but neither age nor his thick robe could hide his powerful physique. His skin was leathery and the color of copper. Forty-nine years old, Brentor spent at least two hours a day practicing with the sword. Ion rifles and blasters were well and fine, but the blade demanded strength, skill and agility. Any fool could shoot someone. There was no honor in it. His belief stemmed from ancient family philosophies, back to when colonists had first tried to claim this world as their own.

A sharp knock on his door drew his steeled gaze. Visitors were the last thing he needed now.

"Enter," he barked much more harshly than he intended.

A slender page timidly poked his head in. "My lord Count, the council is forming. Your presence is requested."

Brentor's thick eyebrow rose. "Requested by whom?"

"Baron Scura, lord."

Interesting. The whelp wants power so badly he's willing to step on the elder members. Emleth's corpse is hardly cold, and power plays are already being made. This will come to no good. Brentor tried to find an advantage in this but couldn't. Events were moving too quickly for him. He needed to find a way to slow them down before disaster paralyzed them all. Damned politics, he cursed silently. He was about to wave the page away when a thought struck.

"Summon Father Stall to my chambers and inform the council I will be arriving shortly," he ordered.

He waited for the door to click shut before shedding his robe and heading to his wardrobe. He slowly dressed in black trousers and a crimson shirt. His boots, immaculately polished to reflect the sun, easily slid up his claves. His cloak, simple and elegant for his station, lay on the back of a tan chair. The light colors of the room often matched his personality and mood. Today was different. He felt dark and slightly ominous. Yet more friends had gone off to meet the gods. Brentor frowned and took a seat. He did not have to wait long. Danja Stall knocked once and entered without bidding.

"Count Brentor," he said.

Brentor's eyes remained hard. "Danja Stall, thank you for coming on such hurried notice."

"The Conclave is always available to support the council of Lethendweil."

Brentor bit back a snort. "Let us cut through the formalities. Three of our more prominent council members were murdered last night, and I want to know why. War is coming, and their voices were the strongest for avoiding it. I smell a conspiracy."

"What is it you are asking of the Conclave exactly?"

"I need to know why this was allowed to happen. Who had knowledge of it?"

Danja squirmed slightly, just enough to raise Brentor's suspicions. "The Conclave is neutral on the matter, you know that. We do not get involved with local matters of state."

"Unless there is reason to suspect heresy," Brentor finished.

"Heresy? The matter seems clear. Members of the ruling body were assassinated in the dawn of a coming war. I would hardly call it heresy."

The Count of Houraf gently rubbed the stubble of his chin. "There is more here than we are seeing, Danja. Simple assassinations are one thing, but this has the feel of something far deeper."

"What leads you to believe that?"

He is clearly keeping secrets, Brentor mused. Some dark event that was best left undiscovered. "Tell me what you know of the prison escape on Prophet Isle."

A pause. "That…is official Conclave business. Even I have not been read in on it. What are you getting at?"

"There is too much coincidence that three leading members of Lethendweil are murdered less than a fortnight after one of the worst prison escapes in recent Conclave history." Brentor sat back, his powerful shoulders flexed. "You know more than you are letting on."

"Prophet Isle was an Inquisition facility," Danja began to protest.

"Established under Conclave orders! Do not play games with me, priest."

His rage washed on a blank slate. Danja Stall was not intimidated by angry words and simple men. "Perhaps you should have summoned Inquisitor Prowl. I am sure he has more answers than I."

"Perhaps I should. You are clearly of little use."

They stared hard at one another, neither willing to change position. Danja tried to quell his internal debates. Born on Crimeat, he was a native son with close ties to many of the ruling families. He wasn't close enough to call any on the current council friend, but they had been valuable colleagues and important sources for information. Their deaths were not entirely unexpected, but they were untimely. Ursal Prowl had come to him the night before telling him everything he knew of the senior Inquisitor and his guardsmen. For all his faults, Brentor was right about the conspiracies. Danja Stall decided to keep that fact to himself until he knew the severity of it.

Brentor stared at the priest, desperately searching his motions and reactions for any sort of double cross. He was loyal to the Conclave and Inquisition, but Lethendweil came first. The rest be damned. Stall's job was to provide council, wisdom and insight. His closed tongue was enough to birth suspicion. Thick muscles bunched under his shirt. He wanted nothing more than to strike Stall squarely in the face and throw him out on his ass, but doing so would not serve his purpose.

"Our discussion grows heated, and such should not be the case," he finally admitted.

Danja nodded. "These are difficult times for us all. A level head is needed if we are to see ourselves safely through this crisis."

"Agreed. I trust you will be joining us in council?"

"I was only just informed of the emergency session. Unfortunately, I have other business to attend to," Danja replied.

Brentor nodded. "Then we are done here."

Danja excused himself with a curt bow, more dismissive than courteous. Brentor shook his head as he rose and attached his cloak. Now was the hour they needed to be strong in unity, not cowering behind half-forgotten allegiances and petty secrets. He already knew what awaited him in the council chambers. The surviving members would be locked in bitter arguments. No doubt Scura was preaching revenge. The young man already held the ears of many of his peers, making him extremely dangerous. Too many of the weaker nobles flocked to his illusion of strength. They needed guidance, not firebrand speeches designed to incite mobs. Ruination beckoned, not just for themselves but for the greater population.

Brentor strode down the marble corridor, marching past countless statues and paintings of past glories and faded memories. He wondered where he fit into such a gallery. The future remained unwritten, but it was as devious as the past. His reflections carried him to the outer chamber doors where a pair of armed guards awaited. Their dark brown uniforms seemed oddly out of place amidst the polished brightness of so much marble. They snapped to attention upon seeing him, saluting with their old automatic rifles. The weapons were the best they had available once Brentor had issued a decree that the guards were no longer to wear their traditional ceremonial swords. Dangerous times required extreme measures. Many guards saw the murders as their own fault and offered to resign and return to their own kingdoms in penance. They were denied to the man.

"Count Brentor, they are expecting you," the sergeant of the guard announced crisply. Grave insult clung to his face.

"I should hope so," Brentor tartly replied. He waited for the doors to hiss open and looked the sergeant in the eyes. "What happened was uncontrollable by all of us. Keep your head high and serve us well."

The sergeant beamed with newfound pride and saluted again. Brentor slapped him on the shoulder and reluctantly entered the council chamber. All conversation ceased as they gradually noticed him. Heads turned. Blathk rolled his eyes, and Lord Klesh of Uberlorn shook his head. Highlighted in the center of the chamber, Baron Scura gently folded his arms across his black-clad chest and offered a curt nod.

"At last, our missing count decides to grace us with his presence," Scura mocked. "One would think the new head of our council would be more prompt considering the circumstances."

"I do not recall asking for your opinion, Scura," Brentor snarled back.

Scura opened his mouth to speak but was cut off by Lord Mans of Berchenfel. "We are in a time of crisis! Three dead council members in the span of an hour, and you two want to trade trite comments. How much longer until we find knives waiting in the dark for each of us?"

Brentor resisted the urge to laugh. "Are you so afraid, Mans? Are all of you? I remember times when we laughed in the face of death. You are Lords of Lethendweil. Do not succumb to petty fears."

"I am not the man I once was, Brentor. Times have changed," Mans replied weakly.

"As they must," Scura added before another could cut him off. "This is the time for change that we must all accept. Our brothers, our comrades demand retribution. Raise your armies and let us be united. The Ugri must pay for their treachery."

"You speak much of war against a foe none have seen for decades," Brentor cautioned. "Tell us, Scura, how do you intend to prove the Ugri are responsible for the assassinations of our brothers? What evidence qualifies their genocide?"

A mischievous glare entertained Scura's eyes, as if he had been waiting for such an opening. He reached into his dark robes and tossed a crudely made dagger at Brentor's feet. "Is this evidence enough? We all know the legends of their ceremonial daggers. Drawn in anger, used for revenge. General Shiramon can attest to the validity of the weapon. Who knows their treachery better than the people of Durn? The Ugri are preparing for an invasion. Now is our time—perhaps our only time. We must crush them before any other innocent lives are lost. Or will you accept our foes sweeping through your cities in the depths of the night?"

Brentor, unsuccessfully trying to hide his scowl, reached down for the dagger. There was nothing special about the blade. Dull and rusting, it could easily have been a farmer's or a trapper's. Brentor looked at each of his fellow nobles, staring deep into their eyes. He raised the dagger for all to see clearly.

His voice was level, unstressed. "This dagger is nothing. It does not represent some grave threat to our future, nor does it imply that we are besieged by dark powers. What sign is there that this blade belongs to the Ugri? Have any of you seen signs of them in any of your kingdoms? I see nothing but a dull blade that could have been stolen from a butcher. Mercenaries and thieves come across the Ugri. Who is to say that one of them did not steal or trade for the blade?"

"Your chivalrous world of honor does not exist, Brentor," Klesh replied. "Our society is more diluted than you would believe. Modern Lethendweil has advanced beyond petty games of political intrigue and honor."

"Do not be so rash as to assume other peoples want to be like us." Brentor's laugh echoed off the white marble walls. "Democracy can easily be construed as weakness. The Ugri care nothing for conquest. They are a secretive race that only wants to be left alone."

He passed a glance over to Danja Stall, but the Conclave priest kept his eyes lowered to the floor.

"You speak as if you hold them in high regard," Lord Al'tek of Curdelean accused. "That is close to treason."

"Have any of you ever seen an Ugri? Or are they just images of our fears? I've seen them, fought them. A good warrior knows when to show his enemy proper respect. Anything less will result in disaster." Brentor turned his attention back to the entire council. "You all sit here, locked away from the real world speaking of battle and killing. How many must die before you remember that war is no game? Perhaps we should have our Inquisition representative summon an army of Prekhauten Guard to take care of our problems. Would that end this foolish paranoia?"

General Shiramon struggled to contain his rising anger. He had heard enough. "You suggest we do nothing? I did not gain the rank of general by resting on the morals of others. I say we end the threat and begin rebuilding the council. Give me your forces so that I may lead an offensive into the Barrier Jungle and finish the Ugri."

"General, your ignorance is enlightening," Lord Grushm scolded. He had the least concern. His lands were the furthest east and safe from any threat. "Do you honestly expect us to deliver our armies to you? What would prevent you from using that power to mount an assault on the rest of us? Your allegiance has been rather dubious of late."

"My allegiance?" Shiramon spat vehemently. "I'll have your tongue for that."

"Enough!" Brentor roared. "Squabbling leads nowhere. Our first priority needs to be discovering who killed our brethren and why. We must stem this fractured tide now before it is too late."

"What would you suggest?" Scura asked coyly.

Brentor paused. "Send the commission like Emleth wanted. We have no positive direction in which to turn. I ask that you all take a moment to collect your thoughts. There must be proof of Ugri involvement before we march to war. Additionally, I would like to know who exactly escaped from the Conclave prison on Prophet Isle. That person may be more involved than any of us give credit for."

Danja Stall cleared his throat, a weak gesture at best. "I am not at liberty to discuss internal Conclave matters. The incident at Prophet Isle is being handled by the appropriate authorities. I can assure you that there is no direct threat to you or your lands."

"Empty words," Shiramon grumbled. His massive arms were folded over his chest, giving him a menacing air.

Danja held up his empty hands. "We all must play the cards dealt us."

"Sit down and mind your tongue, *priest*," Shiramon snapped. "Men are speaking. You and your Conclave are next to useless so long as you guard your secrets. I will not sit by and wait for our world to be pulled down around us. My forces are mobilizing as we speak. This body clearly does not have the stomach for what needs to be done. The mistakes made in this chamber will not be the damnation of my people."

"Sit down, Shiramon," Lord Schuul of Xiolen rasped. "It is well known that your lands stand the watch between us the Ugri. That does not give you freedom to wage war on your own."

Shiramon's eyes narrowed. "What do you know of my people, old fool? The swamp you call home has as much value as a rotten hrangzar egg. I go to war with or without your support."

He rose in one clean motion and stormed from the chamber. Silence dominated his departure. Brentor, helpless as when he first entered, stood and watched as his fellow nobles filed out. Events were slipping beyond his control. Scura came to stand beside him.

"It appears the will of the council has made itself known, Brentor," he said quietly so only they could hear.

"I do not know what trickery has been done on your part, but I will not let you fools rush to ruin."

"Who is there to turn to? The Conclave? They keep their secrets and won't look you in the eye. The Inquisition? I hear rumors of their commandos already scouring Vaade for the assassins. They have their mandate to follow, and it does not match ours. We are alone, Brentor. Join us or be left in yesterday's ashes."

Scura strode confidently from the chamber, leaving Brentor alone. Last to arrive and now last to leave. Lethendweil was disintegrating in his hands, and he had not been head of council but a single day.

"This isn't right," whispered Jers. His weapons and armor felt heavier than usual.

Sergeant Fies harshly snapped back, "Keep your mouth shut and your eyes open. I don't like this any more than you do, but we have our orders."

Jers suppressed a reply, knowing it would ruin his career. Orders were one thing, and he wasn't the sort who held reservations over killing anyone, but this was borderline madness. A third of the ruling body had just been murdered, and his one squad was out patrolling foreign streets in vain attempts at finding the culprits. Brave as he was, Jers was downright scared. The murders could only have been done by professionals, and that meant the Vaumagians nine times out of ten. Regular Guard didn't go after Vaumagians and expect to live.

Haggle, close to Jers's right, shifted his ion rifle to cover forward and leaned close. "Told you he wasn't in the mood."

"I'm going to kill you. You know that, right?" Jers hissed.

Haggle blew him a kiss and returned to his position in the patrol.

"Sarge, I think Jers might be on to something," Annalilly said. "I'm not picking up any readings at all."

She slapped the detection sensor on a cold, black side and shook her head. Nothing.

"We are in the middle of a fucking city. You must have some kind of reading," Fies replied. He winced, a slight pain between his eyes. Fies wasn't the sort to give in to superstitions, but Jers had a valid point. Common sense said to have the city guard and local military executing the search, not offworlders who barely knew where the nearest inn was.

"Negative. It's almost like we are being blocked."

Shit. Fies resisted the urge to remove his helmet and wipe the building sweat from his brow. A sniper's bullet awaited if he make a rookie mistake like that. The sky was filled with gray clouds, blanketing Vaade with a drab atmosphere. The humidity was much higher than his men were used to. Sweat ran freely and irritatingly down their backs.

"Kastor," Fies called. "See if you can raise the Sergeant Major. I want out of this ASAP."

The older Guardsman gave an imperceptible nod, his reaction hidden behind the reflective helmet visor. A seasoned veteran, Kastor seldom felt out of place regardless of the situation. He'd seen combat on a score of worlds. One small night of rebellion here on Crimeat hardly marked an important moment in his life. He pulled up their external net frequency and put the call through.

Fies pulled up his infrared display. Dozens of human heat signatures showed up. His concern doubled. This had to be an ambush.

"Weapons free. If it looks hostile, shoot it," he ordered quickly.

The hum of a handful of weapon charges coming to life was his reply.

"Bout damn time," Jers growled. He glanced over to see Beve cranking the six barrels of his pulse cannon clockwise. The dark purple light glowed from the power pack. Jers could picture the savage grin on the big man's face as he prepared for battle.

Fies came back over the helmet intercom too quick. "Jers, take point."

Jers swallowed hard. He'd forgotten to silence his communicator and now paid the price for that lapse of attention to detail. The squad inched forward. Deep misgivings lay within them all, but none even thought of refusing. This was what they were paid for. A lifetime of service dedicated to preserving the innocent and defending the righteous.

Not more than a minute later, Jers picked up movement in a third story window. He cursed and brought his rifle up. The window was the perfect height for a sniper to drop them all and have little concern for return fire. The only consolation Jers had was the fact that the squad's heavy weapon specialist would be the first target. He swallowed hard.

"Movement, second window in, third floor on the right."

There was a moment of silence, not long at all but enough to unnerve him. "Got it. Beve, cover high. Jers, take your team across the street."

Jers exhaled sharply. He knew he was going to get shot. Part of him wanted to ask if there had been any reply from the Sergeant Major. The bigger part wanted to stay alive. At the end of the day, he was a Prekhauten Guardsman. Duty came with obligations. He did not hesitate in following his orders.

"My team, stack right on me," he ordered.

Bodies hustled in place behind him. He didn't bother looking over his shoulder. His people knew what they had to do. Jers moved, low and quick. His rifle barrel never left the center of the building door. The familiar crack-sizzle of small arms fire coming from the window chased his footsteps. Beve's heavy machinegun erupted from across the street. The small cannon fired hyper-velocity rounds of raw energy, devastating targets with maximum effect. Building parts showered down on Jers and his team.

Adrenalin pumping, Jers held up three fingers and dropped them one at a time. On zero he kicked the door open and stormed inside. The staircase was directly in front, and the foyer was dark except for the random shafts of light slicing in from the few windows. The Guardsmen didn't need light. Thermal imaging on their helmet visors lit the entire building up like a Founding Day celebration back on Vau Prime.

Jers rushed the stairs, keeping his rifle pointed at the most obvious avenue of approach. He paused only slightly before charging up the central staircase. He felt the body heat and occasional bumps of his team members rushing behind him. The clatter of weapons and equipment announced to everyone who didn't already know that soldiers were on the way. Sweating dripping, hearts pounding, Jers and his team gained the landing of the third floor.

"Which way?" he breathed heavily into his helmet's intercom. He blinked to clear some of the sweat from his eyes.

"Shift left, and the target is in the second door on your left. Let me know before you breach so I can lift fire," Sergeant Fies calmly replied back.

Calmly. Of course he's calm. He's sitting down there under good cover waiting for us. "Haggle, take point. Enter left and we'll adjust. Move."

The four armored Prekhauten Guardsmen stalked down the empty hall with murderous intent. Senses were high. Emotions threatened to rip loose, adding fuel to an already dangerous situation. Jers leaned against the wall a moment after Haggle, and the others stacked on the plain black door. Thankfully, most of the doors in Vaade were the old-fashioned turn the knob and push kind. Jers looked at Haggle and nodded. Go.

Haggle mouthed a prayer to the goddess of protection and kicked the door with all his might. Wood splintered into the room, followed closely by four soldiers searching for someone to kill. A loud crack sounded from the right corner. Weapons shifted and opened fire. Ion rounds sizzled, punching holes in everything. Fluffs of furniture blossomed up. Slivers of cabinets spit across the small room. A strangled moan was barely audible over the sound of the rifles. Haze clouded the ceiling. A bloodied hand slammed into the floor from behind the remains of a chair. Dark red blood pooled across the floor.

"Cease fire!" Jers shouted.

"Clear," Haggle announced loudly and was echoed by the other two.

Jers breathed deeply and started to relax. He keyed the intercom and told Fies, "Sergeant, the room is clear. One hostile KIA."

"Roger that. Good work. Search the target and come back down."

Jers unlatched his dull grey helmet and removed it. There were days he hated being in the Guard.

The old rooster crowed softly from atop his favorite fencepost, bringing the sleeping village of Hasjef into the new dawn. Nestled between the city of Durn and the Great Barrier Jungle, Hasjef was ever a village on edge. Strange things happened in the night. The people were spooked and for good reason. No one knew what lay beyond the mists at the edge of the jungle.

Heavy fog blanketed Hasjef, adding a sense of mystique to the thatch-covered homes and barns. Villagers here went about their lives as best as could be expected considering the imminent pressures of war and fright at the doorstep. The Ugri may be figments of imagination in Vaade, but here they were very real. Columns of smoke drifted from the host of chimneys, adding subtlety to the fog. Haslef's constable was already up and making his rounds. Street keepers were out extinguishing the lamps along the main roads. Aromas of fresh baked breads and pastries enticed folks out of bed. The lights flashed on in the chandlery. Farmers were already in their fields and tending animals. Life went on like it was meant to.

No one noticed the score of shadows marching out of the fog. They moved with deadly precision. Bristling with high-powered rifles, hand blasters and swords, they fanned out. Each was dressed in flat black combat armor and used infrared goggles. They pressed against the outlying row of houses and waited. Their leader raised a clenched fist, and they swept into the village. Whole families were slaughtered in their sleep. The constable managed to draw his sidearm before being gunned down on the steps of the general store.

The soldiers tore their way through Hasjef like a plague. No room was left unchecked. No crawl space, no closet unnoticed. Every man, woman and child was shot dead where they were. Many of the homes were set afire. Livestock were slaughtered and left to rot. The village of Hasjef ceased. Ash and smoke drifted across the corpse-littered street, partially concealing the soldier in charge of the raid. His goggles were pushed back over the crown on his head. Sweat and grime streaked down his cheeks. An odd look marred his face. He was not proud of what he had done, but the pay was well worth the price of a few nightmares.

He glanced up at another soldier running to his side.

"Sir, the village is pacified," he reported.

Pacified is a good term, he grimaced. "Very well. We are done here. Sound the withdrawal. I want everyone back on the shuttle in five."

The soldier saluted. "At once, sir."

By ones and in groups, the soldiers extracted from the ruins. Their black uniforms were a visage of death. The village of Hasjef was a memory by the time the sun finally rose. No one would ever know the truth of what had happened.

THIRTEEN

3210 A.G. (After Gods), Vaade, planet Crimeat.

Tolde Breed threw down his datapad. "This is useless."

Matthias finished drinking from his canteen, shaking his head. "We have to be missing something. The Three don't act without reason."

"The Three are becoming a pain in my ass," Tolde snapped back. "I'm sorry. That was uncalled for. My frustrations should not be taken out on friends. I don't like not knowing what to do, Matthias."

"My opinion is the Three have done this through countless generations. This just happens to be our turn. The question remains: why here, and why now?"

"I don't know."

Matthias set the empty cup down. "This would be much easier if we knew what their purpose was."

"The histories tell us all of that. The Three are the sons of the gods, cast out from their father's grace before the great war."

Tolde frowned. He wasn't sure he believed that anymore. Much of what the universe took for granted was twisted into what man wanted to believe. The realities had passed, leaving much that was once known lost. Tolde feared that might be their eventual undoing.

Matthias waved him off. "I know the training program as well as you and have been around long enough not to believe in them anymore. Whoever the Three are, they have a purpose. What if they aim to awaken the gods?"

Tolde looked up slowly, horror dancing in his eyes. "It would be the end of all that we know."

"Meaning the war brewing here is just a cover," Matthias concluded hesitantly.

"The gods might be bigger players than we previously thought," Tolde offered. "We cannot hope to fight against them."

"Not if we want to win."

Fear threatened to take hold. It was an old fear, one ingrained in every new Guardsman and Inquisitor. Each was trained to hunt down heretics or to stop man from finding and awakening the gods. No one ever dreamed that it might actually happen. A hundred different gods were worshipped on seven hundred different worlds. If just one of them awakened, the universe would drown in flames. Tolde and Matthias glanced at one another with forbidden realization. Their task became infinitely clearer.

"That gives us only one option," the Senior Inquisitor stated slowly.

Matthias nodded.

"We must stop Amongeratix."

"It won't be as easy as it was the first time," Matthias said.

Tolde arched an eyebrow. "Easy? He nearly killed us all, and that was with the aid of a Blood Witch."

Matthias nodded again. "I need an easier job. This planet is a powder keg waiting to explode. People are frightened. The deaths of those three nobles spooked half of them and set the other half on the warpath. This isn't a fight we can win."

"I agree, but we have our orders. What are you going to do about yesterday's incident?"

"I gave the weapons free order. It's my responsibility. Fies and his men did what they thought was right. Can't say as that I would have done differently."

"Innocent civilian casualties won't sit well with the local government," Tolde agreed. "What did Strannan have to say?"

"He was displeased but seemed to understand the situation. Still, we didn't make any new friends because of it."

"I was under the impression the target had a weapon," Tolde hinted.

Matthias scowled. "We found a weapon, but it hadn't been fired in who knows how long. There is no telling where the shots came from."

"Have you decided what to do with that squad yet?" Tolde asked.

"Officially, they are on administrative duty."

"Unofficially?"

Matthias broke into a sly grin. "I have Sergeant Fies going through the evidence to try and find answers while the rest of the squad is enjoying well deserved downtime."

Tolde Breed paused. He didn't want to say what they were both thinking, that the entire incident had been a setup. He frowned. The situation on Crimeat was worsening by the day, and they had yet to begin hunting the Three. He couldn't help but feel pulled, like a puppet dancing on strings. Somewhere, cleverly hidden from them, was the puppet master, and he was twisting them exactly how he wanted.

"Interestingly enough, we have yet to hear from the local Conclave representative—or Inquisitor Prowl," Matthias added as an afterthought.

Tolde frowned. Prowl should have been pounding the door in by now. Corruption was not unheard of amongst Inquisitors, though certainly rare. Tolde tried not to think of Ursal Prowl being heretical. The universe may be a dark, foreboding place, but he always thought the best of people until they proved him wrong. He decided to pay Inquisitor Prowl a visit later in the day.

"Excuse me, Sergeant Major," a young private poked his head in the room. "The shuttle has arrived."

Matthias looked up. "Thank you, private. Inform Sergeant Fies that the Senior Inquisitor and I will be departing shortly. He is in command."

"Yes, Sergeant Major."

The private disappeared back into the outer room. Matthias said, "Our Blood Witch has arrived."

"Might as well get this over with. The sooner we can get her in the field, the faster we can start unraveling this mystery," Tolde replied sternly.

His distaste for the witches bled through his words. They were an asset to his work, but dangerous and unpredictable. Belief in the gods was anathema to the order, making their very existence heretical. Deals had been struck long before Tolde's time, and those agreements still stood. He believed the Order held some dark secret over the Conclave that allowed their continued presence.

Tolde and Matthias collected their jackets and headed for the airfield. The day was exceptionally sunny. Few clouds peppered the sky, and a slight chill clung to the air. The short trip was made in silence. Tolde busied himself with his meeting with Prowl. Matthias tilted his head against the cold metal frame of the air car and fell asleep. Tolde envied the man. Soldiers always managed to find a way to get rest without much trouble. His own nightmares prevented him from getting much sleep. He'd seen too much, fought against those dark things that most men were frightened of. Thankfully, the trip was over before his mind took him down shunned corridors of memory.

The Blood Witch stood at the foot of the shuttle ramp patiently awaiting their arrival. Her white-grey robes concealed all her body except her gossamer-like hands and the occasional lock of bleached hair poking out from her hood. Tolde recalled the blood-red eyes and the abject, distant look the last one had given him. He felt very small in her presence and couldn't help but feel judged. Many in the Inquisition felt the same, furthering the mystery of their continued existence. Loath as he was to admit it, Tolde recognized the fact that he needed the witch if he had any hope of success.

She hovered a few inches off the ground as Tolde and Matthias exited their air car and came to her. Sister Abigail cocked her head slightly as she searched through the collective memories of previous Sisters. The Order of Blood Witches had once learned to transfer conscious memories to one another for the greater good of their survival. Abigail scrolled through what the previous Sister had learned from the two men.

"Senior Inquisitor Breed and Sergeant Major Matthias, it is a pleasure to work with you both again," she said politely. Her voice was a gravel whisper.

Tolde reflexively stopped. Common sense told him there was no way the witch standing before him was the same one from fifty years ago, but he couldn't rationalize how she knew them both on sight. Matthias faked a cough, allowing Tolde to conceal his surprise for the moment.

"Sister Abigail, welcome to Crimeat," Tolde said. "Have you been apprised of our situation?"

She shook her head.

"At least two of the Three are known to be operating here. We do not yet know where the third is located."

"Which two?" she asked.

He hesitated. "Amongeratix and Tannus."

If Abigail had a reaction, it was perfectly concealed beneath the thick fabrics of her robe. Sunlight danced off it, giving a rainbow effect. "Where is the Bloody Man?"

"We do not know, but there is sufficient evidence to believe he is here as well."

Awkward silence settled between them. Sister Abigail finally spoke, a hint of reproach in her tone. "We were not informed of this."

"It changes nothing. We must focus our efforts on the two that are confirmed. The Bloody Man is a secondary consideration at best," Tolde said.

"No. All three being on the same planet is an ill omen," Abigail replied softly. "The Three have a singular purpose. The location of the third must be learned."

Tolde passed a cautious glance to Matthias, but the Prekhauten Guardsman merely shook his head.

"Sister, our resources are stretched thin already. We have men out searching for signs of the Three but the quest may prove futile, and the local authorities are conspicuously quiet concerning this matter," Tolde informed her.

"You have reason to be suspicious of them?" she asked.

"I cannot answer that at this point in time."

She pressed. "Cannot or will not?"

He swallowed hard. "Will not. The loyalty of the world is not mine to question."

"Unless you have proof of heresy," Abigail concluded.

"We have proof of nothing. Rumors only," Tolde snapped more angrily than he wanted to. "What we do have is a confirmed escape from a secure facility that one of your kind warded. The trail is already growing cold. Standing here debating the finer points of matters irrelevant to what is happening gets us nowhere."

"Nothing is irrelevant when speaking of the Three, Senior Inquisitor. You humans are still a young race and have much to learn. I wish to go to the prison from which Amongeratix escaped."

Finally. "Sister Abigail, that request I can accommodate. Our shuttle will be leaving at dusk. Until then, Sergeant Major Matthias will see to your needs."

"I have no needs," Abigail replied.

Tolde struggled to contain his building fury. "Be that as it may, I leave you in his charge. I have an appointment."

"Yes, with the local Inquisitor," she finished for him.

Gods damned witches. Tolde screamed silently. Outwardly, he nodded curtly and held out a palm gesturing for her to follow Matthias. The sooner they were rid of the witch, the better life would be.

A thin coat of dust covered the furniture, giving the impression that the building had been unoccupied for some time. Tolde Breed looked around, searching for signs of betrayal he hoped not to find. There was brotherhood in the Inquisition, and that bond was not taken lightly. Oath breakers were caught and executed publicly on Vau Prime. Tolde quietly prayed that Ursal Prowl had not turned his back on the Inquisition. He was going to need every ally in the coming battle.

The door groaned open, causing Tolde to turn. Ursal Prowl entered hesitantly, as if he were expecting such a confrontation. Tolde thought he noticed a wild look quickly disappear once Ursal recognized him.

"Senior Inquisitor, my humblest apologies for not being here when you arrived," Ursal began in his most diplomatic tone.

"The work of the Inquisition calls us, Inquisitor Prowl. We cannot afford to ignore it."

"Of course," Ursal replied shortly.

"I am not accustomed to playing political games, so let me get straight to the point," Tolde said. "Three members of the ruling council were murdered mere weeks after the escape of a very dangerous prisoner."

"What are you getting at?" Ursal asked suspiciously.

"What do you know?" Tolde replied. The look in his eye left no doubts as to what he meant.

"I'm afraid you have me at a disadvantage. The affairs of the council are hardly Inquisition business."

"Do not play games with me, Prowl. Inquisitors are supposed to see beyond the obvious. There is some evil afoot on Crimeat, and we must get to the bottom of it before the hour grows too late."

Ursal hesitantly took a seat, his face scrunched with internal debate. "The current political situation here is delicate at best. The council is split into two distinct factions. One wants the coming war, and the other does not. It is suspicious that the three murdered council members did not support the war. I honestly do not know what this has to do with the prison escape."

Tolde idly rubbed his jaw just below the lip. It was entirely possible the war faction had a part in the Prophet Isle escape. Amongeratix relished corrupting others. The natural question was how would any of the Lethendweil nobles know of his presence?

"Is anything being done to stop this war?" he asked.

"An envoy commission is being assembled, but I highly doubt they will find success. The Ugri are a secretive people, and those who preach war will not be sated until blood is shed. Armies are already being mobilized."

"You are not convinced the Ugri are responsible," Tolde said. *What game are you playing at, Inquisitor?*

"My opinion hardly matters at this point. The council has voted, and they are going to war," Ursal replied tautly. "Am I being accused of something?"

Tolde shifted at the unexpected question. "Are you guilty of anything?"

"It suddenly feels like it. What is the real reason you have come, Senior Inquisitor?" Ursal asked.

"I came at the behest of the Inquisitor General. You would do well to remember that," Tolde scolded. "What is the disposition of your Prekhauten cadre?"

Ursal bit back the foul taste in his mouth. He wanted nothing more than to lash out and strike the elder Inquisitor, but that served no purpose. Instead, he took a deep breath before answering. "Most of them are spread throughout the twelve kingdoms. They serve as additional security for the current nobles. A one hundred-man reserve is stationed here in Vaade."

Prekhauten Guard reduced to providing security for local officials? Strannan would be furious if he learned of that. The Guard was the elite combat force in the universe, and they were now no better than hired guns.

"You should be using the Guard to quell this violence, not protecting the local nobility. That is a job for their own men."

"Perhaps it has been a long time since you were responsible for a single planet," Ursal replied, "but times have changed. I have five hundred men to maintain order on an entire planet. *Five hundred*. There is simply no way I can achieve that without ensuring I have support from the ruling class. I made that decision and stand by it."

"You are letting this planet slip away. I will not allow that," Tolde growled.

"How many worlds have gone to war under the watchful eyes of the Inquisition?" Ursal fired back. "How many lives have been lost because the Conclave failed to act in time? I am trying to keep the peace as best as I can. Not all of us are given the praise and accolades that have been heaped on your shoulders. I am just a man."

Tolde moved close enough to whisper in Ursal's ear. "If I discover you have had any part in this violence, you will be made to answer."

The hiss-snap of an ion bolt drowned out any reply Ursal might have had. The bolt sizzled past Tolde's left ear. The tiny hairs burned away, leaving blistered flesh. Tolde instinctively dropped to the floor before another pair of bolts was fired. Ursal spilled out of his chair in the opposite direction even as Tolde drew his side arm and spun towards his assailant. A chair was knocked over. A dark shape fired again and ducked behind the half-wall separating the two rooms. Tolde fired back. The impact from his rounds tore plaster from the wall. Puffs of chalk-like powder exploded in the air.

Tolde caught the telltale slap of a door closing. His attacker had fled into the alley behind the building. Tolde looked back to Ursal. "Where does the alley lead?"

"To the main council complex," he replied, too calmly for having just been attacked.

Tolde filed that information away and charged towards the back. Ursal Prowl dusted his hands off and watched. A devious smile twisted his lips.

Tolde kicked the door open slowly with the toe of his boot. He crouched low, leading with his weapon. One eye poked around the corner. A handful of overturned trash bins blocked the immediate area. There were no doors, no windows on the ground floor for the assailant to duck into. Tolde guessed the alley ran close to three hundred meters before turning right. Three hundred meters of pure kill zone. He snarled with the knowledge that there was nothing for it but to advance and pray for the best.

Producing the communicator from his pocket, Tolde quietly said, "Matthias, I need your help. I am in the alley behind the Inquisition office. An unknown gunman fired on me and fled towards the council complex. Send your men to secure the area while I pursue on foot."

There was a brief silence. "Acknowledged. Troops en route."

Tolde rushed, clinging to the wall. His heart thundered in his chest. Each footstep was the sound of thunder in his ears. Experience and training kept his pistol pointed down the center of the alley. The world faded. All that remained was the approaching corner where death might lurk. Tolde drew deep breaths, willing his body to calm and focus. He brushed past the tipped bins, leapt over piles of trash. He was almost there, and still no shots were fired. Anger welled. The Senior Inquisitor tightened his grip on his pistol and slowed to a halt a few meters from the corner.

His eyes teared from exertion. The thundering died, allowing him to listen to his surroundings. Tolde mumbled a quick prayer to Aris and crept to the edge of the corner. Sweat greased his palm, and his tongue felt covered in sand. He knew he had to be fast to clear both avenues of approach. His assailant might easily be hiding in either direction. Tolde wished he had a squad of Guardsmen with him. They made missions like this look easy.

Tolde took a knee and leaned into the corner with what he hoped was enough speed and violence of action to make his foe hesitate. A quick check to the left was all clear, and the Inquisitor spun as fast as his aging body could. An empty road stared back at him. Vaade's main avenue was a handful of meters away. He turned back around. Nothing. His assailant had gotten away. The ramifications staggered him. Tolde holstered his pistol and waited for Fies' squad to arrive.

The night held dark secrets for Danja Stall. The aged priest often felt skittish, uncomfortable after the sun sank beneath the horizon. Dried tears stained his plain oak desk from nights when the pain was just too much. None of his training or orientation had prepared him for those things he'd seen. Every shadow represented a path to a terrible place where human souls were torn apart.

Danja dared not ask another priest if they shared his visions of torment. He was not as brave as others wearing the robes. All he'd ever wanted was a simple life without cause for worry or fear. Instead, he was blessed with perpetual horror. Danja Stall was old. By all rights, he should have been dead and would be if not for the longevity research conducted by the scientists of the Conclave. Few outside of the order knew that such existed. Science and faith had been mortal enemies for millennia. The universe would tremble past its foundations if the population ever learned that much of the faith-based truths they clung to were derived from science.

The universe was wreathed in secrets. Danja knew too many. Dark forces came to him, beckoning and tempting with illusions of hollow pleasures. Danja Stall stood the watch against the dark and felt like a total failure. The prison break on Prophet Isle was his deepest secret. He struggled to keep the nobles from learning what had been loosed upon their world. If they truly understood what was happening, they would drop to their knees and whimper.

Of course, Danja was in constant contact with the Conclave. His immediate report had resulted in the arrival of the senior Inquisitor and his Prekhauten contingent. Give them full cooperation was his order. He'd done so, and his initial fears were quieted, at least for a time. But something festered in the heart of Lethendweil. The land was angry, violent. He had thought it might be a side effect from Amongeratix being freed but now wasn't so sure. Baron Scura concerned him, leading him to wonder if the young noble had had a hand in the escape.

His internal debate was disturbed when his computer screen flashed to life. Danja's eyes narrowed instinctively. He was not expecting any communications. The wizened old priest collected his robes and slowly sat down. Typing in his password, he began reading the message that automatically popped up. His narrow eyes flew wide. Danja quickly reread it to ensure he understood what was being asked of him.

Moffo Kain smelled bad. He resisted the urge to throw up after catching the putrid smell coming from his arm pits. Scruffy peppered hair covered his jaw and cheeks. His eyes were raw, bloodshot. His pants felt loose thanks to the lack of proper meals since he had arrived on Prophet Isle. His body ached from sleeping on rocks and broken branches. Unexpectedly, he missed conversation. The hulking monster of a companion was reclusive, hardly speaking more than a handful of words a day. They were demeaning and filled with a putrid mixture of hatred and scorn.

He glanced over his shoulders to the cave where Amongeratix hid. Sunlight struck his face, making him wince. Moffo relished the natural heat soaking him. He felt repressed after hiding in the caves overlooking the northern sea for so long. Every day brought another regret. He cursed his weak will. The bottle held on too strongly, and he wasn't so sure he wanted to break away. Leastwise not until now.

The sound of waves crashing against the black rocks below drew his attention away from Amongeratix. Moffo still had no idea who or what the giant was, and that frightened him deeply. He'd signed on to escort *someone* to the port city of Breld and then to a ship. That was it. Babysitting this nightmare for over a week was destroying his nerves. Rumors of war in the south reached him, leading to the conclusion that this being had a part to play. Moffo feared for whoever had to fight against him. He couldn't imagine anyone besting the giant in combat.

A gull squawked overhead, causing Moffo to look up. The bird's white underbelly blended with the wisps of clouds racing through. He sniffed deep from the sea. The familiarity helped calm him. Moffo kept walking, eager for the feel of the salt spray on his face and the cool waters around his ankles. He tried to find some measure of peace before returning to the fetid caves. Man was not created to hide in the darkness. Life needed to be enjoyed, and that's exactly what he aimed to do once he delivered his charge to the ship.

The waves sounded like thunder. The coarse crab grass covering the gentle slope between the caves and the beach irritated his ankles. Moffo had decided to go without boots in the hopes of taking a late afternoon swim. Perhaps that would take his mind off being trapped in a cave with a monster and no wine. He frowned. Perhaps not. Moffo Kain yawned gently and stretched his upper body. He felt disgusted with himself. *Old and fat, that's what I've become*, he cursed to himself. Shaking his head, he rounded a slight bend in the trail and came face to face with an aged ship of black wood and tattered sail. He frowned again. His swim had been cancelled.

Three men awaited him on the beach, the weight of their leather armor sinking them into the pale brown sand. Two bore the look of privateers, or worse. That was to be expected. It was the third that drew his attention. Wrapped in a cloak the color of midnight, the man stood impatiently watching him with oddly colored eyes. Moffo swore he caught a hint of orange in there, reminding him of fire. He swallowed hard and wished he'd brought a weapon. Bargaining was always easier with a weapon at hand.

"Where is he?" asked the cloaked man. His black hair was greasy from not being washed, and his face bore a haggard look.

Moffo felt better. At least he wasn't the only one unable to take care of himself. "Where is who?" he asked innocently. "I'm afraid I don't know you or who you are referring to, stranger."

The man smiled, wicked and feral. "You don't need to know who I am. All you need to do is tell me where *he* is so that I can collect him and go about my business."

Moffo stood his ground, rubbing the scruff on his chin. "You're not making much sense. I just come down to take a dip in the ocean."

Darka Jorm bit back an angry retort. The last thing he wanted was to play games with some bum from Breld. The rustling over his shoulder told him his crew was getting anxious. Bad things happened when they got that way. Bloodshed served no purpose, not after the lady took him from the chapel and led him to the secret council. Secrecy was his best ally. He glanced back, noticing for the first time the awful sight their ship, the *Wistral*, must be.

The sails were mere tatters of what they'd started as. Boards were warped and cracked. The paint was gone in a hundred places. Darka had to admit the *Wistral* was sorry as far as ships went. He idly wondered why the secret council hadn't just hired a shuttle and flown this man south to Lethendweil. Ships like the *Wistral* were outdated and should have been put to rest long ago. His gaze settled on the carved skull on the prow.

"Let me make myself perfectly clear to you," Darka said as mildly as his mood allowed. "I have been hired by powerful people to transport a very important person south. You would do well not to interfere."

"Interfere? I'm just one man going about my business," Moffo countered, more forceful than before.

"Yes, a swim you said," Darka replied. "Only, you have no towel and nothing to bathe with. That complicates your story, don't you think?"

Moffo swallowed. He involuntarily took a step back. The two pirates behind Darka whipped antiquated ion rifles up, barrels pointed menacingly at his chest. A foul taste crept into his mouth. He was no hero and certainly wasn't about to risk his life for anyone else. Perhaps this man with the strange eyes had a point.

"I am not going to ask again," Darka pressed. "My friends are not nice people. You would do well to listen when I speak. Don't be a hero. Death doesn't care."

The riflemen didn't seem the sort to need much reason to shoot. Pencil thin moustaches accented with equally thin beards gave them an unsavory appearance. Tattoos and markings covered their arms and chests. Neither was particularly muscled, but both were well-toned from years of service aboard a ship. Moffo found them barbaric. Dark thoughts filled him of them slitting his throat and dumping his body in the middle of the ocean without anyone ever knowing what happened.

"Come with me, but only you," he finally said.

Darka looked at his companions and nodded. They lowered their weapons but kept their scowls fixed on Moffo, watching for any sign of treachery. Darka appreciated their dedication, if not their misdirected motives. The captain and crew were only here to make a profit, and a handsome one at that. Whoever the members of the secret council were, they had enough influence to commandeer ships, men and equipment enough to move a dangerous figure halfway around the world.

"Alright, lead the way," Darka said and followed Moffo Kain back to the caves.

Amongeratix was standing in the entrance, massive arms folded across his chest. A dark grin carved his face.

FOURTEEN

3210 A.G. (After Gods), Vaade, planet Crimeat.

Castle Scura had been built into the bluffs overlooking Lake Vendashul nearly six hundred years ago. The location was designed for maximum protection against enemies and worse. The plateau behind it provided enough land for family and servants and had quickly grown into one of the major cities in Lethendweil. Rock dragons had once made their roosts among the broken crags and caves. The dragons were long gone, extinct from overhunting, but the castle lords continued to keep watch over the valley below. The Bothwel Mountains speared into the heavens around the castle like so many broken teeth. Winds screamed between the peaks, angry and mournful. A single road wound up through the mountains to the vast plateau representing the lands of the Scura clan.

The plateau had no natural farmlands. Heavy winds and miserable weather conditions forced the population underground or into specially made environmental suits. Mining was the main industry.

Shuttles and transports provided continual trade from the lower kingdoms, at a handsome price, so that the people on the plateau could live properly. Built four stories deep into the mountainside, the port of Reven was one of the largest in Lethendweil. There were over seventy docking bays and hundreds of storehouses that seldom went empty.

As a result, a sprawling industrial complex had developed. Reven had quickly established itself as one of the premier trade facilities in Lethendweil, even all Crimeat. The Scura clan cultivated an extensive enterprise that reached to the stars. As brilliant as they were at commerce, the Scuras were also warriors. Less than a kilometer from the Reven industrial complex was the barracks and training facility. Several thousand soldiers drilled and trained daily, spending their nights and hard-earned money in the local bars and taverns.

Anti-personnel and aircraft cannons were built into the mountains. The plateau was one of the most impregnable places on the planet and had yet to suffer a major siege. Off-world mercenaries and cutthroats filled the empty slots in the ranks. The pay was good, and the rising prospect of battle kept morale high. Armored hover jeeps convoyed back and forth from the port, and three heavy tanks were always stationed on the parade grounds for the benefit of spying satellites. Scura kept most of his strength hidden underground. Nothing could be taken for granted, not even with all twelve kingdoms uniting for war.

Life on the plateau was hard. Guards patrolled the walls all the way to the edge of the mountains. Their dark blue armor was emblazoned with a golden dragon claw, the standard of the house of Scura. Companies and platoons of infantry conducted basic drill and ceremony under the watchful eye of the current baron. Scura wasn't the sort to take chances, especially not now. Suspicion focused on his house, he was forced to think and plan for the worst.

Crimeat's twin moons were already high in the night sky. Scura had once enjoyed the view. He used to stand on this very balcony and give endlessly up into the night. The stars held such promise, an allure that beckoned to him. He'd longed for the day when he could take to the stars and leave this world behind. Now, those days were no more but crisped memories. His gaze swept down over the bleakness of the plateau. How he hated his lands, hated how his legacy was forced to rely on the goodwill of others. It had been more than a hundred years since the last baron was crowned head of the council. A hundred years spent in squalor begging for scraps. Scura meant to change all that.

He deserved more. The campaign against the Ugri would serve as the catalyst. He gripped the alabaster rail in contempt. Anger filled his heart. Anger that his birthright was nothing but black rock and a windswept plateau. His realm was so far from reality that it was often forgotten by most. The lords of the plateau were a farce, distant relics from a wild time.

"Father?" came a hesitant voice from behind.

Keeping his sigh to himself, Scura turned to see his daughter, Ilsara, standing in the doorway. She was the image of her mother, so much so he saw little of himself in her graceful features. There were times when he envied her innocence. The world was new and exciting despite losing her mother at an early age. He often wondered what it would be like without his dark ambitions. It was much too late for that. Scura had already set his plans in motion. With a little luck and the right timing, Lethendweil would be his.

Scura looked on his daughter with love. They lacked closeness, however. Ilsara had once warmed to both he and his wife, but that was before her mother had started losing her grip on reality. Spitting insanities and lost in dementia, his beloved wife remained locked away in quarters known only to him and Ilsara. Scura had hired the best doctors and scientists Crimeat had to offer, yet none could fix her ailments. Some speculated it was the curse of the dragons, vengeful at having been driven to extinction by mere mortals. Scura could not bring himself to put his wife out of her misery, even knowing that was the humane thing to do. Instead, he had her locked away. A dirty little secret others would kill for.

Scura offered Ilsara his most warming smile. "You should be sleeping, daughter."

She shifted, her beige robe swinging from the movement. Her hair was long and dark, framing her oval face. There was warmth in her grey eyes capable of melting even his hardened heart. Her body was slender and athletic with curves in the right places. She could easily have any man she wanted. Her cheeks were smooth, slightly angled against the jaw. Locks of hair drifted down over her right eye, giving her an alluring look.

"I'm worried about mother," she admitted. "She's been raving again. Something about the bringer of storms."

Scura's heart would have bled for her had he not grown accustomed to his wife's nonsense. Ilsara was only nineteen standard years old, and the safety most children were afforded had been violently ripped away from her. Still, he hardly expected his wife to last the year. The last remnants of love still polluted his heart. He'd turned down a bevy of mistresses out of love.

"I know, but there is little we can do. The doctors have all agreed that it is best this way. Has she harmed herself?" he asked.

Ilsara shook her head. "No, not yet."

Too bad, he thought. That would save all of them the trouble, and he could finally move on to better things.

"Perhaps we can go and speak with her. She might like that," Scura proposed.

Sharp commands from drill sergeants barked across the plateau. His blood rose. He desperately wanted to be down there with the soldiers, preparing for combat. His thoughts turned back to his wife. Both he and Ilsara knew her mood changed with the winds. They'd seen it before. The last time, a guard had died for it. How she had gotten hold of the knife was a mystery. A mystery to all but Scura. He'd given her the weapon and left the room only the day before.

Scura walked to his daughter, throwing his arm around her slim shoulders and giving her a warm hug. His strength flowed through her veins. She was a fighter. Good with a blade as well as a blaster. She held her own against many of the castle guard. Ilsara didn't know it, but she was being trained in the ways of politics and court intrigue. One day, she would succeed him.

"How have your studies been going?" he asked, eager to change the subject.

She shrugged. "School is school. The tutors insist on perfection they cannot produce from themselves. They are remarkably pompous. I'd like to take them into the practice ring for a bout of sword play."

"Embarrassing them serves no purpose, Ilsara. I thought I raised you better. Your instructors were hired because they are the best on Crimeat. They are scholars, not combatants. History and science are as important as battle tactics," he scolded.

"Father, I know all of this, but it does not change how I feel. They waste my time."

Scura checked his frustrations. "We all have our assigned place in life. Yours does not require you to march into battle. You have no brothers or sisters, Ilsara. That makes you the sole heir to Reven. I need you as smart and well-rounded in all areas of academia if you are to successfully succeed me. Our lands would fall otherwise."

He grew weary of arguing. Hints of anxiety crept into his voice. He was expecting an important visitor tonight who was long overdue. Scura forced a thin grimace. Events were proceeding much as he had predicted. Those fools who still thought peace was possible would soon learn the errors of their judgment. Lethendweil was slowly being shaped into the image he wanted. Armies were mobilizing, marshalling on the outside of Berchenfel. Volunteers poured in from all twelve kingdoms. Cooks, tailors, ferries, supply masters and whores flocked to the army. Scura smiled as he envisioned the future, his future.

Suddenly content, Baron Scura decided to lead his daughter down into the caverns so that they might try and comfort his wife.

Crack! Scura shot up, frantically groping through the darkness for his sidearm. His throat was parched from overindulging in Pardekian wine before bed. He couldn't command the lights and barely produced more than a strangled groan. His eyes were gummed shut. His body protested its violation. Through it all, he kept focused on a single thought; get the damned pistol. Crack!

"Baron Scura!"

He finally managed to swing his legs out of bed. Scura vaguely recognized the voice, but it was enough to calm his nerves somewhat. It was Geres Auk, his First Aide. Scura tried to calm his nerves and slow his pounding heart, fears of assassination quelled. He should have known better; after all, he was the one who had hired the Vaumagians in the first place. The weeks since Emleth's murder had been spent in fear of reprisal. Geres needed to be reprimanded for startling him so.

Dressed only in a pair of loose-fitting sleeping trousers, Scura padded across the cold stone floor and opened the slightly rusted metal door. Unlike most of Lethendweil, Reven lacked the power output for automatic doors and windows. He squinted in the halogen lights, even though Geres Auk's hulking form took up much of the doorway. His uniform, always immaculate, was complete, leading Scura to wonder if the man ever slept.

"This had better be good," he growled.

Geres bowed awkwardly. "My apologies, Baron, but an urgent communiqué has just come from Vaade."

Scura frowned. The council. No doubt Brentor was going through another impotent spurt and felt it necessary to rouse them all with some useless bit of information. Scura stalked back to his bed and slid into a silk housecoat. His mood darkened. There was no way he was about to have a pleasant conversation.

"Did they say what it is about?" he pressed, not bothering to show his surprise as they stormed down the halls.

Geres shook his head. "No, Baron. The technician on duty informed me only that this was an urgent matter for the remaining council members. I was to rouse you immediately, nothing more."

Scura looked up at the man. For all his tactical prowess on the battlefield, Geres Auk lacked a developed intelligence. He easily stood closer to seven feet than six and was covered in scar tissue and muscles. He was a natural fighter, having grown up in the combat pits for amusement from a young age. He'd never known his parents nor really cared. All that mattered was the feel of steel in his hands and the satisfaction of victory over an armed opponent. Geres was easily the most dangerous man in Reven.

He had curly black hair ranging down to his shoulders. A thick moustache hid his upper lip, accented by a long hawk nose. His skin was unnaturally pale. His eyes were small, tiny spots on his massive bulk. Geres had an ethereal look that was enough to turn the stomachs of even the staunchest. He reveled in the thrill of the hunt and the iron scent of blood in the air. And he was unbreakably loyal to the Baron.

"Typical," Scura said. "Someone breaks a nail and it suddenly becomes important to all twelve of us. If I only had so few concerns..."

"The Ugri?" Geres asked.

They halted at the entrance of Reven's communications center. Scura appraised his trusted assistant and nodded. "More than you will ever know."

He made a quick gesture, and Geres opened the door. The room was large, bordering on a small cavern itself. Row after row of data terminals, view screens and tactical maps of Lethendweil filled the room. Low-level techs moved with a purpose. They monitored the entire continent, including the capitols of the other kingdoms. Scura prided himself on having an extensive spy network and often used it to his advantage over trade disagreements or the like. Tonight, he used it to further his position on the council and in the coming war.

Scura moved to the rear of the room where a black oval desk was surrounded by ten velvet covered chairs. The walls were paneled with dark oak planks, giving the room an oppressive touch. Scura liked it that way. It served to remind them all what life was like in Reven and on the Plateau. The Baron sat and stared down at the image generator built into the middle of the desk. He admired the technology, favoring this over the tediousness of staring at a computer screen. He looked to Geres and nodded. Geres Auk hit the button activating the generator. Brentor's three-dimensional image flared to life a foot above the table surface. A haunting pale green glow surrounded it.

"Count Brentor, what a surprise," Scura said in a dry tone.

Brentor did not rise to the bait. "I must admit that waking you at this hour amuses me, but I would not have done so without good cause."

"I have a campaign to plan, Brentor. What do you need?"

Visibly upset, Brentor did his best to conceal any emotion. That disturbed Scura. Normally the man was easy to read. "My sources report that a village in Durn was attacked and destroyed early yesterday morning. There were no survivors. I have already contacted General Shiramon. He is mobilizing all of his assets to prevent this from happening again, but I fear the coming days will prove a great strain on the council."

Scura perked up, suddenly interested. Durn bordered the Great Barrier Jungle, but there was no logical reason for an attack. He scratched his chin, mind racing. "This is indeed a tragedy, but I fail to see the relevance in waking the entire council. I will offer my assistance to…."

Brentor stayed him with a hand. "There is more."

Scura felt his stomach twist. "Go on."

"One of the attackers was found in the wreckage. It seems they overlooked him when they left. Baron, he was dressed in one of your uniforms."

The words sounded as hammer blows. Scura fought back the urge to lash out, knowing that he needed to remain calm. Even Geres Auk stood in muted shock. Neither had been aware of any combat troops deployed to that region.

"There must be some mistake. I have nothing to gain from attacking one of Shiramon's villages," he replied tersely. Scura decided to go on the offensive before a witch hunt began and ruined all he had spent decades to emplace. "Uniforms can easily be stolen or duplicated. There are twelve different armies in Lethendweil, and we all know each other. Enough of my men have been to Vaade to have their own tailors. It is not inconceivable for a saboteur to have one made and used it against us, especially on the eve of one of the largest wars in our history."

"I haven't accused you of anything yet," Brentor replied slowly. The smirk was almost hidden but still managed to shine through. "Consider this a courtesy, Baron. I am summoning the council back to Vaade by the end of the week. Perhaps then you will not be so quick to defend yourself without knowing the facts. Good night, Scura."

The image faded, leaving the Baron confused and angry. Geres looked down dumbly at Scura.

"Baron?" he asked timidly.

The words might have been comical if not for the sudden gravity of the situation. Scura wanted the world; those closest to him knew that. But he was in no position to act upon that desire. Too much still had to be done before he could launch his plan. His eyes flared. Plans formed. He had no choice but to move his timetable forward. Scura considered taking a side trip to Durn before returning to Vaade but discarded the thought as useless. Brentor's people would already be swarming all over the scene.

He swiveled his chair towards Geres. His fingers dug into the plush cushioning of the arms, secreting his rage. "Open a channel to Shiramon and Klesh. Then summon my council. I want them seated within the hour."

Geres saluted and went about his tasks.

Alone again, Scura began to plot. The wheel was in motion, forcing him to alter plans and abandon others. At the heart of them all was his desperate need to know who had attacked that village in his name. Failure to do so might mean the ends of all his dreams. The only clear fact was that another was conspiring against him.

"Attacking that village was a brilliant move," a light female voice said. "Turmoil is already spreading through the council. Lethendweil is beginning to fall apart, and our contacts in Breld say that they have secured *Him*. It will not be long now before we are ready to reveal ourselves."

"You underestimate our opponents," countered a deep male voice. "Emotions are high, and the council is not thinking logically. Our time has not yet arrived. Calmer heads will soon prevail. They might even discover our little ruse in Durn sooner than we had anticipated."

"What would you suggest?" the woman asked, not so easily dissuaded by the notion of poor timing. "Events are playing out in our favor."

"Do not be so hasty to abandon caution. The hour is still early, and we have much work left. I will not throw away decades of hard work on a whim."

Rage consumed her. "If not now, when? Our agents are in place across the continent. The twelve kingdoms are ready to fall; all they need is a final shove."

"One that we are not yet prepared to make. There is still strength among them," he reprimanded.

"Scura has done much of our work for us. Not only did he weaken the council, he has also blinded the rest to our threat. They march to war without provocation," she reminded him.

The man frowned, the expression lost beneath the darkness of his hood. "They march to war through misdirection. Make no mistake, if any of the nobles discovers our plot, they will abandon the Ugri and crush us."

"How do you propose to stop that from happening?"

"The council meets in five days. We must attack the Ugri to make them commit to the war before then."

The woman cocked her head, the folds of her cowl shifting slightly. "The Inquisitor from Vau Prime should be of more concern. He is a dangerous factor."

"And has the capability to bring in unlimited reinforcements," the man finished cautiously. "Did our agent in Vaade have any success?"

"No. He was able to infiltrate the local Inquisitor's office but missed."

"That is not good. Now they know another faction is operating here. The future can go either way at this point. I am not comfortable with that."

"Do we attempt to hire the Vaumagians?" she asked.

A pause. "No. They have already done too much. Although we might benefit from their continued presence. The assassins could prove a valuable distraction."

"I doubt that. This Inquisitor has already been to the prison facility, and my spies report that a Blood Witch vessel was sighted leaving the main starport."

She left the obvious unsaid. No one on Crimeat had the ability to counter the power of the witches. Only Amongeratix might be able to stop them, and even he had succumbed to their perverted powers. She began to see his point and reluctantly agreed. Their rebellion was too much in its infancy for unnecessary risks.

She glanced up at him. He was nearly a foot taller and of stocky build. Her soft eyes hardened in an attempt to pierce the darkness of his cowl. His identity had never been an issue until now. The man who had recruited them insisted that no one know who the others were. Only he—and they had no clues to his identity—knew the truth of what he had done. That irritated her, but she wasn't in a position to change it. Yet.

"How do you want me to proceed?" she asked with false respect.

He thought for a moment before answering. The Blood Witch added a new and more difficult dimension to what he was trying to accomplish. "Contact the soldiers who attacked Durn and give them their orders. The twelve kingdoms *must* go to war with the Ugri. I will be in touch soon. Until then, I want you to return to Lethendweil. We are done on this island."

She watched him go, dissolving into the darkness like a wraith in some children's story. Part of her wondered who he was, what were his motivations. That part was small compared to her desire to rise above the others and take control for herself. Smiling grimly, she turned and walked in the opposite direction.

Mistrust was rampant across the kingdoms. The ruling twelve had been reduced to nine on a brilliant stroke by Baron Scura and split into two factions. One sought peace while the other needed the thrill of violence. Amidst this confusion, no one would notice the rise of the new power until it was too late. Lethendweil was changing, just not in the way the nobles anticipated.

The sleek, faded black shuttle touched down on the fringe of the small jungle base under the sound of hissing engines. Hydraulics lowered the back ramp as a flock of blood-red birds burst from the canopy. Eight tired men in stained black uniforms and body armor marched off. Some carried their helmets under their arms; others had them strapped to the assault packs on their backs. All the soldiers were blood stained and ragged. A few had superficial cuts and wounds. Still, their efforts were the better. The mission into Durn territory was a massive success.

The assault team's leader waited until the last man had exited the shuttle before ordering, "Clear and lock those weapons. Drop your packs and prepare for inspection."

They obeyed wordlessly. Heavy packs thumped into the soft jungle undergrowth. They automatically checked each other before falling in at the position of attention. They'd worked together for years, displaying actions that could only come from highly developed trust and confidence in each other. The blood and wounds they wore were badges that reminded them of life's hardships. Not every mission was ideal. The wholesale slaughter of innocents went against many of their morals.

Finished with his own kit, Sergeant Frez Belcum slung his near ancient rifle and went through the ranks. The ritual was the same after every mission. Failure to do so even one time meant a break down in discipline and potential issues later. Frez considered his team among the best and vowed to keep that from happening. He took his time, stopping before each soldier and taking the time to ask a few questions, make small talk, and double check what their comrades had already checked. Satisfied, Frez took his place three paces in front of his squad.

His stern gaze swept over all eight. His nose was thin and hooked just enough to make his cheeks shallow. He had thin lips that revealed razor sharp teeth when he smiled. His hair was peppered and close cropped. Frez Belcum was the ultimate soldier. His entire life was dedicated to the uniform he wore. He looked out on his men with pride.

"Job well done, gentlemen. Let's hope we get a better assignment next time," he barked. "Brevel, get the wounded to sick bay, and have Doc patch them up. The rest of you shower, change and get some hot chow. First round is on me at seventeen hundred! Dismissed."

His team fell out, collecting their kit and heading back to the hard frame tent on the far side of the small compound. One hundred men and women occupied the base nestled in a seemingly forgotten corner of the Great Barrier Jungle. A one hundred-meter field of fire had been cleared around the camp, giving the towers and machine gunners a vast killing ground. Ammunition bunkers had been built into the ground and kept away from the main encampment. Shower tents and a chow hall occupied the middle. The command and control bunker was close to the shuttle pad. Frez knew Captain Partiesh would be awaiting his report.

Frez frowned slightly. They'd been sitting in the middle of jungle for months doing nothing but trying to figure out how to avoid getting nipped by the millions of insects swirling around. Suddenly, the compound was filled with activity. He wasn't sure, but he could only assume the other squads had been given assignments as hostile as his. Something was about to happen, and he wasn't so sure he wanted to have a part in it.

Frez entered the C-n-C tent and saluted. Partiesh looked up from the table map he'd been studying. He was old, aching for retirement, but orders were orders. Liver spots colored the backs of his hands and neck. His body had lost much of its former strength, and he'd had a bad case of diarrhea for the past three weeks. Partiesh swore the jungle was going to be his death.

"Captain, mission complete," Frez announced without the normal flair or arrogance.

Partiesh nodded slowly. "Did we suffer casualties?"

"Only a few minor wounds, Sir."

Partiesh glanced up at his most trusted noncommissioned officer. He, too, felt the pain from killing unarmed civilians. "We have our orders, Sergeant. I wouldn't have sent you if I had my way, but we all have jobs to do."

"They were unarmed. Every last one of them."

"Since when did that matter? War is coming. We either fight or we die. There will be no other option," Partiesh reminded him. His eyes suddenly became sad.

"Command, this is Specter Seven, all troops are on the ground and engaging targets."

The strained voice broke over the far bank of radios. Clerks and scribes hurriedly copied the transmission and began issuing subsequent orders. Partiesh turned towards them but gave Frez a final look.

"Get some rest, Frez. I have a feeling I am going to need you again soon."

The late afternoon air was stifling, but Frez enjoyed it more than being in the command tent. Partiesh was not acting like himself, leading Frez to wonder what was really going on. Frez Belcum breathed deeply. His heart hurt. Too many nightmares occupied his nights of late. He felt old. Right now, he wanted nothing more than to retire and find another world to forget it all.

He kicked open the mosquito flap and entered the NCO tent. One man was sleeping and another reading a data slate, but the other seven bunks were empty. Frez dropped his pack at the foot of his cot and collapsed on the old mattress. He wasn't as young as he used to be, and this last mission made him feel the length of his years. There was a time when his hair had been flame red, but now it was greying and thin. He found he needed more time to recover after each mission. He tried to close his eyes, but visions of the day before tormented him.

Men were violent creatures by nature; he accepted that. The weight of so much killing pressed down on his soul, oppressing him more than he had ever imagined. Killing was natural for him. It was nothing to be proud of, just a job he was particularly skilled at. Killing men was one thing, but women and children went beyond his imagination. As tired and tormented as he was, Frez knew he still had much to do before he could finally get some sleep.

The eight-man squad stormed into the canteen with smiles and slaps on the back. Each was eager for the free drinks promised by Sergeant Belcum. They occupied two tables close to the bar and began talking about inconsequential things. Anything helped to keep their minds off what they had done. Frez may have been torn, but these were the men who had done most of the dirty work. His concerns were nothing compared to theirs. Buying them the first round of the night was the least he could do.

A cheer went up when Frez finally entered the tent. They weren't celebrating their accomplishments so much as the prospect of free drinks. Frez grinned despite himself and tried to quiet them down.

"The Captain is pleased with our performance," he paused, "as always."

"But?" Brevel asked.

Frez looked at his corporal. He could always count on the man to ask the hard question. Frez considered Brevel his conscience.

"But…. we did such a good job that we are now on standby. The old man expects things to start getting hot soon. Enjoy the drinks tonight, and take them slow. There is a three-drink limit in effect."

Groans went up from the men. Most of them had been expecting to snore their way through the dawn. No soldier in his right mind wanted to get put back into the line so soon after coming off a major operation. Brevel's upheld hand quieted them.

Frez motioned for the soldier on duty, and a cooler of drinks was brought out and set down on the table with all the care of a new mother.

"Drink up, boys. You've earned it," Frez announced.

Another cheer went up as the dark blue bottles were passed around. Frez snatched two of them and unceremoniously slipped back outside. He was almost surprised to find Brevel already waiting for him. Almost.

"What's on your mind, boss?" Brevel asked between mouthfuls of the rich Genden ale. He kicked over an empty crate for a seat.

Frez groaned and did the same, taking the time to finish his first bottle. "I don't know. This new campaign doesn't feel right."

"Times are more complicated than before," Brevel countered hesitantly. "Good and bad don't really make much sense to soldiers. Those boys in there look to you for all of the answers."

"Thanks for reminding me."

Brevel shrugged. "It's true. As long as you have your shit together, they feel like they are doing the right thing. The only thing they care about is coming home at the end of the day."

"Even if it means we continue killing women and children?"

"Not our call."

"No, I suppose not." Frez finished his second bottle, tiny streams of wasted ale running down his chin. "Were we ever told that village's name?"

"You're being too hard on yourself, Frez. Let it go. It's done. You brought all of us back in one piece. Well, Doc might argue about that one, and probably Kaj, too, but you get the point."

Frez snorted a laugh despite himself. Brevel was right. Self-pity was about the most useless emotion for a soldier to have.

"Maybe you are right. Kill enough people, and godliness enters the picture. We've become invincible in our own minds," Brevel added.

Frez shot him an accusing glare. "That's shit, and you know it. I think we have been blinded from what is really going on. When is the last time any of us heard from Vaade besides the old man?"

"Thinking like this is bad for business, boss. We just need to keep doing what we're told, and it will all be behind us soon enough. I know you want to retire. Now is the time to buckle down and focus on getting to that point."

"Brevel, I like you, I really do, but one of these days I am going to haul off and punch you square in the jaw. Can't you see? We've put ourselves ahead of our principles. I can hardly sleep anymore. This is wrong. We're not murderers."

Brevel laid a comforting hand on his friend's shoulder. "Perhaps we are now. There is no going back from what we did. Like it or not, we slaughtered those villagers like feed animals. It wasn't you or me that made the call. Let the guilt sit with the Captain and command."

Brevel finished the last bit of ale and tossed the empty bottle into the trash can beside the door. He gave Frez and long look and said, "Hasjef."

"What?" Frez asked, confused.

"You asked what the name of that village was. It was Hasjef."

Frez Belcum sat alone for a long time. Crimeat's moons were rising by the time he finally got up. Brevel's words had struck a chord no amount of alcohol would assuage. His own thoughts offered no comfort. He sighed, wondering when they'd made the transition from Prekhauten Guardsmen to mercenaries. Frez stalked back to his tent and grabbed his shower gear. The hot water felt good, and, at this hour, he was the only one there. Steam and water stole some of the ache in his muscles.

He finally made it back to his cot, but not until the water had turned cold. His cot felt much better than the jungle floor. Frez settled in and found sleep eluded him. Every time he closed his eyes, he saw the burning bodies. Heard the children screaming. Mothers crying. Never in his long professional career had he had to deal with a crisis of morality. He prayed he never had to again.

FIFTEEN

3210 A.G. (After Gods), Berchenfel, planet Crimeat.

The green and red moons cast the countryside in a strange, almost haunting glow. A thin cloud cover sailed across the sky, pockmarking the land for as far as the eye could see. Night crows roved in small flights. Small rodents scurried for cover in the relative safety of the tall grasslands of Berchenfel. Lights from distant cities marred the serenity of it all. Various aircraft half-filled the distant skies, the drone of their engines a hollow echo.

Tannus sat atop a ledge halfway up the slopes of the southern part of the Bothwel Mountains. His strong eyes were weakened from causes only he knew. Troubles wormed through his mind, burrowing deeper until he could find no peace of mind. His muscles ached from inactivity. Still recovering from his wounds, Tannus remained hidden from the world. He'd suffered much worse over the millennia, but the battle on Prophet Isle had been the worst he could recall. The reasons why eluded him.

Questions plagued him. His battle with Amongeratix should not have happened. His brother had always been weaker, both mentally and physically. Tannus had watched his brother's imprisonment all those years ago. The black and grey uniforms of the Inquisition and Prekhauten Guard were stark contrast to the ethereal beauty of the Blood Witch. He had been amazed and frightened by the lethality of the combination of those forces. Never in their long history had any of the Three been captured by humans.

Escape was inevitable, at least in his view. It was the way Amongeratix had escaped that bothered him. Tannus had personally checked the wards after the witch left. They were strong enough to last a hundred years without repair. The only way his brother could have escaped was through an unusual amount of outside power. Add what little he had seen of the blast area, and Tannus knew that Amongeratix had had help. Who, though? The question burned him.

"Ever you torment me, brother," he mused aloud.

The violence of their confrontation replayed in his mind. There was no explanation for the sudden strength Amongeratix had attacked with. His brother had been so unexpectedly powerful that it was all Tannus could do to fend him off. Ever their battles resulted in stalemate. They were genetically equal in almost every regard, sons of a long-forgotten father. As a result, Tannus and Amongeratix were forced to rely on mortal assistance. This time was different. Amongeratix could have destroyed him at the prison. They both knew it. *So why*, Tannus struggled to explain. *Why did you let me go, brother?*

Most of his wounds were already scabbed over. Accelerated healing was a benefit of being immortal. The scars never went away, though. His body and mind were a ruined wasteland of scars. Ghosts of fallen friends and foes trailed behind him, an endless stretch across the fabric of the universe. Darkness ever threatened his soul. Tannus repressed the instinctual urges threatening to drag him down. He refused to become like his brother.

He had come to realize humanity was the key. The answer to the great mysteries. Nothing the gods or their spawn did came close to the simple imperfections of the human race. Even spread across a thousand stars and a million faiths, not one of their race was perfect. And that was the answer. Imperfection gave them a reason for being, for getting up in the morning and grinding through another day. It gave them hope and purpose. It gave them dreams. Dreams that one day they might attain that sought-after perfection and become one with their gods. Tannus understood that now. He and his brothers had been born perfect. They were the immaculate creations of time immemorial. And that was their great failing. Tannus understood that so long as he and his brothers had nothing to strive for, they would never gain serenity.

He and Amongeratix had abandoned that quest too long ago. They'd settled into an existence of hatred and rivalry. Untold millions of lives were wasted in an undying war that simplistic fools like the Conclave dubbed a battle between good and evil. Tannus hated the terms. Neither he nor his brothers were evil. They fought for their beliefs, regardless of which side they fell on. Only Sorrow remained aloof. He alone had transcended the eternal plague of violence and abandoned them to their miseries. Sorrow had always been the odd one. He deplored combat yet made no move to save innocent lives. Tannus was almost positive that Sorrow played a more important part than any living figure understood, including himself. It was no accident that Sorrow only appeared occasionally and covered in blood. He was trying to deliver a message.

Tannus suddenly recalled an almost forgotten piece of information. He had heard once that Sorrow had come here at roughly the same time as Amongeratix was captured en route to Occanum. There had been no word or sign of him in the five decades since. Tannus now believed Sorrow was still on Crimeat. Probably hiding in the back of some cave, he snorted. His opinion of his brother was lessened with time. The sundering took all three to different places, and Tannus had no desire to wander down the twisted roads of his brothers. He believed he still represented the light humanity had lost.

Lightning cracked the black skies in the distance, breaking his ruminations. Tannus lifted his head to the timid wind and closed his eyes. Sorrow. Amongeratix. Crimeat. The Conclave. What did they all mean? Tannus suddenly made up his mind. He had to find Sorrow. Only through that route would he be able to piece the puzzle together and learn what Amongeratix was after and who was aiding him. He rose abruptly. The newfound direction produced eagerness he hadn't felt in centuries. Tannus *had* to find Sorrow.

Unfortunately, he did not know where to begin searching. Fifty years was a long time, even in the span of their eternal life. Sorrow might be anywhere. Tannus was sure his brother was still on Crimeat. Amongeratix's presence practically assured it. The trick lay in finding the village in which Sorrow was last seen. From there, he would easily pick up the trail. Thoughts of swaying his wayward brother to his cause for this one struggle flickered to life and were quickly crushed. Sorrow would not be so easy to convince. Tannus had to take things slowly and proceed with caution.

Satisfied with his decision, Tannus confronted his next problem. Record keeping on Crimeat was primitive at best. Finding Sorrow was going to prove difficult. He had no ideations of a quick discovery, especially for an event from fifty years ago. Tannus traced his jaw line thoughtfully. His knowledge of how his brothers operated gave him great advantages the Conclave and their Inquisition lapdogs wished they had. Even when they thought themselves unpredictable, Tannus often was able to make moves ahead of them. He begrudgingly admitted it was the same with his brothers when he tried to outwit them. Their existence thrived on equal understanding.

Tannus looked out across the vast plains comprising the center of Lethendweil. The grasslands ran from the northern coast all the way down to the southern desert and from the spine of the Bothwel Mountains almost all the way west to the Great Barrier Jungle. There were plenty of villages spotted across the expanse. He grinned despite the uncertainty nagging him. Plenty of places for Sorrow to appear and then vanish without ever being reported, he mused. Satisfied he was at least looking in the right direction, Tannus began working out where the safest place would have been. Sorrow was not one to take unnecessary chances. He was the most reclusive since the events of the war some three thousand years ago.

The moon slid behind a bank of thick clouds, temporarily leaving the world in quasi-darkness. Darkness. Sorrow thrived in a world half light and half dark. Tannus frowned. His brother would not have come here unless it was important. Nor would he risk being discovered carelessly. Sorrow must have picked his village with great care and for a good reason. But where? The grasslands were well over two thousand square miles. How many villages were out there, lost from the record books?

Tannus smiled suddenly. He had it. Reaching into a pouch on belt, Tannus produced a small remote control device. Soon, a single-person craft the color of freshly mined coal was hovering a meter off the rock ledge. The angular craft was specifically designed for atmospheric and stellar flight.

The razor-like feel of long grass rubbing against his exposed ankles was irritating. Tannus knew he should have worn long pants and boots, but his haste to pick up Sorrow's trail drove him. A hundred tiny cuts laced his powerful calves and shins. The dark leather sandals covering his wide feet were stained green and red from the combination of blood and grass. He ignored the miniature pain, shutting down that part of his mind to keep moving at the same pace.

Of course, it would have been easier to just take his flier and avoid the entire situation. He frowned at the thought of soaring into a random village with his stealth flier. Villagers would collapse from fright upon seeing his twelve-foot frame. He knew what he was, but to the common citizen on one of a thousand inhabited worlds, Tannus was so much more. Men whispered and called him a god when they thought he was out of earshot. *If only the fools recognized the truth their trousers would be stained with urine.*

Tannus had landed his flier a league away from his target village and gone the rest of the way on foot. Darkness was falling, and he knew it would provide perfect cover to mask his size and movements. The village he chose—the name escaped him—was a good three hours at least from the nearest neighbor, and it was the only village for a hundred miles that had a records court. Tannus believed he would find what he needed to know here.

Something big snorted in the distance and stomped off, as if sensing the tremendous power marching past. Tannus ignored it, marching deeper into the endless grasslands. His heart quickened. Excitement tingled his fingers. This was the closest he had come to finding his estranged brother in a very long time. It was the closest he had come to finding the answers that continued to gnaw at him. Amongeratix was on a mission, and Tannus had to find out what it was before it was too late.

The village slowly came into view. He picked out the tiny reflections of different colored lights in the distance and slowed his pace. Monitored communications over the past few days told him that the entire continent was mobilizing for war. The idea seemed absurd considering who they thought was the enemy. Still, he didn't need a nervous kid with a gun taking shots at him in the dark. Tannus approached cautiously.

A four-foot stone wall surrounded the village. The granite was in stark contrast to the different shades of green just beyond. Tannus guessed there were close to a hundred buildings inside. A massive steeple rose from the center, dwarfing the other buildings. Most were no higher than two stories. Tannus grinned. This was going to be easier than he thought. His long strides took him closer to the sleeping village.

The explosion threw him into the air, the shockwave jerking him back. An iron taste filled his mouth as he fell. Red mist blossomed up through the smoke and shrapnel. Tannus blinked rapidly, trying to clear his mind. Shrill ringing assaulted his hears. He felt something wet and sticky crawling down the sides of his neck. He couldn't focus. Tannus struggled to break free of the mild concussion and figure out what had just happened. He fell back in agony when he tried to rise.

Tannus looked down at his leg and gasped. His left calf muscle was mangled, the clothing ripped to shreds from the blast. Rock and clumps of dirt rained down around him, striking the ground with heavy thuds. A searchlight blared to life. Tannus tried to rise again, and his world went black.

He opened his eyes to a strange environment. He lay on three mattresses placed together. Ragged bandages, no more than torn bed sheets, dressed his wounds. Pain throbbed throughout his body, and he lay back with a groan.

"You should be dead," a thin voice called.

He looked up to see an aged man bent over a decayed wooden table. Tannus reached up to pinch the bridge of his nose. "Where am I?"

The old man shrugged, giving Tannus a glimpse of the black stripe down the middle of the front of his faded white robe. "Safe. They will not come in here."

"You did not answer my question, priest," he growled menacingly.

The priest chuckled softly. "I believe you have already guessed. My attendants collected you before the soldiers could. I am Father Dye, and you are in my church."

Tannus looked around. Banks of candles, grotesquely changed by thick ropes of melted wax down the sides, gave the church the only light. Several rows of wooden pews faced an ancient stone altar. Statues of various gods formed a semi-circle behind the altar. He frowned.

"How long have I been here?"

Father Dye eased around the makeshift bed. He carried a pot of steaming water and a large pitcher. Dye filled the pitcher with water before dropping in a handful of herbs and tea. Tannus accepted without comment. "You have been here only a few hours. I did what I could to clean your wounds."

"They will heal," Tannus said. "What is the name of this village?"

"Parvelon," Dye answered. "And you have come on the eve of war. Most of the young men are marshalling to deploy soon. They also fear an attack. Rumors of villages in Durn being destroyed have prompted the village council to erect defenses and a perimeter. Ha! As if we needed one. No one has attacked a village in Berchenfel for a very long time."

Tannus cocked his head, taking in the wizened old man. Dye was short, hunched from weakening bones. Liver spots covered his exposed skin, adding color to the dark veins showing. What little hair he had was thin and pure white. His eyes made all the difference. They were soft and compassionate. Whatever else he may be, Father Dye was genuinely concerned.

"You do not seem surprised to see me," he suggested.

Father Dye set the kettle back on the small stove and wearily sat beside the prone giant. "No."

"Why not? Most of your kind would run from the very thought of what I represent."

"I am a man of the gods," Dye told him with a faint smile. "I recognized you the moment they brought you here."

Tannus fought back the urge to smile. If only the fool truly understood he would not be so smug. "What am I? Tell me, priest."

"You are one of *them*."

"Them?"

Dye nodded. "One of the sons of the gods. Out of myth and into the fabric of the universe."

Tannus snorted. Gods. Mankind was so primitive. "If that is true, I would not be here bleeding on your mattresses."

"Your wounds are nearly healed, and I confess I do not understand how." He gestured to the center of the shrine where three distinct statues stood. Tannus recognized the loose resemblance to himself and his brothers.

"I did not think man worshipped my brothers."

Dye smiled again. "Man is prone to worship anything depending on how dark the hour. Several have come and bent knee to you."

"I am not a god," Tannus insisted.

Dye gently shook his head. "That doesn't matter. The men here are desperate for anything that will protect them from the enemy's rage. Soldiers are a superstitious lot. Their needs are no less or greater than any other."

Tannus thought back to the days when he commanded armies. Young men barely old enough to grow facial hair willingly spilled their blood for a cause not their own. He winced. The memories stung, even after centuries. He and Amongeratix should never have been cast out to the stars to find their own way. Violence had seduced them both until nothing but hatred and warfare remained.

He decided to change the path of the conversation. "What war comes to your lands?"

"We go to fight against an enemy known as the Ugri," Dye replied.

Relief washed over him. He'd hoped the old man wasn't going to name Amongeratix. This world was not ready for that kind of war. "What have these Ugri done to any of you?"

Dye shrugged again. "Who can say what the truth is? Some say the Ugri have decided to expand their lands into ours, but I suspect it is the other way around. Rulers here are greedy and forget the importance of humility."

"As is often the case," Tannus added.

"Sad, but true," Dye said. "They all promise to remember where they came from but choose to forget the moment they are elected. I say the hells with all of them. We do not need war."

"I agree. War is a terrible beast."

Dye glanced into the fire, lost to memories. Tannus guessed the man had lost someone dear to an ill-advised military action.

The old priest finally looked towards him. "You must be tired. I will leave you to your rest. Do not worry about discovery. No one will enter the chapel unless I say."

Tannus wanted to tell him he wasn't very tired and the tea had helped fill his veins with lost warmth. Instead, he nodded his thanks and let Dye go about his business.

"Thank you for the tea," he said to Dye's back.

Dye paused long enough to look back. An arthritic hand gripped a pew. "You are most welcome. Good night."

Tannus watched him go and tried to relax. Too many images haunted him, spurred by Dye's comments on the coming war. This was unexpected. He hadn't come to Crimeat thinking to get involved in the middle of an armed conflict. Amongeratix had to be part of the problem. His brother relished the chance to bring people to their knees and shatter worlds.

A soft wind crept between the cracks of the chapel where the mortar had crumbled away. The candlelight flickered, causing shadows to dance on the far wall. Tannus lay watching. His mind was too conflicted to relax.

Father Dye hurried to the front doors as soon as the insistent pounding began. He cursed his luck but knew it was only logical for the searchers to come to the chapel. Good men would search every building in Parvelon before too long. If anything, it would clear their conscience and ease rising troubles. Three more heavy pounds echoed through the arched foyer. Dye eased the door open a hand span and peered out at the unfriendly face of Lorden Hack, the local prefect.

Hack was known as a brutal man when the situation called for it. He excelled at torture and had a head for finding the truth. Father Dye choked down his rising bile and looked up at Hack. A ragged scar ran over his right eye, the bridge of his nose and past the curve of his lips. The eye was dead, glazed over a sick milky color. Hack refused to have it replaced or even to wear a patch. The sight was often enough to break a prisoner's resolve and make him talk.

"Open the door, Father," Hack demanded.

Dye straightened. "What for?"

"I am hunting a fugitive. He is somewhere in Parvelon."

"This is a house of the gods. There is no fugitive here."

Hack grinned, savage and wicked. "Precisely why I intend to search your church. What better place for a fugitive to hide? Open the door, priest. I will not ask again."

"You have no authority here," Dye stood his ground.

Hack pressed against the door. "We can do this your way or mine. Give me a reason to bust these doors in and burn your precious shrine to the ground."

"Do not think to come to me under false authority, Lorden Hack! I am the voice of the gods. Who are you to threaten me?"

Hack snapped, "I am the prefect of this fucking village, not some dandy old man who runs around in a robe preaching to deaf ears all day!"

"You may not enter unless it is to pray." Dye refused to back down.

Men like Hack made a living off the weak. They thought that, because they were bigger and stronger, they could muscle their way through anyone. This time, Hack was wrong. Dye had once been a strong young man, a champion boxer. Those days were decades behind him, but the lessons he'd learned remained. He was not going to back down to a bully. His eyes hardened, boring tiny holes into Hack.

Hack eased back a step. His hands curled with rage. "Enjoy this while it lasts. When I come back, I am going to pull your empty shrine apart one stone at a time."

Hack stormed off, leaving no doubt in Dye's mind that trouble was brewing. He had to get the giant to safety. Collecting his robes around him so that he wouldn't trip, Father Dye hurried back to the prayer hall. Dye was deep in thought. Everything was happening too fast, and he was just one old man. There were no weapons, no hidden mines surrounding the church like the village had. Dye was alone and knew that he would not be able to hold off Hack again. If only the giant could help.

He was forced to admit that he had never truly believed the gods were real. Instead, he believed they were well crafted myths that gave mankind purpose as they went about the mundane task of living. Having the son of one here in his church was enough to freeze the blood in his veins. The intangible wove itself around his life like a dusty tapestry that had lost much glory. Dye wished the giant had come years ago; perhaps then, the newfound aggression in this generation's youth would not have taken root.

He shook his head, forcing the dreams away. He had to think clearly. Time was running out. Dye parted the opaque curtains separating the chambers and gasped. The giant was gone. He grew frantic. Hack would be back soon and with help. *Think, damn it*, he cursed himself. *Where could he have gone?* Dye paced, fingers itching his chin. Tannus emerged from the entrance to the priest's private study.

"You are spooked," he said calmly.

Dye jumped before realizing who had spoken to him. "And with good reason. The whole village is looking for you, and if I know the prefect, he is going to bring them all back here very soon."

Tannus rolled his shoulders, loosening them up. "I can handle a peasant mob."

"That is not the point," Dye said after a quiet moment of thought. "You represent a great threat to men like that. They will hunt you until you can't run anymore and then take their time in killing you."

"Calm yourself, priest," soothed Tannus. "The outcome is far from certain. I need weapons."

Dye stiffened. "Regardless of the situation, this is still a house of the gods. I will not suffer violence of any kind within these walls."

Raised voices sounded down the street. They were drifting closer, fast.

Tannus leaned forward, "Time disagrees with you. Whether you like it or not, there is no stopping what comes next."

"I need to get you out of this village before innocent people lose their lives," Dye insisted suddenly.

Tannus perked up at his tone of voice. "This has happened before."

It was more statement than question, but Dye picked up on it immediately. He slowly nodded.

"Where?"

"Not far from here. I was just a lad at the time. A young girl with flame-red hair came riding in. She couldn't have been more than six or seven. She claimed her entire village had been killed by one of you."

Excitement surged within him. Finally. "Where did she say she came from? Father Dye, I need to know. If there is any chance of stopping this war of yours before the rivers turn to blood, I must know NOW."

"Kovlchen. She came from Kovlchen."

An air of defeat seemed to settle over him. Tannus got the impression it was a story the old man had not told in a very long time and that the memories were still too fresh for him to bear. He could only imagine what horrors Dye had been forced to witness all those years ago when he rode into the remains of Kovlchen. It was a tale all too familiar for Tannus. He was used to the antics of his two brothers. He nodded.

"I must leave now. Time is shorter than you think," he said.

Dye nodded back. There was no life, no fire left in him. "Wait; there is one more thing you should know."

Tannus stopped and turned.

"She kept repeating that the monster who destroyed her village was a giant covered from head to toe in blood."

Tannus broke into a wry grin. "I know. That is precisely who I am looking for."

He turned, marched to the front doors and threw them open. His roar bellowed out across the night, and men cringed. Tannus charged into the night and the coming mob. Father Dye slumped down on the corner of a pew and lowered his head. Tears streamed down his face.

SIXTEEN

3210 A.G. (After Gods), Ugri lands, planet Crimeat.

Dawn held no relief from the night. Elisa rubbed the sleep from her red eyes and did a quick glance around her encampment. Flies and other jungle insects swarmed over her horse's head, leaving no doubt that the animal had died sometime in the night. Elisa choked down the growl in her throat. She suddenly felt trapped and abandoned. The horse had been the last chance she had for continuing. There was simply no way she could expect to go deeper into the thick jungle on foot. Again, she cursed her decision not to invest in a small shuttle.

Elisa briefly considered burying the animal but quickly dismissed the idea. She did not have the time or energy to spare. Her neck prickled from a latent sense of danger. She knew she was being watched, but every time she looked around, her watchers faded back into the undergrowth. Small carnivores edged into sight, smelling the aroma of still warm horse flesh. Elisa would have liked nothing more than to blast them into smoking corpses, but it would only be a waste of ammunition. No, she resigned herself to her situation and tried to find a way out of it.

The sun had hardly broken the plane of the horizon, and it was already sweltering. Humidity levels were high. Sweat soon covered her. Elisa wasn't the sort to worry excessively over her looks, but the deadly combination of heat and humidity dampened her spirits. Her long red locks were plastered to her face and neck. Her hands felt clammy. She winced in disgust. Bugs continued to swarm her. The perpetual buzzing was enough to drive her mad.

Elisa tried her best to ignore the harsh circumstances and began collecting her equipment. She knew it was impossible to carry everything. Fortunately, she was a woman of few possessions. Elisa took her weapons and ammunition along with a healthy supply of food and water. A quick glance at her compass gave her the direction she needed to head in. She'd resigned herself to continuing into the jungle with the simplistic reasoning that it would take less to push forward than to go back. Losing her horse might well prove crippling but the alternatives were worse by far. Regardless, she couldn't stay put.

Elisa had never given up at anything in her life, not even when her village had been smoldering ruins and her family broken shells of the people they had once been. Elisa had spent days crying when she realized she wasn't strong enough to bury her family, but that hadn't stopped her. She'd dug and dug until her hands were raw and bloody. She'd dug until her muscles gave out and she' collapsed in a heap of ragged flesh.

Elisa used the anger from those memories to drive her. She shrugged her pack up higher on her shoulder, ensured her rifle was off safe and started to move. She couldn't explain it, but she felt haunted.

She turned several times, convinced that she was being followed and by more than just howlers. Whatever was watching her melted back into the shadowed foliage before she laid eyes on it. That only served to aggravate her more. She gripped her rifle tighter. Her fingers blanched. She really wanted to kill someone or something.

The day dragged on and with it her nagging suspicions. Her body was covered with sweat. Her vision swam. She was too hot and not hydrated enough for the task she had set out to do. Elisa was forced to stop to drink more water and get salt back into her blood stream. Her legs were wobbly, possibly from endless hours of walking. She dropped her pack and slumped down against a tree that would easily take five people holding hands to encircle. Elisa made sure she had as good a field of fire as was possible and rummaged for food.

She crunched the nutrition bar greedily, not wasting a single crumb. The echoes of each bite dulled her hearing to the point she never noticed the five squat figures move right up to the edge of the underbrush. Elisa downed half a canteen of water and blew out a breath. Reluctant as she was to admit it, she was tired. Buzzing insects had kept her up most of the night. Her eyes were red and ached. The sun was at its zenith, forcing waves of heat down through the trees. Humidity levels soared, making a deadly combination she was unprepared for. She considered finishing her canteen but knew better. Drinking too much too fast was the path to disaster.

Her hunger somewhat sated, Elisa packed up and pulled out her compass. She was still on course but didn't know how much farther she needed to go before exiting the jungle. Her best guess was another day at least. Too long. Doubt crept in. She wondered if she had the stamina to make it. The jungle sapped her strength. She felt drained just from standing up. Elisa considered turning around and going back to Durn. A distant howl high in the treetops convinced her otherwise. She'd barely managed to survive the howlers the first time and doubted she'd be so lucky again.

Her wounds ached. She theorized that perhaps that was where her strength had fled. Her body was combating infection. Malaria and all types of fevers threatened to take hold, desperately working against the inoculations she'd gotten from a doc in Durn before leaving. She might never have been this deep in the jungle before, but she had taken great care to learn every possible threat she might face.

Sweat dripped from her brow into her eyes, stinging them with salt. She tried to wipe them with the back of a grime-covered sleeve but only made it worse. Elisa stumbled a step before recovering. She suddenly doubted she was going to make it out of the jungle alive. Desperation crept into her mind. Her resolve weakened. Elisa knew she had to do something fast before she passed out. Digging into her trouser pocket, she produced a small med kit. Her hand was shaking by the time she managed to pull out the antibiotic syringe and apply it to her arm.

The medicine flared through her veins, making her cry out and slump against the closest tree. Darkness swarmed over her. When she awoke, the sun was setting, casting an eerie half-darkness over the thick jungle canopy. Her vision blurred. Elisa clutched her stomach before rolling over to vomit. Her head throbbed. Residue dribbled from the corner of her mouth. Red lines streaked her eyes, but she had to admit she felt better than when she had passed out. Elisa finished another canteen, leaving her with only two more.

"Ugh," she said, more to hear the sound of a voice than anything else. "I knew I shouldn't have accepted Piett's proposal."

A thick snake crawled through the tall grass not far from her. Black diamonds running down its back were mixed with a putrid green color. Bright yellow eyes stared at her, debating whether it would be worth it to try and eat her or not.

She looked down at the ten-foot reptile and frowned. "You're lucky I am tired. You'd make a good meal right about now."

The snake hissed in reply, forked tongue slithering out before it turned and went away. Elisa forced a laugh. She'd eaten snake before and wasn't averse to doing so again. Instead, she consumed another meal bar and started her trek again. Going back was not an option, but she was a dead woman if she waited much longer. Her chances for survival improved the closer she got to the Ugri savannah.

Elisa pushed through the night. Her body was sore and ached terribly. She felt like she'd gone through a major firefight. Her energy was gone. She marched in a zombie-like state, unconsciously placing one foot in front of the next. Night grew deeper. She wasn't sure how long or far she walked. The soles of her feet burned through her boots. Blisters were forming. The shoulder straps of her pack dug into her flesh. Elisa kept moving, drawing ever one step closer to her goal.

Pure sunlight finally caressed her face. It was all she could do to fight back the tears of joy. Elisa couldn't remember ever feeling so relieved. The heavy undergrowth slowly gave way before separating entirely. Trees thinned out until the jungle was behind her. She stood for a moment and enjoyed the unadulterated warmth of the sun. Without the humidity she was suddenly comfortable. Better, Elisa noticed a small stream not twenty meters away. She nearly forgot her training and rushed straight to the clear, flowing water.

Elisa crouched down, bringing her rifle up to the ready position as she took in her surroundings. Endless leagues of grasslands stretched to the west, disturbed only by boulders spotted here and there. The sky was bright blue, with hardly any clouds. Small birds and the occasional rodent flitted by. Elisa relaxed slightly. None of the dangers of the jungle appeared to have followed her into the grasslands. She marched—more like hobbled—to the stream. Her pack hit the soft ground with a squishy thud, and she dropped to her knees, gently cupping the cool water in both hands before splashing her face. Dirt streaked down her cheeks.

She raised her head and froze. Five squat, gray bodied figures were fanned out in a semi-circle behind her. Ugri. She reached for her sidearm but was clubbed across the back of the head before her hand got close. Elisa felt hot blood stream down her neck. The Ugri snickered and howled excitedly. She tried to get her blaster again but was kicked in the ribs. She skittered sideways. The Ugri closed in on her.

Elisa tried to crawl away. Fresh pain erased the old ones.

"Do not kill her," one snapped in an almost drunk tone.

She still had a chance. Elisa rolled right, wincing as agony spread through her side. One of her ribs was at least cracked if not broken. Her roll was stopped by one of the Ugri's immovable legs. He leered down at her a moment before slamming a thick fist into her face. Elisa mercifully went unconscious.

It didn't take much for Elisa to realize that her predicament was almost hopeless when she finally awoke. She was in the middle of a village, a long way from the Great Barrier Jungle. Dozens of Ugri warriors surrounded her, no doubt chanting for her blood. What little she could make out centered on a surprise attack. The only natural conclusion was that she had a part in it. They dragged her before a massive Ugri with more scars than she could easily count. An ancient, smaller Ugri limped out, supported by a gnarled staff. He clearly had more power than she thought as the crowd calmed around them.

"What is this?" Kulaam Lune asked.

The menace in his tone was unmistakable. She had already been judged.

Her captor stepped forward. "We found her in the jungle. She survived a battle with the *bokua'e*. We followed her and took her prisoner after the attack."

Kulaam glared down at her, boring hatred into her soul. Whatever measure of respect he had for anyone who survived a bokua'e attack was buried beneath the prospect that she was a scout for the men who had destroyed his clan's hatchery.

"You are a spy," he accused.

She blinked rapidly. *A spy? For whom?* "There is a mistake. I am not a spy."

Kulaam barked a derisive laugh. "Then why are you in our lands?"

She swallowed hard. Lying served no purpose. The Ugri were secretive and possessive. Elisa only had one chance and even that was shaky.

"I am hunting someone. He entered your lands a few days ago. I am being paid to take him back to Durn."

The Ugri began murmuring as soon as she mentioned the word hunting. Natural warriors, they appreciated martial ability, even if it came from an outlander. Kulaam Lune noticed the sudden excitement rippling through his warriors and frowned. He knew in his heart that this woman was a spy for the enemy. Hadn't Mollock Bolle warned of a coming war? The attack on the hatchery had left dozens dead. Females and the guards he had ordered there had all been slain, as well as every single egg in the mud brick huts. There was no denying this female had something to do with it.

"You hunt the one who brought us news of your people's war," Kulaam pressed. He decided to change directions. No real spy would ever admit to being a spy without liberal doses of torture. He was unwilling to torture a female, even if she was an outlander.

Elisa frowned. Mollock Bolle must have already been here. She had to move quickly if she had any hope of surviving the next few minutes. "He is not what you believe him to be. I am being paid to hunt him down and bring him to justice. The man is a criminal."

Kulaam Lune did not reply.

She took his silence as positive and continued. "You cannot believe anything he has to say. I know nothing of any war. My job is to capture this man and bring him back to the east. You will not see me again once I find him."

"Why is this man important?"

She paused. Truthfully, she didn't know herself. What little Piett had told her had nothing to do with Mollock's escaping into Ugri lands. She knew of no crime, no insult suffered to the nobility. Mollock Bolle was a wanted man, but for reasons no one was willing to share.

"I...I do not know," she stammered reluctantly. "Whatever crimes he committed are between him and the land of Durn. I am only a bounty hunter getting paid to do a job."

Kulaam looked down on the ancient Ugri leaning against the throne. The Ugri shaman looked back up and shook his head. That was enough for the Ugri leader.

"You are an outlander and dare come into our lands when *your* people attack us," he growled. "I say you are a spy. You have come to do harm to the Ugri. I sentence you to death!"

The Ugri erupted in cheer. Revenge demanded to be fulfilled. Many of them had spawned several of the eggs that had been destroyed. They wanted blood. The outlanders had gone too far.

"Before you die, you should know that my entire army is coming. We will take this fight back to your lands. We will kill your families, slaughter your children while they sleep. The day of the Ugri will come!" Kulaam shouted the last part to be heard by all his warriors.

The roar echoed across the plains. Pride swelled in their hearts, competing with the growing rage they needed to retaliate against their foes. A pair of heavy drums began to beat. It was orchestrated by the shaman, through Kulaam Lune. Even the Ugri needed the normal pomp and flair before going to war. The slammed their spears into the hardened ground. Grunts and snarls drowned out any plea Elisa tried to make. Bloodlust took the Ugri, and Elisa knew that she was going to die. It took a massive effort for the shaman to calm the revelry.

Kulaam Lune rose to his full height, which Elisa found ridiculously limited, all things considered. His hands curled into massive fists she easily imagined punching holes through concrete walls. He raised them to the skies and bellowed. The very ground seemed to shake under his feet.

Ugri warriors reached out to roughly snatch at her arms and torso. She grunted from the harshness of their touch and tried to lash out. Their grip was much too strong, so Elisa was dragged away. That didn't stop her from kicking out once or twice. A strong punch to her stomach brought bile spewing out and ended her resistance. Elisa struggled to contain her tears as the Ugri dragged her away.

Guards shoved her into a small cave. Elisa kept her angry protests silent, knowing they would have no effect but to sooth her nerves. Instead, she focused on how she was going to escape. Elisa stared into the gloom. The ceiling was low, barely enough for an Ugri to stand in, much less a full grown human. A fetid smell came from the back, probably from a growing collection of feces and urine. The stone walls were rough and impossibly sharp in some places. Moss and lichen grew sporadically. Small bones littered the dirt floor. There was a crude bowl half filled with moldy water to her right. Elisa fought back her revulsion.

"That was a pretty foolish move following me into the jungle," a raspy voice called from the rear of the cave.

She froze. "Mollock Bolle."

Mollock leaned forward so she could just make out his face. "And you are?"

"I should kill you right now," came her reply.

He barked a laugh. "Be my guest. It can't be any worse than waiting to be executed because of you."

"Me?" Elisa all but shouted. "You are the whole reason I am in this mess!"

Mollock laughed again, weaker this time. "Doesn't matter. Neither of us is going to make it out of here alive."

"Don't be so sure," she replied. She refused to give up, not after coming so far.

"You think you can beat the Ugri?" Mollock asked.

She gave him a smug glare. "Any cage can be broken out of. Give me some time, and I will be dragging you right back to Durn."

"No, thank you. I'd just as soon let Kulaam Lune take my head as go back to those bastards in Durn."

"You are a wanted man, Mollock," she insisted.

"Perhaps, but for what? Did they bother telling you that?"

She paused. He had a point. Piett hadn't gone into details with her, only that he must be brought back to justice as soon as possible. Elisa was forced to admit that the absence of reason left her questioning more than normal. She hunted people for the right reasons, and Piett had offered none. Looking at Mollock, she couldn't see any of the threat Piett had suggested.

Reluctantly, she was forced to admit, "No. Not that it matters. I am being paid to do a job. One way or another, you are coming with me."

"No," he told her flatly. "My fate is here. You'll never make it out of this cage let alone across the Ugri grasslands and then the jungle. No one will ever find your bones."

"At least I am willing to try," she fumed. "What good does sitting in the reek of your own shit do you?"

Mollock shook his head and retreated into the dark. His initial impression from the tavern in Durn appeared to have been right. She was a fool. He decided to explain himself. Not everything, but just enough to entice her appetite for more.

"A long time ago, I stumbled on something that no one living has ever seen. That is the real reason Shiramon and his puppets want me dead. I know secrets that threaten to undo everything they are."

"Keep talking, Mollock. I'm not going to believe any of your stories. The only thing you are doing is passing the time and keeping me from finding a way out of here."

"Don't be so sure of yourself. I know all about you."

She ignored his taunts. "You know nothing about me. Keep your mouth shut and let me be."

"What was the name of your village? You know, the one that was destroyed by the mysterious man covered in blood?"

She paused. How could he possibly know that? Elisa had thought about that fateful day every single night in the fifty years that followed. She'd checked records in every kingdom, especially Berchenfel. No one even remembered that her village had ever existed. Mollock Bolle seemingly knew the impossible. Elisa decided there was no point in denying anything.

"Kovlchen," she whispered.

"Kovlchen. I went through there a few times," he admitted. "A quaint little place. I remember how good the local pastries were at harvest."

Tears welled unexpectedly. Elisa struggled to keep them at bay. She hadn't spoken to anyone about Kovlchen since the Bloody Man had come. Horrors and nightmares festered long in her mind. Every shadow became a threat. Every person a liability. Elisa was afraid to feel. She kept her emotions guarded lest the pain and suffering happen all over again. It took her a very long time to regain composure and some order in her life. She grew up hard and continued to live a hard life. A singular thought kept her focused. She wanted to find the Bloody Man and bring him to justice.

"I don't remember," she said in the barest whisper. "It was so long ago."

"Fifty years," he added. "About the same time as when I first went on the run from *them*."

"Them?" she asked, suddenly brought out of memory.

"Them. The dark council, as they call themselves. They are the true power here in Lethendweil. The idiot nobles on the ruling council only think they are in charge. The truth is that every foul deed and action for the past fifty years has been done at the bidding of the dark council."

"If they are so powerful, why have I never heard of them?" she asked.

"They wouldn't be nearly as effective if we all knew about them, now, would they?" Mollock asked her with a slight edge of mockery.

She didn't believe him. "Nothing that influential could survive for so long in secret. The authorities would have learned about them."

"Everyone who has is dead. The council has seen to that. They have agents embedded in every aspect of government on the continent. You must believe me. After all, what reason would I have to lie?"

She almost laughed. "Your life, for one. You don't know me. Don't know what I am capable of. I could be one of these agents after all. Convince me, Mollock Bolle, before I take you back to a Durn prison cell."

He held out his weather worn hands. "Look at me. I am broken, pushed to the very edge of what I have left. The world is disintegrating around us. Now isn't the time to bicker on pointless debates. Elisa, I've seen more in this world that you can imagine. Our leaders have been corrupted. If you give me the chance, I can prove it."

The implications were staggering. Elisa couldn't believe her ears. She didn't want to. "If what you are saying is true, there is no one we can trust."

"Yes, I know. And we are all marching blindly into a war with Ugri," he told her. "Which Kulaam Lune blames you for, by the way."

She jerked back, narrow eyes boring into the darkness. "Why would they blame me? I'm just a bounty hunter."

"Do you really think the Ugri care? They know as little about us as we know about them. Nothing you or I do will stop this war. We're both dead already."

Elisa refused to accept that. She had fought her entire life, never once giving up when things got too difficult. She thrived on difficulty and based her life's philosophy on it. Her animosity wasn't directed at the Ugri so much as at the greedy nobles in the east. They wanted war. She understood that. She also understood that it was inevitable, even if she could make it back to Durn with Mollock's news.

"What do you plan on doing?" she asked. Frustrated, Elisa slumped down.

Mollock stretched and yawned. "Right now, I plan on going to sleep. The Ugri won't act rashly. They'll have a big gathering. Kulaam will pound his chest and thump his spear to drum up support before they march. It's a shame, really. The poor bastards don't know what they are getting into. They have nothing that can compete with the air power of the east."

She frowned in disbelief. "That's your big plan? Take a nap? I am not going to die here. You stay if you like, but I am leaving."

Silence for a moment. "Where will you go? Do you even know where you are now? Do not be so quick to act without thinking your actions through."

Picking up a rock, Elisa chucked it into the back of the cave. "Stop talking, Mollock. I'm in no mood."

"No, I don't suppose you are," he replied tersely. "You still haven't asked me."

Elisa wanted nothing more than to smash his teeth down his throat and hope he choked on them. Still, until she came up with some sort of plan, Mollock's tale might be the only thing to keep her sane. She settled back against a slime covered wall and finally gave in.

"Asked you what? What kind of fanciful tale you have to spend my time? Or perhaps you have a tale so fantastical that I won't believe it? I don't know, Mollock, and at this point I don't really care. Go ahead and tell me what secrets you discovered that warrant a price on your head."

Elisa figured she would struggle to stay awake, almost wishing for the boredom to sweep in and put her to sleep. What she got was anything but. Elisa's eyes flew wide as his tale progressed.

SEVENTEEN

3210 A.G. (After Gods), Prophet Isle, planet Crimeat.

Crisp winds tore through the ruined valley. Senior Inquisitor Breed wrapped his black cloak tighter around his body and willed the cold away without any luck. Prophet Isle was much colder than it had been just a few weeks ago. He glanced over at Sergeant Matthias who didn't seem affected. Matthias felt Tolde looking at him and passed a wry grin. A lifetime of service in the Prekhauten Guard had exposed him to every possible weather event. Matthias hardly felt anything now; his skin was that conditioned.

"Do you think she is going to find anything useful?" Matthias asked suddenly.

Tolde leaned his face into his cloak. "I doubt it. We combed every inch of the scene. There is no way we could have missed much. At least nothing important enough to make a difference."

Matthias grunted and looked back over his shoulder. Sergeant Fies and his squad had secured the perimeter. It wasn't difficult considering the prison facility had been ordered shut down and abandoned until the Conclave could figure out a better way to strengthen the wards. Fies took to the assignment like a scolded child. They were all glad to be away from the rising tensions in Vaade. No one had spoken about the accidental firefight three days ago. War was unpredictable, and, as far as Matthias was concerned, they were on a war footing.

Sister Abigail appeared in the prison's main doorway. Tolde would have sworn she was floating at least three inches off the ground. He repressed a shudder. Nothing about the Blood Witches was natural. His skin writhed at the thought of being close to another one. He considered asking Matthias if he wanted to go but decided against it.

"Looks like she's ready," he said. A thin smile crinkled his aged face. "Shall we?"

Matthias choked softly. "We? You are the Inquisitor, not me. I wouldn't want to get in your way."

"Nonsense. We have known each other too long to stand on formality. I insist," Tolde answered.

If Matthias had a reply, he kept it to himself rather than risk getting out of hand. He had to remember that, at the end of the day, Tolde was still a senior member of the Inquisition, and theirs was the rule of the universe. Matthias nodded and reluctantly followed. If the Inquisitor was uncomfortable dealing with one of the witches, Matthias was worse. He was a soldier, trained to fight. Dealing with supernatural powers while investigating prison escapes was well beyond him. He almost wished for a good, old fashioned firefight. Anything was better than this.

Matthias looked back to where Fies stood directing his squad. Fies was handling his reprimand well, dedicating himself to proving he was worthy of the rank. The Sergeant Major held a measure of respect for Fies. He'd been in the same position many years ago when his squad had been tasked to assist Tolde Breed on another hunt. Matthias prayed the results would be different this time. Few of his squad had made it out alive. And now they hunted Amongeratix again.

"I feel like my life is going in circles," he said suddenly.

"What makes you say that?"

"Fifty years ago, we were on another prison planet investigating an escape by the same monster. Do you remember the assault on the derelict spacecraft?"

Tolde did. It still gave him nightmares. He absently reached up to trace the blue-tinged rose on his left breast. "This time is different."

"I don't see how. Amongeratix is loose again. He can't have forgotten who put him here or why. I wouldn't doubt that he is going to try and finish what he started all those years ago."

Tolde froze in midstride. "Wait, what do you mean?"

"He was heading into Wild Space, at least so far as we could guess. What was the name of that planet?"

"Occanum," Tolde all but whispered.

Matthias looked up thoughtfully. He was four or five inches shorter than the gaunt Inquisitor. "Occanum. The final battle of the gods."

"Amongeratix was grasping at straws. I traveled to Occanum not long after we imprisoned him here. It is a dead world. Nothing grows on the surface."

Matthias circled impatiently. The answers to so many questions were just out of reach, frustrating him. "Then why go to all the trouble trying to get there? He knows something we don't, and he's going to be ahead of us until we can figure out what."

"It does not matter now. Our task is to hunt him down and bring him back into custody. Let the Conclave figure out his quest, Matthias. You do not want to go down that path." Tolde had wasted years trying to figure out Amongeratix's motives. The wake of bodies a quarter of the way across the universe had pushed him well past the edge of caution and reason. Tolde had lost himself to the legends of the Three.

"You're not telling me everything," Matthias said.

"Because I do not have the answers. We need to focus on finding this monster before he kills again," Tolde said.

"Fine, but you have to talk to the witch."

Tolde continued to walk; he'd already known that was his job. Broken rocks and fist-sized pieces of the prison's superstructure littered the ground for a hundred meters out. The pair was forced to watch where they stepped lest they came down wrong and twisted an ankle. The ground itself was charred and cracked. Dead rodents and birds that had not been fast enough to escape the discharging power had been burnt to ash. The smell of death clung to the night air even after so many days.

The pair reached Sister Abigail and paused. She made an effort of turning to face each before speaking. "The tides are conflicted. Amongeratix is far, far away."

"What clues did you find, Abigail?" Tolde asked.

She drifted back a step, hovering up and down like flotsam on the tides. "The wills of men and gods clash here. The reading is obscured."

"Can you tell us who freed Amongeratix?"

She paused. "They were human. A man and a woman. They possessed powers mortals should not." There was also an older presence. One she wasn't ready to discuss with them yet.

Matthias winced. Old superstitions resurfaced. He began to regret following Tolde on another quest so readily. Amongeratix had nearly broken him once. The temptation of fate concerned him more than it should have. Matthias ignored the impulse to reach for his sidearm. He shook his head in an attempt at clearing some of the demons haunting him.

"What manner of man would willingly support one of the Three?" Tolde pressed.

"Dark powers are focused on this island. They cloud my senses," Abigail replied candidly without any hint of emotion. "I sense a dangerous faction at work. More than that I cannot say."

Tolde Breed hid his own emotions. He had made a career out of fighting dark powers and supposed monsters, but this was much different. Amongeratix represented foulness in the soul of the universe. Tolde refused to think what might occur should Amongeratix reach Occanum.

"Can you tell us where Amongeratix has gone, Sister?"

She lifted her thin arms skyward, tilted her hooded head back. Bright, pale light burst from the gossamer hood. Tolde and Matthias recoiled, throwing their arms up to protect their eyes. A screech so shrill they barely picked it up shattered glass and stone. And then she was silent. Tolde looked up in wonder at the bright blue line rippling through the sky eastward.

"What heresy is this?" Matthias forced. His hand was dangerously close to unsnapping his holster.

Abigail tilted her head slightly. "Your kind dismisses the natural wonders of the universe too easily. It is not heresy but a natural talent all the Sisters have. Call it a gift if you must label such things."

"Witchcraft is not a gift. It is an abomination."

"You condemn what you do not understand," she glibly replied.

"Enough!" Tolde barked. "We need to focus on the task at hand. Sister Abigail, are you positive this is the direction?"

Matthias scowled but kept his tongue.

Abigail turned towards the wavering light. "Yes. Amongeratix went in that direction."

"We need to move," Tolde said as he turned to Matthias.

The Sergeant Major nodded and strode back to his men. "Fies! Get your Guards on the transport. We have his trail."

The ten Prekhauten Guardsmen collapsed their positions and started boarding a sleek Nexus N-17 shuttle. Camouflaged blue and white, the craft gave only the smallest radar profile. Unlike many similar craft, the N-17 had no angles. It was a smooth vehicle made of the strongest metal composites in the known universe. The Guard used them to ferry troops into combat zones. Fies and his men had more than enough room inside. Each N-17 was capable of delivering thirty troops in full kit.

Tolde turned back to Sister Abigail. "There can be no mistakes about this, any of it. Amongeratix is dangerous enough on his own. Now he has others working with him. Were you able to get any read on who helped him escape?"

"The Paths are muddied. I cannot see much of what occurred here. Powerful forces have been at work. Two of the brothers battled. The one we seek went east, the other south. I cannot be certain, but the ones responsible for freeing Amongeratix are in possession of terrible secrets. We must be cautious." She fell silent.

Apprehension terrorized Tolde, though he refused to admit it. "Sister, will one of your kind be enough?"

She might have given a faint laugh. To Tolde, it sounded fair and melodious. "Would any of you accept more than one?"

He watched her float towards the transport. Dark visions danced just out of reach.

Fies removed his helmet and wiped the thick line of sweat from his eyes. "All clear."

Weapons were lowered, and a noticeable amount of tension was released. Matthias followed him into the massive cave complex where the Blood Witch's mysterious powers suggested Amongeratix had hidden. They'd found food remains, a broken water container and a well-used latrine, but there was no sign of Amongeratix or the ones helping him.

"Any sign of him?" Matthias asked. His tone suggested he already knew the answer.

"He could be anywhere in the universe by now." Fies shook his head.

Matthias folded his arms over his chest. Even after more than a decade, it still felt strange to be in the field without body armor on. He envied Fies, knowing that he was going to need it before this ended. "He could be, but he's not. The bastard is still here somewhere."

"How can you be sure, Sergeant Major?"

"We're monitoring every spaceport and airfield capable of holding space-capable craft. No one has seen or heard from him since, and it is not his style to lay low. This bastard is the sort who likes to be known, especially through violence. He's still here," Matthias replied matter-of-factly.

"What's our next move?" Fies pressed. There was a different quality to him. He hadn't been the same since the wrongful shooting death in Vaade. Fies was trying to prove himself, but Matthias suspected he was trying too hard. Matthias decided to keep a close eye on the man.

Looking back towards the beach, Matthias replied, "We let her figure it out."

Fies caught the distant glimpse of the Inquisitor and Blood Witch conversing on the edge of the beach and lost much of his building fervor.

"They boarded a ship and headed south to Lethendweil," Sister Abigail said.

Tolde stared out into the never-ending waves. White froth tipped each wave as it crashed on the shore. "What kind of vessel?"

"Seaborne," she replied curtly.

He eyed her thoughtfully, only slightly wondering if she was making it all up. More than ever, he wanted to be back on Vau Prime, away from the nightmares coalescing around his ankles. Crimeat was turning into a disaster that he had no idea how they were going to escape. Every step deeper into the mystery left Tolde feeling like he was being sucked under. He wasn't so sure that he was going to survive the coming battle. "Can you narrow down his destination?"

"No. The Paths are still convoluted."

Tolde frowned and decided on another approach. "What are these paths you refer to? This is not the first time you have used that term."

Abigail continued to watch the ocean. "All life in the universe is controlled by Paths. They are the way into the future and the past.

The Paths allow my kind to *see* events. We cannot predict the future or change the past. We can simply *see*. Each Sister *sees* the Paths differently. They give us clarity and guidance. We achieve our purpose through them, and they have seldom failed my order. Yet for all our uses, they remain an enigma to us. Countless Sisters have devoted their lives to studying the Paths, and we know little to no more about them."

"And these Paths allow you to figure out what happened?" he asked.

"Yes, though it takes a great amount of energy and will."

"How far back are you able to see?"

She was silent for a moment. "Normally, I can *see* months, sometimes years into the past. Here…here, the situation is very different. It feels as though someone has knowingly tampered with the Paths, twisting them into unusable visions. We must hurry if we are to stop Amongeratix from leaving this planet."

"Agreed," Tolde seconded. He was about to ask another question when he noticed she was very still, staring out into the ocean. "What is it? What do you see?"

"The ocean. I have never seen water like this before. It is…beautiful."

Tolde felt the hardness in his heart lessen slightly. Perhaps Abigail was not so alien as they were trained to believe. Amongeratix was days, maybe even weeks ahead of them. Tolde decided that letting her stay and watch the waves roll up to her robes for a few more minutes was not going to hamper their pursuit.

"Sister Abigail, I must go speak with Matthias. There might be clues inside the caves. I will come and get you shortly." He felt better about himself as he left her. The universe was an ugly place, and it was all any of them could do to appreciate raw beauty.

"Anything?" Matthias asked as the Inquisitor halted beside him.

"No. She thinks whatever power freed our boy is also keeping her from seeing the past correctly," Tolde answered.

Matthias clenched his jaw. "That's not good."

"None of this is good. There is a menace at work here. I have felt it ever since we returned to this planet. It feels as if someone or something is driving Amongeratix to achieve a destiny not his."

Matthias looked at him sharply. "A conspiracy?"

"Possibly."

Sergeant Fies stood listening to the exchange. Each comment made him feel more uneasy. He seriously began to consider retirement but knew that he more than likely wasn't going to be leaving Crimeat. Death had been hounding them from the moment they'd set foot on Prophet Isle and begun the hunt for a monster. He'd always thought the Three were myths, ancient legends that gave clerics and holy men the gateway to answers that might not be rationally explained otherwise.

Fies didn't particularly consider himself a religious man. He worshipped the gods in his own fashion, choosing to do it privately rather than sit in an overly large building surrounded by dozens of complete strangers. He didn't believe that any man truly spoke for the gods, nor did he believe any man had the right to tell another what he should believe in. Those matters were above mortal man, and rightfully so.

Deciding the conversation was growing too gloomy, Fies excused himself and went back to his squad. He walked absently, lost in thought.

"What's the good news, Sarge?" Annalilly called.

When he didn't immediately respond, Jers hung his head in defeat. "Not good."

"The Inquisitor and the witch are trying to figure out where he went to from here. They seem pretty convinced there is some conspiracy going on," Fies said.

Beve blew out a deep breath, making everyone look up at him. He just shrugged.

Kastor asked, "What does the sergeant major think?"

"Not much."

The older Guardsman ignored the defeatist tone. "Do they have any idea what we are facing here? Theories and ideas are one thing. I would like some concrete proof."

"Nobody has a clue, from what I could gather. The one thing I can say for certain is that this planet is about to get a whole lot more uncomfortable for us."

Jers held up a hand without bothering to look up. "I would like to request a transfer."

Haggle broke out into deep laughter. The heavy sound echoed throughout the caves. He was joined by most of the others. Jers shot him an angry look but remained silent. He was only saying what they all felt. Fies offered no sympathy. It was the one emotion he found absolutely no use for.

"Sorry, Jers. You're at the tip of the sword, and it doesn't get any better. You stay," Fies told him. He turned to the rest of the squad. "That goes for all of you. It's time to get your heads out of your asses and stop feeling sorry for yourselves. The sergeant major thinks we might be heading into a civil war. I want everyone sharp from here on out. Nobody takes unnecessary chances."

"Has there been any word on the local Guard forces? Can we expect them to get involved?" Annalilly asked.

Fies shook his head. "Don't count on any other support. Local forces belong to the planetary Inquisitor, and from what I've seen so far, they aren't inclined to do much of anything."

He didn't tell them what he'd overheard between Breed and Matthias back in Vaade. Suspicions surrounded the local Inquisitor. Compounding matters was how the Guard garrison was spread so thinly. Lethendweil was a powder keg. Fies looked at the Blood Witch coming up from the beach. He frowned. The uneasy feeling in his stomach warned him to look away. There was nothing natural about the witch. He reluctantly made his way back over to Matthias. Sister Abigail was already walking away by the time he got there.

Matthias looked at him with a ragged grin. "We're moving. The witch has picked up the trail."

Sergeant Fies took a deep breath, certain he was about to die.

The *Wistral* arrived in Dretl under cover of darkness. The harbor master had already been bribed off. No records of the ship docking would ever be found. Fog concealed the murky greenish waters. A lone gull squawked from an old pylon sticking up from the burned wreckage of a destroyed pier. Darka Jorm stood on the bow with the ship's captain. His eyes glared brightly in the darkness.

"I trust your people will be awaiting us?" asked the captain.

Darka replied, "If all goes well, yes. We should be off your ship within the hour. Your payment will be delivered after."

The captain eyed him suspiciously. He'd taken great risk in accepting their fare, but the woman who had hired him had been insistent.

"I will feel better once your *guest* is gone."

"Captain, what happened was an accident."

He turned fiercely. "You call killing three of my crew an accident? Or perhaps you refer to the two that are still missing?"

Darka knew there was nothing he could say. Amongeratix had flown into a rage and lashed out. Whatever he was, the monster was evil. Fortunately, the hole in the hull was well above the sea line.

"You will be paid handsomely," he said, even though the words sounded hollow.

"You bring death with you," the captain accused.

"That is not my decision. I am being paid to do a job, the same as you."

The captain frowned but remained quiet.

Amongeratix emerged on deck so quietly none of the crew noticed him until he walked among them. Blackness swirled around him. Men grew dizzy and collapsed in boneless heaps of flesh. A deathly chill spread across the deck, freezing the blood in their veins. One by one, the crew of the *Wistral* died. Darka swallowed in horror as a film of ice spread across the deck and rigging. The captain realized what was happening and went for Darka's throat. Darka Jorm struggled as the fingers dug deep into his flesh. His face turned blue. Each breath was strained. His eyes bulged. And then it was over. The *Wistral's* captain fell dead at his feet.

Darka dropped to his knees, gasping for air. He gagged, spitting up phlegm and saliva. His vision swam. Darkness threatened to consume him. Darka rolled over onto his back and looked up at Amongeratix's hulking form standing next him. Unabated hatred blazed in his eyes.

"You…you didn't kill me," Darka struggled to say.

Amongeratix sneered. "Get on your feet."

The giant walked away, replaced by the meek figure of Moffo Kain. His face was ghastly pale, eyes hollow. Darka wondered what terrible secrets could hold a man captive in the service of such vehemence.

"He does not want you dead," Moffo told him quietly. "You should consider yourself fortunate."

"What happened to the crew?"

Moffo had a sad look. "It is best you do not know. He is… not like us. There must be no witnesses to our arrival."

"Witnesses? They were living beings! No one deserved that fate. What manner of monster is he?"

Moffo could only shake his head ruefully and say, "He is the worst in men. Stay out of his way, and do not anger him unless you wish for a similar fate."

Darka could not understand why any man would choose to follow such nightmares. "What does he hold over you?"

"Ask no questions you do not really want answers for. You do not want to know what is happening around us."

Darka watched him walk off, Moffo's last words echoing in his mind. The combination of events and horrors was too much for him. How any man might comprehend what was happening was well beyond his capacity for rationalization. Darka knew he needed to report back to Ursal Prowl but wasn't sure how to do so without risking infuriating Amongeratix.

The *Wistral* collided gently with the pier. Darka Jorm crawled to his feet and looked over the rail. Dretl was empty. Not even a fire burned along the three hundred foot dock. For a moment, he wondered if Amongeratix had been able to spread his influence over the entire village, but then he caught the clip-clop of hooves coming down the old boardwalk. A large wagon emerged from the fog.

The sides were jet black with no windows and only a single door on the passenger side. A team of four horses pulled the wagon, they, too, the color of midnight. A hooded man drove them to the dock. An ominous feeling settled over the harbor. Darka swallowed hard. The hairs on his arms and neck danced on end. Wheels groaned to a stop. Darka cursed the day he'd let himself get talked in to working for *her*. He needed to report back to Prowl before too much more happened.

"Your transportation has arrived," he managed through his choked throat. "But we must be quick. It is not safe to move freely in Lethendweil these days."

Bruises were already forming where the captain's fingers had crushed. Darka's voice suffered the strain of it, the trauma making it hard to speak effectively.

Moffo Kain stalked back to him. "Can your driver be trusted? Amongeratix has terrible fury. We cannot risk provoking him."

Realization hit him. "You are afraid of him."

Moffo's eyes dropped. "With every right. You do not yet understand what he is. The end of everything rides in his wake."

"Moffo Kain, it is time," Amongeratix's voice boomed across the deck.

Moffo offered Darka a sympathetic glance. "I am sorry. Try to escape this madness before it is too late. At least one of us might have a chance."

Darka thought about telling him to come with him but somehow knew there was little to no chance of that. Amongeratix dominated every aspect of Moffo's mind. He vowed not to let the same happen to him. Darka Jorm remained still as the giant began to disembark. Shifting waves rocked the *Wistral* unsteadily. Death stopped long enough to glare back towards Darka. Hatred radiated off him. Darka Jorm knew he had no choice but to follow unless he wanted to become another corpse. He willed himself to obey.

The wagon master did not move. Darka managed to look up inside the hood. He gasped upon seeing a thick metal bar screwed into his temples. The area around his eyes was red and scarred. He had been blinded before being tortured, Darka concluded. Moffo climbed into the empty seat next to the sightless driver while Amongeratix entered the main body. The door gently closed behind him. Darka saw his chance and took it. He ran for everything he was worth. The whinny of all four horses and the snap-crack of reins was barely audible over the sound of his own heart pounding as he fled.

EIGHTEEN

3210 A.G. (After Gods), Vaade, planet Crimeat.

The main council complex was in a constant state of movement. Clerks and pages scurried through the brightly lit corridors from one office to another. No one stopped to notice the impish figure of Father Danja Stall scuffling through them. He was a welcome and revered figure in Vaade politics. Danja had been born and raised in Vaade and was blessed enough to return once his seminary training on Vau Prime was complete. Not every priest could return to his homeworld. Danja took to his work with devotion and unmitigated passion. The people quickly became his. He lived and breathed so that they might grow closer to the gods and achieve the peace of soul that each deserved before transitioning to the afterlife.

Danja was very old now. Lines wrinkled his skin. Liver spots dotted him like one of the great jungle cats. Flesh sagged off his bones where muscles had once sat. He was hunched now, often forced to use a polished walking stick. The one thing that did not change was the fervor in his eyes. His body may be continually shutting down, but his eyes reflected a sharp mind with keen instinct.

Those eyes scanned every face passing him as he headed closer to his offices in the council building. There was only one man he had to see. The rest could be dealt with at a later time. As the Conclave representative for Lethendweil, he was entrusted with information deemed too damaging for lesser men. Secrets kept the order in power— secrets and the necessity for belief in a higher power that gave purpose to all life. Danja feared some of those secrets might be on the verge of escaping, and he was forced to act.

The message from Vau Prime had sent his mind into a frenzy of foul thoughts. He knew he only had a small window in which to act before disaster struck. Danja walked faster, hoping that the man he needed to speak with was already waiting. He was not disappointed. The outer door to his offices slid open, showing him a slim figure seated on one of the plush reception couches.

"Thank the gods you are here," Danja exhaled.

Ursal Prowl offered a fleeting grin. "Father Stall, the Inquisition is always at your disposal. We are allies in a difficult struggle, after all. How may I be of service?"

The casualness in Ursal's voice put Danja on edge. He was too easy, too free with smooth words. A poisoned tongue, Danja quickly realized. The door hissed shut, and he hurried into his formal office, bidding Ursal to follow.

"We must talk," he said after taking a seat behind his desk. The small act gave him an air of authority and went far to calm his unsteady nerves.

Ursal's eyes narrowed almost imperceptibly. "In regards to? The council vote is about to occur, and I would like to be there for it. Brentor and the others are going to induct new members that might avert this war."

"Yes, the war. Ursal, have you received any communications from the Inquisition headquarters lately?"

Ursal slid into the hard wooden chair, frowning at the lack of comfort. "No, but I do not see why I should with a senior Inquisitor on site."

Danja scowled. Perhaps his contact on Vau Prime was correct. "I fear I have something difficult I must speak to you about. The Conclave has sent me a warning."

Ursal leaned forward just enough to convey menace. "Have they?"

Danja swallowed the lump rising in his throat. "They seem to think that you have a part in this war and the deaths of the council members."

"Ridiculous. I am an Inquisitor, not some hired assassin. Might I inquire where this convoluted information comes from?" There was no mistaking the anger in his tone.

"Those, ah, those names should be kept secret," Danja replied hesitantly. He still wasn't convinced Ursal Prowl was involved. "Look, Ursal, we can work past this. Help me discover those responsible so we can clear your name before Senior Inquisitor Breed returns to Vaade."

"Breed is not my problem. He is here to find Amongeratix, nothing more. In fact, I think I only have one problem right now."

"I'm listening," Danja coaxed, desperate to get to the truth.

Ursal Prowl stood and walked around to the giant bay window overlooking the market district. Slipping his hands inside his jacket, he produced a pair of black leather gloves. One by one Ursal slid the gloves on. "I regret what I am about to do, Father, but it needs to be done."

"What are you talking about?"

Ursal turned. His face was a mask of tranquility. "You must understand that I do not act for myself. There is a new power rising, and our orders are in the way. The transition must be allowed to happen, and the only way to make ensure it does is by removing certain obstacles. You, my friend, have become an obstacle."

"Ursal, stop. We have known each other for years. Let us talk about this before you do anything rash," Danja pleaded.

Ursal shook his head sadly. "No more talk. Amongeratix is finally free, and I have sent Breed on a quest that will claim his life. But I am not totally heartless. Your death is going to be the spark that unites the twelve kingdoms and sets the path in motion."

Danja reached out for the intercom button but fell short. Ursal was on him instantly, gloved hands wrapping around the older man's throat. The struggle was brief. Danja Stall was an old man whose strength had abandoned him long ago. Ursal dug deeper, relishing the feel of the old man's pulse fading. Danja gasped and tried to twist free, but Ursal was too powerful. Drool hung in thick streams. Fingernails dug into the hard wood of his desk. A nail snapped. Blood spurted across the desk, splashing Ursal's sleeve.

"Ursal…please," Danja managed to gasp.

Those were his final words. Tongue lolling out of the corner of his mouth, the Conclave priest's eyes rolled back into his head, and he dropped lifeless to the desk. Ursal Prowl stood back, a mixture of shock and excitement twisting his face. The priest wasn't the first man he had killed, but he was certainly the most prominent. He stared down into Danja's lifeless eyes and felt accused.

"You should have stayed to your own affairs, old man," Ursal said softly. "None of this would have been necessary."

Calmly removing his gloves, Ursal left the dead man and made his way to the main council chamber.

Storm clouds hung over Vaade, threatening a healthy rain. Hurricane-strength winds were blowing in from the east. The Jenis Ocean was nearly five hundred leagues away, giving some the feel that this storm was unnatural. Rumors of the Three running loose across Lethendweil circulated much faster than Brentor had anticipated. People were frightened, and rightfully so. They'd be even more so if any of the council let slip the news that an entire village in Durn had been exterminated. Brentor walked with stooped shoulders. More gray hairs appeared daily. He barely slowed his pace when Lord Grushm caught up to him.

"Brentor."

Grushm was the last man Brentor expected to see. He was an uncharismatic noble from the southwest. His holdings in Torbecca were noted for much, but it was his scientists who brought him acclaim. They were among the premier minds in robotics. Schuul had recognized their uses early on and commissioned a defensive line of automated towers and bunkers. That did little to dissuade the notion of him being ridiculed among his peers.

Brentor looked the man over, surprised to see the ceremonial sword belt cinched around his waist. His yellow and red clothes spoke of a certain rigid formality almost as much as the tense look on his face.

"I am glad I caught up to you before the council began," Grushm said with empty sincerity.

Brentor kept walking. "Grushm, what's on your mind this morning?"

"The council is in uproar. Accusations against Scura have us all in disbelief."

Brentor frowned. "Nothing has been proven yet. The investigation into the assassinations has not been concluded. Do not be so quick to jump to conclusions."

"Even so, I would hate to think of Emleth's sacrifice going unrewarded."

"Sacrifice?" Brentor asked incredulously. "I never thought of his murder as a sacrifice. What happened to the rest of you being so engrossed with your own fears?"

"Time heals," Grushm replied softly, as if offended. "You should appreciate that, Brentor. You forget that my lands sit on the western side of the Geic Mountains as well. The Great Barrier Jungle isn't as formidable as it once was. My machines are ready to defend should the Ugri advance, but they have been untested in actual combat. Emleth's murder is far from my mind."

Brentor halted suddenly. "I assume you are more than willing to accept the new Unified Army because of that? How do your retainers feel about that? Do your townsfolk appreciate you donating most of your crops and supplies just a few short months before winter sets in?"

Grushm's eyes flew wide with rage. "Your accusations come too easily. If my lands were as safe from harm as yours, I would be comfortable as well."

"The placement of my holdings has nothing to do with my decisions. All I have asked for is concrete proof that the Ugri are responsible for the recent attacks," the older lord calmly deflected.

"If not the Ugri, then who?"

"That, my friend, is what troubles me the most. Come, we have new members to induct," Brentor said.

The gavel slammed down, announcing the call to order. Lord Brentor entered the council chambers in a dark green gown, glowering at those assembled. The remaining eight were dressed the same but bore no emotion. The ceremonial robes had not been worn in years, and never for such a dire event. The three empty seats mocked him silently.

"This session is called to order," his gravelly voice echoed around the circular chamber. "Bring in the applicants."

Lord Mans rose, strode confidently to a small wooden door on the far side, and knocked once. Heads turned to follow. The door groaned open, a thin film of dust drifting to the ground. Three figures, two men and one woman, marched into the center of the chamber and faced Brentor in a line with their hands clasped behind them. The gavel banged once more.

"Fellow lords of Lethendweil, today is not one of sadness but one of acceptance. We recognize the passing of our peers and accept new ones into our fold. Are there any last objections to the three standing before you? Any fault you find that disqualifies them from standing to your left or right?"

One by one, they answered, "No."

Brentor nodded curtly. "Then today we welcome our newest peers with the solemn pledge that they put the good of the land before personal interests. There can be no question of loyalty or petty ambition. The twelve kingdoms of Lethendweil must remain united, or all will fall to darkness. These three nobles come to us in uncertain times and do not have the luxury of time to learn their roles. The drums of war beat from shore to shore. But let not that put sorrow in your hearts," he told the three. "These are still glad times, for you will make this council strong as it ever has been. Orthis Gel, turn and take your place as the Lord of Orean."

The old Gel bowed graciously and walked to his chair. Newfound dignity was etched on his stern face.

"Presha Von, turn and take your place as the Lord of Vaade."

She curtsied formally and did the same. More than one man watched the way her body moved beneath the flowing robe.

"Kartis Thu, turn and take your place as the Duke of Carmak."

His dark skin concealed any emotion as he followed suit. Brentor waited until Thu was seated before slamming the gavel again.

"My fellow lords and lady, welcome. You are now part of this council and the voices of your lands," he announced.

Applause circled the chamber, intermixed with an occasional whistle. Yet each noble on the council silently and secretly wondered where the three newcomers stood on the issue of the war. Lines were being drawn, and there was no room for anyone to just stand by and see what happened next. The applause died down, allowing Brentor to continue. Much was left to be done, and this was the first time in nearly two weeks that all twelve kingdoms were represented.

"Council members, I regret to cut this celebration short, but we are facing an unprecedented crisis and must focus our attention on more dire matters."

He paused long enough for them to settle back in their seats and fall silent. "Eight days ago, we received a report that a small village in Durn was attacked and utterly destroyed by unknown forces. There were no survivors. Unlike the assassinations of our fellow nobles, there is no evidence to suggest this was random. We do, however, have reason to believe that agents from Reven were involved."

The council chamber erupted. Scura's face turned deep red despite his foreknowledge of this. His allies demanded further investigation while his enemies called for justice. Brentor watched their faces carefully for signs of treachery, hoping one of them might give a clue to the nature of the true attackers. He slammed the gavel harder.

"Order! There will be order in this council!"

"What proof do you have to make such a claim?" Lord Klesh asked once the commotion quieted enough for him to be heard.

"A body was found among the dead villagers. Whether it was overlooked or left to deceive us, we cannot be sure, but the body was dressed in the uniform of House Scura. Until contrary evidence arises, we must assume that Scura is somehow involved."

The council sat in stunned silence. Scura leaned back into his chair and folded his arms across his chest. The others stared at him, silently demanding an explanation, a reason for them not to believe. Finally, he stood.

"Fellow council members, I stand humbly before you with but a single request. Do not be so rash to dole out judgments before hearing what I have to say. This council was formed on the backs of men who were no strangers to murder and political positioning. It is true that my father was considered mad by some, but his quest for power ended with him on the night he was murdered."

"Genetic manipulations and legions of terrorists razing the lands are not the legacy I would crave," Mans growled. His people had suffered the most at the former Baron's ill desire.

"I am not my father," Scura replied harshly. "His aggressions against the lords of Lethendweil hold no bearing on this matter. Friends, is it not possible that one of my uniforms could have been stolen? Used by my opponents to implicate me? These are not the civilized times that we wish for. In fact, it is very possible that this was not one of my men at all.

"People disappear along the frontier all of the time. Men leave lands for better opportunities, and now we have a combined army massing in the west. It is no secret that some of us in this chamber do not see eye to eye. This man could even have been kidnapped by the Ugri before the raid. Am I to be accountable for everyone wishing to do harm to my name? If so, tell me now so that I may act accordingly."

Brentor held his hands up. "You are not on trial, Baron. I have brought this matter to the council to discover the truth."

"One man's truth is another's deceit," Scura countered.

The two locked gazes, neither willing to break away. Brentor ground his teeth slowly while narrowing his glare. Scura remained unfazed.

"Baron Scura, will you allow a commission to be sent to the Plateau to learn the truth of what happened in Hasjef?" Brentor asked suddenly.

Scura sat defiant. "I will not. If you wish to inspect my lands, then you will come yourself, Lord Brentor."

A light knock thankfully interrupted Brentor's dark thoughts of the approaching war.

"Enter," he commanded.

Lord Mans glided in, followed closely by Lord Schuul of Xiolen and the recently inducted councilwoman Presha Von. Schuul immediately noticed the half-empty bottle of port and nodded appraisingly. His lands were known for producing some of the finest wines in Lethendweil, and seeing a quality selection on the council head's desk spoke volumes. Presha Von folded her violet and crimson dress up and sat in one of the thickly padded leather chairs by the fireplace. Winter was coming, so most of the offices kept fires burning.

The woman was an enigma to Brentor. He knew her by reputation only. Looking upon her was a minor pleasure. She was attractive with long flowing brown hair and almond eyes that sparkled in the firelight. Presha was the kind of woman who spent hours keeping her body in shape, as much for the effect it had on men as for her own conscience. She interlaced her fingers over one knee, manicured nails white tipped and clear. The tight smile suggested impatience and was the only mar to her perfect skin.

She was the first to speak. "Now what?"

Two words. Brentor tried hard not to frown. That was it, just two words powerful enough to convey the implications of the future. *She's not even officially on the council for one day and has the nerve to ask questions that none of the senior members did. Perhaps having her will prove a blessing.*

Brentor finished his glass of wine and said, "The situation is…unclear."

"Unclear?" Mans blurted out. "He's called for the final vote. It cannot be any clearer. Scura must be stopped now while we still are able to do so."

"How do you propose we do that, Lord Mans?" Presha asked politely. She may have been the newest member of the council, but she was well versed in the political nightmare of Lethendweil. "From what I have gathered, your support is thin at best. Grushm is the only other who will vote with you."

"And he is already overtaxed with campaign preparations," Schuul pointed out. He saw the danger pressing in from all sides. "Scura has been getting out of control ever since Emleth's death. We are in a dangerous position, Brentor."

"Surely there is some obscure law that can be used to remove Scura from power," Presha suggested.

Brentor's smile was grim yet sincere. "Scura is hardly the reckless sort he portrays. I believe he wants us to go to Reven, but for what purpose I cannot say."

"What is this talk?" Mans asked angrily. "Baron Scura is nearly as dangerous as his father was. It is a good thing the boy murdered him when he did, or we'd all be under that foul banner. You'll send us all to ruin by going up into those black mountains!"

"Calm yourself, Mans. We have not reached the point of open treachery yet. I think Presha might be on to something," Schuul offered.

"Really, Mans, I thought you made of stronger bones," purred Presha.

"My bones are just fine," he replied with a rueful smile.

Schuul immediately recognized the look in Mans' eyes and tucked it away for future use.

Brentor ignored the murder comment. He, too, had suspicions, but there was absolutely nothing linking Scura to the death. "Scura might be telling the truth. Anyone can get a hold of a uniform and plant a body. More than likely, he was a convict. The real question is why; why would one of us want to commit such a crime?"

"We are already faced with war. Dividing us might give one side a clear advantage," Schuul said thoughtfully. "I think we should give Scura his wish. Vote to send the council to Reven and learn the truth of it for good."

"Risk the entire ruling body on the whims of a man we cannot trust?" Brentor asked doubtfully.

"Scura has many faults, vanity being one of them, but I do not believe he would be so careless as to kill us all on the eve of the campaign," Presha said. "How would he maintain control of so many different armies?"

"Do we keep some of our forces in reserve?" Mans asked. "He wouldn't be able to consolidate power with all of our forces committed in the field."

"Scura is too powerful to defeat without concrete evidence of his treachery," Brentor warned. "We must be careful with how we proceed."

Schuul added, "I fail to see how keeping some of our fighting strength back will avert the potential for disaster. We should act now. Complacency will be our damnation."

"No one has mentioned war between the houses," Presha said cautiously.

The three lords stared down at her in disbelief. No one wanted such to occur, but the possibility was not as remote as they wished.

"Should it come to war among the lords, we will need as many soldiers as possible. General Shiramon is most assuredly siding with Scura. The two of them combined have more military might than the other ten," Brentor told them. "If Scura is planning some sort of treachery, he will throw our forces into the front lines with the hopes of breaking us thoroughly. We would be sorely outmatched in any case. Even without the war, there is no way to meet them on the open field."

Schuul stifled a yawn. "What of the other two newly elected lords? Where do they stand? Can they be trusted?"

"Puppets already in Scura's pockets," Presha Von smiled politely. "They were undoubtedly bought before Emleth's assassination. Do not count on them for support."

"Two, but not three?" Mans asked.

Her face hardened. "What are you trying to say, Lord Mans?"

Mans folded his arms across his chest and nervously ran his tongue around the inside of his right cheek. "You claim the others have already been bought. Perhaps that is true, perhaps not. I only question why you have not been bought as well, unless there is something you would like to tell us?"

Her cheeks flushed crimson, an incredulous look briefly flashing across her face. "I am no puppet, Mans, I assure you. Scura came to me asking for support in the war, but no more. I am not interested in warfare. My sole focus is seeing to my lands and people. Scura does not have enough money to peak my interest."

"Regardless, Vaade is no longer safe. Baron Scura is hiding something sinister, I fear. It is our responsibility to find out what," Brentor cut in.

Presha offered a false smile. "Brentor, you are always so depressing. We cannot even be sure he is up to anything. What if Scura merely wants to end the threat of the Ugri for future generations? You cannot condemn a man if he hasn't committed a crime."

"What, then, do you propose?" Schuul asked. A hint of anger traced his words.

"We hear him out, make him think that we are overly interested," she replied. "He telegraphs his thoughts every time he speaks. Scura may be many things, but he is not a complicated man."

Brentor thought she had already spent a lot of time thinking this through. He couldn't say why, but that disturbed him.

Mans snorted a laugh. "Scura has an army of nearly ten thousand. That is more than enough to secure the entire eastern half of the continent once we are out of the way."

"And do what with them? He can hardly keep an occupying force in every major city, and then there is the Conclave. What do you think they will do once they discover that he has usurped the rule of law?"

"The Conclave?" Schuul asked mockingly. "Vau Prime might as well be in another universe for all of the support the Conclave has given."

"They sent a senior Inquisitor and a detachment of Prekhauten Guards," she countered too smoothly.

Brentor decided that she knew far too much for someone in her position.

"A token gesture," Mans said. "One Inquisitor and a hundred guards are nothing compared to the amount of military power he has."

Presha disagreed. "We all know how fast an Inquisition fleet can be in orbit. Their battleships would make quick work of any concentrated amount of soldiers. All we have to do is discover the truth and show faith."

"Faith?" Brentor asked. "I find it difficult to have faith in ghost forces. If the Conclave were worried about Lethendweil, then why hasn't this Inquisitor come to introduce himself to us? In fact, where is here? My sources tell me that he and a squad of guards took a shuttle to Prophet Isle in the company of a Blood Witch no less. No, the Conclave does not see our political troubles worthy of their attention or resources. The incident at their prison facility has priority. We are alone."

"Could it be that Scura is involved with whatever happened up there?" Schuul asked suddenly. It hadn't occurred to any of them that the lord of the Plateau might be a player in the Conclave trouble.

Presha Von passed him a wary glance that lasted for barely a second.

"To the best of my knowledge, there is no one from Crimeat incarcerated there," Brentor told them. "The Conclave has always been secret about its establishments. I couldn't get Father Stall to tell me anything when the Inquisitor first arrived."

"Perhaps that is for the best. We do not need them involved with our daily lives," Mans said.

"A moment ago, you wanted their help," Presha commented snidely.

"Mind your tongue. I'll not be lectured by a woman who has hardly had time to wear her title," Mans snapped.

"Enough, both of you!" Brentor scowled, hands clenched. "We need to focus on Scura. Let the Conclave worry about their business. I'll get involved once Stall comes to us and asks for help. Until then, we need to find a way to stop this war."

"I think we are missing a key point in all of this," Schuul offered. "Scura may have numbers, but we hold the advantage. He cannot hold any terrain he conquers, should it come to that. The people won't stand for it. There will be an insurgency within a month and civil war shortly thereafter."

"We are getting ahead of ourselves. Scura's ambitions are still unclear. It is easy to sit here and accuse him based on half-truths and suppositions. The bottom line is that we have no concrete evidence that Scura was behind the assassinations or the attack on Hasjef. We are going to have to concede and go to Reven." Brentor wasn't pleased but it was the only way he could see through the problem.

"I don't like it. That path is too dangerous," Mans told them.

"There is no easy way ahead," Brentor countered. "We stand at a crossroads to an uncertain future."

Presha took a sip of wine, enjoying the sweet textures. "Gentlemen, at the risk of being repetitive, I suggest we get the Conclave involved. After all, what point is there to them being on our world?"

Brentor winced, the onset of a headache stabbing tiny blades behind his eyes. He was tired, and this constant bickering didn't do him any good. He almost found himself wishing that Emleth was still alive and running the council but quickly realized that no amount of wishful thinking was going to change the fact that he and two others were dead. The mess they'd left behind would have to be enough. He reluctantly admitted that Presha was right. The Conclave had significant presence on almost every inhabited planet in the universe. The only major exception was Kharsis, the planet of the No God.

Brentor looked to each of his peers before holding up his hand for silence. "I think that Presha Von might have a point. We cannot hope to win alone. Ursal Prowl and Danja Stall have involved themselves in our affairs for as long as I can recall. It is time to call them to task."

"Prowl was in the audience seats during the induction ceremony," Schuul offered, "though I did not see Father Stall."

"He is a busy man. I'm sure there was a valid reason for his absence," Presha said. "We are forgetting one key piece in all of this."

"That being?" Brentor asked.

"The Ugri. I know it has been ages since anyone has even tried to contact them, much less see one alive, but that does not make them our enemies. We still might have a chance at finding peace with them."

"Not once the first bombing run ends," Mans commented.

"That is beyond our control for the moment," Brentor cut in. "Right now, our primary goal must be to determine Scura's guilt or innocence. One way or another, this internal feud must end. I fear it is the only way our society has a chance at surviving."

Presha finished her wine. "I shall go and find Father Stall."

Brentor nodded in agreement. "Good. Mans, go and inform the Baron that we will take him up on his offer to visit Reven. Personally, I would like to see his vaunted military powers for myself before I start having nightmares about them."

They rose and headed for the door. Brentor slammed the last swallow of wine and wiped a drop from his lip. He watched his allies go, all the while wondering if they were going to be strong enough to weather the approaching storm. One thing was certain; once the dust was settled and the bodies were counted, Lethendweil was never going to be the same. Mans pushed open the aged wooden door and was nearly bowled over by a courier in dark brown livery. The youth's face was ashen.

"My lords, come quickly. There has been a murder," he all but cried out.

NINETEEN

3210 A.G. (After Gods), Ugri Lands, planet Crimeat.

Mollock Bolle awoke with a start. His eyes were streaked with red. His hands trembled. Dried tears stained his cheeks, leaving trails through the grime. He couldn't breathe. The air was oppressive. It had been a long time since he last felt like this, almost immediately after discovering one of the universe's terrible truths.

Elisa appeared quickly, offering what water they had. She bore a concerned look. "What is it?"

"Nothing," he said after draining the water bowl. It was brackish and old but helped ease the pain in his throat. "Just a dream I used to have."

That doesn't make sense. Elisa took the bowl back and crouched down beside the old man. She had a newfound respect for Mollock, despite the horror his tale had produced. Under normal circumstances, she would not have believed a word he said, but her experiences with the Bloody Man around the same time left an open mind. No fool, Elisa was both afraid and inquisitive.

"Dreams do not normally have such an effect," she said cautiously.

His smile died as soon as it formed. "This one has. Funny, I haven't had it in a very long time. I wonder why now."

"Could it have something to do with what you told me earlier?"

He titled his head in thought. "Possibly. I never really thought about it like that. Although there was one other time this happened, now that you mention it."

Finally, a little more of the truth. "When was that?"

"I visited a friend, long ago. Oh, not much after they sent their creatures after me. Those were terrible times. No nightmare has ever held so much power. I remember talking with him before *it* came. He asked me what I dreamt of. My answer was a single word. Winter. I dream of winter. The cold, the snows. I dream of a universe covered with the frigid chill of death." He fell silent.

Elisa rubbed her right forearm absently, soothing away the goose flesh. "Why winter?" she asked once she worked up the courage.

"I do not know. The cold reminds me of death."

"You believe this is what is coming?"

He nodded. "Yes. For all of us. I cannot say why, but the winter will be the harbinger of the end for us."

Elisa wished she hadn't gotten him talking. Life had seemed less worrisome without his ranting. She'd spent the last day going over everything she knew about the Ugri and the eastern kingdoms and had come up with the same conclusion as before. The coming war made no sense. There was nothing the Ugri had worth taking, and the Ugri had no aspirations of going beyond the Great Barrier Jungle. She frowned. *What did I miss? Is it man's nature to just take without any thought of those who came first?*

She found the future worried her more than before. Her life had been focused into a singular purpose that, admittedly, was unachievable. The Bloody Man was as much of an enigma today as it was fifty years ago. There were no recorded sightings in all the years since, leaving Elisa to wonder about the significance of his arrival in Kovlchen. Coincidence seemed highly unlikely. The Bloody Man must have wanted something, but what? Elisa was at a loss.

Scrambling to her feet, she left Mollock where he lay and went back to the front of the cell. Elisa didn't see a point in worrying over a twelve-foot giant from her past when the future was decidedly short. She and Mollock were going to end up on a spit, roasting in flames if she couldn't find a way to escape. The Ugri had taken all her weapons. They'd been very thorough in that regard. A quick look around the cave confirmed her worst suspicions. There was nothing she could use as a weapon, at least not effectively. Elisa felt helpless for only the second time in her life.

"Don't mind me," Mollock told her as if sensing her rising despair. "I am an old man. My words hold no meaning."

She didn't think that was true. "Mollock, your words carry more weight than you think. Our lives have been shaped by outside influences. Nothing either of us has done was for ourselves. We've been forced into this position, and neither of us can tell why."

"What are you going on about? I know exactly why my life is a joke," he retorted with false anger.

She shook her head. "I don't think you do. Think about it. The coincidence that my entire village was exterminated at roughly the same time as you making that discovery in the Bothwel Mountains is too much."

Curiosity started to get the better of him. "What do you mean? I knew nothing about the attack on your village."

"I think they are related, and you hold the key. Shiramon knew what he was doing when he had Piett hire me to come after you. It is like wrapping up two loose ends at the same time."

Elisa felt suckered and foolish. She'd done everything they wanted, and it was all a lie. Mollock Bolle wasn't a wanted man; he was an information hazard. The obvious hammered her harder than she anticipated. Should they successfully escape the Ugri, she and Mollock had nowhere safe to go. Shiramon didn't act alone, and if all the wrong people were expecting them to die at the hands of the Ugri, they couldn't go anywhere near a civilized kingdom. Elisa cursed softly at her ignorance.

"Mollock, we need to get out of here, and I need your help," she finally said. "We only have one chance at getting out of this whole damned mess. Are you with me?"

He leaned forward just enough to breathe easier. "What do you have in mind?"

"I need to get you back to Reven."

Her words, simple as they were, carried finality. Mollock recognized it for what it was; a suicide mission. "No. I am not going back to that place. Do you understand what you ask? I barely survived the first time. Gods damn it; my life has been ruined because of what I found. There is nothing in those caves except a lingering death."

"We already live with that death!" she practically shouted back at him. "Wake up, Mollock. No one is going to help us, and…I need you."

His eyes widened. *Here's something new.* "What could you need with a broken man? I have nothing of value left in me."

She struggled to maintain composure. Lethendweil was changing, and unless she wanted to end up in an unmarked grave, she had to change with it. The time for acting alone was gone, replaced by the sudden urgent need for companionship, even from one as odd as Mollock Bolle. He represented answers to the questions that had plagued her for most of her life. Elisa suddenly felt renewed purpose. Her intent changed.

Elisa spun on him, her face tightened. "Mollock, I need you. You can help me find out why my village was destroyed. This is my best and only chance at ever finding peace. We have the opportunity to end it for good."

"To what end? My life is spent, Elisa. I am less than a shadow of what I could have been. The hunt has taken its toll. I have nothing left."

Unacceptable. Old man, I will drag you by your neck all the way to the Plateau if I must. "Listen to me, Mollock. We are getting out of here, and you will take me to Reven. I want answers, even if you have already abandoned hope. One way or another, you are coming with me. Help me or stay out of the way until I am done, but don't dare back down now."

He admired her in new light. There was strength shining through that she never knew she had. Decades of forced vengeance and compounding hatred had shaped her but failed to define her true self. Here, trapped in an Ugri cave far from home, Elisa was discovering the truth. Mollock smiled tightly. She was going to be a very formidable woman in the future.

"Well, then, it seems I am left without choices," he relented.

"Neither of us has had a choice for a very long time," Elisa told him. *I'm done being a puppet, doing everyone else's work while they sit back and wait for me to die. They may have made me what I am, but I'll be damned if I let them break me.* Elisa vowed to destroy the dark council.

Passion flared to life in her hardened eyes as she outlined her plan for escape.

The now familiar scuffling of heavy Ugri feet awakened her. Her fingers curled around the only rock she had found large enough to use as a weapon. It had taken her the better part of two hours prying it free from the cave wall. Half of her nails were broken. Grime so thick it started lifting the unbroken nails away from the flesh pained her other fingers. Elisa worked through the pain. She knew that it was going to get much worse in a short period of time. Even if her plan succeeded, there was little chance of them surviving long enough to see Reven. With no water and no supplies, they would be fortunate to get halfway through the jungle.

Elisa cleared those thoughts away. Her priority was to escape. She slowly opened her eyes, their light blue color lost in the darkness. Despite years of hunting men, her heart quickened. It was unfortunate that she had to do this to the Ugri guard. He was only doing his duty, but he had become the embodiment of all her pent up rage. Elisa watched as the torchlight fell over the first few meters of the cave. *One guard; they are careless.*

The gate opened with an earthy grinding sound that echoed in her teeth. The Ugri slammed the torch into its crude holder so he could deliver their food and water. Elisa waited until he was close enough. She moved fast, leaping up and bringing the rock down on the Ugri's temple. Once. Twice. The stone struck with wet smacks. Dark blood poured from the fresh wounds. Elisa continued to attack. The Ugri grunted, dazed and confused. He managed to slam his elbow back, catching Elisa in the stomach as he staggered under her blows.

The air fled from her lungs. He slammed back again. Elisa curled her free arm around the Ugri's throat in a desperate effort to hold on. Her vision darkened. Flames lanced through her abdomen. Where was Mollock, she cursed. The Ugri roared back, driving her into the jagged rock wall. Tiny barbs of pain spread across her back. Elisa struck him three quick times. She lowered her aim and was rewarded by the Ugri crying out as he lost his right eye. Elisa grinned savagely and continued to attack the wound.

The Ugri sagged. He recognized death approaching. The sharp pain in his chest was unexpected. Heart blood pumped down his bare chest, and he fell dead. Elisa rolled forward over the corpse. Mollock Bolle looked down on her with a mixture of horror and respect.

"I have never seen anything like that," he uttered.

She looked up, noticing the cooling blood dripping off the Ugri's short dagger in his hand. His eyes seemed empty to her.

"I...I've never killed anyone before," he said with a hushed tone.

Elisa was at a loss. Comforting others was not one of her strong suits. Mollock helped her up, and it was all she could do to stand. Her vision went in and out. The pain running down her back was excruciating, but at least she didn't think anything was broken.

"You did well," she gasped. Elisa squeezed her eyes shut. Breathing hurt. Thinking hurt. She wanted to curl up into a little ball and wipe the pain away.

Mollock dropped the blade and eased her into a sitting position.

"Thank you," she managed. Talking hurt.

"What do we do now?"

Elisa wanted to laugh. *Now I need to find medical attention, a bottle of whiskey, and a few weeks of rest*, she thought. Aloud, she replied, "Grab the sword. We need to move before others come."

She was surprised no one else had shown up. The noise from the struggle must have aroused suspicion. Elisa expected more guards any moment. The one chance she and Mollock had for escape was narrowing.

Mollock hung his head. "You need rest."

"There is no time."

"But…," he started to protest.

She cut him off with a withering glare. "Help me up. We need to head as far away from here as possible. More Ugri will be coming."

Elisa bit back a cry when Mollock hauled her onto her feet. She took the sword and tested the weight. While she much preferred her own weapons, especially the double-barreled pulse rifle, Elisa resigned herself to using the crude weapon. She drew a couple of deep breaths. "Now or never," she muttered.

With a curt nod, she motioned Mollock forward. The irony of the pair almost made her laugh. She was not far from being crippled, and he was old enough to be courting death. They weren't going to make it very far, and she was in no condition to put up much of a fight. Elisa let her mind idly wander to the different ways the Ugri might cook her.

Night was at its darkest. Elisa guessed that dawn wasn't far off. There was a chance most of the Ugri were asleep. Newfound hope warmed her heart and gave her strength. Elisa stepped into the open and froze. Her eyes moved slowly over each inch of their surroundings. She didn't sense anyone close, but that didn't mean much. She was lost in an alien land and had no idea which direction the jungle was. They would have to wait for dawn to get their bearings. Time was as much her enemy as the Ugri.

Elisa looked sharply at Mollock. "Come on."

Night sounds echoed across the camp. Insects chirped. Fires cackled softly. Plains bats darted by, but there was no sign of any more Ugri. Elisa urged Mollock to move faster. Fortunately, the caves were near the rear of the camp. Most of the warriors would be centralized around the stone throne Kulaam Lune used.

They made it a few more steps before her blood froze. An Ugri warrior lumbered across their way. Still half asleep, the Ugri had stumbled off to relieve himself. Heading back to his bed roll, his eyes flew wide as he realized what was happening.

Elisa threw the sword as hard as she could. She felt something in her right side tear. Her aim was true, surprisingly. The blade buried itself in the Ugri's throat. His thick hands flew to his neck, but the artery was already severed. Blood pumped through his fingers. The Ugri died with a strained gurgle.

Elisa wasn't the sort to believe in luck. She'd seen and done too many things to believe that an imaginary force shaped the course of her destiny. Mollock was more impressed. She'd performed two miraculous feats within a matter of minutes. He wasn't used to a life of warriors or combat. Such raw death churned his stomach yet left him with growing fascination. He let his thoughts drift idly to doing the same, unsure if he had the ability.

Elisa collected the sword and stripped the dead Ugri of another blade. Better armed, she felt some of the strength return. "Keep moving. There will be more."

Mollock mumbled something unintelligible and kept going. His mind was drifting elsewhere. Elisa eyed him, searching for any signs that he was beginning to crack. Neither noticed the high-pitched shrill of aircraft engines until it was too late.

Explosions rocked the ground. Compressions hammered into their skulls, threatening to drive them mad. Rocks and debris blasted outward. Elisa slipped, dragging Mollock down with her. Flames and shrapnel reduced the Ugri village to ruins. The bombs started a grass fire that quickly spread into the savannah. Screams competed with the fading terror produced by the bombing run.

Elisa clamped both hands over her ears. She tried to close her eyes, hoping to avoid seeing death racing towards her, but the temptation was too great. Ugri were running everywhere. None were interested in the prisoners. Survival instincts took over as waves of sheer panic swept over them. Mollock Bolle stood and raised his arms to the skies. Tilting back his head, Mollock laughed victoriously. Madness took him. His senses were overloaded. The explosions. The indiscriminant death. The cries. The flames. He laughed and kept laughing.

You sick bastard, Elisa thought. "Get down! You're going to get killed like that!"

Her voice was barely discernible above the surrounding chaos. Mollock ignored her. The bounty hunter had served a purpose, but she was so wrong about everything. She was the key to it all. He *had* to get her to the Plateau. She *had* to see what he had found in those caves. It was the only way. Mollock tried to pull her up, but she resisted. He wanted to tell her not to worry, that it was going to be all right. She wasn't going to die here. There was purpose to her life, and she had yet to discover it. All of this was just shaping the future.

A group of silver-bellied fliers swooping in low and began firing energy weapons into the milling Ugri. Bodies disintegrated in red spray. Elisa watched, dumbfounded. For all their bravado, the Ugri were no match for the technology of the east. A blinding beam of golden light lashed up and struck the trail flier. Elisa blinked. Where had the Ugri gotten a plasma cannon? The superheated energy punched a hole through the belly and out the roof. Black smoke poured from the flier as it started to go down.

The remaining fliers broke off and turned away. Hundreds of bodies littered the camp. The Ugri force was reduced considerably, though Elisa had no way to tell how many there had been to begin with. She heard Kulaam Lune's voice shouting orders in their native tongue. It wasn't going to be long before they reorganized and started sifting through the destruction. Elisa forced herself up. She grabbed Mollock by the collar, jerking him out of his daze.

"Move!" she snapped.

Elisa finally had a plan. The flier hadn't exploded when it crashed, and that meant it might still be flyable. She pushed Mollock in front, forcing him to leave whatever sick form of bliss he had discovered. The old man had become a liability, and she hesitated bringing him with her. Unfortunately for her, Mollock Bolle was the only one alive who could get her into the caves of Reven. *The right caves*, she corrected herself. Baron Scura was known for treachery, and there was little doubt the way onto the Plateau was heavily guarded. Once they got past the initial defenses, the rest should be easy enough. Mollock alone knew the location of the hidden caves and the source of all the madness that had consumed her life.

"Isn't it beautiful?" Mollock asked suddenly. His voice was unsteady, as if darkness lurked just beyond reach.

She frowned. "What are you talking about? Get going. We have to get to that downed flier before the Ugri regroup."

He barked a laugh. "And do what? It was shot down, Elisa. We must find another way."

"There is no other way. If they missed the engine and the cockpit, I can get it back in the air. It might be our only shot at getting to Reven."

Mollock snapped up at the name. Reven. Of course, he'd almost forgotten. The lone city on the Plateau. He shuffled along as fast as his old body could go, almost dragging Elisa with him. The odd pair slipped out of the Ugri camp unnoticed and made for the downed flier. Elisa's mind wandered briefly. What little she knew of the Ugri suggested they lacked any sort of technology. The plasma cannon proved that wrong. They had advanced weapons and were trained in how to use them effectively. Perhaps Mollock's dark council was more powerful than she gave them credit for.

They rounded a bank of scarred boulders and were rewarded by finding the wreckage. A body hung from the open canopy. Elisa left Mollock and rushed to the pilot. She gave a quick tug, and the body fell to the ground. She choked back the rising bile. His body was disintegrated from the waist down. She couldn't help but note how young he was. War was a cruel thing.

Elisa climbed the handful of rungs and took his seat. The glass was gone, shattered to oblivion, but the instrument panel seemed intact. Unwilling to leave anything to chance, she scrambled back to the ground and inspected the hull. Aside from the holes, there wasn't much damage. The engines were unmarked. She only hoped they started. The belly was ripped up from sliding across the uneven terrain but didn't pose a threat to flight.

Elisa took a breath. The cockpit was small. It was a one-person fighter-bomber designed for low-level attacks. She wasn't familiar with the model but had enough general flying skills that she *should* be able to get it in the air. A new noise broke her concentration. The Ugri had probably come to the realization that they had shot down one of the enemy fliers. Kulaam Lune would be leading the hunt to claim the glory.

"Climb aboard. Time is up," she ordered Mollock.

Mollock Bolle climbed unsteadily; much of his strength had been stolen during the imprisonment and the attack. He looked into the blood-stained cockpit. "Where am I supposed to sit?"

She grinned wryly. "That's not my problem. Get behind the pilot's seat and hold on. This is going to be a bumpy ride."

"Are you sure?"

Elisa despised being questioned. She shoved Mollock up. He fell into the cockpit and onto his head. "Move, old man."

Looking back over her shoulder, her fears were realized. A mass of angry Ugri warriors surged around the boulders. Kulaam Lune was at their head just like she'd predicted. Each had a feral attitude. They'd been blooded and wanted revenge. Clearly, they intended to take it out on the pilot. Unfortunately for Elisa, he was already dead. That left her and Mollock with two dull swords. Panic drove her faster.

Elisa hopped into the pilot's seat and scanned the instruments. She'd never flown anything this complicated before. A gnawing feeling carved a hole in her stomach. She was used to high-pressure situations, but this was unlike any previous experience. Elisa blew out a calming breath and finally found the ignition. She lightly touched the button and was rewarded by the mechanical purr of the engines firing. Raw power surged through the flier, trembling the surrounding area. Elisa jerked back on the throttle and felt the wounded flier slowly begin to rise.

She cringed as it bounced off the ground once before correcting the angle and accelerating. The flier surged forward. Elisa could have easily turned it to face the Ugri and opened fire with the forward cannons, but, despite her imprisonment, she felt no animosity. They were acting for the preservation of their species, and she just wanted to escape. Elisa gave the Ugri her engines and throttled up. The fumes and inertia knocked down the first three ranks while making the others take cover.

Elisa didn't look back as the wounded flier roared away from the Ugri camp. Fortune had provided her with the means to escape. She doubted it was going to be able to make it all the way back to Reven, but that was going to have to wait. All Elisa needed was for the flier to get her beyond the Great Barrier Jungle and General Shiramon's lands. The comforting folds of night slowly began to fade into a pale shade of grey. Elisa couldn't say why, but she felt like time was against them. She gave the flier more throttle.

TWENTY

3210 A.G. (After Gods), Durn, planet Crimeat.

Dawn was much colder than Seinz Shiramon preferred. He normally slept in past dawn, but there was no way he could remain in bed while thousands of men and women prepared for war. The only true military mind on the council, he had quickly been appointed Supreme Commander for the Unified Army. It was an unparalleled honor. Few had earned the title in the time since the twelve kingdoms ended hostilities. Opposition in the council kept him reigned in, more so than any other in the past. He resented Brentor and the simplistic view that peace could only be achieved through diplomacy. Shiramon scoffed at the naivety. Peace was won with an iron fist. The other nobles had grown weak, threatening to undo everything Shiramon had dedicated his life towards.

Shiramon was naturally shrewd. He viewed the position apprehensively. Scura's plans for war were still in the infant stages, and much could go wrong. Shiramon was only as good as his leash was long. Greed drove him. He wanted more, wanted to be unleashed on the Ugri and any who stood in the path of justice.

"General, a runner just came in for you," Geres Auk announced. The tall aide stood at a rigid position of attention. On loan from Reven, Geres was both an asset and a spy. Shiramon had no doubts that Auk was reporting everything back to the baron.

Shiramon nodded absently. The predawn sky was filled with the gentle lights of shuttles and troop transports streaming in from the kingdoms. The marshalling area north of the Spine River was overflowing with troops and material. Howitzers, light tanks and infantry columns littered the plains. Row after row of dark green tents looked like a small city. Supply trains took up acres of once empty farmland. Shiramon tilted his head back, his stomach rumbling at the smell of cooking meat and fresh brewed coffee.

"From whom?" he asked.

Geres frowned slightly, the gesture fading almost too quickly for Shiramon to notice. "He did not say."

"No one thought to ask?"

Geres's face darkened. "There are not many in your command tent with the ability to act without orders. The man who took the message is a farmer, I believe."

Farmers and stable boys. Shiramon cursed his luck. The majority of the Unified Army was comprised of peasants and volunteers too bored with home life for their own good. True soldiers numbered in the minority. Shiramon knew from experience that the combination was potentially deadly. A great number of men were going to die once battle commenced.

"Very well, I will be there shortly."

Geres Auk excused himself and disappeared back into the fading night. The mass of the Geic Mountains was becoming visible to the northeast, and the sound of rushing water from the river lessened as night died. Shiramon had chosen this land for a number of specific reasons. The river and mountains provided natural defensive barriers. The Great Barrier Jungle lay over a hundred leagues west of the encampment. He was safe here from the Ugri and any treachery from the other nobles who had yet to send their forces, namely Brentor and

Mans. It was no coincidence that neither had committed. They were the chief opposition to the war. Shiramon wondered what Scura's plans were for removing them for good.

He knew what he would do. Since he was a little boy, Seinz Shiramon had exhibited a unique blend of leadership traits. Other boys had flocked to him, eagerly drinking his thoughts and ideas. Leadership and tactics were natural abilities he'd decided to exploit early on. His bloodline was one of the purest military families, and he proudly traced his lineage back to when men first settled Lethendweil. His great-great grandfather had had the honor of leading the Unified Army against eastern invaders, making his now-famous last stand on the walls of Vaade. The walls and the battle were now only faded memories that historians loved to recite. Shiramon wore his great-great grandfather's sword with pride.

When he was still a small child, Seinz Shiramon had joined up with a group of off-world mercenaries looking for recruits. He still remembered the hunched shoulders and look of defeat from his father as he'd walked away in the morning mists. That was the last time Seinz ever saw his father. His mother had remained heartbroken until Seinz returned home some thirteen years later. Seinz had left a boy and returned a man, ruthless and cunning as the great beasts of the deep oceans. He strove to live up to his great-great grandfather's image, ruling with fear and respect.

Seinz Shiramon saw himself as a liberator. Others might look back on history and label him a traitor, condemning him forever. Lethendweil was mired in baseless politics and stagnant leadership. Progress was stalled. He and others like him were bringing new light to the twelve kingdoms. He was one of the few who slept without doubt or worry. A new dawn prepared to slash through the veil of night, and he stood on the cusp. Too many men were content to live through history; he wanted to make it.

Shiramon entered the command tent, a massive seven-tent structure that housed the various aspects of the army's command. Junior officers and senior sergeants moved from pod to pod with papers and data pads. A pair of armed guards flanking the main entrance snapped to attention and saluted with their rifles. He returned the salute and pushed inside. The smell of men in the field for too long assaulted his nostrils despite its familiarity. Battle maps and campaign plans littered numerous field tables and charts hanging from the walls.

Lieutenant Pulson noticed Shiramon enter and shuffled through the crowd of staff officers. A young man, Pulson was on his first duty assignment. His sandy brown hair matched his fatigues perfectly, and his light build suggested he was wiry. Pulson stopped and saluted.

"What is it?" Shiramon asked, taking his impatience out on the boy.

Pulson swallowed hard. "Sir, you have a guest in your quarters. He would not say where he came from or who he represents."

Shiramon resisted the urge to knock some of the Lieutenant's teeth down his throat. "What the fuck can you tell me, Lieutenant, or is everyone in this damned headquarters better suited for a firing squad?"

Trembling slightly, Pulson summoned what measure of courage he had and replied, "Sir, he is dressed in all black and will not remove his hood."

Shiramon flinched. Black robes and no faces could only mean one thing, and that was the last thing he needed in his headquarters on the eve of one of the most major campaigns to begin in a hundred years. He waved Pulson off and adjusted his uniform, if only slightly. The ranks parted to allow him by, and he found himself about to enter his personal tent much too soon. He wished he'd been born a common foot soldier. Then, none of what followed would be necessary.

The figure in black looked up at the rustle of tent flaps peeling back. Any emotion remained hidden behind his hood. Shiramon portrayed a look of leadership he certainly did not feel. The black figures troubled him greatly. They were a scourge, a stain on the nobility of Lethendweil. And they were strong. They always got what they wanted, and for one to arrive at his field headquarters boded ill.

"I am told you have a message," Shiramon said as nonchalantly as possible.

The figure in black, a man, nodded once. "Indeed, General. The winds are changing. Much that you once held dear is bankrupt."

"Speak plainly. I do not appreciate forked tongues."

Shiramon felt the hatred being directed at him. "Do not think me a simple man, Seinz. We have more power than even you can imagine. It would be a shame to find a nasty surprise in your quarters tonight."

"You dare threaten me!" Shiramon roared.

The figure in black stepped forward. "We threaten anyone we choose. The black council is now the true power in these lands. You would do well to remember that, General."

Shiramon puffed angrily but maintained his composure. He had little doubt this man was capable of killing him in his sleep. "The message."

A tense silence filled the chamber. "You are to begin the campaign. Send half of your army to the Great Barrier Jungle."

"What about the other half?"

"They will attack Torbecca first and then Berchenfel," came the reply.

He said it so matter-of-factly that Shiramon was caught off guard. Scura wanted to be rid of the peace sympathizers, but this was too much. Still, Shiramon knew that several of the nobles were preparing to head to Reven. Perhaps Scura had more planned than he had let on. Dangerous times were about to begin. The wholesale slaughter of the nobility promised to be messy and filled with retribution on those responsible. A purge might be necessary and even inevitable, leaving Shiramon wondering where it would stop. Death was not as fickle as men presumed.

He stared hard at the messenger. Questions demanded answers, but he realized there wouldn't be any forthcoming. The dark council, whoever they were, remained the most secret society in all Lethendweil, and they treasured information above all else. "This will not sit well with the men."

"They are soldiers. They get paid to do what they are told. Or perhaps you are not up to the task?"

Shiramon stiffened. "I will burn this continent to the ground if I have to. Do not doubt my resolve."

"Good. That is what we want to hear." He paused. "You will understand that there is the need for us to maintain contact, of course."

"How?" Shiramon asked sternly. He already guessed the answer.

"We will be in touch. Until that time, you can sleep well knowing that our agents are already within your ranks, just in case."

The figure in black bowed and slipped through the door flaps, leaving Seinz Shiramon stunned and slightly frightened. Threats never sat well with him, and now he was left with a spark of doubt for each person working for him. As much as he wanted, there was no way he could downplay the messenger's last words and ignore them. Shiramon reentered the main room of the tactical operations center and watched his staff go about their tasks. Which one was the spy?

New orders were issued two days later. Shiramon took his air car to the top of a sloping rise where he could see the expanse of the army. Hands on his hips, he calmly watched as his men continued breaking down the camp. He was tired. Sleep remained elusive since the visit from the dark council messenger. Shadows jumped at him, whispers behind his back infuriated. Shiramon felt like he was slowly going insane. Trust was lost, and he had no one to confide in.

He yawned. The combination of lack of sleep and growing paranoia prevented his natural passions about life as a soldier from arousing. He'd been a warrior since birth, often called an old soul trapped in a child's body. Shiramon was the consummate professional in every aspect of the term. His uniform was more than just clothing; it was a symbol of what he represented. Life had not been easy; in fact, it was the opposite. Long hours were spent pouring over details, agonizing over potential losses.

He did not have the squeamishness he saw in newer soldiers. They lacked experience and did not yet know if they would break when the sounds and smells of combat took over. Standing beside the corpse of what used to be your best friend was not an easy thing, he admitted reluctantly. Shiramon was a living legend. He'd slain more men than anyone else in Lethendweil. His deeds were sung throughout the ranks, and his quiet acceptance encouraged those myths to spread. Morale drove armies. He wanted men to think he was a god made flesh, comfortable knowing soldiers fought harder when they believed their commanding officer was a hero.

Rising trails of dust betrayed the movement of convoys already en route to Torbecca. The advance party left at dawn; five thousand crack infantrymen from his own kingdom. Shiramon trusted no one else to begin combat operations, especially against his fellow nobles. He prayed they would strike quickly enough to keep Lord Grushm entrenched. Surprise and lethality were everything. All the nobles believed that Shiramon was marshalling the army for a western advance. No one would be looking to their own walls. Shiramon wanted to laugh. Part of him was in disbelief that so many accomplished and senior rulers could be so blind as to truly believe one of the largest armies in history was mobilizing against an insignificant foe like the Ugri.

Shiramon let his thoughts turn back to the subtle comments from the messenger. Baron Scura had never insisted on assassinating Brentor before. The other three nobles were weak. They needed to be removed. While the details were made known, Shiramon correctly guessed the Vaumagians were involved. That presented new problems. He questioned who the assassins really worked for—Scura or the dark council. Could that be the source of the threat?

The decision to ignore Brentor might come back against them. The elder noble would never bow to tyranny. He was a threat. Killing him was a necessity if Scura's plan for domination had any chance of succeeding. Shiramon didn't see what they were doing as treason. The new Unified Army was his tool to wield as he saw fit. The liberation from old traditions and outdated ideals was beginning, and he rode the tide as it readied to crash into the sand. Whether Scura stood at the forefront or not remained to be seen. Shiramon had new doubts that the dark council was going to let either of them rule in the aftermath.

Enough nobles had been killed to make most of the population understand that the old ways were dead. Greed became the new king. Shiramon recognized the value of loss and shock. The unthinkable had been done. Lords of Lethendweil, Emleth especially, murdered in the sanctity of the most secure city in the land. Vaade was no longer safe. If assassins were able to strike down the ruling member of the council in his own quarters, no one was safe. The common citizen would never know that Emleth needed to be removed. He was too dangerous, too much of a veteran to leave loose. Killing him made sense as it had with Whitel. As lord of Orean and the Great Southern Desert, he had too much influence in the center of Lethendweil to be left alive. His desert warriors were among the fiercest in all twelve kingdoms. Now, they were a non-factor.

Poor Lord Parkhol had been killed for statistical value. He was young and relatively harmless, but youth often translated into uncertainty. Scura and Shiramon hadn't been sure which direction his vote would have gone in, so murder seemed the only viable option. But Brentor! The man was turning into a major obstacle. Wise and experienced, Brentor represented everything Scura was not. He wasn't going to be fooled by fine words and modest deeds. Shiramon had never liked him, but Scura would hear none of it. He rationalized that killing such a popular figure as Brentor invited disaster for their cause. Better to play it safe until they were assured of victory. Then Brentor would swing from the gallows.

Shiramon had argued for one decisive thrust into the heart of Lethendweil. The kingdoms were weak, in desperate need of a quick overhaul. He let his eyes wander from the departing vanguard to the early morning sky. Wisps of clouds stretched for as far as he could see. The air was chill, remarkably cooler than normal for this time of year. Winter was still weeks off, but the change had begun. Flights of geese speared across the sky, honking in passing. Swallows swooped down among the command tents before darting back to the distant groves of trees. Late autumn wildflowers bloomed in those areas untouched by the heavy footprint his army left.

"Excuse me, General," a middle aged major interrupted from the back seat of the vehicle.

Shiramon gently closed his tired eyes and turned back to the car. The moment was gone. "This had better be good, Major."

The major stiffened noticeably. "Sir, our long-range scouts are reporting back that they are within visual range of Torbecca."

It has begun. "How long until the main body arrives?"

"The commander assures me he will have the majority of his forces in position around Torbecca before nightfall. A secondary blocking force is moving into position, and the first supply convoy will be heading out near dusk."

Shiramon held up a hand for silence. He didn't need to know the movements of every single soldier in the Unified Army. There was time enough for that sitting through the endless briefings and situation updates that were to come. "Very well, Major. Inform me once the command is ready to move. I wish to be left alone for a while longer."

Clasping his hands behind his back, General Seinz Shiramon strolled off into the patch of wildflowers.

The jungle heat was already murderous, and it was just past dawn. Humidity levels were close to one hundred percent, making life miserable for Frez Belcum and his renegade Guardsmen. He finished his third canteen of the morning and cursed. Sweat soaked through his shirt, running down his face and back in heavy sheets. He hadn't been so miserable in years, and he was going to throw up if he drank any more water. His stomach sloshed angrily with every step he took, not only adding unnecessary weight but making him feel sluggish. Frez hated Crimeat more as this campaign lengthened. He wanted to contact Prowl and tell him the deal was off, but that wasn't his call.

"Morning, Boss," Brevel said good-naturedly.

Frez normally went into the jungle to find a measure of peace before the day started. There was a certain solicitation in the raw power the jungle displayed that soothed his mind. He looked back at his second in command. "I don't like to be disturbed when I am out here, Brevel; you know that."

Brevel held up his hands defensively. "I'm just the messenger."

"What is it this time?" Frez sighed.

"Captain wants to see you. He wouldn't say, but from what I gathered, we got another mission," Brevel answered.

"Hopefully not another one full of sleeping women and children."

Brevel shook his head. "Sometimes you are too cynical. I think this is a genuine military target this time."

That's a start. Feeling slightly better, Frez headed for the command post.

The moon wouldn't rise for another couple of hours, leaving the landscape plagued in near perfect darkness. The jungle was far behind them, and Sergeant Frez Belcum appreciated every moment. A light breeze cooled the grasslands east of Durn. It sent chills down Belcum's back. The oppressive heat and humidity of the jungle left all his force shivering in the late autumn chill.

He picked up his binoculars and stared down at the long, winding supply column inching steadily closer. Pleased as he was to finally have a military target, Frez Belcum couldn't help but wonder why they hadn't set up their base of operations in an area like this. The Prekhauten Guard were expected to fight in any terrain and weather, but the jungle was just damned ridiculous.

Frowning, he looked to Brevel and whispered, "Spread the word. We strike in ten."

Brevel disappeared, crawling back down the gentle slope from the observation post. The rest of the patrol was spread out along a short ridgeline at five meter intervals, weapons ready. Every other man was on watch while the remaining half tried to get a little rest. He never would have seen them if he weren't wearing his night vision visor.

Brevel tapped the closest man lightly on the leg and watched the gesture spread down the line. Random clicks and hums from weapons being taken off safe and energy weapons powering up told him what he needed to know.

He looked at their surroundings one final time before returning to Belcum. A large stream ran parallel to the road on the right, but they had placed two heavy machineguns on the far side just in case anyone got the idea to swim to safety. Three feet of anti-armor mines blocked the road twenty-five meters from the ambush line. Boulders and the ridge provided enough cover for his men to give all at least some measure of security. Satisfied that they were as ready as possible, Brevel wormed back to the OP.

"Here they come," Frez said over his shoulder.

The first of the trucks ponderously entered the kill zone. Running on blackout drive, none of the vehicles used their main lights. The only illumination came from tiny blue-green lights on each side of the front grill. Brevel grinned. They were marching to their deaths and would never know what hit them. The first truck struck the land mines and erupted in a massive ball of flames. Screaming men leapt from the ruined vehicle cab before the ammunition strapped down in the bed superheated and exploded.

Frez's men opened fire with shoulder-fired rocket launchers and a plasma cannon. Most of the vehicles were hit. Enemy soldiers in the rear vehicles jumped out to return fire but were cut down by the twin machines guns on the opposite side of the stream. Bodies piled up. The screams of the wounded and dying struggled to be heard over the massive amount of firepower being poured into the kill zone. The ambush was over quickly. All that remained was to go down there and finish it. Frez Belcum didn't appreciate having to kill wounded men, but their orders were very specific. No survivors; no prisoners. Unslinging his blackened ion rifle, he led the charge down the slope.

Snipers continued to pick off those who thought to use the cover of the wrecked vehicles. Heat from the flames was oppressive, driving black smoke into their lungs. Frez Belcum rechecked his safety for the third time and shouldered his rifle. He moved with all the precision and experience of a trained Guardsman. A body moved. He fired. The body slumped down and didn't move again. Step. Fire. Kill. Move. Frez and his men executed close to thirty survivors before reaching the rear of the convoy.

"Brevel, take a fire team and double back. I want to make sure this was it," he ordered. "The rest of you search the bodies in teams of two. I want a rifle trained on those bodies until you verify they are getting cold."

He blew out a long, deep breath. The adrenalin was fading. His heart rate slowed. Frez removed his helmet and stared at the scene with his own eyes for the first time. Any pride he'd found in his men dissipated quickly. The soldiers of the convoy were non-combatants. Most were supply specialists and mechanics. None of them ever expected to be involved in any real firefight. It was a sad fact of war, but not every fatality was a trigger puller. Men and women died simply because they wore a uniform.

Brevel returned twenty minutes later with a grim look.

"Is it done?" Frez asked softly.

"Done. There are no survivors." He left off the part about there being too many boys hardly old enough to use a rifle among the corpses. Frez didn't need that on his conscience. Too much damage had already been done over the course of the night.

Frez swept his gaze over the kill zone one final time. Strands of hair were matted to his forehead. Despite being pressurized, standard Guard helmets didn't prevent them from sweating.

"Plant frags in all of the vehicles. I don't want any identifying marks left behind for Shiramon to figure out what hit them," Frez said.

"What about the bodies?"

A partially burned corpse glared up at him with glossy eyes, accusing Frez of inhumane crimes. He felt sick. "Leave them for the crows."

Brevel started to protest, "But they are just…."

"They are not our problem. Have the medic check everyone for injuries. Let me know when we are green on sensitive items. Use the hand lamps to double check the site. We leave nothing behind," he snapped.

Brevel stared at him quietly for a moment, anger seething through him. "Nothing but the dead. They deserve some respect."

Frez jabbed an angry finger into Brevel's chest and all but shouted, "Not from me. We are soldiers in the Prekhauten Guard. This is not our world, not our fight. We have our task, and that is to ensure all our men survive. Now get the men checked out and call for the evac, Corporal."

Brevel stalked off. He'd suddenly become unsure of his best friend and squad leader. *This is getting too far out of hand.*

TWENTY-ONE

3210 A.G. (After Gods), Berchenfel, planet Crimeat.

A stiff breeze swirled against Tannus's calves, tickling the exposed flesh. His trousers had been shredded when the land mine exploded, his flesh torn apart by white hot bits of shrapnel. Most of the deep tissue wounds were healed, but the scars would remain for many long years before his skin completely regenerated. The frown on his face wasn't going anywhere, though.

Armed patrols filed out of Parvelon like streams of ants. He could have cut them down, a cold hand of divine justice with horrific splendor and disease, but that went against his core beliefs. Tannus never actually enjoyed hurting people, not even the bad ones, the ones with black rot entwined in their souls. The same could not be said for man. Mankind was petty and weak, at least so far in his experience. They hungered for power, for domination over all else. Those who stood in the way were run down and eliminated under the claim of the greater good. They sickened Tannus.

Son of the gods, he struggled to find some bright spot that might elevate the race to its full potential, but it was difficult. Every time he found hope, an event occurred that stole it away. Tannus very much wanted to leave this village behind and return to his flier, but the overzealousness of the crazed villagers prevented that from happening. They smelled blood and were being driven into a frenzy, probably by the same thug who had threatened Father Dye. Men like that came to power too easily, normally through ruthless means, and secured it by eliminating competition and collecting other malcontents to their banners.

The urge to return to Parvelon and put an end to this nonsense tempted him, but not strongly enough to keep him from finding his brother. He had to know the reason why Sorrow had come to this planet. Coincidence was a mortal concept. Tannus knew that everything happened for a reason. Discovering the truth might mean the difference between life and the deaths of tens of thousands.

The sound of barking dogs drew his attention. They'd be drawn to the scent of his blood. Frowning, Tannus knew what needed to be done and was reluctant to do so. He doubled back the way he'd come, following the path of a narrow stream towards the village wall. This time, he was careful to search for landmines. Father Dye was a good enough man, but he was old and would be unable to distract the others for long. Tannus needed time to distract his hunters and make it safely to his flier.

A small grove of oak trees offered the perfect cover for his twelve foot frame. His strength and size provided considerable advantage over mortals but became an inconvenience when it came to concealment. There were only so many places for a giant to hide. He grinned savagely at the irony as a handful of villagers came stomping across the fields towards his position. They carried torches and crude weapons. Most were outdated ion rifles, but there was the occasional sword and bolt action carbine. Tannus had nothing to fear. His size alone ensured they would panic and run, but he couldn't take the chance and rely on that alone.

"This way!" one of them, probably a tracker by trade, shouted.

The others shouted and brandished their weapons in the air. *Fools. They march to their deaths with little regard for what they hunt.* Tannus decided to leave the regret for after. They were almost in range. Tannus tensed, ready to strike. He noticed this group did not have dogs. *Even better.* When they were only a handful of meters away, he tore from the cover of the trees, roaring angrily. Fear struck them. A few dropped their weapons. One fired a wild shot into the night.

Tannus was among them before they had time to react further. His massive fists hammered into weak human flesh. Bones snapped. Organs burst. Men died with horror etched on their faces. Tannus hated what he was doing, but it was an unfortunate necessity if he had any chance of escaping cleanly. Sorrow had to be found at any cost, and these people were in his way. Less than a minute later, all seven villagers lay dead in a lopsided circle at his feet. Blood dripped from his fists. His heartbeat faster. It was over so fast, he didn't have the chance to work up a sweat. Tannus couldn't deny the empowering feeling he got from the act. He felt connected to his heritage, a part of the deep myths of cultures across the universe.

The blood stained his hands and clothes. His shoulder-length hair was wild, giving him a feral appeal. Fever threatened to consume him, old appetites resurfacing. It drove his passions, whispering to be let loose upon the world. A wild glaze tinted his eyes. The bloodlust was almost too much. He struggled to contain it, lest he be reduced to his brother's level. A noise startled him. The snap of a twig. He spun, hands raised in an assault position.

Father Dye stood there, mouth agape. His face was bruised and swollen. Tannus had readied himself to attack before realizing who it was. Shame burned his cheeks. The priest had been nothing but kind to him.

"You should not be here," he warned. "It is not safe tonight."

Dye hung his head. "I have no other place to go."

Tannus straightened and glanced back into the village. Flames licked high into the night sky. It took little to deduce that the town prefect had burned the church. He turned back to Dye, looking closely at his injuries. "Who did this to you?"

Dye swept his gaze over the dead men, men who had once attended his church and worshipped alongside him. Fears rose. He imagined Tannus sweeping through his entire village in less than a night, and the thought chilled his bones.

Tannus noticed his reluctance. "You have nothing to fear from me, priest."

Emotions finally got the better of him. Dye practically collapsed as he told Tannus how Hack had returned not long after with axes and torches, backed by a mob of angry men. They broke down the doors and ransacked the church, shouting obscenities and defiling many of the statues and holy shrines. Dye tried to stop them but was quickly beaten into submission. Satisfied the one they sought was gone, Lorden Hack had ordered the church burned and Dye put to death. It was only through the sudden change of heart of Ezre Sed, perhaps the youngest of the mob, that Dye snuck out the back door and escaped before his temple burned down around him.

Tannus felt genuine sorrow but did not know how to show it. Millennia of pointless combat and slaughtered innocents had left him emotionally deadened. He looked down on Dye with appreciation, though misplaced. "You are stronger than you want to believe, priest. Not many would have had the strength to stand before so many."

"Do not harm them," Dye said unexpectedly. "Lorden Hack is a cruel man, but he is only a product of his environment. The promise of war with the Ugri has turned many like him mad with newfound power. Cruel as he is, he is not at fault."

"No one forced him to put your church to flame! He and others like him are filth, stains to humanity. They cannot be allowed to continue unopposed," Tannus snarled.

Fresh anger gave him strength.

"He is not evil. I know this in my heart," Dye insisted. "Do not go back into the village. Too many have already suffered."

Tannus shot a quick look at the carnage he'd caused. He felt nothing. "These men were a necessity. You called me a god earlier. Such petty violence is intolerable. I need to get to Kovlchen quickly."

"Murder is intolerable."

"Would they have done differently? To me?" He gestured with his head. "To you? I can see, even in the dark, that you suffered greatly at their hatred. Where does justice lie if not in retribution?"

Dye spread his arms to encompass the bodies. "This is not retribution. Not a one of these men assaulted me or the church. You killed innocent men."

"Innocent is a relative term. These men came here to visit violence on any they found. I merely stopped that from happening. Do not quibble with me, priest. I have seen and done many things, not all of which I am proud of. My actions are my own, and I will live with the consequences."

Barking dogs stole his attention. Another group of hunters was coming. "I must go. This place holds nothing for me."

A pause, only the slightest hesitation. "Take me with you."

Tannus halted. *This is unexpected.* "I do not have time to care for you, priest. My task is my priority."

"I will not be a hindrance. I swear."

The dogs were getting closer. Tannus made out dozens of torches. "Keep up with me. My flier is not far."

Tannus took off at a fast walk, mindful of Dye's human limitations. Still, he outpaced the wounded priest enough to clear the path of threats. Dried blood flaked from his fists. The muscles on the backs of his hands ached from being clenched too tightly for so long. He hadn't been forced to kill a mortal in a very long time, even by immortal standards. The battle rage left him. He was covered in sweat and suddenly very tired. Regret for those lives he had taken crept into his mind, shame for allowing his base instincts free one more time.

A small part of him wanted to go back to the village and bring some sort of reason to the angered mob, but he knew the act would be futile. Hot blood made men do foolish things. The pile of corpses back by the stream was testament to that. Vain ambitions and rash actions often led men to ruin. Tannus was no stranger to killing, but the gut wrenching knowledge that he had caused such harm continued to haunt him.

Tannus spied his cobalt black flier and doubled back towards Dye's limping form. The priest was haggard beyond comparison. His wounds would heal, but they were enough to slow him considerably. The flier was big enough to hold a human, but Tannus doubted the old man was going to make it that far without help. Time was his enemy just as much as Dye's wounds.

"You should go back to tend your flock. They will have need of their faith before this is finished," he said much more harshly than intended.

To his credit, Dye didn't back down. "They are my flock no longer."

"A moment ago you defended them. Why the sudden change of heart?"

Drawing a deep breath, he said, "All men are given choices. Hack chose to become the violent man he is today. I choose to move on, to deliver my message to other villages. Men like Hack cannot be allowed to run rampant across the innocents of the world."

"Men like Hack would drive the universe to ruin," Tannus remarked.

"We are only what the gods allowed us to become."

It was a weak defense but the best Dye could come up with. The gods had not been relevant for three thousand years. Man was alone in the universe, governed only from a distance by the Conclave. Cardinals from every religious sect gathered to discuss and debate the best course of action for countless trillions of lives. Most of their decisions never filtered down to the individual worlds, leaving men like Dye to preach the word accordingly. His greatest fear stemmed from being wrong, misguided. Hack's sudden rise to power added credence to the thought.

"You have doubts," Tannus suggested.

He lacked the telepathic abilities of several others of his kind, but the wound on Dye's face was unmistakable.

Dye offered a weak smile. "Sometimes I think doubt is my only companion."

Tannus succumbed to a moment of sympathy. "Here, lean on me. We must move faster."

Rather than protest, Father Dye accepted the assistance. Together, they ambled towards Tannus's flier. Hack and his mob were close behind.

Fifty years had passed since the Bloody Man arrived in the village of Kovlchen, and the ghosts remained. Charred beams and braces stuck up from the ground like broken spines of ancient beasts. The aroma of death clung to the area, as strong as it had been on the day of the slaughter. Tannus found it strange, but there were rumors of his brother dabbling in ancient magics long forgotten.

Nothing grew within the old borders. The very earth was struck dead. Sunlight held no warmth. Ash and grime scarred the land black. Bones littered the area. Hands curled with pain raised skyward, dead where they lay. Skulls and ribcages made it difficult to walk. Tannus and Dye stepped carefully, for they did not want to disturb the ghosts of Kovlchen.

"What could have done this?" Dye gasped. He walked wide eyed through the ruins, the limits of his imagination stretched.

Tannus struggled to keep his rising sorrow in check. "My brother."

"No one being has this type of power," Dye insisted.

"Would that it was so," Tannus replied with empty words. Kovlchen was not new. He had seen this before on countless worlds. The indulgences of Amongeratix and the unpredictability of Sorrow left ashes in their wake. "Look around, Father. Everything that once grew here is dead for eternity. All of this is the result of the excess of my blood."

Dye offered a soft prayer skyward before replying, "Not everything died that day."

"What do you mean?"

Dye cleared his throat. The acidic taste of ash tainted his mouth. "Most of the towns in Berchenfel heard rumors, whispers that a single child was spared...*this*. I do not know whether it was substantiated or not, but we heard that investigators arrived."

Tannus began to pace. New possibilities came to light. *Could it be? Could the one thing Amongeratix sought be here on Crimeat?* He didn't see how. They had searched for centuries with no results. To have it under their very noses, with one brother imprisoned, was too much to put faith in.

Dye noticed the sudden apprehension changing Tannus and timidly said, "You know something."

It was more statement than question.

"Possibly, but I must think," Tannus replied.

The truth was that he didn't know what to think. He wasn't close to either of his brothers, not since the sundering when their father had cast them down. Amongeratix devoted his life to vengeance, Sorrow to grief. Tannus took the mantle of defending humanity and trying to find a new path through the course of time. Their war never let him achieve his goal. He was constantly under siege or responding to unwarranted attacks.

Tannus began to pace. Each footstep ground desiccated bones to dust. The brittle sound made Dye cringe. Frustration beset the giant. Too many possibilities and legends surrounded the Three to make sense of the desolation before him. Sorrow was ever unpredictable and had done this same deed a hundred times before, though never when either of the other two was on the same planet. Amongeratix wanted to reopen the war against their fathers and desperately needed to return to Occanum to begin.

Tannus growled, a deep throaty noise that would have run off a wolf. The obvious continued to elude him. Why did Sorrow suddenly find it necessary to follow Amongeratix, especially once their angry brother was in the custody of the Inquisition? It made no sense. Tannus resisted the urge to punch something. He kept his anger close, refusing to vent until he stood face to face with his brother again. Then Dye's comment pushed itself to the front. Rumors of a survivor. A young girl. What made the girl important, or was she at all? Tannus wished he could be sure.

Crimeat was far enough out of the major hyperspace trading and shipping lanes to not make much of a difference in the grand design of the universe. It seemed improbable that a woman from this unimportant and technologically inferior world could affect anything to do with the gods. The legend was particular, but he didn't know enough of it to make it useful. Sorrow was always the one who mired himself with useless knowledge and ancient myths.

He cursed his lack of knowledge and tried to refocus on the girl. What was so important about her? He frowned, heavy brow concealing his twilight eyes. The girl. The damned girl! He fumed and raged, but the answers remained hidden until finally a spark took flame. His face paled, his skin grew cold. *It couldn't be. It's impossible.*

Father Dye glanced up at the sudden lack of noise and looked into Tannus's eyes. What he saw frightened him more than the thousand deaths visited upon Kovlchen. He saw pure, stark horror. "Tannus?" he hesitantly asked.

The giant struggled with comprehension. "We may be in more trouble than I believed. Where is this girl, does anyone know?"

Dye cocked his head in thought. He explained what little he knew of the impossible survivor. She'd grown to be an angry woman, drifting through the center kingdoms as a bounty hunter. Men said her heart was rough stone, black as the midnight hour. Dye didn't place much stock in such fanciful descriptions. He had little doubt that her heart was poisoned by her experience and paused to wonder how he would have reacted. The thought was unfathomable.

Tannus listened intently, carefully picking apart Dye's words for any clue that might help. An empty wind surged through the ruins, tickling his nape. The stench of death was insulting. Kovlchen was a permanent scar. Frustrated, Tannus threw up his hands. "Nothing. Nothing you said means anything to me. I cannot imagine a peasant girl having any importance to either of my brothers."

Dye let the obvious question go unanswered. Having all three titans loose on Crimeat represented an unprecedented disaster. Worlds were destroyed with less. Instead, he asked, "What is our next move?"

Not for the first time, Tannus wasn't sure. "This village holds nothing for us."

Dye held a suspicion that Tannus was hiding some key piece of information. "We shouldn't stay here."

"Nervous, priest?" Tannus asked with an arched brow.

"This village is not natural. Great evil rests here."

Tannus agreed but felt no fear. The dead offered him no trouble, for he was the son of gods. The sun started to set, and a fine mist rose from the scorched earth. Shapes took form. Dye gasped as he made out dozens of faces locked in a rectus of fear and eternal torment. Kovlchen's dead stretched up from the earth where they had died. A baleful wail echoed across the ruins, chilling his soul. Father Dye had not believed in ghosts until now. The supernatural held no sway over the depths of his faith, but he could not refuse the truths being exposed to him tonight. Dye reeled back.

Even Tannus paused as the ghosts of Kovlchen formed around him. Fading images of desiccated corpses rippled on all sides. The dead stared accusingly, recognizing him. He was one of *them*. The dead did not care that he wasn't covered in blood. They only cared that he was the same size, for there couldn't be many giants left in the universe. Tannus was amused to see Dye making warding signs and whispering prayers. As if that was strong enough to break the will of the damned.

"Save your prayers, Father," Tannus offered, "they will only offend the dead. Perhaps it is time to leave after all."

Dye did not argue. Ghostly figures swarmed him, reaching out to touch him. He cringed, trying to sneak away, but they were everywhere. More than a hundred ethereal forms crowded him. Dye began to hyperventilate. He felt cold. His breath came out in ragged plumes of smoke. The worst were the eyes. Dead eyes stared into him, past the weak flesh and into the shadowed corners no one dared look. Dye felt exposed as the dead searched his core for answers. The dead wanted to know why they had been so ruthlessly slain that distant autumn day. Father Dye had no answers.

"I cannot help you," he protested weakly.

The dead pushed closer. His skin was electrified. They wanted him to join them, to become one with eternal torment. They needed another soul to remind them, if only for a moment, of their lost innocence. Dye whispered hushed prayers. Strong winds blew up from the west, and the ghosts began to fade. Dye dropped to his knees and continued to pray.

Tannus watched in amazement as the ghosts appeared to flee from Dye. *Could faith be so strong?* Soon all but one of the ghosts had gone. What looked like a middle-aged man hovered scant inches from Dye. This one bore a look of infinite sadness rather than the hatred of the rest. Dye stopped praying and looked up into those soft, dead eyes.

Have you seen my daughter?

Rumors of a survivor solidified into fact. The girl did exist, and he was suddenly convinced she had a part to play in the future. He was finally able to recall the missing pieces of information. Amongeratix was searching for something, and Sorrow had come to prevent him from finding it. It was now up to Tannus to ensure Amongeratix failed and left this world.

The ghost stretched out a thin hand, silently pleading to Dye for help. Dye had never felt so helpless. No amount of words or oaths of comfort could assuage the guilt of being a survivor. Dye wanted to cry. The ghost looked dejected as he, too, dissolved back into the ether. Tannus gave the priest some time to collect himself before striding back to him. His doubts were lessened, and he began to trust Dye a little more.

He decided it was time to include Dye just a bit more. "Tell me, Father, have you ever heard of a place called An'kuruku?"

The nights were getting progressively darker the closer they got to winter. Both of Crimeat's moons were new, leaving the sky an ominous mixture of purple and dark blue. Soft winds cooled Vaade, driving people inside at dusk. The city continued to be on edge. Tensions from the military campaign in the west translated through every household. Armed guards patrolled the streets with merciless attitudes. Fear was growing.

Two figures in black robes stood on the steps of the ancient Duzori Temple, quietly staring up at the alabaster statue of Aris, the goddess of wisdom and protection. She was depicted with long, flowing hair, a sword in her right hand and a torch in her left. The gleam in her eyes whispered security. The two figures stared at her with disdain. She represented everything they despised.

The temple itself was an architectural achievement unmatched on a dozen worlds. Built to commemorate the first colonists' original victory over the native tribes, the temple was one of Lethendweil's most impressive attractions. Twelve steps led up to the temple from all four sides. The steps were each thirty meters long and evenly spaced. Five pillars lined the tops of the stairs. Intricately carved and sculpted with scenes from epic battles in history, the pillars were meant to inspire pilgrims. The Duzori Temple was a bastion to the human spirit. It was a fitting meeting place.

"Events are moving faster than anticipated," the taller man finally said.

This late at night, no one else was around, not even the priests. Local clergymen were in shock over Father Stall's unexpected demise. Messages streamed back and forth with Conclave headquarters on Vau Prime. They wanted safety, but the Conclave offered none. The assassinations of the nobles had stunned them, but Stall's murder drove them into heightened panic. Something dark festered in the heart of Lethendweil.

"Stall's death was unexpected," replied a light female voice. "He should not have been killed."

"We did not authorize that," he replied. "The priest was a minor nuisance, nothing more. This has the capability to prove dangerous for us."

She shook her head. "No, we cannot let it deter us. The people are smoldering. All it will take is a single spark, and the flames will spread. We must push forward."

"Are you sure?" he pressed. "We are taking an awful risk."

She scowled, unseen by the other. "The war is beginning. Shiramon has been given his orders. There are reports of his armored columns moving in to surround Torbecca as we speak. Do not let the priest's death deter you."

"Less than half of the current nobles are in our influence. We need more."

She regarded him with sudden misgivings. "This is not the time for doubt. Our power is rising. The old ways must be eliminated if we are to have any hope of ruling this land. The twelve kingdoms have proven they cannot sustain themselves with the current leadership."

"We rely too heavily on the baron," he insisted.

"Scura is a puppet, nothing more. He does not yet know it, but events will force him to assassinate the remaining nobles when they visit Reven."

He jerked back slightly. "All of them? We are not ready. Our agents are not in place yet."

"Time is our enemy," she growled. "All threats have been removed. The senior Inquisitor and his forces are off on a wild chase, and the local forces are doing our bidding. Inquisitor Prowl is useless to anyone but us. We are about to step into the light for the first time."

"I do not like this new direction."

She resisted the urge to strike him down. "All of us made a pact. Do not be the one to go back on it. Go back to the council building and wait for further instructions."

He bowed and slipped off into the night. Presha Von watched him go from beneath the obscurity of her hood. She had narrowed down the list of potential figures her fellow council members could be and had taken precautions to ensure hers was the dominant will. She alone knew what Baron Scura had coming. Still, her companion offered valid points. Their plan was not ready to succeed, but hers was. Presha Von decided that it was time to bring the senior Inquisitor into the equation to make things more convoluted and interesting. Smiling, she walked away whistling a childhood tune.

TWENTY-TWO

3210 A.G. (After Gods), Breld, planet Crimeat.

Prophet Isle was unsophisticated compared to most of the civilized universe. There was only a single, small airfield for off-world contact. Most contact came from the old ways, horse drawn wagons and sailing ships back and forth with Lethendweil. Senior Inquisitor Tolde Breed remained impressed that any place in the universe remained this outdated.

The town smelled of sea salt and burning wood. Smoked puffed up from the dozens of chimneys, tainting an otherwise pure sky. There was a homey feel that Tolde hadn't felt in a very long time. Fields and pastures surrounded Breld. Cows, sheep and chickens filled the air with a hint of dung. Quaint as it may seem, Breld was nothing like Krenz.

Tolde and Matthias led the way down the two-track dirt lane into the center of town. Sergeant Fies and his squad were behind, spaced out at five-meter intervals in the event of an ambush. After the events in Vaade, none of them were taking chances. Sister Abigail walked in the middle, though the others could have sworn her feet never actually touched the ground. Townsfolk peered through half-shuttered windows and stopped to stare from the side of the road as the formation marched past, making Matthias grin. People needed to be reminded of the might of the Prekhauten Guard lest they grow complacent and let heresy in.

Matthias turned to Fies. "Sergeant, secure your gear from the inn and meet us back here. I want to be off this island in an hour."

Fies left a small detachment to stand guard while the others entered the small wooden inn. Tolde continued to scan the immediate area. He'd had enough of potential assassins and accidental firefights.

"Inquisitor," said a voice so soft Tolde almost thought he'd imagined it.

The Senior Inquisitor spun, hand dropping to his side arm. "Show yourself."

A figure slipped from the shadows less than five feet from where he and Matthias were standing. His hands were out in a display of peace. The hardened look he bore suggested a criminal. The orange flecks in his eyes danced in the twilight.

"That's close enough," Matthias warned. His weapon was already in hand and leveled.

Darka Jorm halted. His heart quickened. No one had warned him that the Inquisitor might shoot him. Frowning, he continued with his message. "No need for weapons; I am only here to deliver a message."

Tolde and Matthias exchanged a wary look. "Go on."

Darka stared down the cold, black barrel disapprovingly. "I've been instructed to tell you that you are looking in the wrong places. Lethendweil is about to erupt in revolution, and you chase ghosts."

"You are not giving me any reasons not to shoot you. Speak plainly," Matthias growled. He, too, was tired of games.

Ursal Prowl had been right. These two were difficult to approach. He took an instant dislike to the Prekhauten. "The war against the Ugri is a front. Certain factions in the council have manufactured a crisis to divert you from discovering the truth."

Conclave policy stated that local politics were not a concern for the greater universe. Inquisitors were not to get involved. Tolde was trying to ignore the local problems, but they were interfering with his ability to locate Amongeratix. Sister Abigail helped, but even her mythic powers seemed dulled. He decided to press Darka to see just what he knew.

"The Inquisition does not involve itself in planetary politics unless they pose a threat to the greater universe. We are here for other reasons."

Darka sighed inwardly. *Finally*. "Yes, the prison escape from a few weeks ago."

"What do you know of it?" Tolde asked, subtle menace behind the words.

"It is the reason behind everything going on. One part of the ruling council had a hand in the escape."

"Impossible. The prison is a Conclave facility. Locals had no access to the inmates," Matthias interrupted.

Darka shrugged. He didn't care what they believed. "So you think. You off-worlders aren't as smart as you want to be. The Baron discovered the truth about your *special* prisoner years ago. The rest of the nobles have been puppets."

"Choose your next words carefully, messenger. Who helped *him* escape?" Tolde edged closer. His hand gripped his sidearm; his anger urged him to draw it.

"It was the Baron."

"He is lying."

They turned to see Sister Abigail hovering, her head cocked to one side as if studying them. Darka's face paled at the sight. Blood Witches were a rarity in the universe, but all knew of their sorcerous ways.

"Get that thing away from me," Darka practically screamed. He took a step back, suddenly desperate to hide in the shadows.

"I don't think our new friend likes you, Sister," Matthias grinned.

Sister Abigail moved closer. A soft red glow burned from under her gossamer hood. "This man tells half-truths. He means to deceive us."

"No…I swear..."

Matthias struck quickly. His thick fingers curled around Darka's throat and then squeezed. He leaned threateningly close and snapped, "Keep lying, and you're going to scream too."

Tolde felt a sudden calm, as if all their troubles on Crimeat had just been explained. He placed a hand softly on Matthias's shoulder pauldron. "Not so fast. He may yet have some useful information."

Matthias reluctantly eased his grip and stepped back. Unexpectedly, Sister Abigail slipped between them. A graceful, feminine hand slipped out and touched Darka on the cheek. "You will speak the truth."

Darka jerked back. His eyes went blank, rolling back into his head. His tongue lolled out of the corner of his mouth. Matthias gasped, sick to his stomach.

"What did you do?"

"What needed to be done."

Her voice betrayed no emotion—no remorse, no guilt, no sense of satisfaction. Matthias felt cold inside. The creature next to him was an abomination.

Tolde wasted little time. "Why was Amongeratix freed?"

"I do not know," Darka droned. His body shuddered once. Spittle frothed around the corners of his mouth.

"Who freed him? Who is this baron?"

"Baron Scura wishes to be the lone lord of Lethendweil. He ordered the assassinations of the three nobles and orchestrated the war against the Ugri."

Tolde passed Matthias a nervous look. "I think we have stumbled into a very treacherous ruse. Amongeratix might not even be part of what is happening here."

"Could be, but how can we be sure? This guy doesn't seem like he was read in on every little detail," Matthias answered.

"You may be sure that he speaks truthfully." Abigail's words reminded the Prekhauten Guardsman of everything he was fighting against.

Neither decided to question her.

"Who is Scura working with?" Tolde asked.

"Ursal Prowl."

The words stung like a slap in the face. Ursal Prowl? Tolde couldn't believe his ears. Prowl was the planet's sole Inquisition representative. There was no way he could be involved in such treachery.

"You must be mistaken," Tolde said and instantly regretted it. He'd gotten a bad feeling from Ursal almost the moment they'd met. The man had an odd air about him, as if he were keeping secrets in the hopes of appeasing Tolde. *Too much damned hero worship left him with a stain.* Cruelty seemed to be a common theme amongst men. It drove them to great acts, both of wonder and violence.

"No. Inquisitor Prowl sent me to Reven repeatedly to coordinate with Scura," Darka explained. A strange hum surrounded him, distorting his figure slightly.

Fies and the rest of his squad emerged from the inn and stopped cold in the street at the sight of the Blood Witch. She had a hellish glaze to her. The whites and transparent colors contaminated with dark red and violet. It was the eyes that stole the strength from their souls. Crimson flames rimmed the hollow places where her eyes should be. Sister Abigail looked like pure evil. Matthias shot them a glare that kept any comment from being uttered.

"What is Prowl's intent?" Tolde pressed.

"He wants to be the power behind the unified throne. He wants the control that he cannot have as an Inquisitor."

Matthias grew angrier. "What about the local Prekhauten Guard?"

"They are being used to make attacks on the Ugri and the eastern kingdoms. Scura and Prowl want each side to think the other is provoking them."

Matthias balled his fists. A lifetime of service demanded vengeance. No Guardsman should have allowed themselves to be wasted so carelessly, regardless of the circumstance. The local Guards had been seduced through evil intent and were a liability. Matthias regretted it but realized there was only one viable solution. The rogue Guards had to be dealt with.

"This is worse than we thought," Tolde said to Matthias.

"I agree. We might be too far behind them to be able to stop them."

Tolde turned back to Darka. "What is Scura planning next?"

"I do not know."

They waited for Sister Abigail's confirmation. Her body flickered, turning totally transparent before re-solidifying.

Tolde changed the subject. Scura would be dealt with, but he was still a minor player. Amongeratix and now Tannus remained the bigger targets. The Three had used numerous human surrogates through the ages; the fools on Crimeat were no different. Tolde thought back to the first time he and Matthias had captured Amongeratix. They had brought him here to Prophet Isle under the expectations that he would remain incarcerated for at least the rest of their lives. Now he was free and undoubtedly going to attempt returning to Occanum. Tannus's unexpected arrival only confirmed their fears and suspicions.

"Tolde, those Guards need to be neutralized. I cannot allow their actions to continue," Matthias said gravely.

"Perhaps we need to call for reinforcements. There is more going on here than any of us believed. The Three are using the local nobility to further their intent," Tolde concluded. "It is only logical that Amongeratix will be where Baron Scura is." He turned back to Darka. "Where is Scura now?"

"Reven."

Tolde snapped his holster shut and told Abigail, "Release him, Sister. We have all of the information we need to proceed."

The hatred and foul energies dispelled. Abigail shuddered as the eldritch strength of the Blood Witches fled her body. "It is done."

"Will he be alright?" Fies piped up.

"I cannot say. Each man deals with the *touch* differently," she replied too easily.

Matthias pushed aside any thought of Darka's wellbeing. "Fies, get back to the shuttle and link in to the council reports, satellites and anything else you can think of. I want to know where Inquisitor Prowl deployed his Guards."

"Yes, Sergeant Major."

He beckoned with his head, and the squad headed out, glad to be away from the unnatural powers of the Blood Witch. Sister Abigail appeared indifferent to their reaction, as if she'd seen it too many times to bother noticing. Her kind often ignored the mortal sensibilities of man. She hardly bothered looking down to watch Darka slide to the ground and collapse in a heap of useless flesh. His body convulsed, and he began babbling in wordless tongues. Tolde suspected his mind was permanently gone. Not that he cared. Darka Jorm was a minor player and an expendable pawn. The real prize awaited in Reven. He stepped over Darka and walked away.

Matthias gave a second glance at what remained of the man. He didn't feel sorrow, though a small hint of mercy ached to be fulfilled. "What do we do with him?"

Tolde paused. "Leave him or shoot him, I do not care."

The words were cold but appropriate. They had been played from the moment they were ordered to Crimeat. Tolde's anger struggled to remain checked. Matthias calmly drew his sidearm, the gun metal black matching his glove perfectly. Kneeling, he looked for any sign of the man Darka had been but found none. He was an empty shell, used and discarded. No man deserved to live like that. Not even the scum on Crimeat. Matthias placed the barrel to Darka's temple and lightly squeezed the trigger.

Baron Scura stood on the balcony of Reven's prominent watch tower. It appeared no more than a spike on the mountainside to any who didn't know where to look. For Scura, it was proof that he was destined for greatness. He'd never been one to waste time staring up at the stars. Men like that never amounted to much, in his opinion. Instead, Scura had dedicated his life to amassing strength and power through guile. He excelled at deception and never hesitated to take the occasional chance that might push him past an obstacle. Tonight was different.

Tonight, Scura watched the stars and stared down onto the winding road up the mountainside and onto the plateau.

Tonight marked the culmination of more than two years of plotting and waiting. Two years since *they* had first come to him with their proposal. It had taken him many sleepless nights to come to terms with what *they* offered. *They* had promised untold riches as well as access to previously forbidden technologies Lethendweil had lost over the centuries and asked for little in exchange—at least, little compared to his overall goal. Still, the promise did not come without risk. What was asked had the potential to send every hard-earned and imagined dream to ruin.

He began to pace. The prospect of losing everything at this stage daunted him. His stomach was twisted. His mouth was dry. He felt as nervous as when he had finally summoned the courage to murder his father. That night had been bittersweet but left him with the knowledge that he had the strength to do the hard task. He prayed that strength did not desert him tonight.

Reven was alive beneath him. Lights from vehicles and various compounds distracted his thoughts. The bulk of his army was already deployed under Shiramon's command, but his reserve forces remained a secret. Elite commando and police units had been pouring into secret barracks for the past year from across Crimeat. He was almost ready to unleash his plans on Lethendweil. The large horse-drawn wagon continued its slow pull up the mountain.

"My lord, it is almost time," Geres Auk's deep voice echoed across the circular room.

Geres idly, freshly returned from the front lines, glanced at the entwined snake sculptures hugging the six columns decorating the room. Superstitions held nothing for him. He was a man of flesh and blood and believed his destiny was made by his own hands. For now, he served Scura's will.

The Lord of the Plateau felt a childish giddiness. Excitement and fear collided violently. He wrapped his cloak around him, black on black, and nodded. "Come, then. Let us see if this gambit is going to pay off."

Doubts still nagged at him. The dark council was dangerous and their intentions still unclear. Scura didn't trust them any more than he put faith in his fellow nobles. Surely they served some nefarious purpose contradictory to his, but that was worth the risk. Visions of being crowned emperor entertained him.

Geres Auk studied him curiously. He'd never seen his master act so bizarrely. Baron Scura went to great lengths to present a confident appearance. The impending arrival of their mystery guest had changed him into a borderline paranoid. The promise of exposure to the universe's most dangerous weapon choked the strength from even the stoutest. Geres was silently thankful that he was not in charge of anything except security.

"The palace is ready?" Scura asked upon noticing Auk's glum nature.

"It is, though I have doubts on how long they will last if this goes wrong."

Scura eyed his aide with sudden interest and approval. "You doubt my decisions?"

"I do not trust what we seek to treat with. We do not know who or what the dark council represents. They would not seek a deal with us if it were not to their advantage. That makes them dangerous."

Scura suddenly found himself reevaluating his opinions of Geres. Ruthless as he was cunning, Scura liked Geres but made a mental note to watch him more closely from now on. Too much craftiness presented new challenges and threats.

He tried to sound confident. "The dark council has its uses and will need to be dealt with at some point. Our first concern is meeting this weapon they decided to send our way. Right now, I need strength to crush all resistance in the twelve kingdoms."

"You do not think General Shiramon will be enough? Torbecca has already fallen."

"Grushm was an easy mark. He never paid enough attention to his borders. Brentor and Mans will not be so accommodating. And now there are the rumors of the Ugri actually mounting an offensive into the Great Barrier Jungle." Scura frowned. He'd used the reclusive Ugri as scapegoats to put Lethendweil on a war footing but never expected them to become involved. If Shiramon's reports were correct, the Ugri were massing in great numbers and making attacks on eastern units.

Scura was starting to believe the war was going to take longer than he anticipated unless this new weapon of the dark council proved as useful as promised.

"The enemy is wily, but they were caught off guard. Brentor will not sit on his heels while our forces advance across the kingdoms," Geres Auk offered. "Still, he does not have the strength to meet us head on in open battle. This will be a long campaign. Most of the battles will be skirmishes and ambushes. Brentor will realize his position and begin a guerilla campaign against us."

Scura wasn't so sure he approved of Auk's newfound conversational skills. "These may be dangerous times but let us not forget that Shiramon comes from a long line of military genius."

Geres shook his head ever so slightly. His gaze hardened. "Overconfidence in him could lead to ruin, Baron. I suggest caution."

"What you suggest handicaps my intent," Scura countered harshly. A ghost of anger flashed across his face. "I hired you for security. Let me focus on the bigger picture." He shifted focus quickly before Geres had the chance to grow angry. "I want our guest kept under constant surveillance. He may be a weapon, but he is also a tool of the dark council. We cannot afford to trust them."

"Yes, Baron."

They walked in silence. Scura contemplated removing Geres before he became too cunning for his own good despite his simple presentation. He'd regret getting rid of the man. Geres was a tremendous asset. They exited the watch tower and climbed into the waiting air car. It was one of the few available on the Plateau, and Scura had spared no expense. Coal black, the car was heavily armored with tinted windows. The seats were small but luxurious, made from the skin of the giant vorsh lizard of the southern deserts. The car sped across the drab rock surface.

Running without lights, the car went past the training fields and then the lone surface airfield. Transports and shuttles streamed in and out of the docking bays in steady rows. Commerce continued despite the war footing. Geres Auk stared blankly out the blackened windows, unimpressed. His mind raced through intricate details concerning his security preparations. The Baron may be easily ensorcelled by whispers and promises, but Geres was a practical man. He only believed in what he could kill. And those things that he could kill could also kill him, especially their inbound guest.

Scura glanced over at his silent head of security. Auk's blank expression was misleading, but there was nothing for it. Both men had their secrets. Scura wondered if the big man noticed anything along their trek.

Geres Auk caught the look of mild disdain from the corner of his eye and kept his smile concealed. Scura was making a bad habit of underestimating him. He'd already counted more than twenty carefully hidden guards dispersed along the main avenue. Most were disguised as civilian workers returning home from a long day's work in the mines. Dozens more lurked in the shadows, dressed in chameleon body armor. The scheme's shifting pattern continuously matched the colors of night. Power rifles and ion pistols were locked and loaded. Each guard awaited Auk's call.

Scura noticed Geres Auk's sudden stiffness but guessed the reason incorrectly. "Patience, Geres. We did not come here for a fight. Let us hear what the dark council has to say before you send in reinforcements."

"I have doubts about tonight. The dark council is too powerful. We are being pulled in too many directions at the wrong time."

He didn't say it, but Scura knew he referred to the impending visit of the council of nobles. Brentor would not pull his punches, scrutinizing every minor detail. More than once, Geres had suggested causing an *accident* to their shuttle. Scura had scolded him for it, but the thought persisted. Removing Brentor opened many avenues; unfortunately, it would also solidify resistance, and he wasn't ready for that.

Scura had the car stop several meters from the meeting place. A lump formed in his throat. *This is surprising.* He'd been in more tense situations than this lately, so why the sudden apprehension? A frown creased his forehead. Perhaps Geres was correct. Events were steadily compounding, making it difficult to keep focus. Lost in thought, he waited for another hour before the massive horse-drawn carriage pulled up.

With a nod, he and Auk got out of the air car. Scura subconsciously smoothed the wrinkles out of his clothes, much to Auk's amusement. They looked up at the obsidian wagon with awe. It was massive. Lanterns hung from both sides of the side door, casting an eerie glow on the dark paneling. There were no windows, no way to see in or out. Scura felt dread pulsing from the wagon. His knees threatened to buckle.

The coachman slowly climbed down and walked towards the side door. Scura couldn't be sure, but there seemed to be something wrong with the man. He passed a cautious glance to Auk, but the bigger man did not move. Together, they watched as the giant door slowly opened. What came out made their jaws drop. Twelve feet tall and so heavily muscled he had to be more than five hundred pounds, the giant wore a look of pure evil. Hatred was suddenly very real.

"My gods," Scura whispered.

Geres Auk, surprisingly, did not move. His mind raced with the sudden manifestation of such malevolence. It did not seem possible. The giant cracked his mighty knuckles, the sound like distant thunder, and then rolled his shoulders. A thick brow hid most of his eyes, but the shine coming off them was not natural. Scura would not have believed that such perfect black would be able to shine at night. His strength abandoned him.

A second figure emerged from the carriage. Scura was surprised that it was only a man. Overweight, balding and surrounded by an air of indeterminable filth, the man appeared as frightened as Scura suddenly was. The giant glared down at the man, silently sending him towards them.

"Who rules here?" the man asked impudently.

Geres visibly tensed until Scura laid a calming hand on his forearm. "I am Baron Scura, lord of Reven and the Plateau."

The man looked him over, as if judging him. "My master wishes to speak only with you. He stays here."

"I will not leave the Baron in your care," Geres snarled.

Scura had a suspicion that the giant heard every word, no matter how quiet they talked. "My associate means no disrespect to your master, but you must understand our situation. We are at war with the other kingdoms. Trust is not an easy commodity to give, and we do not even know your names."

"Moffo Kain," he replied hesitantly. His hand trembled beneath the heavy jacket. Cold winds whipped across the Plateau, making it inhospitable to life on the surface. "Best you let him introduce himself. He's waiting." *Though I would turn and run right now if I were you.*

"Not alone," Geres repeated.

"It will be fine, my friend. Stay here with Moffo while I see to our guest."

Any confidence Scura portrayed in his voice was false. His heart beat so fast he felt like it was about to explode. Never in the depths of his imagination did he think to stand before such a mythic creature. Scura advanced on unsteady legs until he was a meter away from the awe-inspiring giant.

"Where is the tomb, worm?" Amongeratix growled in a voice so deep it threatened to burst Scura's ear drums.

Scura jerked back. "Tomb? I am not sure what you are referring to."

"Do not play games with me, mortal. I want the location of the tomb, now."

"I do not know of any tomb. We burn our dead."

Amongeratix drew back to crush Scura. It had been a very long time since a mortal had dared speak to him so. He felt betrayed. People were messing with powers they didn't understand. Amongeratix thought back over the last few days since his battle with Tannus. Moffo Kain was a puppet and a nearly useless one. The smell of shit constantly irritated Amongeratix. Whatever his faults, Moffo was representing dark forces, ones strong enough to free him from the wards of a Blood Witch.

Then there was the woman in black. She was strong willed and determined, and she knew too much about him and his brothers. She had insisted he come to Reven but remained reclusive with her reasoning. He correctly guessed the tomb belonged to one of his forefathers. That was the only possible reason for coming to such an abandoned place. So why would a mortal woman want him to find it? Why help now?

A sudden gleam twinkled in his eyes. *Could it be? After all the countless centuries of search and toil, could I be close to finding Paradise Tear?* He didn't dare to dream. Instead, he looked back down on the puny noble and asked sharply, "Why am I here then?"

"I was hoping you might be able to tell me," Scura replied as casually as possible. "I was only told that a powerful weapon was being delivered to me, not what that weapon was."

Amongeratix stiffened at the word. "I am no cattle. No one delivered me." He paused, letting his anger abate. "A weapon, eh? I am a weapon more terrible than the black dawn. Choose your words carefully lest I tear out your tongue for my own sport."

Scura cowered as the words settled over his soul. He had heard of the power of the deep space wolves. Surely this giant must be one of them. Ancient hatreds rippled beneath the crust of his flesh like so many serpents. Scura was weak compared to such animosity.

Amongeratix sneered down on him. "You stink of fear. Ever you humans seek to control things you do not understand."

The words were barbs, needles piercing deep. Scura stared up into those black eyes and felt lost. All his carefully laid plans and dreams were reduced to childish inspiration. He groaned softly as the rot took shape in his mind. Scura crashed to his knees. Blood trickled from the corners of his eyes. Unimaginable horror tightened around his veins, choking the oxygen from them.

Amongeratix leaned down, amused with his work. "Do not think to treat with me as your equal again, mortal. I am the death of the universe, the harbinger of apocalypse."

"No, no, no," Scura repeated over and over between delusional sobs.

Geres Auk had seen enough. He keyed the emergency button imprinted on his left thumb, alerting all forces the Baron was under attack. Moffo Kain stood by glumly. His mind was elsewhere. Geres watched, struggling to keep still before his forces arrived. Any move now damned Scura and himself. A soft rustle behind him was enough to drop into a battle stance.

Moffo Kain noticed and stepped back. "I wouldn't do that," he warned quietly.

Geres snarled and readied to attack. A withering glare from Amongeratix stopped him in his tracks. The warmth of his blood fled.

The giant grinned, savage and feral. "Come to me, little man."

Geres took only a few steps before self-preservation took hold, and he stopped. Amongeratix threw back his head in laughter. Three millennia since he had been cast down from his father's grace, and humanity had not changed. Humans were fragile and weak, undeserving of inheriting the universe.

Satisfied the threat was reduced, he turned back to Scura. "Now, then, I need to find the tomb."

Baron Scura nodded helplessly. Amongeratix looked up to the heavens, veiled behind thin wisps of clouds. *Soon, Father. Soon I will be coming for you.* Paradise Tear awaited.

TWENTY-THREE

3210 A.G. (After Gods), Vaade, planet Crimeat.

The sweet smell of lavender and orange spice filled the chamber with pleasant tones. Oil lamps burned along the circular wall. Steam rose from the water already prepared for Presha Von's bath. Luxurious cushions piled against the wall were the only furniture in the private bath chamber. A small table with a tray of fresh fruits and a silver pitcher of water sat off to the side for after.

Two attendants dressed only in transparent shifts stood in the water awaiting their lady. Both were female and barely eighteen. One was a slightly pale blonde with firm, young breasts and a body that still held some of the softness of youth. Her eyes were emerald and surprisingly dull, void of much emotion. Her counterpart had long locks of striking raven hair and a desert tan. Each wore a tight black collar marking them as slaves.

Jars of various scented oils were lined up on a thin board beside the girls. Sweat covered their bodies in a thin sheen. They stood with hands clasped in front of them, both looking down into the swirling waters. The chamber was painted an opaque gold, accented with numerous species of exotic flowers and plants. Presha Von was many things, but she always tried to remind herself of her humble beginnings.

A gilded door opened, causing both girls to turn their heads. Presha Von entered with the grace of a big jungle cat. Her hair was tied back in a loose bun, and she wore a concealing full-length robe of black fur. A male attendant trailed her, wearing the same collar and a loincloth. Many rumors circulated through the various circles of Vaade about Presha's eccentric tastes, but no one knew for certain just what happened in her most private quarters. She had once considered rendering her servants mute but relented after much debate. Still, the punishment for talking was a shade shy of death.

She paused to look back at her manservant, scrutinizing his every move as he closed the door. He was lightly tanned, more toned than muscled. Presha pursed her lips. He quickly moved to her and untied the silk belt around her waist. She let the robe slip to the floor, naked save for the loose gold chain dangling around her flat stomach. Holding out her hands, Presha smiled as the two girls gently took them and assisted her into the bath. She was just past forty but still had a body to make men weep. Her grace and beauty were known to have ruined more than one relationship. There were a few silver strands poking from her full-bodied black hair. Her full breasts had begun to sag, and she had a few extra pounds where once was muscle. Still, Presha Von remained timelessly elegant, a reminder for all women in Lethendweil. There was power in her.

She allowed herself to be seated on the upper step of the tub. Hot water instantly made her skin flush. Presha gasped softly. Waiting until their mistress was properly seated, the girls began pouring cups of water over her. Goose bumps covered her exposed flesh. Presha enjoyed the tingling sensations and tilted her head back. Her soft eyes closed. Once thoroughly wetted, the girls reached over to the jars and began lathering her in oils. Her manservant collected the thick robe and folded it with care before standing patiently behind the women.

Presha opened her eyes to watch the brunette kneel at her feet, carefully massaging every inch of her flesh with the oil starting at her toes. Presha loved having her toes touched, though no proper lady would ever admit such. The blonde simultaneously began working on her neck and shoulders. This was a daily experience, even though the servants often changed. Presha did not keep favorites, either man or woman.

Presha purred as the brunette's hand snaked up her inner thigh. Her legs parted. The brunette wordlessly obeyed, applying more oil until her fingers brushed the dark patch of hair between her mistress's legs. Lust ignited in Presha's eyes as the aphrodisiac powers in the oils took control. She ran her right hand up the blonde's legs, who had begun massaging Presha's breasts. The blonde gasped as her mistress penetrated her with two fingers. Leaning forward ever so slightly, the blonde closed her eyes and squirmed under the expert manipulation. She quickened her pace, focusing on Presha's hardened nipples.

Presha tilted her head back to flick one of the brunette's nipples with her tongue. The oils coating all three women were an imported drug designed to enhance stimulation, making the user lose control of their urges and inhibitions. It had taken just one time for Presha to become addicted. She found herself needing the oil more each day, the sessions lasting longer. One hand dabbling in the blonde, the other caressing the brunette's hair as she expertly used her tongue, Presha Von lost herself to the lust.

She hardly noticed when the manservant waded into the water and scooped her up as if she were a mere child. He carried her, water and oil dripping on the smooth stone floor, to the piles of cushions and lavish pillows. Her eyes were mere slits. Her pupils dilated. Her breath came in ragged gasps. She didn't see her little pretties slink from the water, the lust consuming them too. They crawled beside her and lavished her exposed body with kisses. The man couldn't take anymore and shed his loin cloth. He dropped down between Presha's legs. She readily complied as he entered her in one long penetration. Her inner fire erupted with a guttural moan.

This spurred her servants to greater frenzy.

When she finally awoke, Presha Von felt drained. Her body ached in all the right places. She was a mess. Covered in dried oils and body secretions, she hardly presented the image of a noble of Lethendweil. She rose and stretched. Her muscles tried to rebel. Tiny cramps spread through her body. A soft moan made her look down. Her servants slept in a mass of bodies and limbs. The oils had that effect. Her head was pounding, and she reeled against the minor dizziness. These were aftereffects she knew would soon dissolve. Presha despised herself for what she had done, but the drug was too powerful. The addiction ran too deeply in her blood. She couldn't stop if she wanted to.

Presha didn't know where the oils came from. They'd initially been a gift. Now they came with a price. Presha Von was as much a slave as the three youths at her feet. She struggled to keep this life secret. The council would expunge her without a second thought, and the dark council would simply devour her. Her life was nothing but layers of conflicting secrets. Sooner or later, she was going to get caught. Her only hope lay in Amongeratix unleashing his fury on the universe.

Naked, Presha strolled through the door and into a second, slightly more public bath without the sound-proof walls. Her normal attendant shifted her eyes in what had turned into a reflex. She'd lost count of the times Lady Von had emerged in this state. After a long, hot bath, she helped Presha into a light robe that did little to conceal her body. Presha Von couldn't have cared less. All she wanted was a small meal and some sleep. She rolled her eyes upon seeing the doorman awaiting her at the entrance to her personal chamber.

"Forgiveness, my lady," he said, "but you have a visitor inside. He was most insistent."

Unlike the bath attendant, he made no attempt to avert his gaze.

Presha growled. "I hope for your sake this is extremely important. I am in no mood, Temuth."

The graying Temuth bowed meekly and opened the door. She stormed past with the knowledge of his predatory gaze. The door clicked shut, and she let out a pent-up sigh. The after-effects of the oil were starting. She was weak, exhausted. Her body lacked the solidity and strength she normally commanded. Still, it was a small price to pay for such awakening. Presha tightened her robe, took a deep breath and entered the main chamber. A tall figure in a black robe stood beside the calming warmth of the fire. She froze. A forgotten part reminded her that it couldn't last forever.

"What are you doing here?" she hissed.

"You have grown careless," he replied sternly. "We are starting to have doubts."

She stiffened. The implications of him being here, in the main council building of Vaade, were staggering. Members of the dark council were not supposed to know who the others were. It had been designed like that to ensure continued fealty. They were **NOT** intended to know each other's identities. Presha Von felt the walls close in.

She struggled to maintain composure, forced her mind to work. "You violate our mandate by being in my chambers."

He laughed. "Did you truly believe no one on the dark council knows anyone else? Ridiculous! There is always one who knows the secrets of the rest of us."

"Leave me, now," she commanded, planting her feet square.

"Or what? You'll summon your guards and risk exposing yourself as a conspirator? I don't think so."

Panic took hold. She wasn't sure what to do. He moved to stand beside her, threateningly close. His features were locked deep in shadow, but there was something familiar about his voice. She almost felt she knew him. Gloves concealed the fingers reaching out to trace the outline of her lips. The faint fragrance of flowers tickled her nostrils. He let his hand drift down her neck, pausing between her quivering breasts. Presha's eyes forced close. She gasped. The oil! He must have put a small amount on his gloves. She didn't have much time before the addiction took hold.

He leaned in close to whisper, "You have been a bad girl, Presha. My spies tell me you are working against the wishes of the council."

"I have done nothing," she protested.

"Indeed?" he said mockingly. "Perhaps you can explain why He is in Reven as we speak? The time of ascension is almost upon us, and your selfishness threatens all of our carefully wrought plans."

"Amongeratix will not answer to any man," she replied, struggling against the raw power of the oil. "He has gone to Reven of his own accord."

The tall man drew back and slapped her across the face, driving her to her knees. "You lie! I know you sent him there. Now tell me why."

Presha bit back her tears. White hot pain lanced across her jaw. "I acted with the will of the council. He is a force unimaginable. Agents are escorting him as per your wishes."

"Your agent was found dead in the streets of Dretl." He paused to let the words sink in. "What have you to say now?"

She was confused. Darka Jorm dead? Why? How? Presha had been assured of success. Once certain that the off-world Inquisitor would take the bait and remove all her loose ends, she was now certain something had gone terribly wrong. Presha made the instant decision that she needed to get to Reven, get to Amongeratix before a host of enemy forces descended on him.

She detected hints of sorrow in the intruder's voice. It was a voice she felt certain she knew, but the oil clouded her thoughts. The slightest touch of desire flared through her body. She knew it wouldn't be much longer before she succumbed to the lure.

"Give me five days," she offered, silently wondering how he had managed to get through the massive government building undetected. *Who is he?* "Five days, and I will have Amongeratix in Vaade. Our enemies will be destroyed at last."

He cocked his head, the soft folds of his cowl shifting slightly. "How do you propose to get him to the city if he cannot be controlled?"

"I have my charms," she purred.

Presha trembled; the oil threatened to consume her. She wasn't sure she could hold out. The prospect of becoming lost within the addictive power was frightening, but it felt so good...

"Do not fail us. We risked everything by freeing him from that Conclave prison. We will not be deterred this close." His voice turned grave. "Fix what you have ruined, or the council will be forced to take action. It will not be pleasant."

Presha's head dropped. The lust-rage was burning within. Embarrassment was beyond her. Presha Von realized she wasn't important anymore, only the oil. She needed it, yes, but a primal part of her she'd never known existed wanted it more. Those desires were much stronger than her.

He grabbed her chin, pulling her off the floor. "We will be watching you, Presha Von, every dark shadow and near corner. Nothing you do will go unnoticed. Nowhere you go will be private."

He snarled and stalked off, leaving her quivering where she stood. Her robe had pulled open, not that it mattered. Her eyes glazed over, a telltale sign the oil was assuming control. The door clicked shut, and she nearly collapsed. No longer in control of herself, Presha crept back to her private bath. Any thoughts of the dark council were quickly replaced with the need to fulfill her desires.

The robed man passed a small purse to the doorman and nodded. "Watch her closely."

"Yes, my lord." He smiled openly. The heavy feel of gold coins in his hand was as unfamiliar as it was welcome.

Satisfied, the robed man stalked off and entered the main corridor. Ursal Prowl removed his hood, scanned both directions before heading back to his meager offices. He had much to do. Darka's loss haunted him, if slightly, and set his own plans back. Ursal decided his next course of action was to take care of Tolde Breed, hero of the Inquisition. No doubt the older Inquisitor was ready to call in reinforcements. Ursal Prowl couldn't let that happen.

Brentor started awake at the urgent pounding on his bed chamber door. The aging noble begrudgingly crawled out of bed and dressed in an elegant crimson robe. The anger carved on his face was unmistakable. Sleep had become a rarity of late, ever since the war against the Ugri had begun. Reports streamed in from the front lines of a massive Ugri invasion force striking from the Great Barrier Jungle. Making matters worse was the sudden lack of communication with the Unified Army. He did his best to keep current on the situation but was quickly becoming more appreciative of having an effective staff. There was no way he could keep up alone.

Sleep still heavy in his eyes, Brentor cursed as his feet struck the cold concrete floor. He'd argued with his wife for more than twenty years that they needed larger rugs by the bed or a heated floor, but she preferred the cool touch. He always relented. Cool, he laughed to himself; some nights it was downright miserable.

"What?" he asked sharply once the door opened.

Aenis, his captain at arms, clutched his fist to his heart and bowed. "My lord, I bring grave news from the frontlines."

Damnation. "Reports have come in that General Shiramon has sent half of the army and encircled Torbecca. Lord Grushm is cut off."

And betrayed. Brentor was silent for a moment, making Aenis uncomfortable. They both felt helpless. Torbecca was hours away by air and days by ground. Grushm was on his own, and the nobles were scheduled to depart for Reven tomorrow.

Brentor finally replied, his voice dejected. "Well, Captain, it appears our war has begun. A shame the Ugri aren't the real targets. Summon my war staff and have the other nobles assembled. No doubt he aims to move on Berchenfel and Xiolen next. Time is our enemy."

"Yes, sir." Aenis disappeared back down the long hall.

Never did Brentor expect this unpleasant matter would all devolve into open rebellion. Left with few options, he brooded over his next move.

Fires ran down the outer parapet, thick and rich from oil and a mixture of gases. The walls had been mercilessly battered with light cannon and catapults for two days. Scored and threatening to break, the walls wouldn't stand much longer. Servants and house guards ran up and down the ragged defenses with hoses and buckets of water, but the burning oil was too strong to extinguish with water. Wounded soldiers refusing to abandon their posts stood fast beside comrades looking down at the massive army in the fields surrounding Torbecca. Scattered corpses lay in patches of ruined earth, but the living far outnumbered those within the walls.

The lord of Torbecca, his kingdom diminished to the extent of his city walls, stood atop the highest tower taking in the early morning scene. Once his favorite refuge, Grushm now found it lacking past splendor. His world was evaporating before him. Shiramon had attacked with such ruthless efficiency that Grushm never stood a chance. His forces were surrounded, and communications had been cut off before he'd managed to send a distress call. He was alone. Grushm paused to think what might have happened if he had sided with Scura. A rueful grin was all he managed.

"A damned sight to see, eh, Theseus?" he quietly asked.

The old chamberlain was accustomed to war, but not on this magnitude. He could hardly nod. "It seems a waste of men and time to do such things to former allies. I think compassion has been murdered. There will be no request for surrender, my lord."

"Indeed," Grushm agreed. "No matter the outcome, I think we'll give them enough trouble to slow their advance on the other kingdoms. Perhaps even enough to give Brentor a chance to put together his own army. Have we heard anything from Schuul?"

"No. No communications have come in or out since the siege began."

Grushm lightly slammed his fist onto the stonework. "I should have known better. Shiramon and Scura made too good of an argument to go to war against the Ugri. And now we are doomed."

Thick clouds rolled in from the north, blocking out the sun and bringing thunder and lighting.

"This bodes well for us, my lord," Theseus sagely remarked. The sudden change in air pressure chilled his tired bones, awakening old aches.

Grushm looked at him like he had gone mad. "How so?"

"Our enemy is encamped across open fields, most of which have already been tilled and plowed for the coming winter. A heavy storm will turn those fields into thick mud. Their siege engines and heavy equipment will bog down."

Hope twinkled in Grushm's eyes. "They'd be unprotected. Rouse the watch, Theseus. We'll teach these dogs a trick or two before they knock down our walls."

Seinz Shiramon watched the storm roll in on him with bitterness. Great thunderheads drowned out the sun. He cursed. Most of his force was still moving into assault positions. Camps had not been established, and it was his fault. Shiramon had been adamant about encircling the city and beginning the offensive before Grushm could manage a counter offensive.

This storm was only going to make matters worse. No soldier enjoyed fighting in the rain or snow. Weather had a way of sapping a man's strength or bolstering his confidence. Shiramon feared the worst. Already, the winds were sweeping angrily across the fields. Without a natural forest to block them, the winds bore straight through the army.

"Orderly!" Shiramon shouted to be heard. "Get Captain Zeth on the line."

The communications specialist started broadcasting on an internal frequency to the recon element. Shiramon scanned his field command post. The tactical operations center was alive with activity. Map boards lining the tent walls were covered with so many colored dots and pins that he had trouble making out any of the terrain features. Captains and junior officers strategized over possible outcomes as reports came in on a dozen different radios.

"General, Captain Zeth is on the line."

Shiramon reached for the handset. He would have preferred the up-to-date technology of the Prekhauten Guard, but Lethendweil did not have the vast amount of resources of the Conclave. The Unified Army was equipped with substandard vehicles and weapons but still packed enough firepower to topple kingdoms with ease.

"General, this is Zeth."

Efficient. I like that. "Captain, take command of our armor. I want you to flank to the left and punch a hole through that damned wall before the storm hits. We don't have much time. Breech the walls, and you'll have a column of infantry at your back to swarm in. Don't fail me, son."

"Yes, sir."

The line went dead. Shiramon clasped his hands behind his back and strode back outside. Hopefully, tonight he would be dining in Grushm's hall.

Zeth winced as a beam from one of those damned plasma cannons whizzed past his head to incinerate another tank. One tank already stood melting a few meters away. The heat from the flames threatened to burn him. Another shot, and another medium track went up in a chorus of screams and flames. These were his first combat losses, and Zeth felt like he was on the verge of losing control. Indecision mocked him. His men were being burned alive by an enemy without honor. *Murderers!*

"Sergeant!" he called over the roar of battle. "Move your platoon right three hundred meters and get under the range of those cannons."

"What about the infantry on the walls?" he asked.

Zeth snarled, training his oculars on the city. "We'll deal with them once the walls are breeched. Move quickly and engage any targets you can!"

It was their only chance. A smaller explosion rocked his command vehicle, kicking up a bout of rock and debris. Zeth ducked to avoid most of the lethal spray. The high-pitched whine of multiple engines dominated the field. Zeth immediately ordered a concentrated barrage on the nearest section of wall to cover the advance. Enemy plasma cannons redoubled their rate of fire. Two more tanks were slagged before they got off the line. Zeth was forced to sit helpless as the advance continued; all the while, screams of the dying echoed in his headset.

The fear of failure gripped him. Zeth struggled to regain some semblance of composure. He knew Shiramon was cursing his name from the TOC. He watched men crawl from burning vehicles and drag themselves away. He smelled the finely roasted flesh of his men and damned his own helplessness. Zeth looked down at the ruined corpse of a boy who couldn't have been more than nineteen summers.

Unprecedented emotions clicked. Zeth suddenly found focus, clarity of action. Too many men had died while he sat immobile in his command hatch. He decided to move. Zeth ordered half of the remaining armor around to the left in a separate assault. Grushm simply did not have enough men or cannons to stop both advances.

The handful of heavy cannons left atop the battlements rained down a horrific barrage on the Unified Army. Bodies and equipment were vaporized as the super-heated plasma in each 170 mm shell exploded with the fury of a dying sun. The heavy iron smell of blood hovered like fine mist. Soldiers ran to avoid getting hit; others dropped into craters and prayed. Indiscriminate death continued to hound them, regardless. Columns of thick black smoke dotted the fields. Most worlds had abandoned the primitive form of cannon, but Crimeat lacked the competitive advancements of worlds closer to Vau Prime.

Gunners were ordered to slow their rate of fire and were suddenly able to pick and choose important targets with impunity. Enemy snipers crept closer, taking out any gunner foolish enough to avoid taking cover. Men fell screaming from the ramparts. Lord Grushm patrolled the walls offering words of encouragement and picking up an occasional rifle. An enemy rocket slammed into the wall nearby, driving him onto his back under a flurry of stone and shrapnel. Groaning, he tried to get up but found he couldn't. Blood seeped from a dozen wounds, and his ears rang. Soldiers rushed to his side, but he angrily shoved them off. The last thing his men needed was to see him weakly dragged from the battlefield.

He struggled to his knees. Pain lanced throughout his body. His vision swam. It had been a long time since he last felt these effects. A new sound assaulted the city. His eyes flew wide with horror as recognition dawned. Even above the roar of battle and nature's impending fury, there was no mistaking the aggressive sounds of attacking armor. Grushm knew he had nothing in his arsenal capable of defeating a major armor thrust. They were doomed. Panic spread through the defenders.

Light tank rounds began peppering the walls. Men died by the score. It started to rain, washing some of the debris from his face. A huge chunk of wall disintegrated, throwing random body parts into the air. Grushm watched in horror as his men started to run. The end was in sight. He recalled why he had never pursued a military career. Risking a look, Grushm ducked behind a broken piece of concrete. Shiramon's armor was taking up positions in a crude semi-circle, and that was barely a third of the huge force pushing down the main avenue of approach. Grushm swallowed the lump in his throat.

Every tube elevated simultaneously, converging their deflections until all were aimed at the same point. Grushm turned and fled just as gunners tripped their foot triggers. It wasn't going to take more than a few volleys before his only defense was shattered, but the damage would not be to his walls alone. The morale of his men would die, and he would be forced to surrender if Shiramon would accept it. Shiramon was tactically shrewd, so something or someone else was driving him. Sieges were long, drawn out affairs that were more trouble than productive. This wasn't going to last the night.

Grushm snatched the nearest soldier by his collar. "Go down to the gates. Tell Major Hael to pull back as many people as possible and reinforce the right flank. Infantry will attack as soon as the walls come down."

A long gout of flame exploded overhead, sending ash and fire down around them. Grushm's sole concern was for his soldiers. The civilians would be fine. People lived without much of a say in who ruled them, and his hands were no cleaner than Scura's. Another salvo punished the walls. Out of options, Grushm decided to evacuate the army. Brentor and Mans were seriously outgunned, and every man he saved in Torbecca would be able to fight again. Grushm stumbled off in search of Theseus.

He found the steward exactly where he expected to, near the outer wall directing soldiers. Blood painted the right side of his face, and his arm hung useless. Theseus offered a grim look. "I am afraid events are not going quite as we expected, my liege."

More explosions ripped the ground.

"No, no they're not. I fear it is time to abandon our positions." Grushm's word stung, but he saw no other way out. They were doomed if they stood.

Theseus remained silent. Never in his darkest dreams did he foresee this day.

"Give the order. Abandon posts. Get as many men out through the tunnels as you can. We have to save what we can."

Theseus eyed his lord, silently judging him. It pained Grushm to give the order to his oldest and most trusted friend. Theseus had been his father's advisor and a proud servant of Torbecca. Conflicting emotions twisted his face.

"Do this for me, my friend. One last deed in the Grushm name." His words were barely a whisper.

Theseus cleared his throat. "Sire, you must come first. The men will endure, but our lands will not without their lord."

"No. I must stay. Shiramon is after me. This insanity will end once I surrender."

"They will give you no mercy; you know that."

Grushm nodded sadly. "I must be accountable for my lack of actions. I led us to this disaster, and I alone will accept my fate. Go. Get out while you still can."

The older man pursed his lips before thinking better of it. Grushm was a proud man and, despite numerous character flaws, did not need to be doubted at a time like this. He was sacrificing his future for the greater good of his men and his people. Theseus reached out to clasp Grushm's hand in a last act of friendship before disappearing into the haze, collecting soldiers as he went. The lord of Torbecca struggled with overwhelming sorrow. Theseus was a good man and a better friend who deserved much more than to be sent away at the greatest hour of need. Grushm wiped a tear from the corner of one eye and looked at the destruction. What he saw surprised him. Scores of soldiers had disobeyed his orders and were moving back to the walls. Many of these were already wounded, some gravely. Grushm was filled with pride.

"Cone on you dogs!" he barked. "Let's give these bastards a proper greeting!"

Cheers rose moments before the armor started firing again.

Grushm picked himself up from the rubble and dust. Rain pelted them as much as incoming tank rounds. The hundred or so men still alive did the same, trying to forget lost comrades and their own wounds. Cut off, surrender was no longer an option. They stared out through the rain, dust and smoke as the Unified Army tightened the noose. The cannons were all silent. Most of the crews were dead. That last blast had punched a hole in the walls wide enough to drive three tanks through abreast. Grushm knew it was over. He could hear the cheers of enemy infantry as they charged.

Grushm drew his ceremonial sword and stabbed high in the air. "Give no quarter, for you can expect none! Remember, we fight for our families, for our freedom, and for all Lethendweil. The enemy wants to take this from you. Will you give it to him freely?"

His men roared in defiance.

"Or will you make him pay for every inch of ground, every life taken?"

The ground shook under the assault of thousands of armored soldiers drawing closer. Grushm lowered his sword and opened his mouth to speak again when he noticed the pencil-thin man slip into the ranks around him. His heart warmed as Theseus gave a curt nod. The old man had volunteered for certain death, and Grushm envied him. Not everyone was so fortunate as to choose his own demise. The men around them instantly became more confident. They crouched behind broken parapets and took aim. Shiramon's infantry was almost at the walls.

Grushm didn't need to tell them to fire.

Seinz Shiramon entered Torbecca the same as his soldiers had done three hours earlier. They deserved to see their leader humble as he officially claimed Torbecca. Most of the bodies had been policed. A huge area just outside the walls was turned into a mobile hospital. Hundreds of wounded and dead surrounded the hastily erected tents.

Blood and torn uniforms littered the immediate area. Shiramon detested visiting the wounded but knew it was necessary.

He met Zeth at the city gates, now thrown open to accept the conquerors. The captain had fresh scars and looked twenty years older than he had at dawn. Shiramon both envied and pitied the man. War was a harsh mistress, as unforgiving and fickle as the northern winters. Together, the pair went to the wall where the last defenders had fallen. Shiramon soon stood over the cool corpses of Grushm and Theseus. By all accounts, they had fought bravely, as befitting a lord of Lethendweil. Most of Shiramon's dead lay scattered around the pair. Shiramon knelt and gently closed Grushm's eyes. A fellow noble, regardless of which side he was aligned with, he deserved an honorable burial. He'd fought well and, as Shiramon would discover in the next few weeks, saved much of his combat force.

Shiramon rose and ordered, "See to it these two bodies are cleaned and given a proper burial in the family cemetery, Commander. Bury the others or let their families claim the bodies. These men fought with honor."

"At once, General," he saluted crisply and darted off barking orders.

Shiramon continued into the city proper. There was still a fair amount of sporadic gunfire, but the shot reports were scattered, unorganized. For all intents and purposes, Torbecca had fallen. Armored Unified Army patrols scoured the streets. Dismounted infantry went house to house, rooting out guerrillas. Seinz Shiramon watched his army execute their mission with ruthless efficiency. A satisfied grin finally broke free. He had struck the first blow in the revolution.

TWENTY-FOUR

3210 A.G. (After Gods), Berchenfel, planet Crimeat.

The pair of combat fliers swooped by at subsonic speeds, causing the wounded craft to wobble uncertainly. Elisa spit a curse as she struggled to maintain control. Warning lights bleeped on the instrument panel. She strained her neck to see where the fliers sped to, all the while knowing they were circling like predators anxious for the kill. She knew the Unified Army didn't have many fliers, so they would naturally be curious as to why one of theirs that was undoubtedly reported lost in Ugri territory was suddenly flying over the plains of Berchenfel.

"What do you think they are going to do?" Mollock Bolle asked, his head peeking out from behind the pilot's seat.

Elisa bore a hard look. "I'd say they were going to shoot us down. Find something to strap yourself in with. This is going to get ugly."

"Can we out fly them?"

No. The answer was unequivocally no. Elisa had been lucky just getting this carcass off the ground in the first place. She and Mollock had made it halfway across Lethendweil without being investigated by the Unified Army. Her prayers that the surviving fliers had reported her craft lost were only answered for so long.

"Just strap in," she snapped through gritted teeth.

Mollock fumbled for anything that might save his life. The massive hole in the hull produced a loud sucking noise that threatened to make him deaf. The old man started to rethink his decision. He knew he could have talked the Ugri down, but to what end? There was no safe place left for him to go. He'd been on the run for fifty years—so long, he no longer knew where he was from. Mollock didn't know which home was home. What a family was. Mollock Bolle was the definition of empty.

Perhaps his finding Elisa was meant to be. She had a familiar hurt. Her soul bled from wounds that could never be healed. He pinched the bridge of his nose. There was too much hurt. He almost wished he'd never found that cave on the Plateau, but the secret he'd learned needed to be told. His life had been spent on the run from fear. Dark figures chased him to the ends of the continent and back again. Mollock regretted what needed doing but saw no other option. He had to get off Crimeat. It was the only way.

The roar of engines speeding by his left broke his train of thought.

"They're coming back around!" he practically shouted.

Elisa waved him off.

"Unidentified aircraft, announce yourself and set down immediately," a sterilized voice ordered over the intercom.

Elisa ignored it. She was struggling to keep the flier airborne, and now these assholes wanted her to put it on the deck. She had no intentions of doing so. Glancing over the instrument panel, she was rewarded with a little pane displaying weapons status. The missiles were gone, and she only had a few thousand rounds of chain gun ammo left. She wasn't an experienced enough pilot to dogfight with two enemies. A shrill swoosh followed closely by an exhaust trail blasted across their canopy.

"What was that?" he shouted. Fear strangled his voice.

"Get back! They're firing on us."

Elisa banked the flier hard to the right and drove it down. The enemy craft had expected this maneuver and followed suit. She cursed.

"This is your last warning. Put your bird on the deck, NOW."

"Maybe we should do what they say," Mollock offered. He didn't want to die in a fiery crash in the middle of nowhere.

"Shut up before I kick you out the gods damned hole!" she snapped.

Mollock pressed himself back against the hull and screwed his eyes shut. Better not to see the end before it happened. He was no hero after all.

Red-blue streaks flashed by the canopy to detonate in the air. The concussions rattled the wounded flier. Residue splattered the composite windshield. Elisa ducked to see. The flier shuddered under the assault of enemy chain guns. Mollock cringed as hundreds of metallic pings tore through the rear of the fuselage. Warning lights blinked on. They were going down. Elisa grew desperate. The pilots chasing her were getting increasingly aggressive. It wouldn't be long before a missile rammed up their ass end. Her only chance was to make it to the Bothwel Mountains. Hopefully she would be able to lose them in the soaring black peaks.

"You're going to get us killed!" Mollock screamed.

Like I need your confirmation. "Hold on," she ordered and jerked the throttle back as hard as she could.

The flier broke upward, narrowly missing the pair of magnetic missiles intended to rip out their bottom. Their engines screamed. Smoke began to trail out. Time was running out, and the mountains were still at least fifty kilometers away. She didn't have a chance. Elisa throttled the engines for all they had left. The missiles struck together and detonated. Shrapnel blossomed out, forcing the enemy fliers to juke out of the path. Elisa decided to use the momentary distraction to her advantage and banked right. The flier screamed through the sky directly at the nearest enemy. She tripped the trigger and opened fire.

The twin chain guns erupted with the fury of a dying star. White hot rounds punished the top of the enemy flier, tearing jagged holes down the fuselage. The pilot dropped his stricken craft before Elisa got lucky and put enough rounds into his engines to cause an explosion. She roared by and headed for the mountains at top speed. Only one enemy aircraft followed.

Mollock was in shock. They had just attacked the enemy and came out relatively unscathed. More chain gun rounds hit their tail. Power flickered off for a long second, dimming the cockpit. Mollock closed his eyes again, knowing they would not live long enough to gain the safety of the mountains.

"What in the hells are you muttering about?" Elisa called over her shoulder.

"What?"

"I asked what you were saying," she said again. Elisa didn't care much for conversation, but anything helped keep her mind off the violent demise eagerly pursuing them.

"Nothing, just some old prayers."

Elisa suddenly realized that she hadn't prayed or bothered believing in the gods for a very long time. Not since the day the Bloody Man had come to her village. Faith seemed hollow after watching everything she knew and loved destroyed on a whim. A siren blared to life.

"Incoming missile!" she shouted.

The mountain wall loomed so close she almost believed. More alarms came to life as the missile charged towards them. Five kilometers left. They weren't going to make it. The missile struck them hard, slamming Elisa's face into the canopy. Mollock cried out right after a loud snap. The flier was dying. They were going to have to ditch and make the rest of the way on foot, if either of them managed to survive the crash.

Black smoke filled the cockpit. Mollock and Elisa covered their mouths. Tears streamed down their cheeks. The smell of raw fuel tainted the air. Elisa's eyes flew wide. If the flames struck the exposed fuel lines, the flier was going to explode. They were jerked back and forth suddenly as the right engine flamed out. The crippled flier limped across the sky. Another stream of traces stitched across the left wing, shredding the thin metal. Fliers weren't designed for combat; a lesson Elisa was painfully learning now. She dared a look back at Mollock and wished she hadn't. The older, deranged man had his arms wrapped around his drawn-up knees and was weeping.

The muscles in her forearms hurt from the strain. Elisa pulled the throttle back as hard as she could. Her jaw clenched. The enemy flier continued to pour a deadly stream of chain gun rounds at her. *This is it. I'm going to die so close to the answers I've searched my life for.* More warning lights started blinking. A loud siren screamed above the sputtering engine. *Shit! Proximity warning.* Elisa looked through the smoke and grime and saw only blackness. She squinted. The blackness quickly took shape. Jagged peaks and broken outcroppings rose like angry claws.

Elisa jerked the throttle, narrowly avoiding a massive cluster of black rock. She couldn't miss it entirely. Centuries of hardened rock drove up into the belly of the flier, ripping metal and wiring to shreds. The power flickered and died. They were dead in the air. Their only grace came from having traveled at such a high velocity the flier continued to blast into the mountains. Elisa briefly wondered if her pursuit was still there but found the thought foolish. She and Mollock were about to become a smear on a mountainside.

"I'm sorry, Mollock," she whispered an instant before the flier lost both wings between two monstrous pillars of stone.

Pebbles and debris erupted out, encasing the cockpit completely. Fire and smoke did the rest. Elisa wanted to keep her eyes open, meet death head-on with the same ruthless pursuit she put into every bounty, but panic's grip was too tight. She closed her soft blue eyes and waited for death to strike. She didn't wait long. The flier crumbled on an outcropping, disintegrating into a hail of metal fragments.

Pain. Intense waves of pain rippled through her battered body. Elisa tried to move but lacked the strength. Her vision slowly refocused, and what she saw filled her with cold dread. Instead of clouds and sky, all she saw was the dark black of the Bothwel Mountains. Any relief she might have found was dashed against the very rocks she had sought comfort in. She tried to take a deep breath, but the fire inside forced her to stop. She had at least one broken rib, probably more.

She laughed suddenly. *I'm alive!* The impossibility of it forced her to smile. There was no way either of them should have survived the crash. Elisa twisted her head. The pain was intense but bearable. Against all odds, much of the cockpit remained intact. Mostly. The debris field stretched for hundreds of meters. Small flames pockmarked the surrounding area, only the flames were upside down. Elisa was confused. *Is this the afterlife? Am I in Hell?*

"Oww."

Her heart quickened. "Mollock? You're alive?"

Cough. "It doesn't feel like it. What happened?"

She wished she knew. Divine intervention was out of the question. Everyone knew the gods were gone. It was the age of man, and man was one mean son of a bitch, she thought.

"We crashed," she answered, deadpan.

Mollock cocked his head. A large gash on his forehead wept blood. He wanted to laugh but struggled just to remain conscious. Elisa took pity and explained how they had been shot down and, hopefully, left for dead on the roof of the Bothwel Mountains. He didn't believe it but wasn't willing to argue. It took her close to an hour to work herself free from the wreckage and another hour to dig Mollock out. She was happiest when Mollock produced a med kit and a small pack of field rations. Elisa tended his wounds and the few cuts and scrapes she had that a bandage was good enough to fix, and they split the food.

Cold winds assaulted the mountaintops. Winter was almost upon them, and the roof of the world grew cold. Elisa and Mollock huddled next to each other around one of the larger fires that still burned. She wanted to sleep but doing so meant death for both of them. They'd gained the relative security of the mountains and were so close to reaching their goal. Mollock had promised he could get her into the cave where his secret awaited, but if they didn't last the night it didn't matter.

She found the darkness unsettling. It reminded her of an empty hatred stalking her childhood. Old nightmares loomed on the horizon of her memory. Memories, Mollock sympathized with. He, too, struggled against demons. She shivered.

"We're not going to make it through the night," he muttered.

The comment made her angry. She wanted to chastise him despite the potential truth of it. "Yes, we are. Stop talking like that. I'm going back to the wreck to see if there is any kind of survival kit. We have to find a way to keep warm."

"I'll help you." He struggled to rise and fell back down. His strength had abandoned him.

She shook her head. "No. you sit and try to recover. You took the worst of the blows."

Elisa didn't have the heart to tell him she preferred to be alone. There was a strange comfort in it, like an old friend she could tell anything to without worry or concern. Hobbling because of a twisted ankle, she rummaged through what little remained of the flier. Random thoughts danced through her mind. Every event in her life had led her to this point, darkness on the edge of winter. Mollock had told her that he once had dreams of winter and didn't know what they meant. The chill driving through her torn clothes and deep into her marrow might provide an explanation. Winter was close, and so was the end of her journey.

She didn't know what was so special in Mollock's secret cave, but she was determined to live long enough to find out. Questions demanded answers. Elisa prayed it led her to another confrontation with the Bloody Man. Only then would she feel vindicated for the horrors he'd left her mired in.

The shuttle skipped just above the treetops. Sleek with narrow angles to confuse enemy radar, the craft was pitch black and lightly armed. Small tubes protruded from the belly, each capable of firing dozens of ground flares. Engines rigged for silent running, the ten men inside sat back restlessly as they sped closer to their target. Brood Hammerling looked at each of his men with stern eyes. They had all been handpicked by Sergeant Belcum to perform what was considered one of the most important missions in the budding war. Brood watched his men for weakness, knowing that he would be forced to act should one of them break.

He was a giant of a man, more akin to the ancient barbarians than the sophisticated soldiers of the Prekhauten Guard. He kept his head shaved. His chest and shoulder muscles made it look like he didn't have a neck. Rumors said he'd killed more men and heretics with his bare hands than with an ion rifle. Brood let the rumors grow, knowing the damage they could do before he ever deployed. Momentarily satisfied, Brood leaned back into the mess jump seat, closed his eyes and remembered.

"Let's go, ladies! Rise and shine," Brood snapped a moment before kicking the steel trashcan down the middle of the ten-man tent.

Several Guardsmen instinctively rolled from their cots and reached for weapons. Brood grinned savagely. One managed to sleep through the noise and the sudden assault of a halogen light turned on.

"I said move it! We're wasting daylight. The day's half over, and you slugs are still dreaming about old loves and little boys. Get out on my line before I bust your useless skulls open!"

Brood stormed from the tent and returned to Sergeant Belcum. The senior NCO watched approvingly as the squad poured from their tent like a swarm of ants.

"Wasting daylight? My grandfather used to tell me that," he commented.

Brood shrugged. "It works."

The sun had yet to rise, and the camp was in an uproar. Word had come down that they were officially declared heretics. Loyal Guard forces were purportedly already beginning to search for their camp. Ursal Prowl had been discovered, and now the Guard contingent on Crimeat was going to pay for it. Of course, murdering several villages' worth of innocent civilians didn't make his men any less undeserving of the Conclave's wrath. Brood sighed but quickly realized there was nothing for it. They were damned either way.

What surprised him was the order to mobilize and counterattack. His doubts about attacking fellow Guardsmen didn't matter much. They were going to do their best to kill him, leaving no choice but to try and kill them first. So Belcum decided on letting Brood loose. A man like that was too valuable to be left to rot in garrison during the middle of a campaign.

"We don't have much time," Belcum said. Brevel nodded from behind.

Brood glanced back over his shoulder. Most of the squad was in some ragged form of a line awaiting his inspection. "They'll be ready."

If he had any reservations, they didn't register in his tone. Belcum shot Brevel a wary look. "You have no problems with this?"

"No. One mission is the same as another. Bodies wind up everywhere, and the ground turns red. This is war."

Belcum's eyes hardened. "Do this right. It's the only chance we have before they send in a few divisions."

Brood smiled. "If I find them, I will kill them."

That night, they boarded the assault craft.

"One minute," the crew chief called over the scratchy intercom.

Brood's eyes flared open, dark and menacing. New life flowed through them, and it terrified his men. Brood was a pure killing machine. Muscles bunched beneath his flat black armor, Brood unbuckled the safety straps and rose. His men did the same. *Cut off the head, and the rest will fall*. The thought replayed through his mind. Brood wanted to hunt. Wanted to fight. These pathetic indigenous tribes failed to offer any form of challenge. Now he got to test his skills against his former comrades. The battle promised to be spectacular.

"Thirty seconds."

His squad was all standing, hanging on to thin red straps dangling from the roof. They rocked with the sway of the craft. Only Brood stood immobile, his massive legs anchoring him to the steel deck. His weapon felt good in his hands. It reminded him how simple life was. Life and death all came at the end of a barrel. Brood refocused on the task at hand.

Intelligence was tracking the enemy Guardsmen moving through the grasslands of Berchenfel. Brood snarled when they couldn't narrow it down until the last minute and was oddly pleased when he was told that they were going to be bait. He liked the idea of letting his counterparts come to him.

"Ten seconds."

Brood looked over his squad one last time and offered a curt nod as the back ramp dropped. The giant started heading towards the exit. The craft shook as it lightly touched the ground. Brood jumped into the waist-high grass and barreled forward, weapon raised and biometric scanner actively searching for targets. A nearby brook babbled a constant stream of water. Massive boulders littered the immediate area, concealing multiple heat signatures. Rodents and predatory birds scurried away at the heavy sound of twenty boots trampling across the field.

"All personnel deployed. Good luck," the crew chief whispered into Brood's earpiece.

Brood smiled and pushed ahead as the shuttle silently drifted away. The squad formed a loose wedge at his back. The Unified Army camp was less than a kilometer away. *Camp*, he snorted inwardly. It was no more than a signal outpost. Hardly worthy of his talents. A pair of human-shaped heat signatures flared on his helmet scanner. They'd come across the sentries. *Good. That means there are infantry here.* His hopes of getting a good fight might just be met after all.

Brood clicked his mouthpiece. "This is one. Enemy identified. I am taking the shot."

His rifle flashed twice, and he was rewarded with two cooling figures on the ground. A pair of shadows sprinted forward to drag the bodies into cover. Brood listened to a similar report from a hundred meters west. So far, so good. Without waiting for the all clear, he kept moving. The infantry put up a good fight, but they were sorely outmatched and disadvantaged.

Brood gave the order with glee. "This is one; engage at will."

Rifle fire erupted across the tiny compound. Brood took credit for the first kill. A commo tech was coming back from relieving himself when he ran right into the giant man. Brood snapped his neck and kicked the body away. Men ran by, firing at every target they could. Bodies dropped in sprays of blood. One of his men fired a grenade launcher directly into the communications vehicle. Brood barely had time to close his eyes before the massive ball of orange and red flames filled the night sky, stealing his night vision.

Brood barely waited for the flames to die down before assaulting a machinegun pit on the far side of camp. Ion rounds shredded the sandbag walls and the men cowering behind them. Body parts flew into the sky. Brood relished the horrified looks etched into the faces of the dying. One man made it out of the foxhole and attacked. Brood grinned like a feral savage. Lowering his rifle, Brood drew his long knife and charged. The Unified Army soldier lunged with his bayonet. Brood easily sidestepped the move and drove his blade deep into the soldier's left side just below the ribs. The soldier let out a startled gurgle as Brood twisted the blade up and into his heart. He was dead before Brood pushed the body away.

"Man down." The call broke his battle trance.

Snarling, he clicked the talk button. "Say again?"

"We have a man down."

Brood looked around and was disappointed to find no living enemies. The communication vehicle was bleeding black smoke. Twisted corpses hung from the rents. All four guard posts were drenched in flames. Bodies littered the camp. His scanners read eight life forms. Only eight.

"Collect the dead and leave the evidence. I want there to be no mistaking who did this," Brood ordered.

Brood Hammerling knew that the Prekhauten Guard would be quick to investigate and even quicker to find him. He smiled. Hopefully, his fellow Guardsmen would put up more of a fight than these peasants pretending to be soldiers. Either way, there was one hell of a fight coming.

TWENTY-FIVE

3210 A.G. (After Gods), Reven, planet Crimeat.

Baron Scura ground the tip of a ceremonial dagger into the ancient wooden desk in his private study until a mass of shavings concealed it, but he didn't notice. His eyes blazed with building rage.

His mind was focused on the monster the dark council had unleashed on him. He had never imagined what the manifestation of hatred was until Amongeratix had emerged from that wagon and proved his dominance. Lethendweil had changed that day. Scura realized he was not the power he'd once believed. He never had been. All his plotting and dreaming was nothing but the realization of the dark council's desires. It was a sham. He was a pawn.

Anger reduced his ability to rationalize. The building stones of his legacy had crashed down around his ankles, leaving nothing but rubble. Shiramon's message that Torbecca had fallen should have bolstered his spirits, but he remained cold inside. Perhaps it was the impending winter, perhaps not. His ankle-length black robe with purple trim did little to warm him. The very chill seemed unnatural. He glanced at the gently cackling fire across the room. The flames mocked him.

Scura tried to shake off the feeling of dread and focused on the tabletop map of Lethendweil his father had paid a healthy sum to have engraved. Torbecca had fallen, and the Unified Army was marching against the Ugri and Brentor. Scura reasoned that the Ugri were savages that needed to be dealt with eventually, and this was the best time. The full weight of the army could be thrown into the steppe tribes and claim the lands for the eastern kingdoms.

The Conclave wouldn't bother him so long as he left Prophet Isle untouched and maintained effective communications. Still, Scura contemplated taking the isle for the resources alone. There would be plenty of dissidents in need of imprisonment when the rebellion was finished. The prison was the perfect place to *remove* certain enemies. He highly doubted the Conclave or Inquisition was in the position to send forces to Crimeat. There were too many worlds in need of immediate attention, if Ursal Prowl was to be believed.

Trying to clear his thoughts, Scura took a drink of aged port. The idea of removing Amongeratix was particularly appealing but a waste of time. He was one of the fabled Three, god-like myths striding across the board of the universe. No, he had to think small. Geres Auk was his immediate concern. His chief of security and untitled first minister was perhaps the most dangerous man in Reven. He seldom slept and never needed instructions. It was as if he could read Scura's mind. The Baron frowned. Strengths and weaknesses overplayed each other. He tipped back his goblet, draining the last of his expensive port.

Dangerous. The thought continued to circulate. Scura tried to recall what he knew of Geres Auk. He was surprised with how little that was. The big man had come to him a few years ago with an immaculate resume and the inner drive necessary to succeed up on the Plateau. Geres was a natural killer, a matter he'd proven several times over. Scura didn't trust him, but he was too afraid to let him go.

A troubled look scrunching his face, Scura collected his robes and stormed from his private quarters. A pair of guards snapped to attention, their black uniforms crisp in the artificial hallway light. The Ugri. The dark council. Geres Auk and Amongeratix. Scura couldn't think straight. Too many conflicting thoughts rendered him immobile. He wasn't sure anymore. His thirst for knowledge seemed dry. He couldn't find any weaknesses or strengths, and that left him frustrated beyond reasonable measure.

"What troubles you, Baron?" Geres Auk's voice boomed from behind.

Always where we least expect, eh? "Nothing, I am merely tired."

The big man fell into step and remained silent. He bore a look of quiet disdain before quickly masking it. His sleeveless vest hugged his muscled torso. The twin rows of knives running down his back left nothing to doubt. He was dangerous.

"What have you to report on Amongeratix?"

Geres clenched his jaw. "Not much. He is lost within the caves. Most of my spies have been unable to find him successfully, and the ones who have were all found dead. He is a cunning enemy."

Interesting you use the term enemy. "Is he a threat to Reven?"

"Yes."

"He must not be left unattended," Scura insisted. "We stand to lose everything. Our war against the twelve kingdoms has only begun, and this abomination threatens to drag us under. Are we any closer to discovering what he is searching for?"

A pause. "I believe he searches for a tomb."

"That's what worries me, Geres. Amongeratix is a force too dangerous to remain in Reven."

Geres Auk had no answer. Scura knew there wasn't any logical conclusion. The Three were myths manifested on Crimeat, causing Scura great fear. Perhaps going after Amongeratix was the wrong course. Scura stopped in midstride and faced his aide.

"This dark council, what do you know of them?" He carefully hid the malice he felt, still unsure of Geres's true loyalties.

"Rumors—whispers, really. They are a rising power in Lethendweil."

Scura snorted. "There is always someone else craving power. We are weakened by the war. Our eyes are not focused in the right place. We should have seen them well before they sent *him* here."

"Some say that not even its own members know each other's identities," Geres suggested.

That doesn't make any sense. Scura cleared his mind. "Set a team up to investigate. I want their names and what kingdoms they are from. Geres, I want this dark council eradicated."

"Yes, Baron." A simple reply.

"You seem distracted," Scura questioned.

Geres nodded crisply. "The council's shuttle is en route from Vaade. They will be here shortly."

A fist clenched deep within Scura's stomach. He'd forgotten about Brentor's impending visit. "Are your forces in place?"

"They are. I have men posted in strategic points around the airfield. Brentor will not know what happened until he is in his cell."

Scura scratched his chin thoughtfully. "We are taking an awful risk. There is no room for error. I want them locked away and forgotten before news can get out. The twelve kingdoms must not learn of what we have done until after Vaade is secure."

Vaade was his idea but not an immediate concern. Inquisitor Ursal Prowl assured him the city would be successfully captured and locked down with minimal effort. The problem of Prekhauten Guards dressed in local uniforms was Prowl's dilemma. Of course, there was the obvious threat of Conclave reprisal once word got to Vau Prime, but the Conclave was normally reluctant in dealing with planetary affairs. The implications were dizzying. Scura focused on his own affairs, let the rest be damned.

"Timing must be precise on this, Geres," Scura reiterated.

Another sharp nod. "All will go according to plan, Baron."

"See that it does. Amongeratix changes things but not to the point where we should despair." He paused. "Notify me right before the shuttle lands. I want to be there to see the look on Brentor's smug face when he's clapped in irons."

"Of course, Baron."

The shuttle cruised across the Lethendweil night sky with the grace of an arcing swan. Pure white save for the golden dagger seal of the council, it was nearly invisible to the watching eye. Advancements in radar technology made the shuttle invisible to most conventional radars, but none on the council knew of Scura's dealings through Ursal Prowl. Reven had some of the most superior military-grade equipment for a dozen star systems.

Leather seats lined the shuttle in two rows. A pair of attendants stood patiently in the rear of the craft should one of the nobles required them. Drinks were served shortly after takeoff from Vaade, and the nobles immersed themselves in tactics. Brentor's mood had been soured with the news of Grushm's death. Torbecca was their largest ally in the west. With the city taken, the path east across Berchenfel was wide open. Nothing could stop them before the Unified Army assaulted the walls. All Lethendweil would fall beneath the carefully conceived plots of Baron Scura. Unless Brentor could find some way to stall him.

"This is foolish, Brentor," Lord Mans repeated for the ninth time since taking off. "Scura will not be foolish enough to allow us to march into his home and make demands."

Brentor pushed out a heavy sigh. "What choice do we have, Mans? Torbecca's loss hurts deeply. Not only have we lost a key ally, but we can no longer be certain which units assigned to General Shiramon remain loyal to the council. I have no doubts that many of the senior leaders have been subsumed by Shiramon's men."

"You suggest that our own forces are turned?" Schuul questioned.

"We cannot rule anything out. Gentlemen, I believe we are doomed if we cannot convince Scura to compromise."

"Or should we?" Mans asked.

"Explain yourself."

Mans held out his hands in a desperate gesture. "Everything we know is now threatened. Thousands have already been killed. How many more need to die because of twelve men and women?"

"I do not enjoy the thought of bowing to an upstart from the Plateau," old Orthis Gel added. "Any man who murders his own father is the worst kind of usurper."

"I am not suggesting we cave," Mans quickly followed. "But we owe it to our peoples to find a way out of this war."

"Your tongue bleeds traitorous words," Brentor cautioned.

Mans shot him a foul glare. "I am one of the most loyal sons in Lethendweil. Do not question my resolve to continue the fight. All I am saying is that we are no longer in a position of strength. Scura and Shiramon will drive what remains of our armies all the way to the sea."

"So you want to play games?" Schuul mocked.

"I do not think this is a game at all," Mans defended.

Brentor interrupted. "But it is. It is a very dangerous game, and make no mistake about the consequences should we lose. A short rope and a long drop will be for us all if Scura gets his way. He wants control. That is all it has ever been about. The consolidation of absolute power in Lethendweil. We have long suspected it, but Emleth was never able to prove so."

"Until now," Schuul said.

Try as he might, Brentor couldn't get a good read on Schuul's intentions. He suspected the lord of Xiolen held sinister purpose. Too few of his fellow nobles were sided with him, and that left Brentor feeling hollow.

"Until now," Brentor agreed. "The game itself is very simple. In order to win the world, he must first defeat the world. Scura has proven his desire and prowess with the sack of Torbecca. He moves quickly because he has no choice. We must be just as quick with our response."

"How? All communications have been cut off, and you tell us our armies have been turned against us," Schuul protested.

"Perhaps you can explain how it is your kingdom is still able to communicate with Vaade," Orthis Gel snapped.

Schuul scowled. "You ask too many questions, old man."

Mans quickly jumped in. "He asks valid questions, Schuul."

"Enough of this," Brentor charged. "We are alone. Get that through your skulls. I have reason to believe even our friendly Inquisitor has abandoned us, taking his Prekhauten Guard with him. You can be assured that no one is coming to our aid."

"Then why bother fighting?" Schuul asked, frustration twisting his words. "You present the grimmest of scenarios, and none suggest we can win. This is pointless."

Brentor struggled to maintain composure. "Pointless or not, we are going to try and position Scura to at least end the fighting. No one else needs to die because of the greed of a selfish few. We must finish this now before everything is lost and Lethendweil is plunged into chaos and darkness."

"Surrender?" Mans choked out. "I never thought you'd accept such a notion."

Brentor's face turned gloomy. "If needs be."

"Absolutely not! We cannot surrender just for the sake of lives. What we stand to lose is too great. Scura will not stop his tyranny until every kingdom is broken and in tow with his twisted dreams of power. This continent will bleed for generations."

Schuul passed a carefully crafted glance to each noble but held his tongue. Only Orthis Gel noticed, and he, too, decided to keep his comments private. The council was clearly fractured to the point of ineffectiveness, and nothing seemed capable of stalling Scura's quest. Brentor saw the truth in this. It took great courage to step down for the greater good, but Mans had a valid point. Scura was a tyrant aching to be unleashed. Orthis Gel gently closed his eyes and thought. There was still time to choose sides.

"This conversation is turning to foolishness," Brentor countered softly. "Wars are often won in the shadows, despite what happens on the battlefield. Emleth knew this and tried to warn us."

"You need to stop hiding behind Emleth's failures," Mans snarled. "His death should have shown us all something. Scura needs to be stopped."

Brentor leaned forward slightly, his eyes hard. "How?"

"The same way Emleth and the others were."

"Assassination?" Schuul gasped.

Brentor sadly shook his head. "I cannot condone such a vile act."

"Then we are lost."

Brentor let the conversation die. He was torn by conflict. Surrender was cowardly and not in his character, but he saw little choice. The council was weak. Half were already deep in Scura's pockets, and the rest had been rendered helpless by the betrayal of the army. Alone and faced with impossible odds, Brentor failed to see any hope. He and all Lethendweil stood on the edge of a razor. Already, the blade cut deep. He spent the rest of the trip in silence, quietly contemplating which demise best suited his mood.

The ambassadorial shuttle was the only craft on Reven's long runway. Brentor, looking out the starboard windows, immediately grew suspicious. Important visitors were always escorted into one of the docking bays built within the mountain. Scura was sending a clear message; they were not welcome on the Plateau. The handful of nobles bristled with tension, both from their internal strife and the lack of respect the Baron showed. No one noticed the first snowflakes star to fall.

Baron Scura emerged from his armored air car. The door hissed shut. Scura wore a pitch-black cape that matched his disposition. Satisfaction was his. His cape swirled in his wake. Tiny snowflakes peppered his hair and shoulders. The sunlight was pale, filtered through a veil of bland clouds. A storm was coming. He was the harbinger. Scura halted ten meters from the shuttle and waited. Idle thoughts of Brentor groveling at his feet entertained him while he waited for the nobles to compose themselves. Scura was in no mood for abasement. He wanted blood.

Brentor was the first to exit the shuttle. He looked remarkably old, much older than at the last emergency council meeting. Scura maintained his smug look, knowing it burned the old man up inside to have been played like a fool. He crossed his arms over his thin chest as Geres Auk took his place beside him.

"Welcome, my lords, to the Plateau," he said once the last noble had exited.

Brentor moved ahead of the others in a subtle act of dominance. "Scura. We were expecting a more civilized greeting. Your hospitality is lacking."

"My hospitality is reserved for friends and welcome guests," the Baron spat back. "We value our privacy here, and you assuredly are not welcome."

Cold wind slashed across Brentor's face. "Welcome or not, there is business that needs doing. Baron Scura, you have gone against the will of the council of nobles and subverted the armies of the twelve kingdoms. You have murdered innocent civilians and acted in congress with certain dark powers to become the sole ruler of Lethendweil."

Scura's laugh echoed on the winds. "Now you come to it. All my plans and deceits. All my quiet loathing. You are a fool, Brentor. The rule of Lethendweil was never yours. Emleth knew this. Yes, I had him assassinated along with Whitel and Parkhol. The Vaumagians were more than willing to provide assistance."

"Murderer," Mans whispered harshly.

"There is no blood on my hands, Mans," Scura smirked. "Lethendweil has been rotting from the inside for years. I am merely trying to cut it out so that we can grow again. This continent needs strength. It needs a legitimate ruler who has the understanding. It needs..."

"You?" Brentor asked. "None of this was necessary until you executed your peers. You are the rot, Scura. You and the stain of your family."

"My dear Brentor, you have no idea what is coming," Scura countered sharply. "Hatred has taken hold here. I am just the catalyst. Even as we speak, there is a dark power deep within the Plateau. Do not be so naïve to think I worked alone."

"We know of Shiramon's deceptions," Mans accused. "You have both brought this ruin down on our heads."

Scura laughed in his face. "You have no idea. My spies have infiltrated all your networks, but I am not the true strength here. There is another power that trumps even my foulest desires. None of us saw them rise, not even me."

"Speak plainly, Scura," Brentor growled. His patience was worn. More than anything, he wanted this day finished, but Scura's taunts at another power intrigued him in the worst way.

"Lethendweil suffers from ancient hatreds. The dark council has risen." His eyes glazed over, the faraway look disturbing. "Worse, they have one of the most startling of nightmares. If Lethendweil survives the coming storm, it will not be the land of our fathers. Our reign here is at an end."

Sudden coldness gripped Brentor's core like fingers of ice threatening to rip his soul out. He failed to imagine what could possibly be worse than the promised enslavement of the kingdoms to Scura's will.

Scura noticed their confusion. "You do not understand. That will prove your undoing. Enough of this, I have said too much." He focused on Schuul. "Come, my friend, it is time for you to join us."

"What?" Brentor questioned, the cold getting stronger.

Mans let out, "Traitor!"

Schuul turned on his friends and bowed theatrically. "It was far too easy deceiving you. Emleth knew what was coming and implored me to go deep in Scura's council. At first, I did so with trepidation, but Scura gradually won me to his service. You were always too weak to do what needed doing, Brentor. Yours is the losing side. I acted to save myself and my kingdom."

"Lord Schuul, I would like to thank you for your service. Emleth was a fool to have trusted you to be his spy in my council. You have played your part perfectly," Scura congratulated. Schuul took a step forward to join him. "Unfortunately, I have no tolerance for traitors. Your service is no longer required."

"What is the meaning of this?" Schuul protested. "You promised I would get my due!"

Scura's smile turned wicked. "And so you shall. Geres."

Geres moved so fast he was almost a blur. Schuul went to throw up his hands, but Geres's blade ripped across his throat before he could finish the move. Dark blood sprayed out, drenching Geres's shirt. Schuul's hands flew to his ruined throat, but it was too late. He fell dead with a stricken look etched on his face. The big man casually bent down to wipe the blood from his blade. He rose and passed the remaining three nobles a wry grin before rejoining Scura.

Brentor and the others reeled back from shock. The brutality was too much, so long had it been since any of them had gotten blood on their hands. Anger flashed to life. Brentor wished for his own blade and the opportunity to prove his own mettle against such a casual foe. The long history of warriors in his family demanded retribution. A sudden movement off to the far right gave him pause.

Dozens of soldiers dressed in the black and purple of house Scura emerged from their hiding places, short barrel pulse rifles aimed at the nobles. Reflective masks hid their faces, though their poise left no room for error. They were here to perform Scura's will. Geres Auk nodded once, and his soldiers drew the noose tighter. The snow began to fall more heavily.

"Lord Brentor, I hereby place you and your cohorts under arrest," Scura announced with song in his voice. "Your influence on Lethendweil is at its end. My time has risen!"

Soldiers slipped through the circle to roughly clasp heavy manacles around their wrists. Orthis Gel winced as the cold iron bit into his flesh. A tiny trickle of blood seeped from beneath. They were pushed and shoved towards a waiting transport truck that had been rushed to the flight line.

Only Brentor looked back at the smug Scura. "You'll pay for this, Scura. You can't keep this quiet! The people will rebel."

"The people will never know," Scura whispered after him. He turned to Auk. "Place them in the deepest dungeon. I don't want any of them to see the sun again."

"It will be done," Geres replied but did not move.

Scura was about to comment when another shuttle, this one sleek and angular, came blasting in at low levels. His first reaction was that the Plateau was under attack, but that wasn't possible. Air defense upgrades he'd purchased from Schuul had made Reven and the Plateau almost impregnable from the sky. Whoever was aboard the shuttle had been let in purposely. Scura rounded on Geres.

"Find out who that is and arrest them," he fumed. The very thought of being breeched in such a flagrant manner insulted him.

Geres Auk looked down his hawk nose at him and remained still. Confusion crossed Scura's eyes. The crisp sound of a blade being drawn echoed across the flight line. Geres smiled, almost as harsh as had Scura when Brentor was arrested. The Baron reached for a sidearm before foolishly remembering that he had left everything to Geres Auk. He had damned himself.

"What is this, Auk?" he snarled, venom coating the words.

Geres shrugged nonchalantly. "You said it yourself, Scura. There are bigger, darker powers at work in Lethendweil."

Panic surged up. "Guards!"

Geres laughed in his face. The handful of remaining guards crowded closer as if awaiting a specific command. The snow came down harder, coating their shoulders and helmets. Geres gestured, and they quickly stripped out of their Plateau uniforms. The shock in Scura's eyes upon seeing his men dressed in Prekhauten Guard uniforms beneath the purple and black was priceless. Geres leaned close enough for his breath to tickle Scura's exposed neck.

"Did you truly think you could contend with the will of the dark council? Everything that has happened has been because they needed it to happen."

A range of emotions assaulted Scura, leaving him sunken in defeat. He'd been outplayed, probably from the beginning. He had a hundred questions but knew he'd get answers to none. Still, he had to ask one.

"How long?"

The side ramp opened with a hydraulic hiss. Darkness pulsed from the hold, disturbed only by an unsettling red glow from deep within.

"Since before you murdered your father," he admitted before falling silent.

Inquisitor Ursal Prowl was the first to deboard. The smug satisfaction on his face sickened Scura. He'd never trusted the man. Prowl was always too careful, too meticulous in covering his affairs. It had soured his opinion of the Inquisition enough to embolden Scura in his schemes.

Scura turned to look up at Geres, hatred pouring from his black eyes. "Traitor."

Geres Auk shrugged the moment before the Prekhauten Guards placed Scura under arrest and dragged him off to share the same cell as the others. Nine robed and hooded figures followed Ursal Prowl off the shuttle. His open face broke a cardinal rule of the dark council, one that he had instated and now found useless. It was time for the world to know the true power behind all the madness. Prowl clasped Geres on the shoulder.

"You have done well," he said. "Lethendweil is in chaos, and the ruling body has been removed. Now we may begin our work in earnest."

The rest of the council filed down, humble and seemingly obedient. All but one, Geres noticed quietly. Judging by the slender shoulders and slight appearance under the thick robe, the woman strode confidently and with head held high. His eyebrow arched as he narrowed down the possibilities of who it might be.

"Where is *He*?" the woman asked.

Geres gestured back over his shoulders. "Down in the catacombs. He and that small man went down there immediately after arriving."

Ursal glanced at Presha Von smugly. The darkness of her hood may have hidden her face, but it did little to hide the greed in her voice. *I've been playing you like a fiddle this whole time.* He decided to let her secret remain hidden, if only for a while longer. The Inquisitor had deeper troubles concerning him. Darka Jorm had not been heard from in a long time, and Ursal suspected Presha had something to do with that. The newly elected councilwoman was growing into a nasty little problem that would soon require dealing with. He suppressed a frown. Time was already his enemy, and now he had Presha Von's twisted desires to deal with.

Ursal passed a casual look up into the darkening skies, wondering when the Inquisition fleet would arrive to begin punishing his quaintly crafted insurrection. The botched assassination attempt on Tolde Breed would have pushed the man to the only possible conclusion; Ursal Prowl was a traitor. It didn't matter that his orders came from high in the Inquisition chain of command or that certain factions of the Conclave and Prekhauten Guard were supporting the move. He was a traitor and expected to be dealt with harshly. His one hope lay in convincing Amongeratix where to find the Paradise Tear.

"Take us to him immediately," Ursal commanded. *There is no time*.

Geres stopped him when he walked past. "There is more. We have reports of an unidentified flier down just east of the mountain wall. I have scouts searching for the wreckage, but I do not know who the pilot is."

"The Baron did nothing about this?" Ursal demanded.

"We only just learned of this before Lord Brentor arrived."

Ursal scowled deeply, the lines distorting his handsome features. "Scura was a fool. Our enemies close in, and he allows a massive security breech. I want his daughter taken into custody immediately. Perhaps he will choose to cooperate when he sees her weighted down in iron."

Geres's jaw tightened. "She is in the north tower. It is her father's favorite thinking spot. I have guards ensuring her *safety*."

"I am not concerned with her safety, Geres. I want her humbled and broken in order to make her father pliable. See to it."

"Yes, Inquisitor."

Presha Von listened carefully, storing the information for future use. Ursal Prowl was pragmatic but distracted, and a man like Geres Auk would not stay complacent for long. She began calculating what it would take to steal his loyalty. The dark council made their way down into the hidden caverns and tunnels of Reven, all with the hopes of harnessing the raw power of the Three and bringing Lethendweil to its knees.

"We have achieved orbit, Admiral."

Thin grey hair cut tight against his scalp, Admiral Kildred narrowed his pale blue eyes and nodded. His fleet had been dispatched by the Conclave to stop the insurrection on Crimeat. Sixteen capital ships moved ponderously into blocking positions in high orbit over Lethendweil. Kildred scowled. He did not appreciate being used to hunt down heretics and considered this to be a waste of time and assets. Still, he was a professional dedicated to the preservation of the Conclave. Killing a few hundred heretics was a small price to pay for the continued peace and security of the universe.

"Very well, Commander. Order the battleships into firing positions and begin transmitting the surrender signal to known enemy forces," he ordered with a raspy voice.

Several crewmembers paused to look at him, stunned he had given such a command. Kildred ignored them, knowing all too well what he demanded of them. No, not demanded. The Conclave needed this. Heresy was a disease that required total excision. Otherwise, the rot would spread.

TWENTY-SIX

3210 A.G. (After Gods), The Plateau, planet Crimeat.

Senior Inquisitor Tolde Breed looked up at the Bothwel Mountains and felt a small measure of anxiety. The jagged peaks were the color of nightmares, partially hidden behind wisps of clouds. He was reminded of his first confrontation with Amongeratix aboard the derelict cargo carrier in deep space. Those memories still haunted his dreams. The black rocks felt just as oppressive. Tolde suppressed a shiver and wrapped his navy-blue cloak tighter.

"Those are some damned big mountains," Matthias whistled.

"And filled with perimeter defenses, I am sure. We'll be hard pressed to enter undetected," Tolde replied sternly.

Matthias wasn't convinced they needed to sneak in. They were senior representatives of the Conclave and Inquisition. Such trickery was reserved for cowards and malcontents. Matthias bristled with latent anger at the thought of crawling through tunnels. Still, he understood the necessity of it. Tolde suspected Ursal Prowl was involved with much of the treachery going on across Lethendweil. If that was true, there was no telling how many nobles he had in his pockets. Reven was considered enemy territory. Matthias grinned tersely.

"What?" Tolde asked.

He shook his head. "It's about time we had a stand-up fight. I'm tired of chasing ghosts on this rock."

"The fight is coming to us, I fear. I suspect that Amongeratix is up there as well as our rogue Inquisitor. This will not be easy."

"It never is," Matthias broke into an open smile.

"I believe I can get us inside their main complex without detection," Sister Abigail said softly.

Tolde and Matthias both looked at the Blood Witch hard. Her gossamer robes had an eerie glow, making her appear ethereal. Her voice was melodious, taking them back to childhood lullabies. The memories were soothing, blocking their growing fears and filling them with hope.

"How is this possible?" Matthias asked.

Her head cocked slightly as if amused. "My order knows many secrets less enlightened might consider magic. All I require is your complete trust."

"Heresy," one of the nearby Guardsmen whispered through his helmet.

Matthias, feeling the same but knowing better than to show it, snapped his head around and pointed an accusatory finger. The Guard lowered his head and moved back uncomfortably with his peers.

"We're not going to like this, are we?" Matthias asked her, most of the venom gone from his voice.

Her tone might have been confused with mirth. "Most assuredly not."

"What do you need us to do?" Tolde asked. Time was up, and his choices were few. They needed to get to the top of the Plateau quickly before events spiraled out of control. His only safety lay in the small Conclave fleet scheduled to arrive in orbit. His request for a full division had met resistance, and a meager combat force had been settled upon. Sergeant Major Matthias was entrusted with two brigades, only five thousand Guards to quell an entire continent filled with yet-to-be-revealed foes.

"Gather around me as close as you can. Everyone must touch someone else."

Tolde noticed Matthias's skeptical look and decided to keep it to himself. Now was not the time. The obvious question didn't need to be asked. He knew he was the one expected to touch her. The thought was as repulsive as it was compelling. The Inquisition shared little knowledge of the Blood Witch order, and this provided the perfect opportunity to gain new knowledge. He gave Matthias a nod.

"You heard the lady. Gather around, and make it quick," Matthias snapped.

Tolde waited until the others were committed before reaching out to gently place his right hand on her extended forearm. The touch was cool, like ice taken from distant mountaintops. His breath quickened. His skin prickled. He felt a deep vibration in the corners of his soul. It built, threatening to tear him apart. Tolde's head jerked back. His mouth opened in a silent scream, and the world went black.

The sound of coughing echoed off the cold rock walls. His head pounding, Tolde forced himself up. He waited for his vision to clear before taking in his surroundings. Handfuls of fire littered the walls and floor of the massive storage chamber. Most of the Prekhauten Guards were still down. Matthias lay on his side, a pool of vomit spreading in front of him. Only Sister Abigail seemed un-phased. Once again, he had underestimated the powers of a Blood Witch. Tolde silently vowed never to do so again.

"That was unnatural, Sister," he said after moving beside her.

Abigail floated inches off the ground, her gaze locked on the distant door. "The Order is privilege to many things your kind would consider supernatural. It is an ancient device we unlocked centuries ago."

Violent fragments of memory flashed. Tolde saw them surrounded by a ghostly white light and then a ring of fire. Tiny daggers of pain crept through his entire body. He fought the urge to vomit.

"Magic?" He tried to comprehend what had just happened. One moment, they were standing at the base of the Bothwel Mountains, and the next, they were here. Wherever here was.

"Less educated minds believe so," Abigail replied too casually to be convincing.

Tolde felt torn. One of the main Inquisition mandates was to stamp out the use of eldritch powers, powers that men considered magical. Yet they willingly employed the Blood Witches without reservation. The very subject was anathema in most circles. He looked hard at Sister Abigail and wondered what dark secrets they kept on their comet fortress. He also was filled with the desire to return to Vau Prime and discover what leverage the Order held over the Conclave.

Groaning to his feet, Matthias unslung his ion rifle and approached. His eyes were bloodshot and tearing. He pointed a gloved finger at Abigail and snarled, "Don't ever do that again."

"Get your men up and moving, Matthias. We don't have much time," Tolde ordered and then turned back to Abigail. "Where are we exactly?"

"One of the less used storage hangars. Reven has several of these that are barely in use. We should be safe from detection for a while still."

That was good enough for Tolde. Matthias had his Guards assembled shortly after. Each was eager to do his or her job, if not entirely physically ready. Most suffered nausea and vertigo but used their armor to compensate. The grim looks on their faces told the Inquisitor everything he needed to know.

"We've pulled up the schematics. This is one big damned place, and we don't have a clue what we are looking for," Matthias said after he returned.

Sister Abigail recoiled slightly, as if she had secrets she wasn't permitted to speak. Her robes shifted colors quickly, matching her heartbeat.

"You know something," Tolde reasoned.

"You are not allowed to know the truth of…certain matters," she said carefully. Her tone was soft so as not to be insulting. "This is not my decision, Inquisitor."

"Whose decision is it? I'm not moving until I get an answer, Sister." Tolde planted his feet solidly and hardened his stance. "These men depend on my decisions for survival. I will not betray that trust."

"There is more at stake here than our small group. Many of the universe's great players have converged on Crimeat. There is a time of reckoning approaching, and we are but pawns. Our lives are unimportant." Her robes shifted from light green to metallic white. "Your leaders understand this."

"Why the deception? Why risk our lives casually when so much is at stake?" Matthias cut in.

She fell silent, giving them time to come to their own conclusions. The inevitability of failure frightened her. It was a new emotion, one that she found alluring and dissuading. Her Order knew several great mysteries that mankind was incapable of rationalizing. Part of her wanted to tell Tolde everything, but her life was forfeit if she did. The conflict was tantalizing.

"I am sorry, but I cannot tell you. All you need to know is that I am here to support you without reservation," Abigail said with sincerity. "Amongeratix is above us, and he is searching for a very sacred artifact. I will say no more."

"And Tannus?" Tolde appreciated the additional information and was careful not to ask too much. Abigail may have offered more than she could, but he didn't doubt she would clam up when pressed.

"Not yet, but he will be here. Fate demands a heavy toll for what is about to happen," she replied.

Tolde had heard enough. He nodded sharply. "Good. Matthias, we need to move. Lead us to a command center. We should find everything we need."

"Roger," Matthias said. He whistled low and pointed.

The squad fanned out in a wedge and stalked to the doors on the far side of the hangar. Matthias struggled to push thoughts of Fies to the back of his mind. They were on their own and would have to wait. He prayed Guard headquarters moved quickly and dispatched reinforcements. Otherwise, they were in for a long, hard fight. Inserting himself into the middle of the wedge, Matthias brought his rifle to the low ready.

"Right."

The point man moved with precision, rifle trained on the corridor. Matthias guided them down a service tunnel, reasoning that there wouldn't be much traffic. So far, his guess had paid off. They'd only run in to two maintenance workers. Matthias had both stunned with neural darts. They'd awaken hours from now with no memory of seeing a platoon of black-armored soldiers assaulting through.

Matthias pushed his Guards hard. He wasn't sure why, but there was desperation hanging over him. The Inquisitor felt the same but kept it to himself. There was a strange connection between the Blood Witch and Tolde that had been absent during their first encounter fifty years ago. Matthias shivered at the memory. He'd lost good men on the hunt for Amongeratix, and the survivors had barely escaped. If it hadn't been for the mystical powers of the Blood Witch… He let the memory die. Nothing about this was comparable to the past.

"Movement," the point man whispered over his helmet intercom. A fist shot up, and the Guards crouched into kneeling firing positions.

Matthias crept to the front. "What do you see?"

"Sensors are picking up a lot of movement on the other side of this wall heading in our direction."

Matthias keyed his own scanner. His eyes narrowed suspiciously. Whatever was on the other side of the wall was massive. "Tolde, I think we have something."

Blue-tinged rose almost glowing in the quasi-darkness, Tolde had a sudden apprehensive feeling. *Amongeratix. You have haunted my dreams for decades. It is time to put old dreams to rest. Let us end this tonight.*

"How far away do these corridors merge?" he asked urgently.

"Looks like thirty meters."

"Get your men there and block the exit. I don't want anyone getting through," Tolde ordered immediately.

His senses heightened. Dark spots flashed his vision. Fifty years of tormented nights laced between sweat-filled sheets and countless hours staring up at the heavens questioningly came down to this one moment. Time slowed, and the first slivers of doubt crept in. *What if I am not up to the task? Amongeratix nearly killed me those long years ago. Will he finally succeed and end my misery?*

Passing a wary look of concern, Matthias darted past the Senior Inquisitor. He had his own demons to fend off; Tolde would have to look to himself. Boots echoed down the thin metal floor, echoing like hammers. His breath came in filtered rasps. Soft vibrating hums pulsed off their weapons. Hands clenched the handles; fingers dancing close to the triggers. They had run ten meters when the wall exploded.

Chunks of rock and wall battered the Guardsmen, knocking down half. A dust cloud immediately filled the corridor. Fibers of fiberglass and worse clogged the air vents on the Guard helmets. Vision dimmed, forcing them to adjust to infrared. For a moment, all was still. The Guards recovered quickly and took up hasty fighting positions along the back wall. Not even Matthias was prepared for what burst through the gap. Twelve feet tall and filled with unmitigated rage, Amongeratix charged into the Guards.

Guards cried out. Random ion shots slashed through the debris cloud. The blue-white bolts sizzled on impact. Amongeratix gave a feral grin and attacked. A foot struck the nearest Guard in the chest. The crunch of breaking bones and ruptured organs was loud. Dark blood fanned out from beneath his helmet as he fell dead. He was the lucky one. Amongeratix lashed out quicker than any but Sister Abigail anticipated. A massive hand clamped down on a Guard helmet and squeezed. Bone and brain matter exploded between the giant's fingers.

"Kill that fucker!" Matthias roared.

As one, the Guards opened fire. Ion rounds scorched Amongeratix in a hundred places, knocking him back a step. Blue flames peppered his torn jerkin. Part of his hair caught fire, and he roared. Tolde's knees went weak as tremors ran up his bones. Another Guard fell and another. They were being slaughtered. Matthias aimed and unleashed his full power charge into Amongeratix's chest. The giant lurched back, fists clenched. Matthias knew it wasn't enough, but it did buy his men time to reorganize. He wasn't disappointed when the heavy machinegun suddenly roared to life.

Bouts of rock flared out from the walls. Pulverized wall and stone showered the combatants mercilessly. Tongues of flame shot from the quad barrels. Amongeratix paused, forced to take cover before the Guards wounded him too greatly. He bled from a dozen places, a few severe enough to hurt. He forced the pain away and trusted his advanced metabolism and immortal genes to heal him. The heavy machineguns continued to ravage his surroundings. Amongeratix snarled, savage and bestial. He charged again with the intent to murder the gunner.

He didn't see the Blood Witch until it was too late.

Sister Abigail flung her hands out. Her fingers were bony and fragile; the sheer volume of power pulsing outward was anything but. The Blood Witch unleashed a massive torrent of kinetic energy. Streams of black, purple and red extended from her fingertips. Amongeratix froze. His muscles strained but could not break free. His eyes bulged from their sockets. His face swelled. The roar in his throat threatened to rip his esophagus apart.

Matthias stopped firing, horrified and amazed.

"I cannot hold him like this for long," Abigail struggled to tell Tolde.

"Keep firing! Bring him down," Tolde bellowed.

Ion rounds fired so fast they formed a sheet of white-blue. Tolde threw an arm up and turned away to protect his eyes. Inquisitors lacked the technologically superior armor and equipment of the Guard. Besides, he wanted Amongeratix to see his face. Perhaps he might spark a small measure of fear, though more likely it would be amusement. He pushed past the pair of Guards assigned for protection and confronted his most powerful fear.

"Amongeratix!"

The giant's head cocked ever so slightly. Dull recognition twinkled in his coal black eyes. Tolde was surprised he remembered; then again, Amongeratix had had fifty years in captivity to stew over it. Tolde swallowed hard. Fear threatened to consume him. Age had finally caught up with him. He felt paralyzed, a mirror image of his sworn enemy.

"You," Amongeratix mouthed slowly. He struggled harder. Muscles bunched and flexed. His eyes burned dark with hatred.

Sister Abigail recoiled slightly. Her colors faded. Her fingertips blackened. A guttural scream ripped from her lungs.

"He is too strong," she struggled to say.

Tolde forced one step and then another. He stared deep into those hate-filled eyes and found something unexpected: a soul as twisted and warped as the deep reaches of space. Extinction reflected, and it unnerved him. Tolde carefully raised his issue ion pistol and fired. Time slowed as the round streaked across the distance between them. One watched with abject interest, the other with wishful thinking.

The round penetrated Abigail's kinetic field and struck Amongeratix between the eyes. A black streak stained his brow. Blood trickled down the bridge of his nose. His head snapped back in a deliberate motion. Amongeratix narrowed his eyes. Rage radiated outward. Tolde Breed saw his death approaching.

"Matthias, we cannot win here," he said unexpectedly.

The Guardsman paused, unsure of what he'd heard. They had the monster entrapped and were hammering him down with escalated firepower. Retreat didn't seem plausible. They were *winning*.

"Tolde, I..."

"No. We need to fall back and regroup. He is too powerful."

The Senior Inquisitor stung at his own words, bile filling his mouth. A dark part of him wanted to kill Amongeratix and sent his corpse back to Vau Prime for all to bear witness. It was an impossible dream. Amongeratix was one of the three sons of the god-king. They were immortal. Death was but a cruel joke.

Matthias failed to recognize this fact. Ever the professional soldier, he was lost in the moment. Thousands of ion rounds lanced into the giant. Blood and bits of flesh popped away. One of the ceiling lights shattered. Sparks rained down before that section of the corridor faded to darkness. Sister Abigail's energy rippled, warping back towards her. She dropped to a knee. Savage powers assaulted her, driving her to the ground in collapse. Tolde rushed to her side, abandoning thoughts of Amongeratix. With the Blood Witch failing and Tolde distracted, Matthias made the decision.

"Pull back, everyone!"

No sooner had he given the command then Amongeratix shredded the energy field and burst back into combat. Two Guards dropped quickly, their bodies mere mush within their armor. Matthias cringed while firing off a pair of heat rounds. Each detonated on the giant's neck. Flames curled up over his face. Slowly, the Guards began to disengage and flee back down the corridor, but half were already dead.

His movements were blurred, his hatred unparalleled. Amongeratix waded through the remaining Guards with murderous glee. Blood and body parts sailed across the open area. Men and women fell screaming. Matthias suppressed his tears and continued firing. Amongeratix ducked beneath a plasma rocket, snatching a Guard and ripping him in half at the waist. Desperately, Matthias drew his combat blade and readied to attack. He knew it was suicide, but it was the only thing he could think of to give his Guards more time to escape.

Amongeratix paused suddenly and tipped his head back. His eyes widened in shock and tortured delight. *At last.* "Tannus," he whispered.

The giant dropped the ragged corpse in his hand and bolted down the corridor towards destiny and the hell that awaited. Matthias stared with a blank expression as the monster raced away. His knife fell to the ground. A part of his mind snapped. He felt entirely defeated. Tears sprung forth in an uncontrollable wave. Matthias turned his gaze to the ruined corpses littering the corridor. Failure. He hardly noticed Tolde and Abigail out of the corner of his eye.

Tolde couldn't take his eyes of the ragged remains in his hands. Acrid smoke poured from Abigail's hood. Urine pooled around her lithe body. Her robes, once so pure, were blackened shreds. Tolde was shocked at how light the Sister was. She felt like a feather in his arms. Looking down into her cowl, he found silver eyes staring back, pinpricks in the blackened ruin.

"Sister," he whispered.

Her voice was ragged, the melody lost. "He was too strong for me. I am…sorry."

Unexpected emotions rose. Tolde looked down on the ruined creature, not quite human and not quite something else, without the apprehension and suspicion from earlier. Abigail was dying. He was sure of it. The witches always inspired a certain level of fear. Now that he saw her, he was no longer afraid. He felt…pity.

"Amongeratix will be caught," he vowed.

She coughed violently. "He must be. Everything depends on it. Do not let him find the…."

What remained of her body shuddered. A low rattle escaped, and she went slack. Tolde frowned. Sister Abigail was dead, and she left him with another riddle. A soft hum filled his arms as, horrified, he watched her body slowly disintegrate back into the fabric of the universe.

Are we all just dust in the end?

Ashes drifting across his face, Tolde pushed back to his feet. He heard a laugh from the far wall and was surprised to find a ghostly face staring at him. *Abigail?* She smiled softly and faded away. Tolde felt hope grow. New resolve strengthening, he stepped through the wreckage and bodies to reach Matthias.

His nod answered the unasked question.

"We need track him down. Abigail tried to warn me about finding some *thing*. She died before saying more." Tolde struggled to keep the disappointment and confusion from bleeding through.

Matthias gestured to the dead. "How are we supposed to take him, Tolde? Most of my men are dead. He is stronger than before."

"Stronger or not, we are servants of the Conclave. Amongeratix must be stopped. We are the only ones who can do it."

Anger flared. Fists clenched before Matthias realized it. Pushing his thoughts of failure aside, he quickly remembered that he was a sergeant major in the Prekhauten Guard, the vaunted warrior-defenders of the universe. He was the iron fist that smashed aside heresies and brought rebellions to their knees. He was the face of combat, death's boon companion. Matthias straightened, that old pride returned.

"The remnants of the squad are at the far end of the corridor. We'd be able to cut him off if we had a clue as to his intent," Matthias said sternly.

Tolde knew that was what Sister Abigail was trying to tell him. He gazed down the ruined corridor, following the trail of carnage. "Cutting him off isn't an option, but we can damned sure follow where he went."

"I'll get my men."

Tolde nodded approvingly. "I'm going after him."

Matthias froze. "What? You can't be serious."

A wry grin flashed. "He and I have unfinished business. Don't worry; I'll try not to get killed until you arrive."

Matthias stood dumbfounded and watched Senior Inquisitor Tolde Breed storm bravely, and foolishly, off into the waiting arms of death. He suddenly felt ashamed. No one but the Guard should muster such courage.

He keyed his helmet's intercom. "Sergeant Plous, gather your men and get your asses back here. We have a hunt ahead."

The flier sped over the mountain wall on silent engines. Tannus pushed the craft as hard as he dared. His brother was below and had to be stopped. Heavy snow hampered his vision enough that they almost crashed three times once they entered the treacherous mountain range. Low-power laser bolts flashed from various air defense emplacements. Inaccurate, the bolts struck the black rock in wild patterns. Tannus frowned. He'd expected better. Behind him, Father Dye whispered prayers.

"To whom do you pray?" Tannus asked nonchalantly.

Dye started and caught a dozen crimson flashes speed by. Wincing, he regretted doing so. "Aris. I figured we need the protection."

Tannus barked a laugh sharper than intended. "Save your breath. She will not answer. The gods are gone."

"I am nothing without my faith, Tannus," he replied tersely before throwing an arm out to keep from slamming into the hull as Tannus banked hard right.

"Faith is too easily misplaced. Humanity's greatest flaw lies in your willingness to proscribe deities that cover your weaknesses."

Dye's eyes widened. "You can't possibly suggest the gods are figments of our imaginations! They are your fathers."

"Tell me, priest, how many men have been murdered in the names of those fathers? You should not be so quick to place your faith in those who would rob it."

The old priest made to protest when a sudden realization slapped him across the face. Tannus suffered from self-deprecation. *What torments could one see to make them lose all faith in themselves?* The possibilities were horrifying. Had the gods truly abandoned hope and destroyed each other? Was that what drove the Three to separate means? Dye hung his head, feeling sorry for the giant. Worse, his sorrow carried to the rest of humanity, for if the gods could not withstand the pressure, what hope did the rest of them have?

Tannus's face pinched as he jerked the flier hard to avoid a heavy burst of flame. Shrapnel pinged off the hull, pock-marking the black paint. Respectfully, Dye kept his prayers silent. This was not the time for a theological debate. His fingers bled white from his death grip on the back of the pilot seat. Dye squeezed his eyes shut. The flier jerked and rocked, dropped and banked sharply. Then it was over. Calm washed over the craft. He heard Tannus exhale softly and relaxed in relief. The worst was behind them.

"We're through their main defenses," Tannus called over his shoulder. "Once I find a place to land, I want you to stay behind me."

"My voice will be needed if we are to avoid the promised violence. The Baron must be allowed to learn the error of his ways," Dye insisted. While not a soldier, he was no coward. Hack and his cronies had threatened harm, and he'd stood his ground.

Tannus was mildly impressed, but he'd seen too many noncombatants suddenly find their courage and wind up dead on the battlefield. He wasn't sure why, but he liked Father Dye. Too many holy men were religious fanatics twisting faith with internal desires and greed. Dye remained true to his humble teachings. He truly believed in the gods and what the faith represented.

"The time for talk is past. My brother will be down there, and I would spare you the nightmares of what is to come. He and I do not have pleasant reunions," the giant said with finality.

Dye was not to be shunned. He summoned what courage remained and stood his ground. "This is my world, Tannus. These people are lost. I must bring them back to the fold."

"You know that by doing so you forfeit your life?" Tannus questioned, quietly impressed with Dye's resolve.

A weak smile. "My wants and needs ended the moment I became a priest. This is my calling. One way or another, I will see it through tonight."

Snow pelted the Plateau, harsh winds driving it down in impossible sheets both thick and wet. Visibility dropped sharply, making landing difficult. Oddly, the main landing strip was dark. None of the lights were on. Tannus instantly grew suspicious. Winter had come early, according to Dye. The storm was bigger than either had seen in many years. Like so many dreams wasted on the winds, Dye reflected. *Are we to wither away the same?*

Tannus managed to set the craft down on the far edge of the only runway on the Plateau. Steel grated harshly, the high-pitched metallic shriek reminding Dye of a dying beast. Two other shuttles were nearby, empty yet ominous.

"This is your last chance to save yourself," Tannus offered after they were both on the ground.

Dye had never been so happy to be back on solid footing. He was of the old belief that man was not meant to fly or sail. Much of his travels were on foot or horseback. The old priest shook his head, a meek gesture at best.

He stared up at the giant, noticing how crystalline his eyes were. "No, I must do this if for no one else than myself."

Tannus nodded gruffly. "Very well. Whatever happens next will be on your shoulders. I cannot be responsible for you once battle begins."

"I'm not asking you to be. This is my choice."

Secretly thinking Dye foolish, Tannus dropped the subject. Snow pelted them now. Huge flakes stung his face and hands. He snarled but felt oddly satisfied. Winter was the perfect time to meet his brother in combat. Perhaps the snow would wash the blood away more quickly and purify this tainted land. Lifting his nose to the winds, Tannus sniffed deeply. Any freshness of the first winter storm was drowned by the foul miasma of Amongeratix. His brother had always left a stink.

Tannus glanced down on Father Dye. "Stay behind me. We must move quickly. My brother is already here."

They'd come to find Sorrow, not Amongeratix. His presence complicated matters. Still, Sorrow must be in the general area. Too many forces were at play for him to remain in the shadows. All three brothers had not been working on the same planet since the formation of the Conclave. Tannus rubbed his chin, lost in thought. This world held secrets, and that fact disturbed him. Humanity constantly struggled to find understanding from the universe. Little did they know what truths lay among the stars. Tannus feared what might happen should man learn the truth.

He took off at a fast run. His thigh was mostly healed, tiny jolts of fire shooting through his leg reminding him of the consequences of failure. Somewhere deep in the bowels of these black mountains awaited a secret. He had to get there first, or all was lost.

TWENTY-SEVEN

3210 A.G. (After Gods), Berchenfel, planet Crimeat.

A night owl broke the eerie calm. Crimeat's twin moons hung low in the sky. The green and red bodies appeared to touch the distant mountaintops. Sergeant Fies found the colors disconcerting despite having been on Crimeat for almost a month. Knee-high grasses swirled around him, kissing his armored legs. *This land might be nice if it weren't for all the fucking locals trying to kill each other*, he mused. A low whistle made him turn his head right.

Kastor edged through the grasses at a low crouch. Helmet strapped to his pack, the old Guardsman wore a sour look. Fies frowned.

"What do you have?"

Kastor shook his head. "There's a ruined village about five hundred meters due west. I picked up their trail and followed for a little. Fies, they aren't covering their tracks."

"They want us to find them."

Kastor agreed. "It looks that way. There are too many places out here for an ambush. We might be in trouble."

Fies snarled. The insult of rogue Guards murdering innocent civilians sickened him. They were the military elite of the universe, expected to uphold standards the normal populations thought unachievable. For a unit to turn so easily suggested grave consequences for those still loyal. Fies looked around. A bad feeling pestered him. He was no philosopher, but he was smart enough to know when things were turning sour. Bad things were approaching.

"We need to move fast," he said unexpectedly. Kastor gave him a blank look. "Sorry, I drifted. They may have the advantage of knowing the terrain, but we have the advantage of knowing their tactics."

"What's the plan?" Kastor asked flatly. He'd seen too much over the course of his career to be impressed, or scared, at what was coming.

"Find them and turn their ambush."

The old man shrugged. "It shouldn't be too hard. We've got satellite access again. The biggest problem I can see is that there is a rather large army heading this way. It might get complicated."

"Or we lose them in the confusion." Fies grunted. "I need eyes on. We can't move until we know exactly where they are."

A harsh rustle. "Movement!" came the hushed shout.

Fies spun, raising his rifle. "Direction?"

"One o'clock. Fifty meters," Annalilly replied.

The click-hum of Beve powering up the heavy machinegun comforted Fies. He knew the rest of his squad was quietly moving online into firing positions.

Fies whispered back, "Can you identify?"

"Negative, Sergeant. I'm reading close to twenty heat signatures, but I can't make out who they are."

Shit. "Keep scanning. I don't want anyone firing until I give the order."

He left his thought unfinished. Part of him wanted them to be refugees heading to safety. The bigger part of him wanted them to be the rogue Guards. He almost ached to be done with this foul task and back with Matthias. That's where the real fight was. Not in some empty plain halfway across the continent.

"Talk to me, Annalilly. Who are they?"

He imagined her frown at not being able to answer.

The bright flash barely missing his right ear told him all he needed. "Fire! Fire!"

A fifty-meter section of the plain erupted in ion fire and was returned with twice as much. Flames sparked, igniting the grasses. Smoke and embers blew over the battlefield and threatened to cloud normal vision. Fies spat.

"Visors down. Switch to thermal vision," he shouted into his helmet. "Beve, pin these bastards down. Annalilly, get your fire team on me. We're going to flank right."

Machinegun fire intensified. Hot blue ion bolts scythed the tall grasses. Fies was rewarded with two heat signatures rapidly cooling. He grinned. Two down. Perhaps these Guards weren't so tough.

Tracking them down proved easy enough. They'd left a trail of bodies across Lethendweil, calling cards that dared Fies to come and get them. The stark severity struck him. His squad had been led here purposefully. The two deaths were a gift, pure luck. Fies keyed his intercom a moment before the plasma round erupted behind them. A trap!

Rock and dirt slammed down in great chunks. Part of a stone clipped Fies in the back of his helmet. The impact knocked his sensors out, leaving him blind. Ripping his helmet off, Fies shouted, "Annalilly!"

Jers scanned his sector of fire, surprised that his nerves jumped. A veteran of many years, he wasn't the sort to get overly excited under fire. The ambush in Vaade had proven that. Of course, he had gunned down what turned out to be an unarmed civilian. He and the rest of the squad had been unofficially reprimanded and sent out to hunt the enemy. An enemy that was once an ally. Jers wasn't sure how he felt about that. Fighting other soldiers and heretics was one thing; going toe to toe with another Guard unit was unthinkable. He wondered if he had friends on the opposite side and what it took to get them to turn against the Conclave.

"Haggle, I don't like this," he whispered.

The bigger man shrugged. "What's to like? Either we're going to kill them, or they're going to kill us."

"Exactly. The odds are too even."

A quiet chuckle. "I like it. Never really been tested in a good fight before."

Are you crazy? "Locals with old laser rifles are all well and fine, but these are Guards."

"Go back to the shuttle if you're scared."

Expression soured, Jers abandoned the conversation before Corporal Annalilly snapped at them. His right hand developed a nervous twitch, distracting him from doing his duty. He stifled a yawn. They'd been going hard for almost twenty hours. Sergeant Fies was tireless. It was almost as if he took the renegade Guards as a personal insult. Jers understood the implications of fighting rogue Guardsmen. He didn't understand why they were more important than finding the prisoner they'd been sent to Crimeat to recapture. It was times like this he was glad that he wasn't in charge.

A snap. Jers stiffened suddenly. He dropped down behind his rifle scope and scanned the line. Was that movement, or was the quasi-dark playing with him? Squinting, he swept his rifle across the immediate area to his front.

"Hsst, Haggle, did you hear that?" he whispered.

"No talking," Annalilly snapped.

Jers bit back a curse and resumed his search. A dark red signature suddenly appeared on his helmet scanner, and then another. *Shit, here they come.* "Corporal, check your scanner."

Annalilly resisted the urge to reach out and slap Jers in the back of his helmet, instead choosing to humor him. Her heart raced when she noticed more than a dozen man-sized signatures stalking towards them. *Looks like Jers was right all along.* She frowned.

"Movement!" she whispered into her helmet.

The firefight started with expected intensity. The enemy was, after all, a trained and equipped Prekhauten Guard unit. She instinctively ducked despite already being as low to the ground as she could be and opened fire before Fies cried out.

"Annalilly, get your fire team on me. We're going to flank right."

She grinned, glad to be moving. If there was one thing Annalilly hated, it was staying immobile while a fight raged. "My team on me. We move on the signal."

The four members of her fire team crawled close, ready to burst out of the line of fire and move on the enemy. She felt hot, the sort of eagerness she always had just before she risked her life. Annalilly did a silent headcount before returning fire. Beve's machine gun erupted in a long, steady burst. The hollow, ominous drone drowned out everything else. She imagined the look on Beve's dumb face and grinned.

The battle picked up, suggesting that their enemy wasn't walking blindly into them. This was planned and well executed. The plasma cannon detonation twenty meters behind them made that point painfully clear. One of the other fire team's men screamed in pain. Annalilly regretted it. She winced at the brilliant green flames ravaging the entire left side of the Guard's body. Death came swiftly and mercifully. What was left of the corpse dropped with a squishy thud.

"Annalilly!"

Throwing an angry arm out, she pointed and shouted, "Move!"

Six bodies leapt up with surprising grace and dashed away. Ion bolts slashed between them, coming close but not enough. Fies thundered close behind, flame spitting from his rifle. Sweat coated them quickly. Each footstep was like thunder in their ears. She judged they'd gone far enough and dropped to a knee. Her breath came in ragged gasps. Annalilly hadn't felt so out of shape in a long time. She hoped it was only the stress of the situation and not a sad reminder of age.

"Check your sectors," she said unnecessarily. Each man and woman in the squad knew their jobs. Guard training was long and intensive, the perfect lead-in to what they had to do tonight.

"Clear."

"Clear."

Fies dropped beside her, ignoring the strange look in her eyes. He hadn't intended to lead a flanking maneuver without his helmet and didn't have the time to explain.

"We're good," she confirmed curtly.

"If they follow standard procedure, they'll reload before advancing. We move as soon as they do," Fies said. He adjusted his grip on the now hot ion rifle.

Annalilly refrained from asking the obvious. "Want one of my scarves to cover your head?"

Fies frowned. "Funny. Get ready to move."

"Take humor where you can find it, Sergeant," she replied glibly.

He tended to agree. Life in their line of work often ended unpredictably short. Fies wasn't under any false impressions. There was a very good chance that one or more of them were going to die on this maneuver if the enemy was as good as he believed them to be. Still, he nearly broke out in laughter. Let death come. Unencumbered by augmented hearing devices, Fies instantly noticed when the enemy rate of fire slowed. *Now*.

Annalilly read his face and signaled her team to attack. She was glad no one was able to see the childish glee etched on her face. Her weapon roared to life as she charged across the short distance to the attacking squads.

Brood Hammerling barely noticed the man beside him drop dead. He kept firing, eager to be done with this hunt and back in the jungle. The zeal he had burned deeply. Brood *wanted* to kill his fellow Guardsmen. A cry announced another death. Brood believed that some losses were acceptable, but he wasn't willing to take many more.

"Drop a plasma round on them, now!" he bellowed.

His heavy weapons team shouldered and loaded the forty-pound missile launcher. The blast report was deafening. A green-orange tongue of flame licked behind the streaking round of pure energy. Brood gave a savage grin after hearing the explosion and following screams. He still wasn't satisfied. The loyal Guards were outnumbered and down a man, but they were in no way out of the fight. He needed to get his men moving quickly if they were going to complete the assault and kill the others.

"They're going to flank, Sergeant," a trooper called out. Faint terror clung to his words, giving Brood cause for concern.

The animal was begging to be released. Brood continued to struggle, holding back all the rage, hatred and insanity. Loyalist fire dropped, making him spit angrily. It was time to let the beast free and bring the ambush to a close.

"Shift right and wait for them to assault through before you fire," he barked. "I'm taking the rest of the squad into the base line."

The same trooper balked. The order took him off guard. It was his last act before Brood put an ion round through his forehead. Brood broke into savage laughter. He hadn't murdered anyone since before joining the Guard.

He leveled a snarl at the closest trooper. "Get moving or you're next."

The trooper ran off, eager to be away from the madman. Brood turned back to the firing base. Eight Guards surrounded him, just far enough away to avoid being snatched by his massive hands. Brood almost failed to recognize friend from foe. His blood boiled through his veins. The kill was what he needed. Brood raised his twin barrel ion rifle and attacked.

Meters sped by. Grass fires tried to burn him. He didn't care. The only thing that mattered was closing on the enemy and breaking them before the assault element engaged his own forces. Brood ran so hard he didn't notice the others had fallen behind by nearly ten steps. Not that it mattered. He didn't need them. Ion fire slashed left and right. More men fell—dead or wounded, he didn't care. Brood left them on the cold ground. Winter's kiss caressed his cheeks. His only armor was around his chest. The rest obstructed his senses, left him feeling helpless. He wanted to see the men he was going to kill. Brood smiled when the first one popped up.

Blue flames spit from his barrel. Ion bolts sawed down the enemy Guard, stitching a bloody line across his chest. The man fell as Brood leapt over him and into the enemy line. Guards dropped back in chaos and confusion. None were expecting the charge by a single enemy soldier. Stark realization finally sunk in when they noticed the unit insignia and dull grey of the familiar combat armor.

Brood moved furiously. He planted a boot in the nearest Guard's chest and fired. Ion rounds shredded helmet and face. Brood jerked back after being struck in the right shoulder pauldron. He snarled and spat a mix of foam and blood. Ion bolts flew past wildly. A stray round caught his rifle, ruining it. Brood threw the useless weapon down and drew a long curved blade.

"Come to me! Who's first?" he snapped.

Two bodies already at his feet, Brood didn't need the rest of his squad. Vengeance fueled him. He wanted to kill, wanted to feel the lives of his enemy drip away in his hands. Brood Hammerling was a killing machine. Nothing else mattered. He attacked with reckless abandon.

Kastor threw his rifle down and drew his combat blade in one fluid movement. Brood's size was daunting, but he had faced larger opponents and lived. Size and age were against him, but Kastor knew he was the only one capable of stopping the beast of a man rampaging through their positions.

Brood picked him up out of the corner of his eye and broke into a devilish grin. *Finally, a challenge.* The two charged towards each other. Kastor swung wide, trying to rip Brood's throat out. The bigger man ducked, punching up towards Kastor's gut. The impact drove the wind out of the older man. Kastor groaned. Redoubling his grip, Kastor drove the razor psharp steel down through Brood's left boot and into the ground. Brood threw his head back and roared. He punched down, catching Kastor on the side of his helmet.

The impact ruptured optic circuits, forcing Kastor to discard his helmet. Brood jerked the blade out. Ropes of blood splashed across the trampled grass. Kastor shook his head as he tried to clear his vision. The blow had been stronger than he anticipated. The entire side of his head throbbed.

"That the best you can do?" he coughed.

Brood laughed. "You should have stayed in bed, old man."

Pushing back to his feet, Kastor raised his fists. "This old man has a little left for you, traitor scum."

Brood rushed him, limping slightly. The bigger Guard drove his knee into Kastor's side, sending him sprawling to the ground. Brood struck harder. His blows hammered down through Kastor's meager defense. Bones snapped. Blood sprayed from nose and mouth. The gleam of teeth knocked free spurred Brood on. Kastor spit blood and lashed out with what strength he had left. His leg swept behind Brood's knees and knocked the bigger man down.

The sound of armor scraping stone made Kastor wince. Groggily, he stretched out for his blade. Brood was on his feet much faster than a normal man should have been. Driving a knee down on Kastor's chest, Brood pushed his full weight down. Ribs snapped. Kastor cried out. Brood delivered punishing blows to the side of Kastor's head. The knuckles of his gauntlet dripped blood and ragged strips of flesh. Kastor stabbed weakly. The blade barely dented Brood's armor.

Cruelty twisted Brood's features. He'd never felt so alive. He slapped Kastor's knife away and drove his own deep into Kastor's exposed throat. The older Guard wrapped his hands weakly around Brood's throat. Wet gurgling sounds whispered from his lips. Brood punched Kastor in the face one last time and jerked free. Heavy winds slashed across his face and body. His breath was ragged. Brood spat and turned to look for the next target. That's when he noticed the battlefield was changed. The enemy line was shattered, but his own forces were nowhere to be seen.

Confused, Brood looked up and saw a handful of Prekhauten Guard atmospheric troop transports streaking towards him. Not even he could fight off a company of Guards, though the prospect excited him. Brood sheathed his blade and withdrew. He never saw the sniper take aim at the back of his head. He never heard the shot that ended his life. The traitor Guardsman dropped face down. Blood pooled out in a crimson puddle, pure and bright on the plain white canvas.

"This is Captain Zole of the battle cruiser *Star Breaker*. I have a company of Guards inbound to your position, Sergeant."

Fies had never heard a more welcome voice, if a late one to his needs. He paused to look around. Most of the heretic Guards either were dead or had pulled back to the ruined village. Annalilly's charge had broken them and allowed Fies to double back to his original line. Kastor's corpse had driven him past the tipping point. He hadn't been surprised to see Brood trundling off. The man had always had questionable loyalties. Fies had raised his rifle and fired without thinking.

Brood Hammerling lay dead at his feet, his face twisted in mockery. They'd been friends once, but Brood turned his back too willingly against those he had sworn to defend. There was no mercy for beasts like that, not in the ranks of the Prekhauten Guards, not in the universe. Fies finally lowered his rifle and took a deep breath. Vindication was not what he had imagined it to be. An emptiness clung to the hollow places in his soul. He thought of Kastor and the others so casually murdered by Brood Hammerling. Professional soldiers accepted death as a price, but there was no honor or glory in this. Such reckless slaughter twisted his stomach, leaving him with an ill feeling. His men deserved better.

Fies swept his gaze across the battleground one last time, struggling against the rising sorrow. His part in the war was over, and he was more than glad to pass the responsibility on. This planet sucked. He only hoped Matthias and the remaining Guards were having better success.

The skies over the jungle were filled with incoming Prekhauten Guard craft. Fighters and low-level bombers roared overhead, searching for the enemy. Drop ships carrying combat platoons plummeted to the earth. Thruster flames burned branches and drove birds and monkeys away. Frez Belcum watched the sight in awe. Fond memories made him nostalgic. There was a time when he had played a part in planetary invasions. A time when his career had mattered. Frez shook his head ruefully. Those dreams were nothing more than dust now, lost to the pages of history and the cruelty of the victors.

"What happened to us, Brevel?" he asked quietly.

Brevel didn't have answers. They had once been the pride of the universe, kings of the battlefield. Now, they would forever be known as traitors, heretics. "We should go."

Frez laughed. "Go where? The universe is against us. You know what the Inquisition will send after us if we run. I don't want to die like that."

"We can still escape. This is a big jungle," Brevel insisted.

"No. I've done too much that I'm ashamed of. There are crimes that need answering, Brevel."

"The Inquisition will not show leniency. You know this, Frez. We'll be strung up and quartered even if we do surrender."

Frez was beyond caring. The guilt was too much. He saw the crisp faces of the dead haunting him every time he closed his eyes. Too many injustices demanded retribution. His smile was empty. Lifeless.

"There was a time when that would have mattered. Brevel, I am past that point. If you want to try and escape, take some of the boys. Remember there is a very angry Ugri army out there in the jungle."

Brevel passed a quick glance to the oppressive jungle. The prospect of facing a determined enemy in unfamiliar terrain left him feeling uneasy at best. He didn't know much about the Ugri, but he wasn't a fool. No good would come from heading off into the jungle without support and only limited supplies.

"I don't want to die here, Frez," he said flatly.

Frez feigned a smile. "I doubt they're going to be quick in doling out the gallows. No, there will be a show trial broadcasted across the universe to quell future rebellions before they catch fire. We'll be made the scapegoats."

"That doesn't seem fair."

"Rank has its privileges, Corporal. Hopefully some of the men will be spared death. No one needs the laughter of crows haunting them in the underworld."

Brevel scowled but held his tongue. Dying for those damned fools in Vaade wasn't part of the bargain. He wished there was just a little more time so he could tie up loose ends—those ends being the people in command.

"I think I'm going to take a stroll over to the command tent," Brevel said suddenly. The mischievous twinkle in his eye bordered on murderous.

Frez arched an eyebrow. "That won't solve anything. We're still going to hang for this."

"Maybe not, Frez, but it's going to make me feel a whole lot better," Brevel replied tersely.

Frez shrugged, instantly deciding to follow Brevel just in case. If the incoming Guards followed standard procedures, they would wait until there was at least company strength before storming the objective. That gave him a little time yet. Perhaps offing Captain Partiesh would be seen as an act of redemption and reduce their sentence to life on a prison world rather than hanging.

The shot rang across the disheveled camp. Guards were too busy running off into the jungle or staring dumbly up at the sky as their doom edged closer. Brevel and Frez exchanged a quick glance and began to jog. The shot had come from the command tent. Racing across the compound, they passed several Guardsmen rushing from the area. He had a sinking suspicion as to what had just happened.

Those suspicions were confirmed by the shaken form of Lieutenant Piles emerging from the tent. His eyes were red and had a faraway look. Piles pulled a stem-stick from his breast pocket and lit it. A thick stream of bluish smoke filtered through his nose as he took a seat on the protective sandbag wall ringing the tent.

"You can go in and look, but he's dead. Blew his brains all over the tactical map," Piles said absently.

Frez frowned. The man was acting like he was a dead man too. "Lieutenant, we need to get out of here before they can mobilize fully."

Piles laughed. "What's the point, Sergeant? We've done wrong here, and nothing anyone says changes that. Maybe Partiesh had the right idea. Too bad I don't have the stones to do it myself." He sobered momentarily. "Good luck, Belcum. You're a good man. Too bad about all of this."

Piles tossed the half-smoked stem-stick down and ambled off to meet whatever end fate had in store for him.

"That whoreson!" Brevel cursed angrily and launched a series of brutal kicks at the ground. "He stole the only decent thing I could have done. Fuck!"

"That's it, then. We're screwed." Frez cast his eyes down and turned away. The future darkened considerably.

The Inquisition was not going to be as forgiving as an ion gun. Pride kept thoughts of suicide away, much to his chagrin. Regret would come later, once he was secured in chains and standing before a tribunal. Heretic. Traitor. His name would forever be lost among the fallen, a scourge better left forgotten. Heavy rustling in the trees told him it was time. Moments later, dozens of heavily armed and armored

Prekhauten Guards emerged from the canopy, weapons trained on anyone foolish enough to pose a threat. Frez caught a frosty glimpse of a blue-tinged red rose etched over the heart on a figure dressed in pure black. The Inquisition had arrived.

Away in the jungle, Kulaam Lune watched the metal birds drop from the sky, wreathed in fire and screaming like wounded dragons. His eyes softened, if only slightly. The men in the metal birds had come to make war on his enemies, and that left Kulaam confused. Humans were a disgusting race. It made no sense why one tribe would attack another with such ruthlessness. He watched the scene unfold from atop a small hillock.

Thousands of Ugri warriors waited for the command to attack— a command that was not going to come. This new tribe of humans had come to cleanse the treachery of the eastern kingdoms. The Ugri were safe for now. Kulaam Lune kept his gaze on the skies, always wondering what might have been and why it had been prevented.

TWENTY-EIGHT

3210 A.G. (After Gods), The Plateau, planet Crimeat.

"Are you sure this is the right way?" Elisa asked again.

Mollock Bolle shrugged her impatience off. "I know where I am going. You keep watch for guards, or worse."

Worse? What could possibly be worse here? Elisa looked back over her shoulder even though the need was minimal. They'd run into nothing but the occasional human skeletal remains and rats and cobwebs since entering the tunnel system that spanned the entire under-levels of Reven. More than once, she had wondered what could have brought Mollock so far down. Finally, she couldn't take it anymore.

"How did you find this place?" she asked in hushed tones.

Mollock hesitated enough to amplify her concern. "I was a…guest here once. But the Scuras forgot about the tunnels. I think they go back to the Founding. People always forget. Ha."

Elisa translated guest to mean prisoner. "What did they arrest you for?"

His shoulders hunched slightly. "I had the character to speak out against the ruling house when no one else would. The Scuras cherish power above all else. They crush those opposed with the flick of a hand."

So, a political dissident. Elisa began to understand the enigmatic Mollock Bolle. Too many people found themselves caged away, never to see the daylight again. She tried to imagine him creeping through these tunnels in desperation. Living had that habit.

"You have nerve coming back here," she said approvingly.

He scoffed. "Bastards like the Scuras often forget the people they step on. I doubt they'd remember me."

She disagreed. If what she had heard of the current Baron was even half true, Mollock might be in serious trouble if they got caught.

"How much further?"

He shrugged. "Not far, I think. The chamber should only be a few hundred meters away."

Elisa decided to keep her doubts silent. Madness seemed a common theme these days, and she didn't care to provoke him. Mollock Bolle was a fragment of the man he might have been. She was sure Scuras torturers had done more than just abuse his flesh. His mind bordered on broken, but there was a depth of knowledge and understanding locked deep inside that threatened to undo the balance of power. She wasn't sure if it was reserved for Crimeat or the rest of the universe. The secret he promised to show her potentially changed everything. If it was true.

Common sense demanded that she abandon this fool's quest and return to her quiet life as a bounty hunter. Only it wasn't so quiet anymore. Shiramon and his crony Piett had effectively seen to that. She harbored little doubt that her name was plastered on wanted posters already. Elisa frowned. Her situation had continually worsened since she had been discovered in that barn in Durn. Provided they survived the night, there was no way she was going to be able to work in the twelve kingdoms again. Mollock might be her only way out.

"What exactly are we looking for down here, Mollock?" she decided to ask. His allusions earlier did little to assuage the fear growing in her heart. Elisa reminded herself that finding and killing the Bloody Man was her only goal. Nothing else mattered.

Mollock tried and failed to conceal his exasperation. The little he'd mentioned during their escape from the Ugri should have been enough to satisfy her. "I don't really know, to be fair. There is a power festering in the heart of this world. The nobles are ignorant of it. That's part of the reason the Baron decided to torture me for his own guilty pleasures instead of learning the truth."

"What kind of power? Mollock, I am in no mood for games. I should never have taken the job to find you." She muttered the last under her breath.

He offered a sincere smile. "Finding me just might have saved your life."

Elisa brushed a string of dusty cobwebs from her face. "Not much of a life."

"All life is precious," he scolded. "You have spent the same amount of time letting the desire for revenge twist you as I have running from the truth. I think we are destined to go through this together."

"I'm starting to think you're a lunatic. You told me this is going to help me find the Bloody Man. You're on your own after that."

She found his toothy smile disturbing. He knew something, like a lover with a terrible secret in the dark shadows of the night. They went on in silence, each contemplating what the other had said. Foul omens plagued their movements. Every footstep echoed like the crash of waves on the rocks. The tunnels wound and turned so much, Elisa quickly lost her sense of direction. None of the equipment she'd managed to salvage from the downed flier worked, leaving them alone in the dark.

Slowly, so much so she hardly noticed, the dark gave way to a faint blue light so pale it reminded them of death.

"What is this?" she whispered.

"The power. Quickly, time is our enemy."

They pushed faster, despite Elisa's misgivings. The glow intensified but kept the same shade. Elisa wasn't sure, but she felt that the very walls hummed. Time had worn the passage smooth. Gone were the cobwebs as well as any sign of life. The path almost looked crafted, lacking the natural roughness of blasted rock the rest of the complex harbored. Promises of danger begged her to turn back before it was too late. Sheer stubbornness compelled her to go on.

"Mollock, I…"

He turned, an almost angry look on his face. "Quiet. You must not speak, or the spirits will not answer."

Will not answer? What spirits? She swallowed her rising fear and steeled herself for the worst. Mollock led her into a massive chamber where she froze. Sculpted pillars lined the circular walls. The vaulted ceiling was so high it was lost in the natural gloom. Strangely, Elisa felt calm, almost as if she belonged here. As impressive as the chamber was, it was the massive structure at the center that drew her attention.

Nearly twenty feet long and placed upon an alabaster pedestal was an enormous glass coffin. She rubbed her eyes. *What is a coffin doing this deep in the earth, and why doesn't anyone know of it?* Elisa knew the answers would never materialize. Mollock Bolle watched her with smug satisfaction and something else—awe, perhaps? Some strange gel-like substance coated the coffin. She reasoned it served as some sort of stasis field for the sleeping giant within. Her first thought went immediately to the Bloody Man. Surely the being trapped in the coffin was of the same species.

Emotions assaulted her from every angle. Rage. Inspiration. Hatred and hope. The collisions threatened to shred her sanity. One step at a time, her legs carried her to the steps leading up to the coffin. Further inspection showed her that it was more than just a resting place for the dead; it was a machine, and it still worked. Elisa realized the being trapped within might not be dead at all.

"This should not exist," she said.

He nodded quickly. "No, it should not."

"Do you have any idea what he is?"

The sleeping giant's face was void of the typical signs of aging. He bore a serene look, almost angelic, for those who believed such things. A thin white robe covered him from wrist to ankle. The body hadn't atrophied or begun to decompose; no doubt due to the effects of the coffin. Muscles rippled beneath the robe, pushing it out obscenely. Shoulder-length blonde hair framed his rounded face. The cut and chisel of his jawbones suggested strength. His heavy brow left a sour feeling in her mouth. He was almost handsome. Elisa was slightly disappointed to find he looked nothing like the Bloody Man aside from sheer size.

Mollock shuffled uneasily. "I have my suspicions, though I can't confirm them yet. What I do know is that whoever or whatever this thing is, he doesn't belong in our universe."

She didn't doubt that, but his opinion changed nothing. This being was here, and she was certain there were others. Just a hundred could rampage across the universe in an unstoppable wave of destruction. Images of dead worlds left in their wake taunted her. *Was this what Mollock discovered all those decades ago and has been pursued for? What dark force wants him dead so badly to keep this secret?*

"Do you think he is related to the Bloody Man?" she asked suddenly. Elisa frowned. *Where did that come from?*

He hoped not. Her stories frightened him on a primal level. Creatures like her Bloody Man belonged in children's nightmares. It was disturbing to learn the boogeyman did, in fact, exist, and his heart bled black.

"I've never seen anything like him, and I pray I never will," Mollock answered without satisfying her question.

She looked closer. Thick cables of an unknown material ran from metallic base down into the earth. Elisa guessed they were plugged in to some sort of generator deep underground. There was no way to know the cables ran to the heart of the planet and used natural thermal power. The purity of it was simplistic and unlike anything mankind had managed to replicate in three thousand years, not since the glory age of the gods.

The shadows in the back of the room stirred, and a monstrous figure emerged. Mollock Bolle felt his jaw drop as the massive blood-covered man stared down on them.

"You!" Elisa snarled and immediately drew her sidearm.

Sorrow held up his hands, offering a meek smile. "If my troubles could be solved by such mundane means, but no, you cannot kill me, child."

Elisa fired anyway. And fired. And fired. Fifty years of pent up rage and a wasted life sped from the barrel with each shot. Sorrow stood and took it. The ion rounds singed the hairs on his chest, left blackened marks on his blood-stained flesh. Elisa screamed and then cried when her sidearm emptied. She tossed the weapon down and followed it quickly to her knees. She dropped her face into her trembling hands and cried.

"You stole everything from me. You killed my father, my mother, my entire life. Why? Why? We did nothing to you." Her voice cracked and broke under the strain of a lifetime of repressed emotions finally breaking free.

Sorrow watched with muted awe. Never in the millennia of his existence had he witnessed the human capacity for grief in such mastery. Tears flowed freely, just as they had those long years ago in the aftermath of his rage. Self-pity doomed Sorrow. His had a specific purpose in the universe, but that path was long and lonely.

"Child, there is nothing I can say to take back the grief I caused. I am a creature of my fathers. All I can tell you is that you are *chosen*."

Mollock felt the warm trickle of urine run down his leg. He squealed when Sorrow spoke, drawing attention.

"Ah, the Prophet. My thanks to you for bringing her back to me."

Mollock Bolle was lost for words. So much suddenly fell into place. He knew now that he had been god-touched by the sleeping giant, that this being was, in fact, one of the fabled forgotten gods. Fifty years of dreams circling winter finally made sense. Mollock was a tool of the gods. They were going to awaken, and it was his calling to spread faith. How could he have been so blind? This was the only reasonable explanation for why the dark council had spent so many resources and lives hunting him.

"Yes, Master!" he proclaimed with newfound love. "I am your humble servant."

Sorrow cocked his head, too many thoughts going through his mind. Mollock Bolle was a tainted man, but Sorrow had *seen* the future. This twisted, broken creature had a great part to play in the coming nightmare. Sorrow wished it were not so, but a great cleansing fire was coming, and there was nothing capable of preventing it.

"There will be a time and place for your humbleness, but not here, Mollock Bolle." He turned back to Elisa. "Child, you must strengthen yourself for what's to come. More will be asked of you."

"Murderer," she seethed.

"I did what needed doing. Do not expect to understand powers far older than the universe itself. I apologized to you the day I committed my crimes. I will not do so again. All you need to know is that you, too, were chosen for a purpose," Sorrow explained almost too quickly.

Elisa looked up. Tears streaked the layers of grime on her face. Her eyes were bloodshot and ached. Worse was the realization that her last fifty years had been spent futilely. The Bloody Man was not the mythical figment her mind created to accept and cope with the guilt of surviving. He was empty and just as fragile as she. Elisa thought hatred would see her through to the end, but she was wrong. Hatred continued to steal the memories of her family and friends, crushing them to fine powder useless to anyone.

Her heart threatened to break. It was all a waste. Everything she had ever done was a waste. "I don't want to be part of anything."

Sorrow sympathized. "Fate seldom asks our opinions. A time will come when all is explained, and you will not doubt. That time is unrevealed to me. I ask only for your trust, Elisa."

The laugh that echoed throughout the chamber bordered on insanity. "My trust? You kill my family before my eyes and walk away without so much as a glance behind, and you expect trust? You are a monster! I will kill you one day."

Death was an elusive dream, but no more. One of the Three, the Bloody Man was immortal. "And I will welcome the deed, but time is now against us. My brothers will be here soon. We must flee before they arrive."

"Brothers? There are more of you?" she asked.

He nodded. "Two more, and the nastiest one is on his way. I can feel when he is near. Hurry."

Mollock touched his forehead to the cold floor. Mindless babble streamed from his mouth. Elisa paused to consider him, finding disappointment. Clearly he was not the strength she had assumed. The Bloody Man towered over them. His long black hair was plastered to his skull. He wore only a loincloth. Fresh blood covered his massive frame. The absurdity of it stunned her. Where did the blood come from?

"Elisa, I need you to cast aside your doubts and take my hand. There is no time for further conversation."

A drop of blood splattered on the alabaster marble. The contrast was almost alluring. It reminded her of…what? She couldn't remember. A great commotion from down the tunnel stole her attention. Even Mollock snapped back to coherence. Sorrow's eyes widened. Time was up.

"Sorrow!"

Amongeratix burst into the chamber, smashing holes in the rock frame. Hatred poured from his eyes. He had come to do murder. Blood stained his clothes. His knuckles were raw, torn and ripped from his encounter with the Prekhauten Guard. The Blood Witch had weakened him. Rage sustained him. Amongeratix squared off against his lost brother, fists curled to strike.

"Run," Sorrow urged Elisa and Mollock.

Amongeratix noticed the humans and dropped back to block the door. "Not this time, *brother*. I am going to kill Paleish, and you can't stop me."

"I must try. They are our fathers, Amongeratix."

He raged. "They betrayed us long ago. Why do you insist on defending them?"

"Humanity needs them, whether they know it or not."

Elisa was having trouble following them. She assumed Paleish was the sleeping god in the glass coffin. After that, she was lost. Survival instincts kicked in, and she desperately searched for an escape route. A quick glance to the side confirmed Mollock was next to useless. She was on her own.

Amongeratix spit as he laughed. "Humanity is a sickness that needs expunging. We deserve to rule, Sorrow. Join me, and we can right the course of history. Help me take my rightful place on the throne of the universe."

"Tannus does not see it the same," Sorrow cautioned. He had spent countless years in seclusion, selectively avoiding the petty confrontations between his brothers. True strength and power had been corrupted. All that remained was the hollow shell of brotherhood. Useless excuses for crimes and atrocities committed in the name of higher power. Sorrow remained hidden for his own reasons.

A mighty fist smashed into the wall, sending boulders crashing down. "Do not speak to me of Tannus. I have beaten him once already on this miserable rock. He is not a problem."

Sorrow considered his words. He had not known of Tannus' involvement. The true path remained obscured despite his manipulations. The Prophet and the Paladin had been born from his plans. They were the true hope for humanity and, perhaps, the entire universe. Tannus should not have been on Crimeat.

"Stand aside, Sorrow. I have business to attend to," Amongeratix warned with unmistakable finality.

Sorrow balled his fists. "You know I cannot let you do that, brother."

"Then you die first."

Amongeratix attacked. His movements blurred, but Sorrow was just as quick. Punch after punch caught nothing but air. Elisa snatched Mollock by the collar and managed to drag them both to safety before one of the titans crushed them underfoot. The battle escalated. Sorrow ducked right, avoiding a blow aimed at crippling his throat, and lunged. He caught Amongeratix in the sternum with his shoulder and drove him into the wall. More rock burst free. Dust filled the air in a fine powdery cloud.

Elisa watched in mute horror as the titans hammered and assaulted each other. She found it difficult to imagine how brothers could share so much hatred. Amongeratix dropped a heavy elbow into the small of Sorrow's back, forcing him to let go. Stunned, Sorrow failed to stop the knee to his face. Fresh blood sprayed across the wall. Sorrow reeled back, one hand in front to ward off the next attack and the other on his ruined nose.

"I warned you," Amongeratix growled. He attacked.

Sorrow was helpless to do anything but fend off the blows. His brother attacked with ruthlessness no human ever mastered. He was the instrument of vengeance, hatred's very soul. He was merciless. Elisa caught the snap of bone. The resulting scream shook the ground.

"Mollock, we need to get the hells out of here," she urged.

Death had come. She saw that clearly now. Nothing the Bloody Man had done to her village compared to the raw hatred unleashed in the tomb. Boulder-sized chunks of ceiling began crashing down. Fragments struck her like the tiny bites of a million flies. The titans tumbled and blocked the way, forcing Elisa to pull Mollock back a moment before he was crushed. Dust choked her. Fine particles scratched her eyes. Elisa's nose bled. She was about to make a break towards the glass coffin when fresh chaos exploded.

Dazzling blue-white bolts sped in from the tunnel and struck the titans in the heads and arms. Amongeratix roared, more at being disturbed than from physical pain. Several grey-clad soldiers crouched in the entrance, firing as fast as their rifles could cycle. Ion fire shredded skin; gushes of flesh and blood sprayed disgusting patterns. An acrid haze added to the pall.

Sorrow used the distraction to break Amongeratix's choke hold by delivering a series of blows to the ribs. Ignoring the ion strikes, he continued his assault with the knowledge it was all that stood between Paleish and doom. Amongeratix was not one to be thwarted easily.

"What's happening?" Mollock screamed above the battle.

Elisa could only shake her head. Matters had gotten increasingly more complicated. She wasn't sure who was on whose side. The only thing she understood was that they were all dead if she didn't act fast. Snatching Mollock by the collar, she yelled, "Move!"

They stumbled over debris and past battling titans, all the while praying the soldiers would notice them in time not to shred them. Amongeratix seemed to have forgotten about his brother. He turned to vent his whole rage on the soldiers.

"Run!" she heard Sorrow command. "Head to the starport. I will find you."

Elisa needed no further coaxing. She ran as fast as they could. It was not easy. Fate seemingly conspired. She peered through the fog of battle and was relieved to see a helmeted soldier waving them on. The battle intensified. Two soldiers were already dead, leaving the remaining handful doubting their commitment to Reven and House Scura. Elisa avoided the stares and snuck past the battle line.

"What are you doing here?" a captain demanded. "It is not safe."

No shit. "We're just leaving."

A scream was cut short. Elisa jumped to the side as the severed human head rolled by. Reven was going crazy. They were going to be lucky just to make it to the runway. The captain left them. She had a feeling it was the only time she was going to cross paths with him or any of the rest of his squad. Elisa grabbed Mollock by the arm and dragged him on.

Bodies filled the tunnel, broken and abused. Amongeratix clearly enjoyed his work. Signs of a running battle enveloped the tunnel. Elisa almost felt pity for the fools trying to fight the sons of the gods. Death seemed the only outcome. A massive series of explosions threw them both down. Elisa cracked her forehead on a sharp rock, slicing to the bone. Blood flooded her face. She knew from training and experience that the face bled more than any other body part, so she wasn't overly concerned yet. Dazed, she managed to pick herself and Mollock up and kept running.

She didn't stop to look behind.

Amongeratix delivered a blow to the nearest Scura house guard that punched his ribs through his spine. The man died with a bloody gurgle. The titan turned to his next victim and was thrown violently into the nearest wall. Plasma rounds burned through the ancient black rock, melting everything in their path. Slag dripped to the floor, sizzling on the ruined marble. A giant figure emerged slowly, challengingly, through the wreckage.

Amongeratix lifted his head slowly and smiled. It had only been a matter of time. "Tannus, welcome to our little reunion. A shame you came last."

Tannus rolled his shoulders, stretching for the coming fight. His gaze whispered hostility, so engrossed in Amongeratix he hardly turned his head towards the crouched figure of Sorrow.

"Sorrow, I hope you have come for good purpose. He and I have unfinished business to attend to."

The Bloody Man rubbed the bruising on his chin. "Tannus, I had not expected to see you here."

"Where are the humans? They know too much to be let free."

"I won't let you kill them." He withheld the fact that they were the Prophet and the Paladin. Such would only enrage both of his brothers. "Too much blood has already been spilled in the name of this madness."

Amongeratix smirked. "You know all too well about such things, don't you brother? Where did you send them? I will crush the life from their tiny hearts and bring you the heads."

"Neither of you may have them," Sorrow affirmed. He dropped into a fighting stance and waited.

"Our wayward brother wants to play," Amongeratix taunted. His cold eyes never left Tannus, and Tannus didn't move.

"This has nothing to do with him," Tannus said.

"Agreed."

Amongeratix attacked. Tannus fired off another pair of plasma rounds, narrowly missing his brother's head. Tossing the expended weapon tubes down, Tannus drew a wicked curved blade and slashed a gouge across Amongeratix's chest. Bellowing in pain, the bigger of the two brothers tucked into a roll to avoid being decapitated. The blade was ancient, a weapon from his father's wars. Fortunately, he'd contracted his stomach the moment before being struck, saving him from spilling his guts on the chamber floor.

Seeing no point in continued struggle, Sorrow used the distraction to escape after Elisa. No one stopped him. His brothers were consumed with destroying each other. He knew Paleish was out of danger. Tannus wasn't going to let Amongeratix succeed, not now after three thousand years. Their struggle was eternal and not about to be solved this winter night on Crimeat. War was coming but not here. The Prophet and Paladin must get off this planet and to the proper places if disaster was to be averted.

He lumbered after them, ignoring soldiers and corpses. When he finally emerged into the open night, he was met with heavy snows. Visibility was reduced to a handful of meters. Random lights blinked on and off, matched by the ferocity of fires and the sounds of combat. A battle was consuming Reven, and it wasn't related to the Three. Sorrow wanted to know more, but any pause might find his two charges murdered before they gained the starport. At last, he caught sight of them, limping and dragging themselves towards a jet black flier.

Elisa gave a shout when Sorrow reached down to pick them both up and helped them the rest of the way to the ship. She struggled, but he was too powerful. He didn't stop until both were aboard. Fire spit from her slit pupils.

"You will not believe me, but you are the promises of hope for the universe. My brother won't stop until all is ruined. You must stop him. Spread the word across the stars. Let the heavens know that evil has awakened. The sparks of Crimeat will fan the coming conflagration."

Elisa thought he was mad. He had to be. What kind of creature was almost naked, covered in blood and preaching about the end of the universe? "This makes no sense to me. I have never been anywhere but Lethendweil in my entire life."

"That doesn't matter now. You must take the Prophet to An'kuruku. Find Paradise Tear. Warn the universe before it is too late. Go!"

A massive explosion rocked the ground, throwing Sorrow down. He spat a mouthful of dirt and snow and turned his head to see his two brothers burst out from underground. Fires poured from rents in the mountainside, reminding him of dragons. Men and women fled. Soldiers rushed out from access tunnels. Some threw down their rifles and ran while others made a bold, and futile, stand. Sorrow watched the colors mesh together in a rainbow of destruction.

He had seen all this before. Too many times. If Amongeratix got his hands on the Prophet and the Paladin, the universe was doomed. Sorrow picked himself up and shouted, "Go now!"

He didn't wait to see if Elisa listened. Instead, the titan charged towards his brothers, expecting the fight of his eternal life.

TWENTY-NINE

3210 A.G. (After Gods), Reven, planet Crimeat.

Explosions rocked the Plateau. Civilians fled by the hundreds. Every transport available was being pressed into service. Rumors of massive giants and soldiers in grey shooting and killing everything that moved circulated out of control. One thing was abundantly clear; Reven was being destroyed by forces far greater than any in the Baron's employ. Screams echoed through the once Spartan halls.

Ursal Prowl stood over the bodies of the dark council. Smoke trickled from the end of his double-barrel ion rifle. Blood cooled on the floor. They had outlived their usefulness, particularly since he had learned that all the Three had converged on Reven. Only Presha Von had the forewarning to escape his trap. The woman was becoming a serious threat to his vision of the future. Prowl vowed to post her head on the end of a pike over the gates of Vaade before this was through.

Still, he wasn't about to let thoughts of Von steal him from his true purpose. He had come to Reven to find the god and help Amongeratix claim his revenge on his fathers. Dark promises had been made in the shadows. Ursal wanted, needed to be part of the new world order. He had to stand at the front of the wave of purifying flames about to cleanse the universe of unbelievers. More, Ursal Prowl wanted to feel the exhilaration behind each shot fired in the name of personal gratification. The blood gave him a rush.

A chain of explosions tore the guts out of the Reven industrial complex. Alarms and sirens went off. Black smoke rushed in to fill the hallways and tunnels. Aftershocks continued deeper into the bowels of the Plateau. Ursal scowled, instantly thinking the worst, but it was too soon for an organized Conclave strike. Communications had been severed in time for his coup. Ursal stumbled to the communicator on the nearest desk.

"This is Auk."

"Geres, what is happening? It feels like the whole mountain is about to collapse."

A pause. "We're still trying to find out, but it appears enemy agents have sabotaged the main fuel reserves. Fires are spreading on levels eight through fourteen."

"Get fire suppression teams down there and fix this. The dark council has been removed. Send the word to our commanders in Vaade. I want the city under martial law before dawn. No one gets in or out."

"Yes, Inquisitor."

Ursal toyed with turning Geres Auk loose on Presha Von, but that was a detail he wanted to keep private. Her survival threatened too much, and men like Geres sold their allegiance too easily. Common sense said she would be heading for the docking bays. It was the fastest escape. Ursal dropped the power charge in his rifle and slapped a fresh one. He was going hunting.

The halls were mostly deserted. An occasional body lay shoved against the wall. Smoke clung thickly to the ceiling, making it difficult for him to find his way. Tiles lay shattered on the floor; some hung dangerously low. Cables and wiring looped down with the promise of death. The going was slow. Ursal worried about being ambushed, though it was unlikely. He crept down the ruined hall. Smoke drove down his lungs. He coughed and spit. Ursal moved faster. Fears of the entire mountain collapsing around him were not unfounded.

It took effort, but he managed to stumble to the main corridor. The wreckage was beyond imagination. Ursal had expected structural damage from the continuous explosions, but his mind was amazed by what he saw. Bodies and parts littered the corridor. Blood stains covered the walls in a mockery of fine paintings. Massive holes lined both walls, clearly having been either punched or broken by sheer brute force. What few lights still worked flickered off and on.

There was only one logical conclusion. No accident caused this. Ursal swallowed his rising fears. Amongeratix was on the rampage. They had taken a terrible risk by freeing the monster, but Ursal's masters had been adamant. Amongeratix needed to be freed to evoke the change the universe needed. Ursal Prowl was a believer, but this bordered on insane. No human power could contain the Three. He was sure of that now. The prospect terrified and excited him.

Many of the dead were from Scura's private army, but the closer he got to escaping, the more he noticed the gradual change in uniforms. Too many dead were Prekhauten Guards. Ursal scowled. None of his contingent were anywhere near the Plateau. The ones not deployed to the west were preparing to occupy Vaade. That meant Tolde Breed and his men were here. Fury surged through him. The hero of the Inquisition had come to end his mad quest for domination.

Clutching his rifle tighter, Ursal stormed the remaining fifty meters to the exit. His dislike for Breed was growing, and it could only be sated with the old man's death. Breed was a relic needing to be placed in storage. Ursal planned on making Breed's coffin the perfect place. He slipped between the broken doors and stepped out into the year's first blizzard. But that was the least of his concerns.

Three giants battled on the main runway. Ursal caught the momentary glint of his sleek black flier darting up into the clouds. Without sufficient airpower, there was no way he could catch whoever had stolen it. Ursal turned back to the titanic battle. Such an event had not been witnessed in centuries and was the stuff of legend and myth. Inquisition teachers preached and warned of the Three, but Ursal had scoffed them off as insecure old men too immersed in fanciful dreams. He'd never imagined being so wrong.

The airspace around Reven seemed like a hive of angry bees. Lights and engines from hundreds of craft, large and small, filled the air as citizens made a desperate attempt to flee. War had come, though not the one promised by Baron Scura. This war threatened to rend the very fabric of the cosmos. Any foolish enough to get close were struck down in blind rage, casual victims in a senseless struggle. Ursal Prowl stood and watched, mouth agape, as his carefully developed plans crashed down.

Ruined, Ursal knew it was time to abandon Lethendweil. Failure lurked in the corner of his mind. His masters on Vau Prime were very specific about his mission, and, despite personal grievances, he had fulfilled his task perfectly. Ursal turned to head for one of the fliers on the runway and stopped abruptly when a new group of combatants emerged from the underground city. His eyes hardened with unbridled hatred. Tolde Breed! So, Ursal smirked, the old man still lived.

Thumbing the communicator attached to his jacket, Ursal said, "Geres, get up to the runway now."

A delay. "Things are heating up down here. I am still needed."

"Gods damn it, I said now! Breed is here, and I need help."

Much quicker this time. "En route, Inquisitor."

Ursal was no fool. He was no match for twenty Prekhauten Guards and a Senior Inquisitor. More than anything, he wanted Tolde dead at his feet, to be the last sight the relic saw before death's cold embrace. He quickly checked his rifle's charge and began creeping his way across the battlefield.

Matthias took point, barreling after Amongeratix with a recklessness seldom enjoyed. Animal urges took control. Matthias let the beast win. Too many good men and women lay dead in Amongeratix's wake. Matthias became the instrument of vengeance. Pent up emotions finally won free of the rigid professionalism instilled by the Guard. Matthias grinned savagely and continued to run.

What remained of his platoon followed as quickly as they could. Battered and nearly beaten, they ignored the bloodstains of their comrades, men and women with whom they had served for years. Boot steps drowned the steady hum of energy weapons. They were just as furious as Matthias and eager to prove their worth against such a demonic foe. War steeled men in ways civilians couldn't imagine.

Tolde jogged behind them. Pain twisted his features. His mind was confused by conflicting emotions. Sister Abigail's loss haunted him. He'd never seen a Blood Witch so casually slaughtered; in fact, until tonight, he hadn't been sure they were mortal. Amongeratix was beyond a monster. He needed to be stopped. But with the Sister gone, Tolde wasn't sure the meager band of Guardsmen was enough.

Fate took the decision out of his hands. They emerged into a raging blizzard that did little to conceal all the Three battling one another. Tolde froze, newfound fear crippling his desire for revenge. Matthias ignored the impossible and dropped into a kneeling firing position. The rest of the Guard pulled online, waiting for his command. He squeezed the trigger. Blue flames spit from the flash suppressor. His ion rifle barked, followed closely by the others.

The roar of the plasma cannon was deafening. Tolde watched the golden trail of energy arc through the snow, angelic and destructive. The round struck Amongeratix squarely in his back and propelled him forty feet through the air. Smoke and flames poured off him. Matthias laughed and continued to fire. Blue-white ion bolts danced off the ground around the other two titans. Sorrow threw his arm up to block a burst headed for his face.

Tannus leveled his gaze on them, instantly deciding they were the enemy despite targeting Amongeratix. He titled his head back and bellowed a challenge. Tolde's blood froze as the monster charged.

"Matthias! We cannot win here. Order your Guards to retreat," he shouted above the howling winds.

Matthias shrugged him off. The berserker threatened to break loose and take hold. Tolde surged through the Guards and slapped Matthias hard across the face. Stunned, he stopped firing long enough to look up. Shame edged into his eyes, replacing the quickly fading rage.

"Order your men back," Tolde ordered.

Matthias saw Tannus charging them and knew Tolde was right. They couldn't defeat one, let alone all Three. "Back, everyone. Back into the city."

"Tannus!"

The titan skidded to a stop and turned. Amongeratix pulled himself off the ground, burned and bleeding. Tiny pockets of flame crackled across his body. He limped.

"This is not over."

His fist clenched. Tannus passed a cautionary glare at the humans. "I will see to you as soon as I am finished with my brother. Do not be here when I am done."

Tolde needed no further encouraging. He helped Matthias up and raced back inside. They'd barely made it back when Tolde noticed the unmistakable figure of Ursal Prowl slinking towards them. Tolde drew his sidearm and aimed. Six crisp bolts peppered a metal shipping container just inches from Ursal's head, forcing him to drop back under cover.

"What was that?" Matthias asked, rifle already trained.

"Prowl."

"What? He's here?"

Tolde nodded. The obvious was unnecessary. They needed to get him before he escaped and spread his heresy to other worlds. Machine gun fire from inside the entrance tunnel made them duck. Tolde and Matthias exchanged apprehensive glances. They were under attack by a new foe.

"Go deal with that. I'll go after Prowl," Tolde said.

"Are you sure?"

Screams accompanied the sadistic rapport of the machinegun. Answer enough for Matthias. He gave Tolde a quick slap on the shoulder and charged off to help his men. Tolde exhaled, his breath frosting in the chill night air. A pair of shots whizzed by, not close enough to harm him. *Good, Prowl shares my sentiments.* Tolde circled around a pair of loading vehicles. All the external lights were out, an unwelcome result of the substantial explosions tearing through Reven's heart. Any advantage he might have had was nullified. No doubt Prowl was using the quasi-darkness as a shield.

Another shot struck where he had just been.

"Old man! Come out. We can end this like professionals."

Prowl's taunts bore little effect. Older, more experienced, Tolde continued creeping closer. Another shot too far away. Bitter realization mocked him. Prowl wasn't trying to see where he was; he was trying to see where Tolde *wasn't.* That cleverness wasn't going to be enough. Tolde was determined to end this tonight. The Three were beyond his means, but one rogue Inquisitor was too easy.

"This is pointless, Breed. We could have been allies."

Prowl's voice held a hard edge, tempered steel against the rising night. He dared not risk mentioning anything more than necessary to draw Tolde out.

"Make this easy. You're a relic. No one remembers what you did fifty years ago. The universe has changed. What happened here is just the beginning, and you aren't necessary."

He fired and took out the fuel lines to one of the external generators. Flames squirted up in a wide arc. Sparks showered the surrounding area, forcing Tolde out from cover. Ion rounds lanced the air over his head, tracing his movements perfectly. Part of his hair ignited. He quickly patted the flames out. The smell of burnt hair gagged him, but he couldn't stop. Tolde fired blindly and ran. His legs betrayed him. He fell.

"Time is fleeing you, Breed," Prowl continued. Victory felt in his grasp. He bolted, recklessly charging through the wreckage.

Tolde ducked behind an overturned crate, desperately trying to catch his breath. He felt every bit of his seventy plus years. Tolde paused to check his rifle. There was still half a charge.

Ion rounds peppered the storage wall where he had just been. Good. Prowl was too distracted to focus. Tolde drew his only flash grenade from the ammo pouch attached to his belt and depressed the trigger. Throwing it as hard as he could in what he hoped was Prowl's general direction, Tolde silently counted. One, two, three. There was a bright flash and a loud boom, amplified by the heavy amount of metal containers. Prowl screamed, more from shock than pain. Tolde took aim and fired the remaining charge. He was rewarded with a cut off shout and the heavy sounds of boots running away. Tolde burst around the last corner, full power charge slammed in. His rifle trained on the spot Prowl had abandoned.

A small pool of blood cooled in the winter snow. Tolde had blindly, and luckily, wounded Prowl. He suppressed a grin and started following the blood trail. Then the world went dark.

The explosion shredded most of the smaller structures on the flight line. Fires licked up into the chill air. Water cooled where the snow had melted. Ursal Prowl slowly drifted back to consciousness, bright flashes obscuring his vision. His head pounded. His body ached. The ion wound on his right side caused great pain. At least one rib was broken, maybe more. The superheated round had cauterized the wound. He was fortunate Breed had fired blind; the wound was two inches below his heart.

Ursal looked around, weapon dancing back and forth. There was no sign of Breed. He knew better than to hope the explosion had killed the man. Wounded, disorientated, Ursal recognized the desperation of his situation. Without Geres Auk, he knew he couldn't win. There was at least one more shuttle, and he quickly decided to abandon his quest for domination on Crimeat. His masters on Vau Prime needed him alive.

He came across Geres Auk halfway to the shuttle. The big man was lying face down, still alive. Ursal started. Geres's skin had turned bright orange. Worse, colors danced in the sky. Every shade of blue, purple and green collided and reformed in the sky over the Plateau. Some dark sorcery had been unleashed in the explosion. Ursal knew it was time to go.

"Get up, we're done here," he scolded the slowly awakening Geres.

Geres focused on Ursal and resisted the urge to smash his face in. The weasel of a man was his only ticket off Crimeat, and, after the atrocities he'd committed in the name of conquest, he needed to escape quickly. Geres struggled to his feet and started to run. The shuttle was close and relatively undamaged.

Brother charged brother. They collided and rolled to the ground in a mass of battered flesh and flailing limbs. Amongeratix rolled away, coming up on one knee. His right arm drew back, fist clenched. Blackness surrounded it, darkness so pure it threatened the continuation of existence. His sneer confirmed what Tannus had long suspected. His brother was subsumed by the foul powers in the universe. Memories of a time when Rengu, the Death God, rode a terrible comet across the stars as he collected souls and sowed the seeds of anarchy angered Tannus. Humanity deserved better, and his brother threatened to bring that plague back.

"You have a taint on you," Tannus accused sharply.

Drool fell from his brother's lower jaw. "Taint? You have always been a puppet of these pathetic mortals."

"They need us."

Hatred flashed behind Amongeratix's coal black eyes. "They need new masters. It is time for us to assume our rightful place in the order of the galaxy. You can still join me, Tannus. Help me finish the work Rengu began."

"Rengu is no longer relevant. His wickedness is finished," Tannus countered. His focus remained on the building power in Amongeratix's fist. He couldn't think of a way to counter it, despite countless centuries of existence.

"Wrong answer," Amongeratix whispered and launched an attack.

Tannus tried to block but was too slow. His brother moved with supernatural speed. Fist flying forward, the black was unleashed with the hatred of a thousand damned souls. Rot spread across the places it touched. Puss oozed from multiple lesions. Tannus bellowed in torment and struck back. His knuckles drove repeatedly into his brother's temple, hammering him as hard as he could. Spurts of blood decorated the snow.

Finally able to break free, Tannus kicked Amongeratix in the ribs with the toe of his boot. A loud snap followed. Vapors sizzled from his wounds, but Tannus knew he couldn't stop. Even the gods could die when they sustained enough damage. He passed a quick glance to Sorrow, confirming what he already knew, and picked up one of the oversized fuel barrels awaiting pick up for delivery across Lethendweil. He started heaving the barrels, striking Amongeratix in the face and chest. Fuel spilled everywhere.

Sorrow watched as his two brothers beat on each other mercilessly. Tears struggled to break free. The great failing of the gods had been passed down to their sons. Enmity unchecked, the sons of the gods had murder in their hearts. It was all too much for Sorrow to bear. He'd spent centuries in exile, refusing to give in to simplistic urges. An unending war continued, but he wanted no part of it. Thoughts danced around his finding of the Paladin. She was the answer. The key to ending this pointless struggle and restoring hope to the universe.

He tipped his head back and screamed. Sonic vibrations kicked up the top layers of snow. Ripples tore through the storm. Drops of blood flew from his skin, staining the purity of the first snowfall. Sorrow strode between his brothers, ignoring their fists and kicks. His nose broke. A rib bruised. Sorrow fought. He caught Amongeratix under the chin. An elbow drove into Tannus's sternum. He managed to wrap his hands around their throats and squeezed.

"ENOUGH!"

They struggled harder, trying to break free to continue the carnage. Fires sprang up around their ankles, burning hotter as they gathered momentum. Sorrow ignored the flames. He looked first to Tannus, then Amongeratix. Neither was inclined to stop struggling. He squeezed harder. Faces started changing color.

"Let…me…go," Amongeratix growled.

Sorrow shook his head. "I will not. You threaten everything with your childish impulses, brother. But no matter. It is too late to change the course of the future now. I have sent the Prophet and the Paladin to An'kuruku. You have failed."

Rage pulsed from his flesh. The blackness returned, swirling around his entire body until the cloud enveloped all three brothers. Tannus' eyes flew wide with shock. Sorrow was slower to react.

"What is this dark magic?" he asked cautiously.

It was too late. The collision of power was beyond anything seen in the universe since the mythic war of the gods on Occanum. Tannus tried to break free, knowing it was useless. Blinding white light formed a shell around the black, compressing energies that should not exist. The ground vibrated. Blood leaked from ears and eyes. Amongeratix clenched his fist tighter, desperate to unleash his fury.

Sorrow finally realized what was happening. "NO!"

The explosion was greater than any in the history of Crimeat. A crater went a hundred meters down, causing cave-ins and collapses throughout the underground city of Reven. The Plateau started to die. Brilliant colors brightened the heavens and could be seen half the continent away. The holy proclaimed it a miracle, a sign the gods truly existed even in their slumbering state. Only those precious few who were trapped in a battle for survival in Reven knew the truth. Unspeakable horror had been unleashed, and when it was finished, there was no sign of the Three. They had disappeared. The war on Lethendweil was over.

THIRTY

3210 A.G. (After Gods), The Plateau, planet Crimeat.

Elisa was thrown back into the pilot chair as the orbital thrusters engaged. She and Mollock rocketed through Crimeat's atmosphere and into the cold emptiness of space. Only it wasn't so empty. Hundreds of ships—some the massive capital ships of Coromoor but most small, more closely related to atmospheric combat—choked the heavens above Crimeat. Mollock's demented laugh refocused her.

"What is so damned funny?" Elisa snarled.

"Winter," was all he said.

She resisted the urge to put an ion round through his skull. Instead, she blew out a steady breath. "What about winter?"

"I was once asked what I dreamed of. My answer was winter. It all makes sense now," he told her. "My whole life has led me here, now. Can't you see? Winter was the key. Never has my path been clearer. Do as Sorrow said, Elisa, please. I don't know why, but this is more important than anything either of us has ever done."

His thoughts lingered on the fantastic display of raw power they'd seen as the flier rose through the thin layer of clouds. Mollock was instantly convinced the gods remained power players. Combined with his discovery of the sleeping god in the catacombs, Mollock saw the explosion as a sign. He was meant to take their message to stars again, a herald of the coming dawn. His eyes narrowed as they shifted to Elisa's back. Was she going to be a problem? If so, he knew how to deal with her.

Elisa, oblivious to the internal deliberations of Mollock Bolle, punched in the coordinates for Deisies II. From there, she figured they'd be able to find out what they needed to know about An'kuruku and the Paradise Tear. She still wasn't sure what had happened but knew there was no going back. Whatever the future held for her, it wasn't on Crimeat. Elisa engaged the sublight engines and sighed.

Cold winds assaulted Tolde's face, bringing tears. He winced into the frigid morning sun but felt no peace. Events had not transpired as he'd predicted or hoped. Crimeat was now under martial law. The Grand Inquisitor himself was en route to see firsthand the effects of the Three and to decide what level of occupation the planet required to be pacified. Prekhauten Guard units continued to be ferried into the system and deployed to strategic points across Lethendweil. Inquisitors and Conclave priests scoured the rebel towns and cities. Heretics were put to the stake and burned.

Still, Tolde found a small measure of comfort. Baron Scura's body had been found in his bedroom. He had put a pistol to his head upon realizing the end was near. All the political prisoners were freed and emplaced back in their primary positions. Brentor vowed a campaign of retribution against heretical kingdoms. Only the heavy presence of the Inquisition and Prekhauten Guard stalled that movement. Besides, Tolde read reports that bodies were beginning to pile up in those kingdoms.

General Shiramon was the only one who had yet to be captured. Some speculated that he had taken a small army and disappeared into the Great Barrier Jungle with the intent to continue the war against the Ugri. It was only a matter of time before he was captured. There was no room for rebel warlords on Crimeat anymore. Tolde remained troubled by the escape of Ursal Prowl and Geres Auk. The pair was extremely dangerous. His concerns were not shared by the Grand Inquisitor; Prowl would be dealt with appropriately, but he was not the grand threat Tolde reckoned him. Tolde was wise enough to keep his comments to himself.

The Three were gone, back to the stars. Tolde knew he was going to run into them again soon. It was inevitable. His entire career had been defined by Amongeratix. The monster haunted him day and night. Tolde had never had a nemesis before, certainly nothing like the life-defining enemy he now understood. Amongeratix was pure hatred. All the bad things in life were rolled into his DNA. Tolde no longer questioned why events had transpired to keep the son of the gods in his life. He accepted it for what it was: a challenge—almost insurmountable, but a challenge he had survived twice already. Tolde Breed did not want to have a third. No one had that much luck.

Perhaps the most curious thing to come out of the events on the Plateau was the finding of the old priest and a rather unsavory character from Prophet Isle. Father Dye claimed to have been sitting at the bar in a deserted tavern helping himself to as much local spiced wine as he could possibly drink when Moffo Kain had stumbled in. Moffo was bloodstained and barely able to stand. Dye invited him to a drink, and they soon discovered that each was associated with one of the Three.

No one was able to explain to the Inquisitor how or why two such odd men were in each other's company. Officially, the Inquisition denied their existence, stating they had no knowledge of either man. Tolde knew better.

Conspiracies formed between them. Moffo remained silent, almost incoherent, as Inquisition interrogators questioned him. Father Dye was more enigmatic. He'd already decided that most of what he had to tell wasn't believable by ordinary men. Both men were placed under Inquisition custody and escorted to a waiting shuttle. They had an audience with the Cardinal Seniorus. Neither would be seen for a very long time, at least not until the mystery of the Three was finally solved. Tolde sympathized, for they were ordinary men who had managed to get ensnared in extraordinary times. He wondered if his fate was going to be the same.

Matthias eased up beside him. His wound had healed, but the scar was irreparable. He laughed it off, claiming it added to his character. Tolde suspected there was more to it but was discreet enough not to press.

"Cold day," he commented, not sure where to begin. Twice in his career he had followed Tolde against Amongeratix and both times come away scarred. Matthias didn't care for another encounter but knew it was inevitable.

A short nod. "I like it. It reminds me of simpler times."

"Those times are gone, Tolde."

"Unfortunately. How are the men?"

Matthias suppressed a frown. "Doc says we might lose Felbrig and Luy, but the rest should pull through. Sergeant Fies is taking his losses harder."

"It is a difficult thing to fight former comrades."

Matthias shrugged. "They turned traitor. Ursal Prowl had more influence with local politics than he should have. That made it easy to sway his Guard detachment. Thankfully, this is a small world. I'd hate to imagine those effects on one of the more populated planets."

Tolde held his own suspicions. There had to more than simplistic greed involved. Ursal Prowl was an Inquisitor, and his Prekhauten Guards were trained professionals. Tolde believed Amongeratix had somehow managed to spread his influence. Combined with the taint of the now-dead dark council, it was only a matter of time before good men fell. He had no way of knowing whether Prowl was one of those good men, though he doubted it. Men like that were cancers.

"We should be receiving orders soon," Matthias changed the subject quickly.

"I have requested extended leave for your men. They performed admirably and deserve it," Tolde said.

"No arguments there. I only wish we could do more."

"And I pray that they never need do more."

Tolde avoided asking how Matthias felt. The wounds on the right side of his body were as bad as they looked. He was fortunate to be alive. Neither had ever seen such raw hatred manifested into physical power. By all rights, Matthias should be dead. Perhaps fate had deemed him worthy of life and intervened. Regardless, Tolde was heartened to see his friend still alive.

It hadn't stopped snowing since the night of the battle. Over two feet of snow concealed the landscape, for which Tolde was grateful. The black rock of the Bothwel Mountains was too oppressive, even for his standards. Snow was pure, serene. It took Tolde back to early childhood, now almost lost to the recesses of time. It represented a new beginning, a time when men could look on one another with renewed confidence and not fear the cold nights. Lethendweil deserved that.

Thousands had died in an ill-advised war. All sides were victims of the greed of a handful of men and women.

Two people approached them, a man and a woman. Both wore dull grey armor and long black cloaks that swept out behind them. Snow drifted up with each passing step. Tolde felt an odd tremble in his stomach.

"You're not required, Sergeant Major," the woman said without looking at him.

Matthias knew better than to speak and bowed curtly before leaving. He had his own masters to report to.

"Senior Inquisitor Breed, I am Luma Kai of the Office of Heretical Persecution. The Inquisitor General has ordered me to debrief you."

Her voice was as cold as her ice-colored eyes. The paleness of her skin was matched by her light blond hair. Tolde nodded. So, the Inquisitor General has unleashed his Hunters. Tolde had nothing to fear for himself, but Hunters were notorious for finding heresies where questions waited. They often jumped unnecessarily.

"Of course, I will be more than compliant on this matter," he replied honestly.

He glanced at Luma's partner, meeting the man's intense glare evenly. Luma feigned ignorance. "You understand that any contact with the Three is to be treated as highly classified?"

Another nod, though he doubted how even the fabled Hunters were going to be able to hide what had happened on the Plateau.

She continued. "The Inquisitor General also commands an audience. You are to be commended for your actions."

"What of my men? I couldn't have done much without them."

"The Prekhauten Guards will be dealt with accordingly. It is not the Inquisition's place to assume that responsibility."

No, only to use them mercilessly and discard them when finished. Tolde sensed Luma was withholding certain bits of information. She clearly had more to say but seemed reluctant.

"There is more?" he asked, uncharacteristically.

Luma Kai stepped closer so only he could hear her next words. "I am to invite you to join our order. The Office could make good use of your specific talents. I do not expect an answer now, but one must be given soon."

They left him standing on the edge of the mountains. It had stopped snowing, and the sky was a dazzling blue. Cloud banks lined the horizon, offering Tolde a glimpse of temporary peace. Much of his childhood had been spent in fear of the night. He had thought it was cured after his first encounter with Amongeratix. How wrong he had been. There were worse and meaner things in the night than just one of the Three. Tolde understood that now. And it terrified him. He rubbed the rose emblem on his left breast but kept his fears to himself.

Luma Kai watched him, though not as closely as her partner. She'd been briefed that he was suspected of heresy. It was a natural concern after prolonged exposure to the Three. She unexpectedly found herself reluctant to continue monitoring him. Tolde Breed was a legend and had defeated Amongeratix twice now and walked away with his life. Men like that ought to be revered, not persecuted. Her opinion did little to temper the fervor of her partner.

"Senior Inquisitor Breed, if you will follow us. The Inquisitor General is awaiting you in the headquarters tent."

Tolde consented and followed them to the temporary headquarters established by incoming Prekhauten commanders. Inquisitor General Alain Nye stood just outside, encased in a circle of personal guards.

"Ah, there you are. Truth be told, I didn't expect your luck to hold. You continue to impress myself and the Cardinal Seniorus. This episode is a dark stain on our order."

"Agreed, Sir."

Nye nodded absently. "What of the prison escape? Were you able to discover anything useful before Inquisitor Prowl turned traitor?"

Tolde wasn't positive, but he detected an ironic tone. There was also the fact that the head of the Inquisition shouldn't be able to name any of his planetary Inquisitors. Tolde was inclined to assume he knew Prowl's name due to the stream of reports he and Matthias had managed to sneak out before all signals were shut down.

"No, Sir. Amongeratix clearly had outside help, which I believe was in part due to Inquisitor Prowl's interference. Sadly, Sister Abigail was slain before we could learn more."

"Yes, a shame the Blood Witch died. I expect the Grand Mistress is already fuming." He quickly shifted focus. "Once you are finished with your debriefing, I want you to take some time off. The

Inquisition will have need of your services again soon, I have no doubt."

Tolde bowed and left, audience finished. The Inquisitor General was an enigma that didn't quite fit in to how events were developing. Tolde was smart enough not to voice his opinion, especially not before a date with the Office of Heretical Persecution. His breath caught as he stepped back into the frigid air.

"Winter came early this year," Brentor's deep voice said from behind.

Tolde turned. "It is cold."

Brentor squared off. "I have trouble saying this. There is little love left in the twelve kingdoms for the Inquisition, but you have done us a grand service. Thank you, Master Breed. We are indebted to you."

Tolde blushed. "I was merely doing my duty, my lord. The Inquisition does not accept debts."

"I don't know how you do it. Scura's war was bad enough, but you fight demons."

A flash of a grin. "We all have our demons, my lord."

Brentor walked a few feet away, staring thoughtfully into the freshly fallen snow. "What will you do now?"

Good question. "The Inquisition never sleeps, Lord Brentor. Heresy is never wiped out, despite what we choose to believe. I suspect the Grand Inquisitor already has another task lined up for me."

"A thankless job." He extended a hand. "You are a great credit to the universe. If only others had your same quality. Good fortune wherever your travels take you, Senior Inquisitor."

Tolde shook Brentor's hand and watched him return to the command tent. He did not envy Brentor or any of the surviving council. Lethendweil might never recover to past glories after the damage Ursal Prowl committed. Tolde couldn't help but notice the similarities to his own position. Wrapping his cloak tighter, he stared off into the howling winds and wondered what the future held.

EPILOGUE

3211 A.G. (After Gods), Abbey of the Order of Blood Witches, Acumensiis Comet.

Ruma Zzein watched the stars blur by. Tranquility was lost. The scene no longer held the promise it once had. The Grand Mistress of the Order of Blood Witches had felt the death. It ran through her veins, dropping the ancient witch to her knees. Sister Abigail was more important than she ever knew. Zzein struggled to collect herself from the floor.

She feared all her carefully manipulated plans were for naught. Amongeratix was once again free and sure to continue his campaign to destroy the gods. Ruma Zzein had warned his father that Amongeratix was too dangerous to let live, but the king of the gods had refused to give in. Fatherly love, such as it was, might be the doom of all things living.

The comet continued its great loop around the universe, unaware of time and the trials of humanity. Forever Night was coming, and Ruma Zzein knew none of them were prepared for it. Life as everyone knew it was crashing to the end. Death was the only certainty.

The adventure continues in The Madman on the Rocks

THE FRACTURED UNIVERSE II
THE
MADMAN
ON THE ROCKS
CHRISTIAN
WARREN FREED

THE MADMAN ON THE ROCKS

ONE

3190 A.G. (After Gods), The Deeves, planet An'kuruku.

The Bone Father stalked the Deeves until he reached the shores of Bo. His morning ritual was sullied by ill portents and bad omens. His ancient shoulders were hunched a little more than usual, his face soured. Dawn was spoiled by the portent of a falling star. The Bone Father had felt his blood chill. Such events simply did not happen. Dark clouds blackened the far horizon. A bad storm was brewing and likely to hit land soon. Experience told him these storms were hazardous and often deadly. He would do well to get back inside.

Sighing, the Bone Father used his staff to propel him away from the Deeves. The soft sand shifted beneath each sandaled step, making the going more treacherous. He was old, some said as old as the founding of the world. His skin was brittle, a coppery color reminiscent of a dying sunset. His hair, what little remained, was long and stringy. There was barely enough to cover his spotted head. His teeth were dull, ground down over the years.

He had seen too many winters with no luxury. Aged fingers curled tightly around the iron and wood of his staff. Sand tickled between his toes, his nails long and broken. His knees were knobbed. The Bone Father was tired, but he could not stop to find rest yet. Chosen by the spirits of the gods, he was forced to endure until a replacement could be found. His was an endless path, one he was both accustomed to and disappointed with.

A pair of black-winged gulls coasted overhead, squawking warning of the coming storm. The Bone Father paused to watch their flight. He sighed again.

"So much like time," he muttered. "The winds steal away our moments until we are nothing but dust."

His bone necklace clinked in the wind as if in response. As the Bone Father, he was attuned to the needs of the world. The Deeves had been his home for as long as he could remember.

His robes rustled against his skin, irritating him. The storm was approaching faster than he had guessed. He wasn't going to make it back to the relative shelter of his mud hut.

Fierce winds drove in from the Bo, rippling waves of the great ocean into a frenzy. They knocked him down. He groaned and spit out a mouthful of sand. He tried to push himself up, but pain lanced through his shoulders. Confusion twisted his face. This should not be happening. He had read the bones this morning. They whispered nothing of this. The Bone Father began to panic. Fear bled his strength as black clouds filled the sky.

"What is this?" he asked the skies, praying to the bones for answers.

There were no answers. His entire life had been dedicated to prolonging the ancient peace passed down by his forefathers. The Bone Father felt hatred on the winds, a fury seeking to undo all his life's work in the rabid howls assailing his ears. Using the last of his waning strength, he managed to rise. His knuckles were white from their grip on his staff. The Bone Father slammed the iron-capped staff on the ground three quick times. Lightning wreathed the skies around him. The ground trembled.

For a moment, the storm abated, and he was once again able to see past his arm's reach. His jaw dropped. Never had he seen the Bo so volatile. Waves crashed upon the shores of the Deeves, threatening to wash away the ancient beach and carry on into the continent. White-capped with froth and filled with flotsam, the waves stole great swaths of sand when they receded. The Bone Father felt death's icy chill deep in his soul.

A supersonic boom roared across the heavens. He cringed, strength fading with each passing moment. Concentric rings of fire burned through the atmosphere. The Bone Father recognized death and once again dropped to his knees with grim acceptance. He had failed. The end had come to An'kuruku. Doubts and wasted opportunities troubled his fragile mind. He had been the hope for the planet, and now Fate had stepped in to rob him of success. The sullied name of the Bone Father would be drowned in history.

Tears formed. He could not cry; he was a keeper of secrets. The last defender of ancient prophecy and the promise of the future.

He was a failure. The Bone Father shook his head. No. Defeatism served no purpose. His staff struck the sand harder. Ages-old mysticism pushed back against the unnatural storm. He gritted his teeth and focused his strength into the earth. Power flooded through the staff and into him.

Eldritch colors pulsed from the tip of the staff, tingling his fingertips and teasing his hair wildly. A pale-yellow glow surrounded the Bone Father. He felt renewed. Youthful vigor, long lost to the vagaries of time, expanded his conscience. He saw events before they happened. Watched the decay of lives and the sudden growth of new birth. The Bone Father became strength unabated.

He rose to his full five-foot height and thrust the staff into the sky. Circles of power penetrated the pitch black. Clouds roiled in new turmoil. Little by little, the strength of the earth beat back the unexpected hatred assaulting the Deeves. Despite the strength given to him, it was all the Bone Father could do to maintain his denial of the sudden affliction threatening An'kuruku.

Shells pelted his frail body. Fish slammed down around him. He heard whispers on the wind, dire warnings of impending doom. Still, he held his ground. The raging tempest was an abnormality needing to be purged. The Bone Father grimaced as a particularly large fish slapped his chest. The very depths of the Bo were tossed into the sky, offending the gods of earth and sea. He immediately set to stem the insanity and restore order to the Deeves.

Uttering ancient words, the Bone Father thrust up the staff again. The explosion tore holes through the storm. Endless power plunged down on his weary shoulders, desperately trying to shatter his protective shell and render him back to ashes. He resisted, though it stole much. The Bone Father felt his life sKain shorten. Too many years bled back to the earth. He doubted he could survive the full fury of the storm. There was too much raw strength bearing down.

Finally, he could take no more. The Bone Father screamed, a mangled sound that inspired hope and plead ruination. Tears appeared in his flesh. His eyes, once magnificent blue, were dulled as if the slow progression of age marched too quickly. The fury abated. Blue skies seeped through the black. A single ray of light shone on his face, offering warmth and the unspoken reassurance that it was all going to be alright. The Bone Father cried. His shoulders sagged. He had won.

The clouds broke, scattered like so many empty dreams lost to time. The Bone Father collapsed. Fresh pain wracked his right arm. Horrified, he looked down at what remained of the hand holding the staff. The skin was gone, melted off until nothing but bone was left. Blood dripped on his tan robes. It pooled in the sands. The smell of burnt flesh sickened him. The earth had answered his pleas and took what it needed in return.

He felt older, more worn and used. The Bone Father knew his time was ending. Sudden urges took hold. He must find a replacement before death's long fingers took him forever. The prospect of death had never bothered him before. He knew it was the logical conclusion to all things. What is born must also die; such things were unquestionable. It simply *was*. But here, now, he felt urgency in the need to complete his task. He was in a race against an unfeeling enemy he could not avoid.

His eyes searched the Bo for any sign of the cause. The sky had returned to normal, restoring his faith in all things and the grand designs of the gods. The Deeves were safe. The Bo still chopped with angry surf, but it, too, seemed normal. Still, the Bone Father was confused. Victory was his. The earth was satisfied. Why was the Bo still angry?

Drifting across the waves he spied the glint of sharp silver bobbing with the tide. Even from a distance, he could tell it was unlike anything natural. An'kuruku was a desolate world with limited technology, far from the main interstellar trade lanes. He looked to the now passive skies and wondered what magic had come to the Deeves. The Bone Father used his good hand to tear a bandage for the wounded one, shifted his staff to the left and half dragged his battered body to the edge of the Bo.

Cool water sloshed over his feet. He lost himself in the refreshing feeling, trying to ignore the premonition nagging him. The object drifted closer. The Bone Father made out soft edges and the occasional glimpse of a window. He was reminded of a casket, memories from his childhood when his father had taken him to watch the funeral procession of the last king of Tenemenah.

The dead falling from the sky? He wished for companionship for the first time in decades. The Bone Father seldom spoke to others and hardly felt the need to. It was enough that he roamed the sparse grass and sand dunes of the Deeves to keep his people safe. He lived alone, friendless. That was what it meant to be a reader of the bones. Chosen solitude was a small sacrifice for the security of the many. The Bone Father never regretted the decisions leading him to this point.

The silver casket was closer. He traced the lines of thick cables running the three-meter length. The top was rounded, contrast to the blocky sides. Rows of sharp green and red lights blinked from banks at both ends. Perhaps it was not a casket at all. The Bone Father knew little of such things. He had never been off world, never witnessed the grandness of the promises technology offered. What he saw seemingly drifting straight for him was anathema.

Strong winds pushed the casket to shore. The Bo discarded the unnecessary. Alien items had no place in the sacred waters. The bulky frame washed onto the sand, coming to rest only a few feet away from the Bone Father. He eyed it suspiciously, half-expecting some mythic figure to emerge. He scolded himself. A lifetime of solitude had taught him many things, and fear was not one of them. He hobbled to the casket, eager and apprehensive about seeing what rested within.

Long, the casket was only a meter high, so he was easily able to peer into the small window. The Bone Father gently wiped the sand away and looked inside. His heart hammered. Resting quietly, almost deathly, was the most beautiful woman he had ever seen.

OTHER BOOKS BY CHRISTIAN WARREN FREED

WHERE HAVE ALL
THE ELVES
GONE?
CHRISTIAN WARREN FREED

Everyone knows Elves don't exist. Or do they? Daniel Thomas spent years making a career of turning his imagination into the reality of bestselling fantasy novels. But times are tough. No one wants to read about elves and dragons anymore. Daniel learns this firsthand when his agent flatly says no to his latest and, what he deems, to be greatest novel yet. Dissatisfied with the turn to zombies and vampire lovers, he takes his manuscript and heads out to confront his agent.

His world changes when he finds his agent dying on the floor of her office. Too late to help, he watches as her dead body disintegrates into a pile of ash and dust. Daniel doesn't have time to ponder what just happened as a band of assassins breaks in, forcing him to flee to the Citadel and the home of the king of the high elves in order to survive. Daniel soon discovers that all of the creatures he once thought he imagined actually exist and are living among us. His revelation comes at a price however, as he is drawn into a murder-mystery that will push him to the edge of sanity and show him things no human has witnessed in centuries.

Everyone knows Elves don't exist. Or do they? Daniel Thomas spent years making a career of turning his imagination into the reality of bestselling fantasy novels. But times are tough. No one wants to read about elves and dragons anymore. Daniel learns this firsthand when his agent flatly says no to his latest and, what he deems, to be greatest novel yet. Dissatisfied with the turn to zombies and vampire lovers, he takes his manuscript and heads out to confront his agent.

His world changes when he finds his agent dying on the floor of her office. Too late to help, he watches as her dead body disintegrates into a pile of ash and dust. Daniel doesn't have time to ponder what just happened as a band of assassins breaks in, forcing him to flee to the Citadel and the home of the king of the high elves to survive. Daniel soon discovers that all the creatures he once thought he imagined actually exist and are living among us. His revelation comes at a price however, as he is drawn into a murder-mystery that will push him to the edge of sanity and show him things no human has witnessed in centuries.

ARMIES
of the
SILVER MAGE
CHRISTIAN WARREN
FREED

Malweir was once governed by the order of Mages, bringers of peace and light. Centuries past and the lands prospered. But all was not well. Unknown to most, one mage desired power above all else. He turned his will to the banished Dark Gods and brought war to the free lands. Only a handful of mages survived the betrayal and the Silver Mage was left free to twist the darker races to his bidding. The only thing he needs to complete his plan and rule the world forever are the four shards of the crystal of Tol Shere.

Having spent most of their lives dreaming about leaving their sleepy village and travelling the world, Delin Kerny and Fennic Attleford never thought that one day they would be forced to flee their town to save their lives. Everything changes when they discover the fabled Star Silver sword and learn that there are some who want the weapon for themselves. Hunted by a ruthless mercenary, the boys run from Fel Darrins and are forced into the adventure they only dreamed about.

Ever ashamed of the horrors his kind let loose on the world the last mage, Dakeb, lives his life in shadows. The only thing keeping him alive is his quest to stop the Silver Mage from reassembling the crystal. His chance finally comes through the hearts and wills of Delin and Fennic. Dakeb bestows upon them the crystal shard, entrusting them with the one thing capable of restoring peace to Malweir.

THE
LAZARUS MEN
A LAZARUS MEN AGENDA
CHRISTIAN
WARREN FREED

It is the 23rd century. Humankind has reached the stars, building a tentative empire across a score of worlds. Earth's central government rules weakly as several worlds continue their efforts toward independence. Shadow organizations hide in the midst of the political infighting. Their manifestations of power and influence are beholden only to the highest bidder. The most powerful/insidious/secret of these, The Lazarus Men, has existed for decades, always working outside of morality's constraints. Led by the enigmatic Mr. Shine, their agents are hand selected from the worst humanity has to offer and available for the right price.

Gerald LaPlant lives an ordinary life on Old Earth. That life is thrown into turmoil on the night he stumbles upon the murder of what appears to be a street thief. Fleeing into the night, Gerald finds himself hunted by agents of Roland McMasters, an extremely powerful man dissatisfied with the current regime and with designs on ruling his own empire. To do so, McMasters needs the fabled Eye of Karakzaheim, a map leading to immeasurable wealth. Unknown to either man, Mr. Shine has deployed agents in search of the same artifact and will stop at nothing to obtain it.

Running for his life, Gerald quickly becomes embroiled in a conspiracy reaching deep into levels of government that he never imagined existed. His every move is hounded by McMasters' agents and the Lazarus Men. His adventures take him away from the relative safety of Old Earth across the stars and into the heart of McMasters' fledgling empire. The future of the Earth Alliance at stake. If Gerald has any hope of surviving and helping save the alliance he must rely on his wits and awakened instincts while foregoing the one thing that could get him killed more quickly than the rest: trust.

Pick up a sword and join the team!
Evil never rests and neither can we.

Warfighter Books

Signup for our newsletter today and follow us on social media for updates, new releases and more!

Newsletter:
https://www.subscribepage.com/warfighterbooks

Facebook: https://www.facebook.com/Warfighterbooks
Twitter: https://twitter.com/ChristianWFreed
Instagram: www.instagram.com/christianwarrenfreed/

BIO

Christian W. Freed was born in Buffalo, N.Y. more years ago than he would like to remember. After spending more than 20 years in the active duty US Army he has turned his talents to writing. Since retiring, he has gone on to publish more than 20 science fiction and fantasy novels as well as his combat memoirs from his time in Iraq and Afghanistan. His first book, Hammers in the Wind, has been the #1 free book on Kindle 4 times and he holds a fancy certificate from the L Ron Hubbard Writers of the Future Contest.

Passionate about history, he combines his knowledge of the past with modern military tactics to create an engaging, quasi-realistic world for the readers. He graduated from Campbell University with a degree in history and a Masters of Arts degree in Digital Communications from the University of North Carolina at Chapel Hill. He currently lives outside of Raleigh, N.C. and devotes his time to writing, his family, and their two Bernese Mountain Dogs. If you drive by you might just find him on the porch with a cigar in one hand and a pen in the other.

www.ingramcontent.com/pod-product-compliance
Lightning Source LLC
Chambersburg PA
CBHW010700100726

47900CB00010B/2743